MATCH MAKER

ALAN CHIN

Dreamspinner Press

Published by
Dreamspinner Press
4760 Preston Road
Suite 244-149
Frisco, TX 75034
http://www.dreamspinnerpress.com/

Match Maker

Cover Art by Reese Dante   http://www.reesedante.com

ISBN: 978-1-61581-587-6

Printed in the United States of America
First Edition
September, 2010

eBook edition available
eBook ISBN: 978-1-61581-588-3

Sincere thanks to Stephen Gregoire, Doug Slayton, Kyle Childress, Rob McCann and Victor Banis for their valuable input and their attempt to keep me honest in the telling. I am also deeply indebted to my husband, Herman Chin, without whom I would still be floundering around page 200 and wondering how three years of my life had flittered by unnoticed.

In the shadow of every great tennis match
tread the coaches who groom the stars to perform
at their peak. These men and women working behind the
scenes essentially make the match.

CHAPTER 1

CONNOR LIN'S eyes grew large as the ball bounced short of the service line and sailed into his strike zone. He drew his racket back while planting his body in perfect balance; his arm swung, shoulders rotated, and his racket arched up through the ball and continued into a follow-through. The ball seemed to shriek from the impact as it sped bullet-fast toward the sideline. It scorched a pale mark on the green court a half-inch from the white line. But once again, it was the half-inch on the far side of the line. The lineman's hand flew up, and he yelled, "Out."

Connor dropped his racket and blinked at the mark, obviously not quite believing that he had lost another game.

Sweat dripped from his nose and chin.

He glanced at the chair umpire, attempting to coerce an overrule, but the chair awarded the game to Connor's opponent.

Connor lifted the flap of his shirt, mopped his face, and bent to pick up his racket.

Watching him from the bleachers, it occurred to me that he must have dreamed about this match for most of his teenaged life. He had begun the first game with all the charisma of a champion poised for a run at brilliance, but the match had mutated into his worst nightmare. No brilliance materialized. Point by point, his entire being shriveled. His confidence and composure evaporated.

There was nothing anyone could do to reverse his downward spiral. I felt his frustration, a searing tightness in my abdomen. I had experienced

the same ordeal many times, and even though half a decade had passed
since then, I knew precisely how he felt: like a man alone at thirty
thousand feet without a parachute. He was playing a quarterfinal match on
the show court of an ATP satellite tennis tournament, set within the
twisted pine forest between Carmel and the craggy cliffs of Big Sur. Five
hundred shrieking, stomping fans packed the bleachers, and the loudest of
them was Connor's father, who sat three rows below me in the players'
section.

Cold fear. It first appeared in Connor's eyes when he must have
realized that, without the help of divine intervention, he would lose to a
sixteen-year-old whose groundstrokes resembled a caveman swinging a
club. His fear visibly gave birth to hatred, seething, and finally,
humiliation. What Connor's eyes showed eventually revealed itself in his
body language. He looked like a pro tennis player—lean, agile body, good
legs, coffee-colored hair gathered into a ponytail and covered with a ball-
cap turned back to front, and the prettiest almond-shaped eyes I'd ever
seen—but his slumped shoulders and marred facial expressions gave him
away. He was out of his league, and he knew it.

I mentally listed his technical problems with a practiced eye. He had
a decent first serve, but a weak, loopy second serve that my aunt Betsy
could wallop for a winner. And when serving a critical point, his toss fell
an inch or so shorter than normal, making him hit down on the ball and
dump his serve into the net. He scrambled from side to side with the fluid
steps that produce great footwork, but he seemed unsure of himself
anywhere in front of the baseline, and three volleys hacked into the net
and a botched overhead told me why.

Other than that, all his troubles lay between his ears. His problems
stemmed from impatience. Instead of working the rallies while waiting for
a weak ball to attack, he tried to crush winners from a defensive position.
He won enough points to keep him pulling the trigger, but he also sprayed
enough balls long, wide, and into the net to lose every game.

Nevertheless, even with his obvious technical and mental issues, he
was thrilling to watch. His grace, explosive speed, and physical beauty
sent chills up my spine. I was not in love with him. How could I be? I had
never even met him. But I loved watching him play.

Connor lost the first set with a bagel, and his father shrieked
hysterically. At first, he directed his outburst at Connor, telling the boy

how to play, then at the opponent, for not being good enough to be on the same court with his son. The chair umpire notified security on his walkie-talkie, and we all waited while two uniformed men escorted Connor's father from the bleachers. He screamed obscenities all the way to the parking lot.

Connor sat through the whole scene crouched forward on his bench with a white towel draped over his head. I would have bet fifty bucks that tears were flowing under that towel, but I doubt I would have found any takers.

Connor's game continued to disintegrate through the second set. After a heated argument with the chair umpire over a questionable line call, he turned to flip the bird at a heckling spectator and received a code of conduct warning for "visible" obscenity. Two games later, another out call had him tomahawking his racket and unleashing a screech. It was a sound of pure anguish. I could only shake my head and watch as that temperamental athlete, with the sublime groundstrokes of a top-ten player, suffered a mental meltdown in public view.

I longed to cradle him in my arms and explain that it was only a game, that it should be fun. I wanted him to know that he didn't need to battle against the pressures that the world threw at him, but he was in no condition to listen to anybody, least of all a has-been like me.

In Connor's last service game, while he waited for his opponent to step to the baseline, he glanced into the stands. We made eye contact for a dozen seconds, and he looked right through me, as if to say, "Fuck you, you know-it-all bastard. At least I'm down here, still in the fight. What the fuck are you doing?" I saw something flicker deep within those beautiful eyes, something more than defiant pride. Or maybe I just chose to see it. Even though his emotions had run away with him, I saw his courage as clearly as if he were holding up his heart like a metal shield.

I sucked in my breath and held it until he looked away.

CHAPTER 2

TWO weeks later, I ambled from the Windsor Country Club parking lot to the fastidious fleet of tennis courts carved into the hillside skirting San Francisco's most exclusive golf course. Being the club's tennis pro, I spent my days giving lessons to fortyish housewives and pre-teen children while their husbands and fathers played eighteen holes.

That cool August morning dawned overcast, and gusty winds drove an occasional flurry of mist off the ocean (anywhere other than San Francisco, it would be called rain), which is pretty much the cliché weather pattern for that part of the city during summer. As I strolled down the damp stone path, I noted with some satisfaction that the courts were dark from the mist, telling me that I would have a quiet morning to get organized before the ladies arrived for their lessons.

When I passed by Mr. Tottori, the head groundskeeper, he bowed and said in slow, precise English, "Hello, Mr. Bottega. A fine day."

"Yes, Mr. Tottori," I said, bowing equally as low. "Couldn't be better."

When I arrived at the clubhouse, I found the president of the club, Carrie Bennett, waiting for me on the covered terrace. She looked slim in her navy blue business suit, and she sported a fresh, boyish haircut with streaks of blonde that erased ten years from her face, making her look thirty again.

Having Carrie down there anytime before noon meant trouble. I smiled and waved a hand toward my office, but before I could utter a word, she lifted two paper cups and said, "Morning, Daniel. I brought us some coffee. Just the thing to warm us up on a summer's day."

I stared at the steaming coffee. In four years of working for her, that gesture was a first. Recovering, I led her into my office, where I had to clear a space on my desk for her to put the cups down.

The desk was crammed with neat stacks of tennis magazines, equipment catalogs, instructional literature, and such. It's amazing how much time I spent pouring over those publications, but for a perfectionist like me, that's what it takes to stay at the top of my sport.

At the edge of the desk sat two yellow plastic trays. One, labeled "Tournaments," held entry forms for an upcoming club event. The second tray was labeled "Other" and held a faded employment application for a prestigious Santa Barbara tennis academy, a magazine advertisement entitled "ATP Instructors Needed," and a newspaper article about a sixteen-year-old prodigy from Long Beach who was burning up the courts and ready to tackle the pro tour.

I settled my lanky body into a swivel desk-chair and took the coffee she offered, sipping, enjoying the rich bitterness. Over the cup's rim, I watched her eyes scan the room as she relaxed into the chair beside my desk. The four walls were the color of tobacco spit, and the only window was rusted shut. A paddle-bladed ceiling fan wheeled above my desk, gliding around in slow rotations, but it moved too slowly to stir the air. It made a clock-tick sound with every rotation, announcing each second that passed. The stringing machine had a dozen stringless rackets waiting on the floor. The bulletin board on the wall posted the lesson schedule in different colored inks.

Her gaze settled on the six photos hanging on the wall behind me, framed pictures of me posing with McEnroe, Becker, Edberg, Courier, Sampras, and Agassi. Each one fading yellow with age.

I had moved from L.A. to San Francisco four years ago, and I took this job as my respite from an unkind world. I found comfort and safety within these dingy walls. Over the years I'd made it my own, with pictures, trophies, and a bookcase for my sports books and magazines. It was more comfortable than it looked.

"When you played on the tour," Carrie said, pointing an index finger at the pictures, "you hobnobbed with these guys?"

"Sure, I met them all. Got to play with most of them."

"You must have been good."

Finally reduced to a must-have-been. I closed my eyes and listened to the tick, tick, ticking of the ceiling-fan. I opened my eyes again and glanced up to study its action. The movement had no beginning and no end; it just kept going in a circle—tick, tick, tick.

"What brings you down here, Carrie?"

She withdrew a pack of Winstons from her purse. When I shook my head, she tossed it back where it came from and, frowning, said, "Ever hear of a kid named Connor Lin?"

The name sounded familiar, and I had to reflect for a moment before the light went on. I nodded. "Saw him play in Carmel two weeks ago."

"What did you think?"

"Terrific strokes and plenty of courage, but he's soft upstairs." I pointed to my head. "Can't handle the pressure. His old man's a real piece of work. In fact, I think dear ol' dad is the root problem. Connor could be a top player if he'd dump his old man and hire a professional coach."

Carrie's lips spread into a wicked little grin. "I'm thrilled you said that, because you may be the remedy that Doc Bottega just prescribed."

Slowly, I set my cup on the desk. My unblinking eyes riveted on her. I hadn't coached a big hitter in four years. They all trained in Southern California or Florida, and nobody remembered me—"fallen off the map" would have been a gross understatement. "He wants to train here? With me?"

Her grin blossomed into a smile. "They're eating breakfast in the dining room. You should see that kid eat. What I wouldn't give to be eighteen again." She patted her waistline.

"Why me? A dozen coaches would hock their family jewels to train a kid with his potential."

"The father wants to keep him close by, wants to help with the training. He thinks he's the Chinese equivalent of Richard Williams."

She explained that the father worked all night driving a forklift at a wholesale produce warehouse in Oakland. He trained Connor in the afternoons and slept when the boy was at school. The mother managed a

Cantonese restaurant on Clement Street. They had sent Connor to the Huntington Beach Tennis Academy for three summers, but he had stopped improving after the first year, so they were now looking for some local one-on-one training. They apparently couldn't afford a big-name training camp if he was not improving—no surprise there.

"Besides," she continued, "the old man is hard-core Chinese. He wants an Asian coach, so you fit the bill. As for the Windsor Club, having an up-and-coming tennis star as a member would be a prestigious feather in our cap. We're waiving the initiation fees and annual dues. We want this to work."

For the first time ever, I was being offered a job because I'm half-Chinese, and I couldn't help but chuckle. The situation seemed absurd, but I noticed a slight trembling in my hands. "You're serious? You want me to train this kid?"

"Daniel, relax. Just give him a look-over. If you like what you see, we'll work something out. If not, he walks."

We strolled up the path to the clubhouse dining room. Memories bombarded my consciousness, some painful and some glorious, all jumbling into something that began to simmer. At the same time, a secret little dream I'd held inside for four long years, like a tightly woven cocoon, began to beat with new life.

CHAPTER 3

As CARRIE and I approached the elegant dining room from the terrace, I scrutinized the father and son through the picture windows. The father sat rigid, his spine pressed to the chair-back and his feet spread apart. He had Pekingese eyes, unfeeling and bulged, and a salt-and-pepper crew cut, paled at the temples. Set under a wide nose, his tight, thin lips seemed chiseled in granite, incapable of smiling. His gray, quilted Mao jacket buttoned all the way to his neck, and his black slacks only partially covered his white socks and orthopedic sneakers.

Beside him, Connor slouched in his chair with gangly arms and legs sprawled in all directions. His leather motorcycle jacket, T-shirt sporting a picture of Che Guevara, saggy jeans, and backward baseball cap all fused to resemble the rap musicians on MTV.

Attitude, I thought. *That costume broadcasts sheer attitude*. My expectations dropped a notch. As we came closer to the window, I saw my own reflection on the glass superimposed on Connor's lolling figure, and a shiver raced up my spine.

We passed through the open French doors and walked to their table. Roy Lin stood and gave me a firm handshake, introducing himself. He motioned toward his son, who hadn't moved, and said, "This is Connor." If Roy had tried to hide the pride in his voice, which is customary for the Chinese, he failed.

Connor nodded his head, glancing at me through dark Oakley glasses. *What a pity*, I thought, *that he hides those haughty, candid eyes*, but the smirk on his face gave me the impression of an insolent child.

I shook that image from my head and proceeded to size him up with a professional's astuteness: eighteen years old (although he looked twenty), six-foot-two, one hundred sixty-five pounds, lanky frame, slender legs that could prove injury-prone, and I had the feeling, from watching him there and from seeing him play, that beneath his disinterested façade, he was sensitive, proud, and high-strung.

His hairless complexion glowed a rich amber, and he had the high cheekbones of the northern Chinese. He would have been handsome if he had not inherited his father's wide nose. His hair swept back into a ponytail, which accentuated the thinness of his face.

I found him appealing, which was unusual with someone so young, but at the same time, I became irritated that he didn't stand and shake my hand. A snub like that wouldn't work. If I couldn't gain his respect, I was wasting my time.

"So," I said, easing into the chair facing Connor, "I saw your quarterfinal match in Carmel." A gleam sparkled through those dark circles of glass. "That guy took winning ugly to a whole new level."

Roy Lin popped a Tums into his mouth, chomping down hard. Between crunches, he asked, "What did you think of Connor's game?"

"Decent first serve, clean groundstrokes, dominating forehand, and smooth side-to-side footwork."

My compliments registered in Connor's eyes, and the thin suggestion of a grin played at the corners of his mouth.

Roy, however, realized I had omitted a long list of negatives. His eyes narrowed to a squint, and he began to operate on me, making deft little exploratory incisions. He asked several direct questions that I answered with my unvarnished opinions.

Nothing I said diminished the grin on Connor's face, but each time I stole a glimpse of him, my heart shrank. He stared out the window, pulled a loose strand of hair into the corner of his mouth and nibbled it absentmindedly, then plucked at a dangling thread on his coat sleeve. The one time he did look my way, I saw through the dark glasses that his eyes were frosted over.

Roy asked, "So what do you think? Does he have it?"

"Does he have what?"

"Natural talent. Has he got what it takes to be great?"

"You know, when I coached on the tour, I noticed a funny thing: the more time a player spent on the practice courts, the more natural talent he had."

"Yes, but you can't discount natural talent," Roy said, shaking his head and waving a hand.

"Takes more than talent to win matches," I said, turning to Connor. "That kid who beat you in Carmel had zero natural talent, but he found a way to win."

"A pusher," Connor spat. "I'm much better."

I smiled, ready to remind him that a "pusher" had served him up a double bagel, but with the words on my tongue, I swallowed the thought, saying instead, "Show me a pusher who keeps the ball in play and I'll show you a room full of trophies."

A waiter sauntered up to take our order. I shook my head. Carrie ordered coffee, Roy asked for a tea refill, and for a moment, I thought Connor was going to order a second breakfast, but he turned his head toward the window, ignoring the waiter's gaze.

"Connor should have beaten him," Roy said, interjecting an edge to his voice. "A fluke. It happens to everybody."

"That kid didn't beat Connor," I said. "Connor beat himself." Connor's grin evaporated. "You see, in a winning game, fifteen percent is stroke production, fifteen percent is footwork and speed, and seventy percent is what's between the ears. That hacker who beat you proved that perfectly. So far, you've developed only thirty percent of a winning baseline game and zero percent of a net game."

"That's why we need your help," Roy said. His froggy voice croaked with excitement. "Ms. Bennett tells me that you know the Xs and Os as well as anyone. I'll work with him on his physical game. You work on his mental attitude and play strategy."

I felt uneasy. I cocked my head and stared out the window, beyond the plush verdant golf course to the pristine white houses perched on the hillside. I was convinced that Roy was a hindrance, and to help his son, he should step aside. I was also annoyed at Connor's lack of enthusiasm, but it occurred to me that it might be a façade to hide his deeper feelings.

I decided to gamble. After an uncomfortable silence, I glanced back at Roy and said, "I don't work that way, Mr. Lin. Either I take charge of his entire training, or I back away. It's no reflection on you, I just can't work any other way." It sounded so good I began to believe it.

"Perhaps we can compromise?"

"Mr. Lin, as a father, what are your goals regarding Connor?"

"My boy will be the first Chinese player to reach number one in the world."

I turned my attention to those dark circles of glass. Connor's eyes brushed the table, and the tips of his ears grew pink, deepening to blood red. He gave me the curious impression that he was not in sync with Roy's grand vision. Either he didn't want it, or he didn't believe he could achieve it.

"What training have you done?" I asked.

"He began at age seven," Roy said, even though I had directed the question to Connor. "I coach him three hours a day during the school year, and for the last three summers, I sent him to the Huntington Beach Tennis Academy. He stayed home this year because of financial constraints."

Carrie had mentioned that Connor had stopped improving at the academy in addition to the money issue. *The old man's holding back on me*, I thought.

"Mr. Lin, when it comes to tennis, compromise is not a concept I'm familiar with. I'm sorry." My reply unsettled him, and I felt sorry I had closed the door so abruptly. I glanced at my watch and, although I had nowhere pressing to be, I started to rise. Carrie began to protest, but I silenced her with a glance.

"Hold on!" Roy reached over and gripped my wrist like a hydraulic vise. "I respect a man who doesn't compromise." A wooden smile veiled his face, but I saw the emotions churning in his eyes. "Perhaps you and

Connor should get to know each other before we decide. If he prefers you, I'll step aside."

An audible change in the rhythm of Roy's breathing accompanied the pause that followed. I had won the first skirmish, but my inner voice told me to back away. I began to say no a final time, but the word caught in my throat.

Why not? I wondered. Life, a meaningful life, comes from a man's unflagging struggle toward his grand ambition. My last four years had pointed to no goal beyond a paycheck; my job was a sanctuary from bashing my head against the world's wall. I had once thought of myself as a cowboy galloping over a prairie in chase of a dream, but I couldn't remember what that felt like. How many more years would I hide, seeking refuge while others struggled and triumphed?

I shrugged my shoulders and nodded. Roy released my wrist. Rubbing the soreness away, I focused on Connor's eyes through those dark circles.

"Your dad is a determined man. I like that." I smiled. He returned a cautious grin, his first friendly gesture. Mine too, for that matter.

"If you find a way to make him swallow a 'no'," Connor said, as if Roy weren't sitting there, "let me know how. I've never learned the knack."

"Let's walk. I'll show you the facilities."

We left Roy and Carrie and ambled downstairs, where we toured the athletic facilities: weight room, sauna and steam room, lockers and showers. I explained that I was big on cross-training with both weights and cardiovascular workouts like cycling and running, and I was also keen on using tai chi and meditation to strengthen concentration. He surprised me by admitting that all of his father's workouts were spent on court hitting balls, which partly explained the lack of focus I had witnessed in Carmel.

We left the building and strolled toward the courts. The mist had passed, but the morning still held its freshness. The sun would soon make an appearance and dry the courts. *A fine day*, I thought, scrutinizing my little world.

I asked about his training at Huntington Beach, and as he described his experiences there, I read between the lines to get my own picture of why he had stopped improving. The powers that be must have labeled him as lazy, or too high strung, or unteachable.

Whatever the reason, they had decided not to grant him precious one-on-one time with the top instructors. Instead, they placed him into group lessons with younger students and then matched him against better players in order to boost the confidence of the better players. They expected him to lose, and of course that was what he did, over and over. By making him fodder for the top players, they inadvertently taught him how to lose. No one had ever taken the time and energy to teach him how to win. The experts had written him off as a lost cause, so it was no surprise when he told me how he had hated the academy.

"Tell me why you play tennis," I said, "what you like about it."

"Winning. I love winning."

"What else?"

"There's nothing else."

Wrong answer. I suspected that was his father talking.

"That's all tennis means to you, winning or losing?"

"That's the whole point of the game, to crush the opponent, right?"

"I always thought that the point of any game was to have fun."

We walked a dozen more steps in silence. Connor swiveled his head back toward the clubhouse, as if to make sure that his father couldn't overhear.

"Everything about tennis is awesome. The feel of the ball on your racket, the way your body moves through the stroke, hitting a difficult shot just the way you mean to, it's all totally killer. But what I love are those times when my game kicks into light speed and I'm not there anymore. It's just the ball and the racket, and I'm whooshing around the court making impossible shots look routine. When that happens, I can't miss. I mean, I play wicked tennis, but it never lasts more than a game or two, sometimes a whole set. But that's what I love, when that thing happens."

A warm wave, fired by hope, surged through my core. "That's called being in the zone."

"Duh, I know what it's called. I didn't just tumble out of the cradle."

"You said that you loved winning. What if I guarantee to teach you how to win every time you step on court, regardless of the score?"

Silence filled the aftermath of my implied promise. He inched closer, and I felt something gel between us.

"That would be awesome, but how can you discount the score?"

"We'll get to that later. How do you feel about me replacing your father?"

"If you help me to win, it's cool. It's not about him, it's about me." A condescending tone interjected itself into those last three words.

"Wrong. It's about your game. There's a big difference, and you need to learn that." He had plenty to learn and plenty of attitude we'd need to cut through before we could start clicking in sync. "Connor, I only know one way to teach: you do what I say, every time I say, with no back-talk and no attitude."

"Now you sound like my dad. I'm sick of his bullshit and the pressure he dumps on me. If you're like him, then fuck it."

We had gotten to the heart of it. He couldn't take the pressure, and judging from the way Roy had behaved in Carmel, who could blame him? He didn't believe he could be great, so he wanted the training to at least be fun. And he also had a point: I could lose some attitude myself. *Lighten up, for Chrissake*, I silently scolded myself.

I realized that my toughest job would be to convince him that he could be great.

The ends of his mouth lowered into a pout. *What is it*, I wondered, *that makes a young man's pouty expression so damned sexy?*

"Okay, okay…. Let me point out that the advantage I have over your father is that I've been there, done it, and I know what it takes to get there. And one thing I've learned is, if you can't take pressure, you won't go far. I'm saying you need to consider whether you're cut out for professional competition. I'd also like to say that you're right: I came on too heavy. If you want my help, it'll be hard work, but I'll make it fun. I'll meet you halfway if you do the same."

"Suits me."

"Mr. Bottega," I said with a slight edge, still trying to establish some boundaries.

He paused. "Suits me, Mr. Bottega." His pout turned into an embarrassed but pleasing grin.

"And anytime I sound like your father, you let me know."

"I'll nudge you in the ribs."

"You give me a swift kick in the ass."

"Deal."

We wandered through the maze of courts that were drying nicely. He asked me what I loved about tennis, and I explained, "The fact that you are in control of your own destiny. You're not at the mercy of a coach calling the plays or benching you, and how you perform depends on how you prepare before the match and how you keep your composure during play. The thing I love most is when I'm pressed to the wall and forced to dig deep, when I hit rock bottom and have to pull out a jackhammer to dig deeper until I find that hidden vein of strength I never knew existed."

I paused for a moment, realizing the truth of my statement.

"Yes, that's what I love most," I said. "When I surprise myself."

He took off his dark glasses and revealed a shine in his eyes.

Something had gelled, but I still needed to tread carefully.

"If you're serious about the pro tour, we'll need to work out twice every day. Three hours in the morning and the same in the afternoon."

"What about school?"

"You'll take correspondence courses over the Internet. Most of the teenagers on tour finish school that way."

"But if I'm on court six hours every day, when will I have time?"

"At night. Connor, becoming a pro is a full time job. Greatness doesn't happen without a price."

"Okay, Mr. Bottega. School sucks anyway."

"There's one other thing I need to know," I said. "I have the feeling that you don't share your dad's goal of you being number one in the world. What's with that?"

"That's his agenda. I dream about going to college and becoming a top surgeon. You know, healing sick people, especially kids, or doing clinical research to find cures for shit like cancer and AIDS, but we can't afford college, let alone medical school. And if I can't be a doctor, well, being a tennis pro is like, you know, the next best thing. I mean, it beats programming a computer or flipping burgers."

"Are your grades good enough for pre-med if you had the money?"

"Totally. I mean, it's all about memorizing shit in books, writing papers, and taking tests. How hard is that?"

He had forfeited his chance at an athletic scholarship by playing the pro tournament in Carmel, which bumped him out of amateur standing, but I explained that with enough hard work and a few good years on tour, he could win enough prize money to pay for college and medical school. "That's easier than attaining number one," I said, "but if tennis is your passion and you're willing to pay the price, becoming a top-twenty player is achievable."

He didn't respond. I knew he felt that his dream was too remote even to hope for, but I couldn't tell which option he yearned after.

"Anything you want to know about me?" I asked.

"Why did you quit? You coached Jared Stoderling, and he was skyrocketing up the rankings until you both vanished."

Bingo. Just the question I had hoped for, because I didn't want any uncomfortable surprises down the road for either of us. "I met Jared at tennis camp when we were teenagers, and we became lovers. On the tour, I relinquished my aspirations of being a player to help develop his career. After four hard years, when our dreams were coming to fruition, the ATP found out we were gay, and they blackballed us."

Connor looked gut-shot. His jaw dropped, and his mouth made a perfect round opening, just about the size of his unblinking eyes. The bond between us shattered. He stepped back, shaking his head, visibly grappling with the shock of it.

In for a penny, in for a pound. "If we work together, some people might assume that we are intimate. They'll whisper behind our backs at every tournament. You'd better be sure you can handle that before we get started, because once the rumor mill starts rolling, it's unstoppable."

A ladies' foursome trooped by us on their way to the clubhouse. Their jewelry sparkled in the sunshine that had broken through the clouds. "Hello, Mr. Bottega," they all crooned.

He waited until they had moved out of earshot before saying, "I'm straight!" His curt tone broadcast that he didn't want anyone believing otherwise, not me and not anyone on the pro tour. He slipped his sunglasses back on and looked as though he was about to cut and run, but he asked, "You're not interested in me? I mean, sexually?" His voice had turned shy.

"No, Connor. I'm not a chicken hawk." I smiled, but he didn't acknowledge my lame attempt at humor, so I pushed on. "Jared and I are still lovers. We have our problems, but there's nobody else for me. Your virtue is categorically safe. It's your reputation that may suffer."

He visibly relaxed, even showed the hint of a grin. He stared at his sneakers and shook his head. "My dad's a straight fascist. He hates gay people. Of course, he hates anybody that's not Chinese."

"If you still want my help, we'll tell him and let the stuff hit the fan."

"Why? It's none of his business what you do off the court. None of mine either."

I began to protest but stopped because his sudden attitude change baffled me. One minute he looked ready to bolt, the next he seemed accepting. Could his only issue have been fear of me hitting on him?

"Does this mean you still want to work with me?"

"I need time to think."

"Fair enough. Let me show you the rest of the layout here before you decide."

The facility had a dozen pristine hard courts, but the two clay courts were my pride and joy. As we approached them, he veered off the concrete walkway and stepped onto the nearest court, sliding his foot across the moist clay. "If I could win any one tournament, I would choose the French Open. Can you teach me how to be a great dirt-baller?"

The clay court tennis that dominates Europe and Latin America connects more closely with my core values than the hard court tennis that prevails in North America. For me, clay courts represent the true spirit of the game, which champions finesse, patience, strategy, and endurance, whereas the hard court game is primarily one of aggression, short points, and instant gratification from blasting winners. Clay court tennis gives me satisfaction from playing long, grueling points and from the tactical thinking that goes into every game. Connor's interest in becoming a dirt-baller hopefully meant we shared the same core values.

I nodded. Again, I saw my reflection in those dark circles of glass hiding his eyes.

I thought I felt something gelling again, but I couldn't be sure. The fact that my facility had the only clay courts in San Francisco gave me an edge, but was it enough? "Talk it over with your father. Make sure you're both comfortable with everything, and I mean everything."

"Tell me one thing," he said. "Can you make me a top contender on the terre battue?"

"I know what you need to get there. Whether you can learn from me is another question. We'll just have to roll the dice and see."

He took off his dark glasses again. The tentative set to his eyes transformed his entire face, making him ravishing, at least in my eyes.

"I know you can help my game, Mr. Bottega, but I'm not sure I can handle this gay thing. I mean, I don't care that you're gay, but it feels weird that people will assume I am too."

His reluctance felt like a knife twisting in my gut, but I understood: he was proud. I liked that about him. I hesitated, knowing he needed more coaxing and that this opportunity was too momentous to let slip away, but I didn't know what else to say. My safe job, my entire life, seemed like a low-salt, fat-free, sugarless diet. I wanted this badly.

"Go home and mull it over. If you're interested, be here Saturday morning and we'll make it happen. If not…." I paused and shrugged. "I wish you luck." I tried to sound matter-of-fact, like it didn't matter one way or the other, but I couldn't mask the pleading tone in my voice.

Connor reached out and clasped my hand, shaking it firmly. "I'll think it over, Mr. Bottega."

He turned and jogged back to the clubhouse, leaving me in the center of my sanctuary, which suddenly felt way too small.

CHAPTER 4

BY THE time I began grade school, I was already haunted by visions of the perfect tennis player: Stefan Edberg. Watching him on television, scampering gazelle-like over the court, his hair falling across his boyish face like golden thatch, he overwhelmed me with his understated elegance. His ethereal serve-and-volley game—a balletic arch to his back and nimble glide to the net—seemed effortless. And ever since my first glimpse of his toned body squeezed into those virginal white shorts, I have worshiped at the altar of the male tennis player. As I neared puberty, his image meshed with the sexual energy that began to simmer in my chest. Since then, I've wanted to be, and wanted to love, a tennis player.

My father, half Shoshone and half Spanish, felt that his two hitches as a Marine helicopter pilot in Vietnam were the high point of his life, after which he became an insurance claims adjuster in Los Angeles. He pushed me toward team sports, football and basketball, as a way to toughen me, but to me, those sports had no grace, no symmetry. Edberg had demonstrated to me that sports were meant to be poetic, where you pit yourself against an opponent and the execution is breathtaking: a ballet solo spotlighting you while sumptuous music fills the surrounding void.

My mother emigrated from the province of Canton to Saigon, where she met my father during the war. She was by no means beautiful, but she had the most unique features of any mother in our neighborhood—tall and slender, a longish face with high cheekbones and slanted eyes, silky raven black hair—all of which she passed on to me. The only attribute I inherited from my father's bloodline was hairless skin the color of sun-baked iodine.

Devout, dutiful, and Buddhist, my mother never assimilated into my father's Catholic family. His clan sang the praises of Catholicism, but it played too many false and hypocritical notes for my ears. My mother's lessons also troubled me, but for different reasons. Buddhism stretched my mind into new dimensions, but the pure sound of the Dharma always brought clarity whenever I achieved a still mind.

I felt the same way about my mother, drawing close to her in ways that I never could with my father. Early on, she recognized my love for tennis and for tennis players. During my pre-teen years, before the sexual part of my obsession blossomed, she enrolled me at the local tennis academy, where I learned the game.

But she, more than anyone, taught me the inner game. Relying on her knowledge of Zen, she taught me to focus on the razor's edge of the unwavering present. That, she explained, was how to expand the chi, the Chinese word for the indwelling force. The Japanese call it *ki*, the Hindus call it *Prana*, the Apache call it *diyin*, but it's all the same force.

She taught me how to do what she called a power-shift—that is, through posture, breath control, and an empty mind, to shift my focus from the thoughts in my head to the feelings in my abdomen, where chi energy generates. That lowered my center of gravity and energized my body with this chi force. This shift in perspective is like flipping a switch. The tension and anxiety that accrue in the mind dissolve, bringing about a greater awareness, balance, and composure—all of which helped my tennis game.

I met Jared Stoderling during my first year at Piedmont Hills Tennis Academy. Already in his third year, he had developed a strong, tawny body. His fawn-colored hair and a Milky Way of freckles scattered across his face gave him a farm-boy image that matched the calm wonder in his pale gray-green eyes.

I began loving him before I realized we shared the same passion for tennis. I heard him play the piano in the players' lounge, which impressed me. Even at that young age, he could sight read well enough to pull off a Bach invention, but only because he played fast enough to hide his mistakes.

We became inseparable; took the same classes at school and practiced tennis together for three hours every weekday afternoon. On weekends we augmented our tennis with hiking the hills, boogie-boarding at the beach, and lazing around the yard daydreaming about winning the French Open Doubles Championship on the red clay at Roland Garros stadium in Paris: the legendary terre battue.

Jared slept at my house every weekend, mine rather than his because I had bunk beds. We stayed up late doing homework and making plans for the next day. We never discussed girls, sex, or any sport other than tennis. When my father called for lights-out, we stripped down to our jockey shorts. Jared took the top bunk and I the lower. I loved drifting off to sleep with the rhythm of his soft breathing in my ears.

By morning, we'd be snuggled together in the lower bunk. Every sleepover, before dawn, Jared would slip in next to me, and I would wake up cocooned in his warmth. For six years, we never did anything more than cuddle as morning sunlight bled through the blinds.

The summer before our senior year, we made love for the first time while camping with six other boys at Yosemite Valley. The hike from the valley floor up Vernal Falls trail to Little Yosemite Valley took all day. As the sun set, we raised our two-man tent beside a gurgling stream about a stone's throw from the other tents.

We all slurped spaghetti and tomato sauce around a campfire while the sky turned a deep shade of lavender. We all wished on the first star, which was probably Mars or Venus, but we didn't care.

James Glader, our tennis team captain, brought out a quart bottle of Wild Turkey, unscrewed the cap, and passed it around the circle. As I tilted my head back to swallow, I saw black clouds boiling over the treetops. Gusts of wind rolled through the trees and drowned out the buzz of insects and the chirp-song of frogs. The bottle made its way around the circle again before the fire hissed from a raindrop falling on the embers.

I glanced up, and an icy drop of water stung my cheek.

"Fuck," James moaned.

"What are we going to do?" I asked, all wide-eyed and nervous as the sky swelled with rainclouds.

Jared patted me on the shoulder and signaled with a nod of his head, saying in his relaxed, easy way, "You boys can sit around soggy ashes eating cold marshmallows if you want, but I'm heading for my tent. See you in the morning."

I stood up. The wind, now armed with flints of rain, struck my face. I turned my back to it, followed Jared to the tent, and crawled in after him. The world collapsed behind a veil of rain. Jared lit a candle. I placed it in the candleholder and hung it from the peaked roof. We knelt side by side like alter boys waiting for the sacraments, peeling off our clothes and spreading out our sleeping bags.

He sprawled on his bag with his head resting in the crook of his arm. The wet strands of hair plastered to his forehead merged with the candlelight to form a halo around his freckled face. I stared into his eyes. They widened, but he did not look away.

I had admired his nakedness in the gym hundreds of times and had pressed into his warm curves every weekend, so I don't know why this time felt different. It could have been the effect of the whiskey or perhaps the distinct feeling of being abandoned by the rest of the world, but for the first time, an irresistible intimacy flared between us, as if something tangible had ignited our insides. Even at that age, I knew from the way he offered himself to me that I would love him and he would accept my love. Those were our destined roles: me the lover, he the loved. He would always maintain an aloof control, while I orbited him like a lesser moon.

What happened next is seared in my memory for eternity. He pulled me toward him, bringing my face to his until our lips brushed. My hand rested on his chest. The heat under his skin felt like a fever rising. Our hearts pounded to the same cadence. After a hesitation, I kissed him back, a long and supple kiss.

A delicious rush of electricity spilled down my spine, exploding in my genitals. His tongue conquered my mouth; all the while, I felt my head reeling. Those lips, their sumptuous softness, set my mind adrift in intoxication. His breath slid down the nape of my neck, curling over my chest. The universe tumbled away, and nothing existed except the feel of his lips on mine and the mounting need in my groin.

My cheek rubbed his and found its way to his hair: silky, smelling of rain. My body quivered like the galvanic response of a nervous animal. He ran a hand down my flank, gentling me like an unbroken colt.

The rain became a steady rhythm on the tent, its syncopated melody merged with our breathing. As the candle burned down, my lips and fingertips explored his contours. His eyes half closed, lips parted, he moaned from somewhere deep below his sternum. I tasted every part of him—neck, nipples, flanks—feeding on the muscles rippling beneath his honeyed skin. His hips thrust against me, grinding his erection into my flesh.

His thighs parted, and I buried my face in the hot silkiness of his genitals. Every nerve ending in my body ignited. We both cried out, barely audible groans that came up from the pelvis and echoed in the tent. The rain muffled our cries. Sweat-drenched and panting, our body rhythms slowed, falling into harmony with the sound of the rain. A heaviness overtook me, and I nuzzled into his warmth as sleep took me.

As dawn's light filled the interior of our tent, the harsh sounds of clanking pots and raw cursing voices echoed from around the fire pit. I awoke to the imposing weight of Jared's body pressing down on me. His face nestled in my hair, and his legs threaded with mine. I pretended to sleep so that I could enjoy the feel of him for a few minutes longer, but he lifted his arm, and his fingertips brushed the hair from my face. He kissed my cheek. I opened my eyes when he whispered, "Morning, lover-boy."

I gazed at him, and he became shy until I kissed him back and whispered that I loved him, that my feelings would never diminish, that I would love him with my last breath. We made love again, making the others wait, not caring if they knew.

Our passion had survived the daylight, and from that morning on, I have kept my word.

WE SPENT our senior year on the practice courts, playing the junior circuit, and making love. School became an afterthought to keep our parents off our backs. Neither of us saw ourselves as gay, which shows just how naïve we were at that age. The utter lack of gay role models contributed to our naïveté. The ones that were visible—effeminate, fluttering, affected men with high, breathless voices—didn't seem to apply to us. We were two boys who happened to fall in love. Our schoolmates couldn't begin to fathom the bond we shared.

On the junior circuit, we both played singles, and we always paired together in doubles. Jared became the more aggressive player both on the courts and in bed. He excelled at doubles but preferred singles. With him, tennis was a fight for supremacy, pitting himself against an opponent, one against one.

I loved doubles: two moving as one, backing each other up, talking strategy between points, setting him up for the put-away, smacking high-fives after big points. For me, tennis was all about merging with my partner to form one cohesive force.

After graduation, we both applied for and were granted full athletic scholarships to the University of Southern California, majoring in Physical Education. Our plan was to transfer to Stanford eventually for advanced degrees in Sports Medicine. My wish upon a star that night in Yosemite had been granted: we would room together, take the same classes, play on the same team.

That summer before classes began, Jared won back-to-back tournaments in Long Beach and San Diego, which earned him enough points for a slot in the US Open Juniors competition in New York. The Open is played over the two weeks surrounding Labor Day, which meant that it would finish just as our fall semester began. We flew to New York, crazed with excitement.

On opening day, we roamed the expansive grounds like puppies. We joked that we should feel right at home because the National Tennis Center is built in the borough of Queens (and although it didn't register then, that was the first time I can remember either of us referring to ourselves as gay). Our laughter soon turned to wonder as we meandered through the maze of twenty-three hard courts and three stadium courts, each one showcasing tennis's brightest stars warming up for round one.

The first round of the junior competition didn't begin until the second week, giving us seven days to saturate ourselves in the euphoria of the tournament before Jared's first match.

The top stars played in the 23,000-seat Arthur Ashe Stadium or the 10,000-seat Louis Armstrong Stadium. Both were loud, chaotic, and electric: the quintessential New York experience. I preferred watching matches on the outer, less populated courts where the players' rankings were lower, but we could sit close enough to see the sweat dripping from their faces.

As week one progressed, we arrived every morning by nine o'clock for an hour-long practice. We spent the rest of the day zigzagging from court to court, stargazing. We caroused the grounds ten hours each day and were bushed by sunset.

Each night we mustered just enough energy to find an Italian or Indian or Chinese restaurant and wolf down dinner before dragging ourselves back to the hotel, where we watched the night matches on television while holding each other between the sheets. Just when I believed life couldn't get any better, week two hit me square in the face like a lightening bolt.

Jared played an eleven a.m. match each day as he fought his way through the draw. We arrived at the practice courts early, drilled for an hour, then hustled to the players' cafeteria to tank up on carbs. More than anything, I loved preparing Jared for his matches, but it was also thrilling to stroll around the grounds in my sweat-soaked tennis clothes while carrying my gear, basking in the crowd's reaction to me. They stared at me like I stared at the top stars. I treasured those looks of homage even though I didn't deserve them yet.

Jared fought his way through four rounds without dropping a set. His killer forehand dictated play and his single-minded attacking style crushed his opponent's confidence. He dropped a set in his quarterfinal match and fought off a match point before winning his semifinal match.

That night in the hotel room, exhausted and happy and proud, we made love five times. The vitality of his winning kept driving us on. By morning I was spent, but Jared's sexual energy had only begun to peak.

It dawned bright and balmy the day Jared played for the juniors' title. We performed our usual routine: warm-up, carb-packing, rubdown. I expected Jared to show signs of nervousness, but he seemed to drift in an interstellar void, a quiet zone I'd never seen before, as if he had played the match in his mind, point by point, and already knew the outcome.

His opponent, a lanky Swede named Tomas Becham, had a monstrous serve, dominating forehand, and cocky swagger that broadcasted he was equally as confident.

The match became a baseline slugfest. Jared faced an adversary who could not only chase down his forehand bullets, but could rocket them back with equal force. They split the first two grueling sets without either player breaking serve. At four-all in the third, Jared rolled his ankle while trying to spin on a dime for a ball hit behind him. From the painful way he limped to his chair, I assumed he would concede the match, but he showed more heart than I gave him credit for. He called for the trainer, who gave him a handful of painkillers and taped his ankle, and play resumed.

At six-all in the third set, Jared stepped to the baseline and served an ace for the first point of the deciding tiebreaker. Each player honed his concentration and amplified his aggressiveness, which produced the kind of unprecedented theater found in the game's elite competitors.

Becham got up a mini-break at 5-5 and served for the match at 6-5. Jared fought back from the brink, winning the point with the last thing anyone expected of him: a drop volley. Becham smashed a service return winner to stay in it at 7-8. Jared saved another match point by sticking an angle volley winner at 11-12. The match ended in dramatic fashion at 15-16, when Becham attempted a drop shot that clipped the tape, hung over the net for a heartbeat before dropping back on his side of the net.

I screamed and jumped five feet straight up out of my seat. I had never been more in love than at that moment when Jared raised both fists over his head and glanced up at me. When our eyes locked, a pinch of nitroglycerine detonated inside my head, and the entire universe aligned into one throbbing sensation of perfection.

That night, during a tandoori chicken dinner in Little India, just off 3rd Avenue, Jared told me that he was turning pro. I shouldn't have been shocked, considering his championship win and the thrill we had experienced of being on the inside of the tournament, but we were supposed to fly home the next day and start classes the day after. It was a done deal and a day away. My dream of our attending college together imploded, leaving me stunned and crushed. The real shocker came when he reached across the table and laced his fingers through mine.

"I can't do it without you," he said. "Be my hitting partner. We'll do it together."

I didn't know what to think. It happened too fast. I was not willing to give up my college aspirations, but they seemed empty without Jared. I shook my head.

"Give it a year," he said. "If it doesn't work out, I'll quit and we'll go back to school. This opportunity may never come again. Who knows what will happen if we don't do this now? Daniel, we're an awesome team. Together we can be great."

Every part of my intellect screamed "no," but I caved into his pleading, gray-green eyes. And it was simple, really: he could never be happy in college, knowing what he'd given up, and I could never be happy without him.

I HAD assumed that my life's work was a matter of my choosing, but when I told my parents I would bypass college to tour with Jared, my father ranted for five full minutes before putting his fist through the kitchen wall.

"Your ass is college-bound," he hissed with a dangerous tone. "Discussion over."

My mother stared down at her hands, her eyes moist with disappointment. She would not, however, try to stop me. She knew why I had made my decision; I saw the comprehension in her tearful eyes.

"I'll give it a year. If it doesn't work out, I'll go back to school."

"If your butt is not in a classroom tomorrow morning," he said, "you're no son of mine. Don't come back home and don't expect anything from me when you fall on your ass. You hear me?"

I hugged my mother. "I'll miss you."

"You've always been more stubborn than him," was all she said.

"You don't get it," Dad continued. "Those bums who scratch out a living with their rackets are the dumb ones. They have shit for brains, too stupid to make something of themselves. But you, you can be any damned thing you want, a doctor, a lawyer, a politician. You're so damned smart that people are throwing opportunities at you."

I grew angry because the larger part of me agreed with him. For the first time in our lives, he and I were on the same wavelength but still on opposite sides of the fence. I wanted to shout at him how much I loved tennis, that I loved a tennis bum (who no doubt had shit for brains), but it was pointless. He could never understand, and she already did.

I packed a bag and walked away without looking back.

CHAPTER 5

ON TOUR, Jared worked with the diligence of a seasoned professional. His work ethic and boyish good looks earned him the reputation of being the small-town, red-blooded American Boy personified.

He dominated his peers with a blistering forehand and sheer hustle, darting about the court and smashing bullets every time he could hit a forehand. He put a hundred percent effort into every point. He always wore the same understated white outfit, and he loved to take on the flashy rivals who followed the Andre Agassi proclamation that "Image is Everything," giving the crowd a farm-boy vs. Hollywood match up. His forehand and his determination took him into the top twenty in just three years.

While Jared played leapfrog in the rankings, I played the challenger circuit, which is tennis's version of the minor leagues, trying to break into the top hundred. My game was pure retriever. Strategy, speed, and stamina were my weapons. Nimble as a cat, I flew over the court, sending every ball back with heavy topspin and no pace, baiting my opponents to go for powerful, low-percentage shots. With each ball I struck, I sent a message across the net: I can do this all day.

I rarely hit an ace, but I never double-faulted, and I didn't crack many winners but seldom missed a passing shot. My strategy usually put me in a winning position, but often as not, I would choke and lose.

My demons surfaced when closing out the match and related to the very nature of competition. In tennis, one player wins and the other loses;

it's unavoidable. One player establishes who is tougher, faster, and/or smarter. The winner earns a sense of superiority, and the loser feels inconsolable. On tour, a player's self-esteem hinges on his most recent performance, and playing well and winning are life-and-death concerns.

I would invariably choke because I would begin to pity the player I was thrashing. I knew I was not a superior person. I also knew how he would feel regardless. Once sympathy crept into my thoughts, my focus crumbled, and the wheels fell off. I could not perform at my peak while carrying that extra mental baggage.

My handicap kept me out of the top echelon, and after two years of being ranked in the one-thirties, I abandoned the challenger circuit to focus on helping Jared.

I poured my frustration of being a second-rate player into honing Jared's game and organizing his tournament schedule, practice agenda, diet, interviews, cross-training, and gym workouts. I pumped him up before a match and calmed him down after. I became the Parris Island drill sergeant of the practice courts, pushing Jared to develop his weak backhand and volleys in order to round out his game. Whatever the drill, I always did it with him, unlike those beer-gut coaches who load up a ball machine and bark encouragements from the sidelines.

My favorite part was giving him rubdowns after a hard-fought match or a grueling practice. I became an expert on every nuance of his muscles and tendons, where he was prone to injuries, and how to treat those injuries. I even tailored a gym routine to strengthen his more fragile muscle groups. If there was ever a hog heaven, I was living it.

After four arduous years of crawling our way up the rankings, with the endorsements and other perks beginning to come our way, Jared played the match of his career in a French Open quarterfinal. Suzanne Lenglen Stadium overflowed with twelve thousand fans. An estimated two million Americans watched on ESPN. Jared pranced off the court as radiant as a shooting star.

That night, we hit the town to celebrate. We wandered through the Marais wide-eyed and breathless. The heavy beat of music oozing from the gay clubs and the parade of beautiful men along the narrow streets had our blood pumping.

We squeezed into a club, the Blue Frog, known for its clientele of elegant men and lovely boys. The men sat along the walls sipping drinks from long-stemmed cocktail glasses. The boys jammed onto the dance floor to perform a gay version of the Hip Hop Shuffle.

We snaked our way to the bar and downed two Cosmos. Jared pulled me onto the floor. He danced loose and cool, with all the attitude of a Justin Timberlake video.

In street clothes and locked in a crush of shirtless, sweaty dancers, we became confident that no one recognized us, so we pulled off our shirts too and began to be sexy with each other, the way we did in the privacy of our apartment. The multi-colored lights glistened, prism-like, through his sweat, and I became hard watching his swaying torso and gyrating crotch. The sexier I felt, the closer I drew to him, until we were an inch apart with the music vibrating between us. Our bodies merged, panting, sweating. We kissed. Under the spell of that throbbing music, I fused into the softness of his lips and became ravenous for more. I cocked my head and ran my tongue along his neck; his salty sweat became nectar.

Someone yelled, "Lick it, baby. You know how," and I knew he meant me. I remember being surprised that they taunted us in English, but I guessed it was obvious we weren't French.

He unbuttoned his jeans and lowered his zipper to half-mast. In street clothes, he never wore underwear, so as his fly peeled open, his pubic hair came into view. The boys around us whistled. I felt swept away by my lust for the creature weaving in front of me. He reached over and unhooked my belt, pulled it from my waist, and draped it around my neck like a dog collar, which he used as a leash to pull my face toward his open fly.

I dropped to one knee, and my face nuzzled his belly. As my lips followed his treasure trail, a bright light exploded over us.

Jared whirled around and zipped up while dancing away, leaving me breathless and alone. The crowd howled in disappointment. I sometimes wonder how far I would have gone if that flash had not made Jared pull away.

That bright light had been a camera flash, and the next day our picture, with my face pressed to Jared's open fly, showed up on the tournament director's desk. We were summoned before the director and told that the ATP had paid a tidy sum to keep that photo out of the papers. Any more publicity of that nature, he explained, and we risked not being invited back.

Adding to our injury, a day later, Jared lost his semi-final match in straight sets to fellow American Nicholas Ahrens. That tournament proved to be the pinnacle of both Jared's career and our relationship. Once rumors of our sexuality leaked to the International Tennis Federation, we began a downward slide, imperceptible at first, then avalanche-like, building in speed and force.

In 1973, Billie Jean King made history by beating fifty-five-year-old Bobby Riggs in the Battle of the Sexes, giving women's tennis some well-deserved recognition. In 1977, Renee Richard, who was Richard Raskind before her sex-change operation, played in the women's draw at the US Open after a legal battle that had denied her entry the year before. In the eighties, it was common knowledge that several top women players were lesbians.

But when it came to sex, the powers that govern professional tennis would be pushed only so far. In our case, everything was whispered behind closed doors, but the message became all too clear: there is no place in professional tennis for gay men.

Jared became the game's whipping boy. The officials shunned us. The endorsements dried up. Competing became a nightmare to get fair treatment. Chair umpires made bad line overrules against Jared, tipping the matches in his opponents' favor.

We trained harder than before, and the fatigue from our workouts helped to anesthetize our frustration, but fatigue alone could not quell all the anger building in both of us. During the worst times, we clung to each other and said, "Screw you bastards," which was the only way we survived as long as we did.

Our last six months on tour transformed Jared into a renegade. He flew into a rage when umpires made bad calls, turning matches into circus-like forums of obscenity, umpire-bashing, and hysterical meltdowns. He plummeted out of the top fifty, then gave up altogether.

We moved to San Francisco and settled into an apartment on Russian Hill with a view of downtown, the Bay Bridge, and the Berkeley hills. After months of bumming around and burning up what money we had put aside, I met Carrie Bennett at a tennis event in Golden Gate Park, and she offered me the job of tennis pro at the Windsor Club. I wrapped that job around me like a cocoon, letting myself be content with teaching people the game.

Jared posted a want ad in the local gay rag offering lessons, and he lined up a dozen students who shelled out fifty bucks each week for a one-hour session. I sometimes wondered what would have happened if I'd gone to college. When those thoughts haunted me, I'd smile and watch them fade away. I had my job and my man. I was happy—as Hemingway said, "as happy as it is safe to be in life."

Then Connor Lin breezed into my little world and ignited a force in my heart that threatened to blow it all away.

CHAPTER 6

THE Saturday following my interview with Connor Lin dawned cool and humid. Broken clouds drifting off the Pacific smudged the morning sky with wide streaks of gray. Being both late and angry had me jogging through the parking lot with my pulse throbbing at my temples. Beside the stone path that led to the clubhouse and at the end of a line of BMWs, Mercedes Benzes and Cadillacs sat a twelve-year-old Chevy delivery van with a crumpled right fender and a sign on the door that read Oakland's Prime Produce. They were at the courts, waiting. That should have pleased me, because until then I had no idea if they would show, but the fact that I had kept them waiting for an hour only fueled my anger.

My morning had begun on a sour note when Jared stumbled through our front doorway at three a.m. after a night of pub-crawling with friends. I tore into him with nine hours of built-up frustration, but I didn't get ten words out before I saw the pain behind those bleary eyes, pain that a deluge of alcohol couldn't drown.

There is a kind of vagueness among drunks, even when they're sober, a look that usually passes for stupidity, but being one of the initiated, I know it's a shield from their pain. As my rage crystallized into pity, I led him to bed, peeled off his clothes, and tucked him between the sheets. Slipping in next to him, I held him until we both fell asleep.

When morning's light turned the windows blue, Jared's body purged itself of its self-induced poison, followed by the shakes and a hangover. I dumped him into a hot bath while the coffee brewed and I changed the bedding. It took an hour to pull him from the tub, force pancakes and painkillers down him, and lead him back to bed.

The drive to work had my stomach performing slow, agonizing somersaults. That was partly due to my car, a '68 VW Bug we lovingly called Slug because of its mustard yellow color. Slug's broken odometer registered all nines, the front windshield had a starburst-patterned crack, and heater-warmed gasoline fumes seeped into the passenger compartment, which often made me nauseous.

That morning, though, my nausea came from being unable to help Jared. His nights out were becoming more frequent. Day by day, I watched him disintegrate. I pleaded with him to see a doctor, but his eyes frosted over, and he gave me the silent treatment. At times, he ignored me for five or six days straight, as if his pain were somehow my fault.

His drinking had robbed us of social interaction with our gay friends, because they would invariably invite us to go out clubbing, and I was intent on keeping Jared as far away from alcohol as humanly possible. His binges always started building a few weeks before a big tournament, particularly a Grand Slam, like a pressure cooker gathering steam, and that first week of play, the lid would blow off and he would focus his hostility inward, incinerating his insides and lashing out at anyone who tried to comfort him.

I HEARD Connor before I saw him, heard the sound of a sweet spot striking the ball in a smooth, metronome-like rhythm. I pulled my thoughts away from Jared and refocused.

Connor was on the show court, dressed in white shorts and a faded blue sweatshirt. But something looked different, and I realized what had changed: he wore clear, wire-rimmed glasses, not the dark Oakleys he had on when I first met him. He must have used contact lenses when he played in Carmel. I took a moment to appraise this new look. It suited him, giving his face a slight bookkeeper's fragility.

Across the net was a blond, about the same age and body type. He wore red shorts and a gray hooded sweatshirt. Both boys were hitting out, smashing the ball with every stroke, and it was easy to understand why: on the clubhouse veranda overlooking court one stood a bevy of teenaged girls dressed in their skimpy tennis skirts and tight blouses. They all squirmed with excitement as they ogled these new boys.

Roy Lin sat at a table on the veranda sipping tea, his eyes glued to the boys. He resembled a stone-faced Mandarin watching two Tae Kwon Do Black Belt Masters in mortal combat, willing his man to defeat the opponent.

I pushed back my parka hood, feeling the sunshine spread over my face.

Connor glanced up at me, smiled, and continued to crush the ball. He put some extra mustard into each swing, no doubt to impress me.

I was impressed, not at how hard he hit the ball, but at the sheer dexterity of his movement: his explosive strides to run down a wide ball, the tiny adjustment steps as his racket looped back and the forward stroke began. The technique of his groundstrokes carved rounded Os through the air with machine-like precision. His footwork and timing were efficient and had that unreal athleticism of Pete Sampras or, I dared to think, Stefan Edberg.

I couldn't blame those girls a bit; he was ravishing. They both were. For a moment I forgot all the practical elements like footwork and timing and I simply admired their poetry, a pair of Appaloosa colts racing across a spring meadow.

A nervous excitement suffused me, obliterating the anger of a few minutes before. Even the sun on my face gave me new optimism.

I strolled into my office to grab a racket and towels, then headed to the show court. As soon as I stepped onto the court, Connor hit a screaming bullet down the line before jogging over to me. His face radiated energy. Up close, I caught the pleasant scent of the sweat that dampened the front of his sweatshirt. I hesitated for a heartbeat as I watched a perfect tear of sweat journey down his temple and hang on his jaw.

The other boy wandered over and stood beside Connor, trying hard to look as if he belonged.

I tossed them each a towel and refocused on tennis.

Connor swiped the towel across his face and shook my hand. He introduced the other boy, Spencer Young, as his regular practice partner. Spencer stood as tall as Connor, but he carried more weight and definition.

His hair, tawny streaks of gold mixed with albino-blond, framed his fine-boned face, which was speckled like a robin's egg from too much time in the sun. A girlish loveliness softened his eyes, which were very large and teal blue.

"Hope you don't mind me bringing Spence here, Mr. Bottega. He wanted to meet you."

I shook Spencer's hand, thinking, *This could be great*: if Spencer chaperoned our practice sessions, Mr. Lin had no reason to take issue with my being gay.

A sheen of sweat moistened Spencer's forehead and sparkled in the sunshine. He looked like the Caucasian equivalent of Connor, only softer, more sensitive, and his youth combined with his innocence to give him a slightly dopey air that I found very alluring. *Yes*, I thought, and I encouraged Spencer to join every practice. The notion struck me that Connor had already thought of that. Did he feel the need for a chaperone?

I led them to the middle of the court, and I sat on the service line beside the net. They joined me, the three of us sitting in a tight circle. I did this to give them a different perspective of the court. A note of confusion marred Connor's face, but he played along without comment.

Before I could begin the lesson, Connor spread his legs and toweled them off, starting at his calves and working his way up his inner thighs. His shorts bunched up, exposing more of his thighs: pale skin as smooth as porcelain and laced with thin blue veins.

The words caught in my throat like a hummingbird in a net. I noticed a series of fine muscle tremors moving under the skin of both legs. They had overdone the warm-up, and I reminded myself that Connor's legs could be injury-prone or fall prey to cramping.

"Drape those towels over your legs so you don't cool down too fast."

I turned my head in time to see a look of sexual interest etched on Spencer's face. He couldn't draw his attention away from Connor's exposed thighs. His eyes crept further up Connor's legs to the fullness in the crotch of his shorts. Spencer's mouth hung open, making a little red O. His story became crystal clear. He was aroused by Connor's fresh, kid-brother sexiness. His adoration of Connor made me like him all the more.

"Sure thing, Mr. Bottega," Spencer said with a mild voice. He grudgingly pulled his attention away from Connor to cover his own legs.

Spencer's obvious puppy love made me grin, but I hardened my resolve and put on my poker face. "Your first mistake," I began, "was coming onto this court without a plan. These club hackers can do that, but we must always act with purpose and intelligence."

Connor's smile faded. His mouth opened to say something, but I cut him off.

"Your second mistake was showing off instead of warming up. If you want to impress those girls, get your butts up there and talk to them. Impress them with who you are, not how hard you can hit the ball. Any time you're on the court, you must zero in on executing our plan."

Connor dropped his head and studied his sneakers.

"Your third mistake was hitting the beans out of the ball without a proper warm-up."

"Sorry, Mr. Bottega," Connor said without looking up. "We've always done it that way."

I reached over and patted his shoulder to let him know I understood. "Before I show you how to perform a proper warm-up, I want to give you my most valuable lesson." I paused until Connor looked up and we locked eyes. "The first time my partner, Jared, gave me a piano lesson, he taught me about perfect practice."

Connor grinned. "You play piano?"

"Connor, are we here to discuss my personal life?"

"Sorry, Mr. Bottega."

"You've heard that practice makes perfect?" They both nodded. "Well, that's bullshit. Practice reinforces what you practice. If you practice with bad form, you reinforce bad form. The only way to perfect technique is by doing what Jared called perfect practice. Understand?"

"Everything except what perfect practice is," Connor said.

"For the piano it means to play a piece of music as slowly as is necessary to perform it perfectly, to move your fingers from one note to the next without making any mistakes in finger position or cadence. If it takes an hour to play the Minute Waltz perfectly, that's what you do. Make a mistake and you stop and do it again, only slower. You see, your body learns. The second time, it will take fifty-eight minutes, and fifty-two the third time. Before you know it, you're playing it as it was intended, and because you've always played it perfectly, you never develop any wrong habits."

"But this is tennis," Connor said. "You can't take an hour to hit the ball."

"I'm feeling resistance here."

"Sorry, Mr. Bottega."

"First off, I want us to perform a perfect warm-up, the way I want you to warm up every time we step on court. We'll start with you both on one side of the net hitting balls to me. Don't swing any harder or any faster than I do. Mimic me. Focus on breath control and seeing the ball. By breath control, I mean inhale into the lower abdomen so that your belly expands like a balloon. That gives you a fuller breath, which makes you take in more air. As you hit the ball, I want you to grunt."

They both gave me a queer look as I demonstrated the technique.

"Grunting makes you exhale so that you automatically inhale after hitting the ball. That keeps you breathing during a rally, and focusing on your breathing keeps your mind free of thoughts. Understand? Correct breathing keeps your mind empty as difficulty and exertion levels increase. That's what I'm after: for you to keep your mind blank."

"But that makes no sense." Connor said, a whiny note creeping into his voice. "You said that seventy percent of tennis is between the ears. Why keep our minds empty?"

"Connor, you play your best when you're in the zone, right?"

He nodded and tilted his head to one side.

"When you're in your zone, what are you thinking?"

"I told you, it's like I'm not there. I'm not thinking anything."

"So you play your best when your mind is silent; your body takes over and it all tumbles into place, right?"

Connor's eyes drilled into my skull.

"That's what I plan to show you," I continued, "how to put yourself in the zone every time you play. I'll teach your body to play perfect tennis and your ego to stay out of the way so your body can do what I teach it. Now, what I'm trying to get across here is that breath control and keeping the mind still are the chariots of creating the zone, what my mother called the power-shift."

Connor nodded, even though I was sure he didn't understand.

"Good. Let's start with the two of you on that side of the net and inside the service line."

Connor glanced up at the group of girls still huddled at the edge of the deck. He turned back to me and groaned, "That's baby tennis. I haven't done that in years."

"Show me you can do it perfectly and we'll up the ante."

"But Mr. Bottega—" He looked up at the deck again.

"Connor," I cut him off, "if you're concerned about what those girls or your father or anybody else thinks, then you're wasting my time. If you're too good to do things my way, then you're too good, and we'll shake hands and call it quits. Otherwise, get your butt over there and let's hit some balls."

With a visible surrender, he abandoned his protest and they dragged themselves into position. I told them I wanted to see their bellies expanding with each breath, and when they were, I floated balls to one, then the other, like a slow-motion ballet. I hit the ball perfectly each time: split-step when either of them hit the ball, full upper-body turn and back-swing, seeing the ball all the way to the racket, grunt, good follow-through. I wanted to demonstrate, let them see rather than think about what I wanted from them.

Spencer had no problem concentrating on his breathing and floating a clean ball back to me each time, but Connor had trouble constraining his strokes. He sprayed balls past me. The exercise stymied him like a thoroughbred racehorse forced to pull a milk wagon.

Roy Lin's raw voice boomed over the court, telling Connor to focus.

"Don't listen to him," I said. "Focus on mimicking me, nothing more. When the body is free of the ego, the chi expands, and it will surpass your expectations."

Too much telling fills the mind with obstacles to overcome. Images are better teaching tools than words, so I minimized my verbal instructions and focused on doing the exercise flawlessly. Spencer began to enjoy himself, perhaps because he did it so much better than Connor, who couldn't return more than five balls without spraying one too deep or into the net. His cheek muscles tightened with every mistake, and his lips pressed together in an effort to force concentration.

Roy's voice cut the air again, telling Connor to split-step.

"Damn it," Connor mumbled after knocking one into the net. "Eyes on the ball, blockhead."

I stopped and walked to the net. "Connor, who are you talking to?"

"Just reminding myself to see the ball."

"This is important," I said. "Tell me, who spoke and who was he speaking to?"

"I just told you, I was talking to myself."

"So, you're telling me that your 'I' and your 'self' are two different entities. Otherwise there's no need for conversation between them."

The same baffled expression crossed both their faces. I explained that each of us has two selves, the ego (conscious mind) and the body (unconscious mind and nervous system). Connor had made all those errors because his ego kept trying to control his body. His ego dictated what to do and blamed the body when the communication broke down and it made a mistake.

They both shook their heads, still baffled.

"The funny thing is, your body already knows what to do, and it doesn't need anything controlling it. But your ego is like Mr. Lin: it can't just sit back and enjoy the game; it's got to try and run the show."

Connor smiled and glanced at his sneakers.

"That's why Spencer has no problem. His ego is so small, it's easy for him to silence it."

Connor punched Spencer in the arm, and they both laughed.

"Okay, so we're going to focus on breathing into the lower belly to expand our chi and at the same time, try to quiet the ego so the body can do what it already knows. Let's do it again, and if you hear that voice in your head saying anything at all, that's a warning that Mr. Ego is taking control. That's the time to concentrate on just breath control and seeing the ball."

We continued to float balls back and forth. Connor relaxed a bit, but he visibly struggled to harness his inner voice. Spencer had found something that he could do better than Connor, and he glowed.

We drilled for two hours, always hitting softly. Whenever Connor returned twenty consecutive balls, we backed up one step while putting more pace on the ball, working our way to the baseline. Whenever he made an error, we stepped forward and took pace off.

After we reached the baseline and hit out long enough for them to demonstrate they could control their shots, I waved them forward.

"That's how I want you to warm up," I told them, "starting inside the service line with no pace and work back to the baseline. Now that you know how, it should take ten to fifteen minutes. Then you can hit out."

They had learned a hard lesson and done well. Inside, I beamed, but I didn't let it show. "Grab some water and pull on your sweats," I said. "We'll take a run to build up your legs."

They piled into the clubhouse, and I strolled over to Roy. He popped a Tums into his mouth and chewed with force, as if he were crunching my skull with every bite.

"I don't understand," he said, "how this baby tennis helps Connor's strokes?"

"It doesn't, but like I said, there's more to this game than strokes. Give it time, Mr. Lin. The Great Wall took four dynasties to complete."

"But what's the point of all this?"

"I'm getting him to tap into his chi," I said, getting a little annoyed. "The lesson stems from the esthetic poise of him striking the ball with his inner force and from the beauty within the flight of a well-struck ball, that is, man transformed into pure action." I could see he was not satisfied with my answer, but I was in no mood to find another way to explain it, so I said, "It's not something that can be expressed with words. It has to be felt."

I darted into my office and grabbed a book from my bookcase: *A Book of Five Rings* by Miyamoto Musashi. Connor and Spencer were back on the veranda by the time I walked back and handed the book to Roy.

"I want you all to read this carefully, and read it again. It explains why we expand the chi so much better than I can."

Roy grunted and handed it back to me. "This was written by a Jap."

I was stunned. I felt heat rising to my temples. I took a deep breath to make sure my voice came out smooth, with no trace of anger. "It's arguably the finest book ever written on strategy and the warrior mindset."

"Do you have any idea, Mr. Bottega," Roy said, "what the Japs did to our people in the thirties and forties?"

"Mr. Lin, Musashi was born in the fifteen hundreds. I assure you he never set foot on Chinese soil. Musashi fuses Zen, Shinto, and Confucianism in order to form a philosophy that every champion needs to utilize."

Roy's back stiffened. "I will not allow this book in my house."

I felt my whole face redden as I handed the book to Connor. "I guess you'll have to read this on your porch."

He slipped the book into his tennis bag while staring at Roy with an obstinate expression that challenged his father's stern glare. Turning to me, he asked, "Ready?"

Good, I thought. Roy had just learned a hard lesson himself: in the game of professional tennis, coach always trumps parent.

We sprinted through the woods at the edge of the golf course, heading toward the sea. Connor took the lead, setting a brisk pace. Spencer and I dogged his heels. I loved to run through those woods, and doing so made the day's frustrations vanish and produced an exhilarating, glad-to-be-alive energy that exploded through my system.

Waves of wind rolled over us, drenching our faces as we plunged through pools of sunshine and shadows. I noticed everything: the tangled colors of Spencer's hair flashing in the noontime light, the sound of our feet crunching the moist dirt, the trees and greens and golfers going by lickety-split.

Before reaching the northern-most fairway, we squeezed through a gap in the fence and crossed over the Great Highway. We ran along the pavement until we came to Ocean Beach. Running on sand was a great exercise to strengthen Connor's legs. We flew past sunbathers lounging on the sand and ran for two miles with nobody in sight. Waves trounced the beach with a steady rhythm that merged with my thumping heart.

I had not run on loose sand in over six months. Three miles had my legs burning. I slowed the pace until I came to a standstill, looking across that blue plane at the point where the horizon stretched into infinity. I told them to catch their breath before we headed back, but before I finished saying the words, they had tossed off their sweats and run all-out and bare-assed for the surf. Their naked skin shimmered in the strong sunlight.

"That water's freezing!" I yelled, but they were already knee-deep and howling from the cold. A spray of fine mist haloed around them as they tumbled through the boiling surf. The sun's rays electrified the spray and gave it a cool golden color that looked like bullets of liquid gold pelting those two perfect beings.

Connor tackled Spencer, and they disappeared beneath the swirling foam. For a split second I felt a stab of concern, but they appeared in the next heartbeat with rivers of water running off their skin. The cold had them shrieking. Spencer tried to fight his way to shore, but Connor kept dragging him back into the oncoming waves.

Their frolicking brought a smile to my face, then had me doubled up with laughter, then caused an aching in my chest. I felt a space open just under my sternum, about the size of a fist and as dense as silt. I seemed to tilt to one side, which pulled me off balance for the time I stood watching them. I realized that the heaviness that pressed against my heart was envy. I yearned to join them, to be eighteen and naked and defying the cold, but I stayed on the beach, unable to pull my eyes away.

I have experienced envy twice in my life, and that was one of them.

CHAPTER 7

CONNOR and Spencer knocked on my door at six thirty p.m. for an informal meeting to discuss their training program. I ushered them into my large and sunny living room. Connor wore a white cotton shirt buttoned to the collar, faded jeans, spectacles, and his coffee-colored hair pulled back into a neat ponytail. Spencer had on a baby-blue wool sweater and the same style jeans as Connor, and his hair hung around the borders of his face.

They glanced around the room as they shucked their jackets and tossed them on a chair by the door. The room had an austere openness. The few pieces of comfortable furniture were of Asian design, and the intricately patterned Tibetan carpets covering the hardwood floors gave the room a cheerful complexity. The dining area nestled on the far side of the room, where a row of bay windows spanned the east wall, overlooking downtown and the Bay Bridge.

Spencer sauntered to the corner beyond the dining table to study a five-foot high bronze statue of the Buddha, cast in the Thai style. He looked around the room, his attention lighting on the four other Buddha carvings, three sitting and one reclining. Bright bits of gold flake covered the reclining Buddha, and it glistened in the light pouring in through the windows. He moved to the fireplace to study the four Chinese porcelain statues on the mantle. They looked antique and expensive, but I had found them at a thrift shop in Chinatown and picked them up for next to nothing.

"This place is sick," Spencer said. "Like the Asian art museum."

"Sick?" I asked.

"That's a good thing, like totally awesome, only better." He scanned the room again with a puzzled look and asked, "So like, where's the tube?"

"We don't watch television."

He stared at me as if I had suddenly grown a second head.

Connor stood in the middle of the living room absorbing every detail. His attention gravitated to the only non-Asian artwork in the apartment, a large canvas on the wall behind the ebony baby grand piano: a Gauguin copy, four naked Polynesian women done in reds and browns with a smudge of mustered yellow slicing across the background.

"You're Buddhist," Connor said. "This décor seems more Japanese than Chinese. Very Zen. I expected a wall of trophies and pictures taken on the pro tour."

My orange tabby cat, Mr. Toa, brushed against Connor's leg. He bent and scooped Mr. Toa to his chest, stroking the cat's ears. Mr. Toa scrambled to his shoulder and perched there, pawing at Connor's ponytail as if it were knitting yarn.

"We like to stay in the present as much as possible," I said, avoiding any discussion of how painful those past memories were. "Make yourselves comfortable. Tea and juice are in the fridge, bathroom's down the hall. Who wants to help in the kitchen?"

Spencer nodded and followed me across the dining room. He froze, however, as Jared sauntered down the hallway wearing a bath towel more or less draped around his waist, his feet making wet footmarks on the hardwood floor. Jared leaned against the wall looking somewhat sodden and perplexed; then a cool grin spread his lips. I had come home earlier and found him stumbling drunk, so I hustled him into a cold shower, where he'd been for a long time. Long enough, I hoped, to sober him up.

"Well, well. Who do we have here?" Jared said, gazing at Spencer. He marginally slurred his words, which gave me hope that he had sobered enough to avoid embarrassing himself in front of our guests.

Spencer's mouth dropped as he stared at Jared's water-softened face and virile torso.

"Connor, Spencer, meet Jared," I said, noticing the tip of Jared's tongue sliding over his lower lip. "Jared, perhaps our guests would feel more comfortable if you put some clothes on."

Spencer cleared his throat. "I don't mind."

A line of red rose above Connor's collar and spread over his face. Was he embarrassed, I wondered, or jealous?

"Nice to meet you," Jared said. His grin widened into a smile, and he winked at Spencer. Turning, he sauntered back down the hallway and disappeared into the bedroom.

The kitchen was as sparse as the rest of the apartment. Nothing cluttered the green stone countertops, cabinets, or the deep copper sink in the corner, as if gale force winds had swept everything away. Evening light poured through the window above the sink. On fogless days, you could see Alcatraz and Angel Island and white sails dotting the bay from that window.

Spencer stepped to the sink to wash his hands before handling any food. "Wow, your views are awesome. This place must cost a wad."

"Not really. The owner's a tennis fanatic, and Jared gives him three lessons a week for a break on the rent."

"I can't wait to get my own place."

"You don't like living with your parents?"

"They're cool, but I want a place that's more me and less them."

I had him pull dumplings out of the steamer and arrange them on a serving platter and pour the boiled soybeans and unsalted peanuts into serving bowls. While he busied himself with that, I sliced a beautiful red slab of raw tuna and began making sushi. I held a slice toward him.

"You like sashimi?"

He leaned toward me and snatched the fish from my fingers with his open mouth. He made an "ummm" sound as he chewed.

"You're off to college next year, right? You'll be on your own?"

He shook his head. "Stanford is close enough that I'll stay at home and commute by car."

"So where does Connor fit into these plans?"

"Nowhere. With any luck, he'll be globetrotting on the pro circuit."

"Does he know how you feel about him?"

A long silence spanned into minutes as he arranged the dumplings around the dipping sauce bowl. He drew a deep breath and said, "Con and I never talk about that. I don't know anyone I can discuss those feelings with."

Jared ambled into the kitchen wearing a red polo shirt and blue jeans, but he was barefoot, and his breath still smelled of whiskey. He came up behind me, wrapped his arms around my waist, and kissed the back of my neck.

"Honey, you smell great." He hadn't called me "Honey" in four years. He growled in my ear that he was starving and reached for a slice of tuna, popping it into his mouth.

I turned to face him, our noses an inch apart, and I gave him my best who-are-you-trying-to-impress look. He smiled as he chewed, not backing away. The doorbell rang, and I said, "Jared, honey, make yourself useful and answer the door."

Jared filched another slice of tuna before strolling to the living room. Spencer's teal-colored eyes sparkled as he said, "You're so lucky."

I began to tell him that everything has its price, but I stopped myself. *Yes*, I thought, *I am lucky, price or no price*. I winked at him and said, "If you ever need to talk about those feelings, I'm a sympathetic listener." I wiped my hands on a dishtowel and patted him on the shoulder, moving past him to welcome the newly arrived guests.

Carrie stood inside the front door, introducing a young woman to Jared and Connor.

I welcomed Carrie, who wore a soigné business suit and high heels that made her tower above everybody. She introduced Shar Paulot. Shar shook Jared's hand and gave him a bottle of wine.

She was tall for a woman, slender, perhaps twenty-two years old, and neither black nor white but rather a golden rum color—obviously the product of varied bloodlines. I was struck by the fact that she wore a man's Homburg hat, dark brown with a small yellow feather tucked into the black silk band. Her dark hair swept straight back, accentuating the thinness of her face, and a purple ribbon held her hair in place behind her neck. She also wore a black one-piece bathing suit, a sheer flower-print skirt that draped from her waist to just below her knees, and lizard-skin high heels. She epitomized the cool and colorful Caribbean look.

I took her hand and stepped back to look at her—no makeup, serenely immaculate, a flawless figure—*chic*, I thought, and the hat lent a unique impression.

"You look ravishing," I said. "I'm so pleased to meet you. And this is Spencer."

Spencer balanced a tray with six glasses of mint-flavored iced tea.

"Hello, Spencer. And thank you, Mr. Bottega. You have a lovely home," she said with a smoky, cultivated voice that reminded me of melted chocolate, all sweet and warm and somewhat self-amused. "But when does the rest of your furniture arrive?"

"Oh, we like to keep things simple," I said, annoyed. Actually, I was proud of the apartment's austerity.

"It's more lovely now that you're here," said Connor, whose face had grown ashen. "I love your hat. It makes you look dangerous, you know, like a gangster."

"Dangerous? Oh my, darling, thank you. It belonged to my ex-roommate. She's a dyke, and she made me wear it everywhere so people would think I was her butch. When I moved away, she gave it to me." She laughed, covering her mouth with her long and graceful fingers. "It was too embarrassing for her to be seen with a straight girl." She glanced at Carrie, and I got the distinct impression, from that gleam in her eye and from Carrie's slight blush, that she was talking about Carrie.

She turned her attention back to Connor. "And you're the dear boy who's to become the best tennis player in the world."

Connor said, "I used to pray every night for that to come true, but it's such a long shot that I gave up hope. I'll settle for winning a Masters Cup or a Slam."

Shar smiled. "Be careful of what you pray for, darling. Saint Therese once said, 'More tears are shed over answered prayers than unanswered ones,' and you never know, God may decide to shine Her undivided attention on granting your wish, and that would be dreadful."

"Dreadful?" Connor asked.

"It's been my experience that as soon as someone achieves whatever it is they desire, dear boy, they no longer value it. I'm afraid that's human nature. I think most people are only happy when dreaming about what they covet, regardless of what treasures they already possess. It seems their happiness comes from things they lack."

"I disagree," I said. "I believe people are happiest when they are working, inch by inch, toward their life's goal. But you're right, as soon as you achieve it, the shine dulls and you take it for granted. The trick is to have lofty goals that you can never attain, like world peace or ending hunger."

"Or becoming the best tennis player in the world," Connor said, grinning.

Shar noticed the Gauguin painting and sauntered toward it. Her lizard skin shoes seem to ripple as she walked, as if they were still alive. Posing herself at the piano, she studied the painting until Connor gravitated to her side.

The women in the painting had supple and haughty postures. Connor cleared his throat and told her, "You look like you stepped out of this painting."

"That's my Senegalese blood. Did you know, darling, that Paul Gauguin painted on my home island of Martinique before living among the Polynesians?"

"You lived in the Caribbean?"

She smiled. "*Oui. Oui.* Born on Martinique, high school in New Orleans, college at Stanford."

Spencer offered her tea, and as she lifted her glass, he said, "I'll attend Stanford next year."

"My apartment is close to campus. Perhaps we can room together and share expenses?"

"Wish I could, but I'll be staying with my folks here in the city."

"Pity. It would be amusing to live with such a sensitive-looking boy."

Spencer blushed as he glanced at his tray of drinks. I became convinced that she enjoyed embarrassing anybody and everybody, and that somehow made me like her.

"So what's Martinique like?" Connor asked in an attempt to take back the conversation.

"You should see for yourself, darling, but you must come during Carnival. Carnival on Martinique is a small affair compared to New Orleans, without the racket and stench and drunks stumbling over themselves."

"Sounds wicked."

"The sequined gowns and Marie Antoinette wigs, the beautiful men in skimpy costumes, and the rumba dancing 'til dawn are all wonderful, devilishly so."

"We can start on dinner if everybody's hungry," I said. "Jared, honey, can you pour the wine, and Spencer, will you help bring everything to the table?"

Dinner was a simple affair: bowls of warm ginger-marinated shrimp and rice-noodle salad, steamed pork buns, shrimp and leek dumplings, four different sushi rolls, and an assortment of raw vegetables arranged on bamboo platters.

Jared poured wine into bone china rice bowls, explaining that we never drank wine, so we didn't have suitable wineglasses. The wine, a French Bordeaux, was a shocking ruby red, tannic, and lovely against the pearl white china. The overhead lighting filtered through the wine; the bowls' insides glowed crimson, a warm sunrise within each rim.

Raising our bowls with all eyes locked on Connor, I said, "We're all here to contribute to the career of this talented athlete. His success will be a team effort."

Bewilderment spread across Connor's face. As dinner progressed, his confusion visibly deepened until he asked Shar, "How will you contribute to my success?"

Shar sipped her wine before answering, "Darling, Carrie has hired me to help with your physical conditioning. Has no one told you?"

He shook his head. "You sure don't look like a fitness trainer."

Shar's eyes grew less friendly. She made a slow pronouncement. "I've earned a degree in sports medicine. What I bring to this party is the intelligence to create a total fitness program and the drive to encourage you to follow it. But perhaps you'd prefer some jock whose only talent is pumping iron…?"

Before Connor could defend himself, I added, "There's another reason she's on the team. You see, I don't regret my decision to coach you, but my being gay will make things difficult. People love gossip, and I'm afraid they'll whisper that we're an item—the classic older gay seducing the boy scenario. If they suspect you're gay, they'll do anything to drive you out. I know because Jared and I lived it. They'll push and push until you take one little step out of line, and boom, they'll hit you like a freight train."

I locked eyes with Connor and let a silent moment pass before continuing. "But with Shar at your side, people will assume she's your girlfriend. That should defuse any suspicion about you. So when we play tournaments, we follow all the rules: no drugs, no drinking, no on-court drama, in bed by ten, up by dawn, and you and Shar will be very, very chummy. Agreed?"

Everybody except Spencer nodded.

"We need a comprehensive strategy," I continued, "that will deflect anything they throw at us, and Shar plays a key role."

Spencer shook his head. "You're like, asking Con to live a lie?"

"I'm suggesting that he spend time with a beautiful woman, which I'll wager won't take much arm twisting. Then we'll let people think what they will."

The suggestion of a grin crept onto Connor's lips, and he glanced up at the Gauguin nudes. "Does this mean we'll share hotel rooms?"

Shar tossed her head back and laughed, a harsh and very unladylike sound. "You glutton! You're getting a physical trainer and a companion on tour at no cost to you. Don't expect any good fortune beyond that. Besides, I don't think a man learns how to appreciate a woman before he's thirty-six. So you see, darling, I prefer older men. The older, the better. I once dated a man who was fifty-seven, and he was utterly charming. Better to be an old man's sweetheart than a young man's slave, I always say. Oh, don't be angry, you dear boy. I'll be very good to you. Just be sure and bring your Palm Pilot." She giggled, more ladylike this time. "No worries, darling, you'll love my post match rub-downs."

Spencer bowed his head and glared at his food. I felt sorry for him and began to regret my part in creating the lie. Jared must have felt the same way, because he reached over and squeezed Spencer's shoulder. He glanced my way. Fortunately for me, looks can only maim.

Shar spent the rest of dinner describing Connor's new fitness program, and by the time we had finished the raspberry sorbet dessert, the sunset had colored the houses across the bay. The living room smoldered with golden light. We polished off the last of the wine, and Carrie and Shar said their good-byes.

The boys grabbed their coats, but I said, "Hold on, men. Spencer helped get dinner together, so Connor pulls cleanup duty." I wanted a chance to talk with him alone, and to my delight, he smiled and started to clear the dishes. Jared sat at the piano. He ran through some scales to limber his fingers and began to play Mozart, a sonata in A sharp. Spencer folded into the wing chair and closed his eyes, letting the music carry him away.

I filled the copper sink with hot soapy water. Connor washed and rinsed while I dried and put away. We worked in a comfortable silence, and I became happy that we could be quiet together. I felt a current of cool air moving through my chest.

Jared finished the Mozart sonata and began another.

"So what do you think of Shar?" My question brought a rose color to the tips of his ears.

"She's pretty saucy, and what a fox. I sure won't mind her rubdowns."

"What's your girlfriend going to say about that?"

He gazed at me strangely and told me he didn't have one. When I raised an eyebrow, he explained, "I dated a girl named Vicky last year. She was smart and pretty and Chinese. Dad loved her. We had good times, but things went bogus. She got jealous because Spence was always hanging around. She accused us of being lovers, so we had this harsh scene and she dumped me."

He turned to me with his head cocked to one side and asked, "Why is everybody so hung up on sex? I'm mean, I totally don't get why it always comes down to fucking. Why are people so obsessed?"

"Wish I knew."

"Is it fear? Insecurity? Stupidity?"

"I suppose."

His brow wrinkled with a troubled expression that made him appear much older. "Everyone assumes that if you love someone, you're fucking them. But it's not true. I'm not wired like that, but because everybody assumes I am, I don't have any other friends. We're outcasts. All we have is each other." He paused, becoming aware of me staring at him. "You think I'm bonkers."

"No, I'm just surprised that you love him so deeply."

That flustered him, and I was sorry I'd said it.

"So how does Spencer feel? Is he gay?" I said, trying to shift the focus slightly.

"Duh! Can't you tell?"

"Well, yes, I suppose I can. I just wondered if you knew." *So*, I thought, *he has already experienced the brunt of sexual bigotry, and this is why he accepted my sexuality but was concerned about people assuming he was gay.* I felt closer to him. Yes, we were so much alike. "How long has Spencer been interested in you, sexually?"

"Since about day one," he said, and he chuckled. "And you're right, I totally love him. We're like two halves of the same person: he's yin, I'm yang."

"How will he react if you and Shar become close?"

"Spence needs to find someone he can roll in the sheets with. Once that happens, he won't be so possessive. I mean, did you see the stars in his eyes when Jared strolled out wearing a towel? Right then, he didn't even know if I existed or what." His voice had a teasing quality, and it found its mark.

I smiled and nodded. Jared finished the Mozart and switched to Beethoven. I fought off the urge to walk in there for a look-see.

"So that's your love life. Tell me about your family, about Roy."

"He's on Saturn, I'm on Pluto. He's like, totally Chinese, like my grandparents, and very proud. He wants to carry on the family traditions, but I couldn't give a rat's ass about that stuff. I'm not Chinese; I'm American. I've got a sister who ran off with an African American, which is why she and Roy haven't said squat to each other in like, seven years."

"That sounds extreme. There must have been more to it."

"As you've no doubt figured out, we don't have any money. It's not that my folks aren't making enough, but my dad has some complicated gambling issues. I'm sure that's the reason he pushes me so hard with the tennis; he thinks it could lead to some fast money. Not that I mind. I mean, I'm nothing without tennis. It's my only talent, other than being good at school. But if I can't afford college, what good is that? A high school diploma gets you nada."

"So tennis is just a means to get the lifestyle you want?"

"Tennis is my ticket to being somebody."

His words nagged me like a catchy tune as we finished the dishes and ambled back into the living room. Jared still played Beethoven, and Spencer watched him with such a pained expression on his face that I asked if he was feeling well. Connor found my question funny, and I realized that Spencer was drifting in a cloud of Jared.

The boys pulled on their coats and said their goodnights. Connor's statement about wanting to be "somebody" haunted me long after they left.

In bed, I held Jared close and wouldn't let go, all the time knowing he felt the same, that tennis was his only means to be extraordinary, and he had lost his chance. As I wondered how to give him another chance, segments of a Truman Capote poem surfaced from my memory, the gist of which was something like: to be somebody, to be remembered—that was what everyone was after, wasn't it?

CHAPTER 8

SUMMER faded, and the holidays crept near. Connor progressed steadily. A combination of tai chi, Zen meditation, and tennis drills taught him to concentrate without thinking. He became adept at silencing his mind, which allowed his actions to flow as free and smooth as the autumn wind. His daily improvements nurtured a growing inner assurance that he could play in his zone without forced effort. This new freedom, this non-striving, had him centered and performing spontaneously. Most importantly, for the first time in a long time, he began to enjoy tennis.

Connor and Spencer met Shar every weekday morning for thirty minutes of Zen meditation followed by two hours of cardiovascular exercise and weight training. While Spencer attended school, Connor and I drilled from nine to noon. We broke for lunch and rested until they both showed up at three o'clock sharp. The afternoon session mirrored the morning one: fifteen minutes of tai chi to empty our minds, fifteen minutes of easy warm-up, then drill, drill, drill.

In my book, there are three types of tennis players. The first are the aggressive baseliners who stalk the back of the court, attack with heavy groundstrokes, and only move forward when forced. They rely on driving their opponents out of position and then cracking a winner into the open court, all from behind the baseline. Both Jared and Connor fell into this category.

The second type is the serve-and-volleyer, who rushes to the net at the first opportunity and tries to win the point with a sharp angle volley, giving his opponent no time to react.

Then there is the category I fell into, the retriever. This style of play relies on footwork, speed, and patience to race down every ball and send it back until the opponent gets frustrated and makes an error going for too big of a shot.

I tried to mold Connor into the type of well-rounded athlete who merged the attributes of all three styles. The underlying purpose of every drill, however, was to quiet Connor's mind. He tended to lose focus because of his strong inclination to judge his performance. As soon as he judged a shot as either good or bad, the mental wheels began to turn, and once turning, they spun faster and harder.

Judgment opens the door for worry, fear, regret, hope, and distraction, all of which create tightness and stifle spontaneity. So when we practiced a particular combination of shots, I paid close attention. At the first sign of a frown after an error or a grin after nailing a difficult shot, I stopped him and we spent a half-minute silencing his mind before continuing. The idea was not to stop him from making judgments (an impossible undertaking) but to train him to realize when he did and to recover his inner composure.

His mind became strong, as did his body. He worked out five times a week, and Shar had him on a muscle building diet: moderate amounts of lean red meat, fish, yogurt, fresh fruit, raw vegetables, whole-grained cereals, and plenty of brown rice.

Connor eating red meat morphed into a battle with Roy. As Buddhists, the Lins were predominately vegetarian. Roy stood firm that his son would not eat any food that had to be killed. When I pointed out that both he and Connor ate fish, he blushed and avowed that fish did not fall into the same category as animals. I responded by telling him that even plants are living creatures, and hundreds of them were killed each day to fill his family's rice bowl.

He stopped crunching his Tums. "So, now I'm a hypocrite?"

"I'm suggesting that you both need to make sacrifices for Connor to realize his potential."

That more or less won me the argument, but I had the feeling that Roy regretted hiring me.

I probed Connor about his religious beliefs and found that we were similar in our approach to Buddhism. Neither of us endeavored to attain a higher level of spiritual enlightenment. We tried to sustain a lifestyle that engendered compassion and respect for all living beings.

Our differences lay in the fact that I always strove to stay in the now, not bothered with past regrets or future hopes. Connor had learned to do that while on court, but it was slow to take root in the rest of his life.

One gray November afternoon, however, as the three of us performed our routine, I had trouble staying in the now because I had a surprise for Connor, and the anticipation nagged me. After two hours of volley drills, I had the boys play a set to incorporate what we'd worked on, as we did most afternoons to wrap up.

Two games into the set, Connor began to dominate, which always happened when he found his zone. He overpowered Spencer, who, like me, was purebred retriever.

The clouds broke open, and the sun spilled warmth over the back of my neck. Over the sound of the ball popping and sneakers squeaking, I heard a raw voice behind me:

"Who around here do I have to fuck to play a match?"

"That would be me," I said, turning around.

Jared pulled me into his arms. He hadn't shaved in three days, and his shadow burned my cheek. I didn't care. His affection was such a welcome surprise that my eyes teared.

A dirty little thought wormed its way into my head: was he putting on a show for the boys? His breath touched my cheek, and I instinctively inhaled, checking for the odor of whiskey. Finding a trace, I dismissed it. Caught up in his magnetic field, I didn't care.

I reached up and touched a vein that ran along the soft of his throat. The muscle under his skin trembled. I kissed him and brushed my cheek over his stubble, burning myself.

"Hey, lover man, you sure about this? You haven't played a competitive match in years. Might dent the ego to have a teenager stomp your beautiful butt."

"Any body parts he bruises you can kiss and make better."

"Promise?"

"Besides, it'll be fun to see what I still have."

I leaned my hips into his groin. "Lover man, you still have plenty. It's just rusty."

He pressed his head against me, forehead touching forehead. "We'll see about that." He kissed me again, and in the quiet wake of his kiss, the surrounding sounds became loud: rustling leaves overhead, the pop of the ball, the chirp of tennis shoes on pavement, the boys' insistent grunts.

My knees went weak. After ten years, he could still turn my insides to quivering jelly. I glanced at my office and thought about hustling him in there and locking the door.

"After," he said, reading my mind. "We'll shower together."

He squeezed my hand and turned to watch the boys play, studying Connor's strokes, footwork, and attacking style of play during an amazing twenty-five-ball rally. He whistled softly. He glanced back at me, and I saw it in his eyes: the boys were far better than he imagined.

"You'll do fine," I said, realizing that his pre-match butterflies had quadrupled in size.

"Christ. With a kid this good, you're walking right back into the lion's den."

"Your help will guarantee that happens."

I felt him shudder, and he looked like a lost child. I couldn't tell if it was concern for me or the thought that I was leaving him behind. Perhaps it was both. I leaned into his side and whispered, "This time will be different. Trust me."

"Is he as good as I was?"

"I'd hate to stake my life on the difference."

He shouldered his bag, and we ambled toward court one. Connor nailed a winner to win the set. Surprise lit up their faces as they jogged to the sideline and shook Jared's hand.

"I've entered Connor in the Sacramento tournament. That gives us two weeks to prepare," I explained. "It's a challenger event that attracts players who are ranked from one-fifty to two hundred. They'll be good, but not the same caliber we'll see at the tier one and two tournaments. I asked Jared to give Connor some practice playing against a big hitter."

Connor's mouth opened slightly. He watched Jared pull two rackets from his bag, each one labeled with a pet name: Thumper and Bambam. Connor's eyes widened as Jared measured the string tension on both by tapping them against each other. He selected Thumper.

I asked Spencer to warm up Jared while I strategized with Connor. Spencer jogged to the baseline, but Jared called him back inside the service line. Spencer's eyebrows arched as he realized that this ex-pro wanted to warm up as I had taught him and Connor, starting off slow at the service line and working their way back to the baseline.

Connor studied Jared's strokes, becoming as quiet as a crypt. His face paled to near white, and his hands began to tremble. He turned and peered right through me. Emotions churned in the depth of his eyes. "He's too good," he said with a slight quiver in his voice.

"You're letting him beat you before you start. Don't be impressed with him until after the match. Do exactly what we've worked on."

He shook his head as if to say I was asking the impossible.

I shouldn't have surprised him, I thought. He needed time to warm up to the idea.

"What's the worst that can happen?"

"He'll mop the floor with me."

"You've already lost zero and zero to a player half as good as you, and with five hundred people watching. What's more humiliating than that? Losing to Jared is a stroll in the park."

Connor dropped his head and stared at the hard rubber toes of his sneakers.

"The worst thing that can happen is if you kick his ass, which is possible but unlikely."

Connor glanced up. "What's so bad about that?"

"Because you'll realize how damn good you are and you'll expect that kind of performance every time. That's not bad as long as you understand you can't always play to your potential. No one can."

He studied Jared again. Silent moments passed before he asked, "So how do I beat him?"

Bingo! Pride surged through me, and I almost hugged him.

"The pressure is all on him," I said. "He's the pro worried about losing to a nobody. This is your first chance to play someone of his caliber, so cherish each point, have fun, and keep your mind empty—just like we've worked on. As far as how to play him: keep the ball deep to his backhand, let him crack a few forehands but keep him away from the net. The main thing is bust your butt to keep every ball in play. Let him pound the ball, but make him pound it over and over. Make him believe that you'll never give up. That will frustrate him. Any questions?"

Connor shook his head. His chin trembled, but at least he grinned. Again, I felt an overwhelming desire to hug him.

Jared smashed a few practice serves while Spencer loped over and joined me on the bench. Connor grabbed his racket and stepped to the baseline.

As they played out the first game, I couldn't help but stare from side to side comparing the two. Connor's Asian features—slim hips, thick dark hair, amber complexion—all fused into an exotic yet youthful countenance. He sometimes seemed frivolous, a bit of a dreamer, and was quick with a laugh. Jared was rugged—more compact and muscular, fawn-colored hair, gray-green eyes, freckles, stubbly beard—giving him an all-American manliness. He had a compelling manner and uncommonly quick reflexes.

Connor was a giver, always concerned that the people around him had what they needed. Jared was a taker; he came first, and the people around him could fight over what was left. If you took them both to a restaurant, Connor would study the menu for nutritional value versus price, order vegetarian dishes, and only enough to slay his hunger, while Jared would be gluttonous for everything and would order twice what he could eat. Earth and air were not more opposite, and yet their style of play was so similar that you would think they were Siamese twins.

It occurred to me that many of these differences were caused by experiences that Jared had suffered while on tour, events that reshaped his personality like a pressure-cooker changes the texture of its contents.

Had Jared been so different from Connor at age eighteen? I remembered his playfulness, his easy smile, his passion for life. I shook my head, admitting that they were shucked from the same pod. The strain of competing combined with the discrimination had overhauled Jared's personality. I leaned forward, scrutinizing them, knowing that Connor would undergo a similar makeover. I hoped I would be a better mentor this time around.

Jared rolled over Connor in the first four games, winning almost every rally. Jared's confidence grew with every point. His body language exuded his growing arrogance. He was physically large, but he began to look like a giant.

Watching Jared play was like reading certain poems that caused an ice-blue river to tumble down my spine. He was rusty but still showed remarkable talent. He held serve to go up 5-0. He jogged to the bench at the changeover. Confidence made his freckles glow even redder against his tawny skin.

Connor dragged himself to the bench, head bent, sweat dripping from his face. "You're not letting yourself into the zone," I said. "What are you afraid of? You think he's better than you?"

His head jerked up, and he impaled me with those almond-shaped eyes. He flushed a scalded red, and his face pinched together, causing creases to form across his forehead. For just a heartbeat, I thought he would walk off the court.

"Because if that's what you think, you're probably right: you'll never be as good as him. But it's not too late to change your mind."

"Come on, Con," Spencer said, handing him the water bottle. "He's good, sure, but you're better. Just pretend he's me and play your game." They glared at each other, and I swear I saw something tangible pass between them. It reminded me of that first day on the beach when they frolicked naked in the surf. Something twisted in my gut that felt like shards of glass, but this time it was hope, not envy, that inflamed me.

Connor glanced back at me, and I saw his eyes pleading for help.

"Change something, anything," I said. "Try something he's not expecting."

Connor jogged to the baseline and drilled an ace down the centerline. The creases across his forehead visibly relaxed. He scored the next two points with hard first serves to Jared's body followed by coming forward and sticking his volleys. His forehead grew smooth again. He clinched the game with an ace out wide.

Spencer leaped straight off the bench. "COME ON!"

Jared held serve to take the first set and rode his momentum to win the first two games in the second, breaking Connor at love. But overconfidence made him relax enough to allow Connor to step up his game.

I witnessed my wildest hopes coming true. Connor tuned out everything but his breathing and seeing the ball. That allowed him to anticipate where Jared would hit to, and he got there faster, giving himself more time to set up and hit a superior shot. As he strung together points, then games, I saw a pure athletic aura surround him, shimmering in the sunlight.

He hit a drop shot to lure Jared to the net, nailing a perfect topspin lob to break Jared and tie the set at two-all. In the next game, Connor repeatedly utilized the one-two punch—serving out wide and hitting to the open court.

Spencer leaned toward me. "He's zoned in now."

"He's beginning to believe."

So was I. Fire surged down my spine to ignite my testicles. If this stallion could maintain this level of play and stay injury-free, we'd be knocking on the door of the top fifty within a year. "Giddy with excitement" is no mere phrase. My nerve endings sizzled with joy and fear.

Concern showed in Jared's body language. He had assumed he would win, but that plan had derailed. His composure dissolved. If Connor could somehow secure the set, he'd probably win the match. I felt sorry for Jared; losing after securing a commanding lead is demoralizing.

They both held serve through the next four games. Jared served to stay in the set at 4-5. He double-faulted the first point and snarled at himself. He picked up the pace, hitting harder and playing fast, as if he wanted to end the match as soon as possible. I winked at Spencer, who sat biting his nails to the quick.

Connor returned Jared's serves and rallied fiercely. At 30-40, Connor had a set point. Jared looked stunned. He hurried through his service motion and double-faulted again, handing Connor the set with a red ribbon. He swiped at the court with his racket and unleashed a chilling growl.

At the changeover, I asked Connor, "Are you having fun?" I already knew the answer.

He flashed a wide smile. "Totally!"

The first four games of the third set were more of what I'd hoped for. Both players ratcheted up and played superlative tennis. Jared brushed his disappointments aside, and he flowed in the moment. Connor hung with him, toe to toe. The surprise of it pushed up through my chest and lodged in my throat.

Word spread throughout the complex, and a dozen people rushed to the bleachers. Soon thirty spectators cheered each point. It had the feel of a championship match. Carrie Bennett sat in the first row, astonishment visible on her face. Even she had begun to believe.

Jared broke Connor and gave it right back. The set went to five-all. Spencer was as white as a sheet. The crowd sizzled with tension.

Goose bumps covered my arms when Connor spanked an ace out wide to go up 5-all, 40-15. One more point and Jared would serve to stay in the match. Jared let out a primal, guttural howl. His right arm flew up, and he tomahawked his racket. The frame bounced, somersaulted twice, and tumbled into the net.

At that moment, I saw something register in Connor's eyes. He had played in a dreamlike bubble of composure for two sets, but Jared's paroxysm had ruptured that bubble, making him conscious of the enormity of what he was about to accomplish, and once aware of it, he peeked ahead to the finish line. Creases reappeared on his forehead.

On game point, he missed his first serve by a foot and spun in a weak, nervous-looking second. Jared chipped and charged. The move threw Connor off, and he sprayed the ball wide. The next point was a carbon copy.

Jared's tantrum had triggered a momentum hemorrhage, and I realized he had done it on purpose. His outburst was no fit of uncontrollable anger, but rather a deliberate bit of gamesmanship.

Smart, I thought, *very smart*.

Connor played the following point conservatively, obviously hoping that Jared would make an error. His defensive play let Jared seize control, running Connor side to side until he cracked a winner off Connor's weak reply.

My mouth went dry. The match was over. Breaking Connor's serve gave Jared a huge mental boost, and he held serve to win. That's tennis: the momentum in a match can swing one way or the other on just one or two critical points, or in this case, on a tomahawked racket.

They shook hands. The spectators cheered. I was elated for them both. Jared had stepped up his game when he needed to, and Connor had slugged it out punch for punch right down to the bell. Connor had experienced a tangible breakthrough, and that had me glowing.

Connor staggered to the bench, his head down and his shoulders slumped. His face took on a greenish hue, and I thought he might vomit. I knew what he was feeling, having been there myself so many times. Serving a game point at five-all in the third set had thrilled him, but the fall had been too sudden and too steep, like a spaceship plummeting through the atmosphere.

He sat on the bench with his head between his knees. Sweat poured off his face, dampening the court between his feet.

We all stood back to let him work it out internally. I saw the green hue fade and the knot in his throat give way to the realization that he had pushed his game to a bold new level.

He laughed. With his head still between his knees, he laughed. He swung around, nailed me with his gaze, and laughed again. His eyes sparkled. I laughed with him—we all did—peals of laughter. There were two glistening pearls of tears caught in his eyelashes. He stood up, and Spencer rushed to hug him.

Jared wrapped me in his arms, and for the first time, it dawned on me that I was enmeshed in an awesome responsibility that affected each one of us.

I gave them a ten-minute rest before we paired up for doubles: Connor with Jared and Spencer with me. We played a point, then stopped to dissect what had happened and discuss how to play it better. We played and analyzed, again and again.

With Jared's support, Connor catapulted his game to an even higher level. Their chemistry as a team ignited, and they crushed us, so much so that after the practice, I called the Sacramento tournament organizers and entered Connor in the doubles with Jared as his partner. When I broke the news, Jared shrugged his shoulders as if it meant nothing, but he grew quiet.

During the weeks leading up to the tournament, the four of us met every afternoon to hone Connor's reactions and improve his shot selection.

To my delight, not a single drop of whiskey passed Jared's lips during that fortnight. He even joined the boys for their morning workouts with Shar. As his body responded to the physical exertion, his determination and confidence grew steadily.

Working together revived all our old cohesive feelings. Each night, he devoured my body like a starved animal, then held me close until dawn. Those two weeks gave me a taste of what had been missing for four long years. I hadn't realized how I'd missed it until then.

What would happen after the tournament? Would our relationship sink back to that painful separateness? Would he revert to making love to the bottle instead of me?

One thing I knew for sure: it would crush me to lose him a second time.

SACRAMENTO is a two-hour drive from San Francisco—three hours in Slug, who topped out at fifty miles per hour. The whole Lin family came to cheer: grandparents, aunts and uncles, cousins, nieces and nephews, about thirty in all.

The cool autumn breeze gave me chills, but sweat oozed down Connor's face. He was the second match up on center court. We stood behind the bleachers waiting. Although I thought Connor's fragile legs would be his biggest hindrance, I soon found that his nerves were the real problem. Fear of losing ravaged him, giving him the shakes.

"Breathe," I told him. "Clear your mind. Once you're on court, those butterflies will shrink."

"I'm going to be sick."

A cheer went up as the first match ended.

"Hear that?" I asked. "It's the sound of happiness. Now's the time for you to show us how good you've become. You're going to make us all happy."

"What if he's better?"

"Are you kidding? I pity that poor bastard. I do. He'll be outclassed by an eighteen-year-old, and there's not a damn thing he can do about it. Trust me, this time next year, he'll be bragging to his buddies that you kicked his ass before you were famous."

Connor's lips spread into an apprehensive grin. He looked down thoughtfully. "You've helped me so much. I just don't want to disappoint you. No matter what happens, you should know that I'm grateful." He leaned against me and gave me a tender hug.

An old man, who I assumed was Grandfather Lin, shuffled up and tapped him on the shoulder. Connor released me and faced the man, who unwrapped a red velvet cloth to reveal a tablet of green jade carved in the shape of the sitting Buddha: his *chang*, his personal good luck charm. He pressed the tablet into Connor's hand and whispered, "For luck." Connor hugged him before grabbing his tennis bag and heading for center court.

Before he got ten feet from us, Shar rushed into his arms and kissed him, a rather sensual good-luck kiss. She whispered something in his ear, and they both smiled. He kissed her again and ran his fingers through her hair. His name blared over the loudspeaker, and he rushed off, leaving her staring after him.

As I predicted, the five-minute warm-up emptied his mind and relaxed his body. His fear visibly turned into eagerness. The match lasted just sixty-two minutes. He demolished his opponent 6-2, 6-1. In the afternoon, he and Jared won their doubles match just as easily.

After that first tournament win, Connor rode a wave of momentum into his following matches. He still became sick before each match, but once the warm-up started, he got right down to business. With each victory, the wave grew in size and force. I kept my fingers crossed that the wave didn't collapse too soon and drown him in self-doubt and disappointment. But he rode the crest with the nimble dexterity of a champion surfer.

Jared was equally impressive. I saw glimpses of his old form. It was thrilling to watch him compete, dominating his opponents with his will, his confidence, and his court presence.

The tournament spread over four days. Connor marched through the draws and into the final in both singles and doubles. He clinched the singles title by trouncing John Silva, ranked #116 in the ATP world rankings.

The doubles final, on the other hand, turned into the kind of hard-fought match everyone hopes to see in a championship match. They played against the number one ranked doubles team in Northern California. There were no breaks of serve in the first set. The chair umpire overruled two critical line calls in the tiebreaker that would have given the first set to Connor and Jared.

Anger inflamed Jared's eyes. It felt like the same tactics the ATP had used to drive him from the sport years ago. Three more overrules in the third set were so blatantly bad that the crowd booed. Those three points tipped the scales toward the opponents, and my boys lost.

Connor and Jared shook hands with the opponents, but they refused to shake the chair umpire's hand. Instead, Jared pointed an accusing finger in his face and called him a cheating bigot. A few spectators booed Jared, but just as many cheered.

As they dragged themselves off the court, Roy, Spencer, Shar, and I were there with hugs and smiles. The joy that they had performed so well in their first tournament overshadowed the disappointment of being robbed of the title.

As we flooded them with congratulations, I noticed that Spencer hugged Jared a few seconds too long and somewhat too intimately for my taste. It wasn't the first time. Spencer followed him around with those puppy-dog eyes and rubbed against him whenever possible. I didn't blame Spencer. I simply wanted Jared to stop leading him on.

Before Connor's family mobbed him, he invited us to the celebration party at his grandparents' house. He enticed us with a promise that we would slip away after dinner and go clubbing. I ignored the clubbing part because they were too young to get into the dance clubs.

Jared remained silent on the long ride home. I blathered about how marvelously he played, that he won the match and the trophy didn't matter. *Déjà vu*, I thought, the same empty script from years before with the same effect. I stopped and listened to Slug's whining engine.

As we drove over the Bay Bridge, storm clouds rushed across the Pacific. When I suggested we take umbrellas to the party, he mumbled that he wanted to stay home and soak in a hot bath. I offered to scrub his back, but he insisted that I drop him off and go to the party alone.

"Don't stay out late," he said. "I'll need you later."

CHAPTER 9

I WAS home long enough to shower, change clothes, and watch Jared sink into a steaming tub.

I drove Slug twenty minutes across town to the grandparents' house, a two-story, reddish-pink house on the edge of the Sunset District. I heard the party noise from three houses away, reminiscent of a gaggle of geese.

The front door opened, and an odor of Chinese cooking drew me in. The house reeked of that wonderful, homey aroma. The air felt heavy with ginger and grease and sweet incense. In the living room, eleven graying or near-graying adults clustered in pods of twos and threes. They were outnumbered by mangy-looking teenagers and clean-cut grade-school-aged kids who sprawled over every sagging piece of furniture.

Above the mantle hung two black and white pictures that had speckled brown with age, one of an old man and one of an old woman. I recognized Connor's eyes in the woman's face.

A red shrine perched on a table in the corner with a jade Buddha statue. Beside it was a bowl of sand spiked with a single incense stick, a thread of white smoke drifting toward the ceiling. A sheet cake with green frosting and white lines that resembled a tennis court sat on the coffee table. It had yellow script saying, "Congratulations, Connor, Tennis Champion." *A store-bought cake*, I thought. *Good job he won the singles.*

Connor ushered Shar across the living room. They held hands and made an alluring couple, but I couldn't help wondering if Shar was mixing her personal and professional life or just being friendly.

Connor introduced me to the group nearest the door: Uncle Harvey, a fiftyish, pudgy stockbroker, and his perky, blonde, Caucasian wife Delores. Harvey pointed out his three boys from the crowd, Christopher, Curtis, and Carl. Delores leaned closer to explain that Christopher had graduated at the top of his economics class at Davis, Curtis started Harvard Business School in the fall, and Carl was the lazy one, which I took to mean he had no college plans.

I met Kitty, Connor's mother, whose pretty face and easy smile let me know who Connor took after. There was Uncle this and Auntie that. It got jumbled pretty quickly. I smiled as I shook hands with each one of them, having no idea which were Connor's relatives and which were family friends because to the Chinese, even friends are considered family.

Uncle Harman stood out in this throng of normalcy. Late twenties, six-foot-two, lean, exotic facial features, he seemed too elegant to be straight. He stared into my eyes, and I felt warmth surge through my head. I shook his delicate hand and gave him a knowing smile, which he returned. When he introduced himself, I thought he said Herman, pronounced with a Chinese accent, but no, he corrected me, Harman, two As, no E. He looked like an older version of Connor, so he was no doubt a blood uncle.

A gray-haired man squinted at me through thick glasses, and I recognized him from earlier in the day. He was Connor's grandfather.

Connor took the old man's hand as delicately as if it were made of Ming porcelain, leading him to me. The old man tottered a few steps toward me and introduced himself as Lincoln Lin. I found the name amusing because it reminded me of Lincoln Logs, a childhood favorite of mine.

Bent with the weight of eighty-plus years, Mr. Lin wore the same style Mao jacket and pants that he must have worn in China. He welcomed me into his home and seized my arm with surprising strength, pulling me toward the kitchen.

As we made our way across the room, he pointed to several children playing a card game around the coffee table and told me their names, which he mixed up, and they poked fun at him. He laughed with them, and his cheeks glowed. His family was clearly his greatest pride, perhaps his only pride.

"We are grateful for your help," he said. "You know, I am helping him too. Yes, I'm teaching him to meditate, to forget himself. All greatness in art, music, architecture, sports, even love, comes from what lies beneath words and thoughts. This is Zen, which comes from China. Everybody thinks it came from Japan, but no, from China first. We practice together."

"I'm sure it helps," I said.

"Why didn't your friend come, the one Connor played with? I felt sorry for him. They cheated him. Even my old eyes saw that. Why did they do that?"

"The judge was prejudiced."

He nodded as comprehension spread across his face. "I have been a Chinese man in this country for sixty-eight years. I know about prejudice. People think they're better than me. We all breathe the same air, eat the same food, leave the same stink in the toilet. But people think they're better than me. We all come from and go back to the same source, but they don't know. They think their big cars and fancy clothes make them special."

Seven adults were packed into the sweaty kitchen, all jabbering in Cantonese while cooking various dishes. I had no idea where they planned to put all the food. The dining room table was already crammed with bowls and platters, and yet the cooking was still in full swing.

The women wore slacks, loose-fitting blouses, and sturdy walking shoes. In the center of the kitchen table sat a bowl half-full of a gingery-scented mixture of chopped shrimp and leeks. Four women sat around the table dabbing mounds of the mixture onto thin wonton wrappers, folding and sealing them into dumplings the shape of clamshells and laying them in rows on a flat aluminum pan.

I felt the urge to pull up a chair and help wrap, but the kitchen was so crowded I could only stand at the doorway.

Mr. Lin said something in Cantonese to an elderly lady at the head of the table. Her short, stout figure reminded me of pictures I'd seen of Chinese farm peasants. She smiled and said a lengthy sentence in the same dialect. I shook my head and apologized that I didn't speak Cantonese. She nodded and said something in Mandarin. I apologized again.

"Aii-ya," she exclaimed, using a scolding tone, then rattled off a sharp phrase in Cantonese.

Mr. Lin cocked his head to one side and asked, "You don't speak Chinese?"

"I'm afraid not, Mr. Lin."

"I'm so sorry for you," he said, patting me on the back as if my deficiency made me pitifully uncivilized. "Your family must be disappointed you have not learned our language."

"I often disappointed my mother. When she was mad at me, she would scold that I wasn't really her child, and she cursed the woman who left me on her doorstep."

"Very funny; very Chinese! When my wife gets mad at her boys, she says she found them in a garbage dumpster. Ha, ha."

Mr. Lin introduced me to everyone, but it became a jumble again. I nodded to each one. Roy Lin was not among them. Surprised, I turned to search the living room again, but he was not there either.

Spencer sauntered over, and he also scanned the room. I frowned. "He didn't come," I said. "He needed some alone time."

"But we're going dancing later." Spencer's face twisted into an expression that was not quite disappointment and not anger but had attributes of both.

"I know you're disappointed; so am I. But there's no need to take it personally."

"But it won't be the same. Who will I dance with now?"

"Spencer, has it occurred to you that Jared and I have enough relationship problems without you following him like a puppy and flirting with him whenever you think I'm not watching? Please don't deny it, I've seen you. I'm asking you, as a friend, to find your own boyfriend and stop making my life more challenging."

He dropped his head. "I'm sorry, Mr. Bottega. It's just that I'm so lonely and he's so...." His voice trailed off to nothing. He glanced across the room at Connor, who had his arm around Shar's waist. "He's fucking her, ya know. He scarcely knows I'm alive anymore."

"No, Spencer, I didn't know." Anger flashed through my chest like a breath of fire. *Bitch,* I thought, *mixing personal with professional at a time when Connor needs to focus on tennis.* It all became clear: this impish, impassioned spirit that was Spencer felt abandoned and desperate to find a replacement. I saw the hurt mar his face, and I draped my arm across his shoulder, giving him a meaningful squeeze.

"Honest, Mr. Bottega, I didn't think Jared even noticed me."

"Of course he does. We both do. You're a beautiful person, how could we not notice?"

He went soft-voiced. "I dream about him, about him loving me like he loves you. But I'll stop. I promise."

"Thanks." I gave him another squeeze. "Say, if you're going out, you should ask Uncle Harman to go. He could be fun."

"We're going to the Engage. It's a gay Asian dance club." I raised an eyebrow, so he added, "Shar got us some fake IDs."

"Well, if it's a gay Asian club, he's probably a regular there."

Spencer's eyes grew huge, and he scrutinized Harman, who sat across the room. "You think?"

"Go talk to him and see for yourself."

"Thanks, Mr. Bottega." He almost sprinted to the couch and squeezed next to Harman.

Auntie Rose brushed past me balancing a huge bowl of fried wontons. She told me to eat before it was all gone, and I laughed. They laid the food out buffet style, and I grabbed a bowl and helped myself to the wonton soup. I sat in the only available chair in the living room and luxuriated in the delicate flavor as it carried me back to my mother's kitchen.

A child's loud voice announced that Uncle Roy was at the front door, and, sure enough, Roy swept into the living room like a wind-rush, carrying an aluminum tray and leading another man like a dog on a leash. Roy took the tray to the dining table and somehow found room for it in the middle of all the pots and platters. He peeled off the cover, and the tangy aroma of roasted crab permeated the room.

Grandmother Lin shouted something in Cantonese, and Roy replied, "No, not at Hu Wong's. I bought it on Clement Street, the kind with the spicy black bean sauce."

Roy led the stranger to me and introduced the sun-lamped and greased-back-haired Caucasian as J.D. Lambert. He wore a pale blue rayon suit with wide lapels and the collar of his white shirt opened at the neck. He smelled of cigars and Old Spice cologne. His shoes sported elevated heels that lifted his height to about my shoulder blades. All he needed was sideburns and dark glasses to resemble an Elvis impersonator. I envisioned him in pegged jeans and a guitar slung over his shoulder, and I had to suppress a smile.

I stood and shook his hand while holding my bowl of soup in my left hand. It became clear to me that he expected recognition, and I would have loved to oblige him, but I didn't have a clue who he could be. There was something familiar, however, about his deadpan eyes, about the way his lacy lids furled down at the corners.

"And this is Connor," Roy said, dragging Connor over to meet Mr. Lambert. "Connor, Mr. Lambert is our new agent. He's going to negotiate our contracts and manage our publicity."

Connor and I gawked at each other. My soup had cooled, so I set it on the table next to my chair.

"An impressive win today," J.D. Lambert said. His face grew animated as he ran his hand through his glossy pompadour. "Congratulations. I wasn't there, but Roy gave me a blow by blow. That win will get me in the door of any equipment manufacturer. You use Babolat rackets, right? No problem. You'll never have to pay for rackets again. Of course for the big money clothing contracts, Nike or Adidas, we'll need an ATP ranking, and it takes three tournament results before the ATP issues a ranking. That's no problem. There are two tournaments in southern California next month. That means I'll start negotiating a clothing deal before we head to Australia in January."

Roy beamed as Connor glared at me with a question etched on his face.

"Australia?" I said, looking Mr. Lambert in the eye. "We're not going to Australia. Not next year, anyway."

"But if Connor qualifies for the Aussie slam, why not? Even if he loses in the first round, he'll get American television coverage, which translates into mucho cashola when I close the clothing deal. And if he wins a round or two, we'll be livin' on Easy Street."

"Look, Mr. Lambert. We already have a game plan. We'll keep improving his game through the winter, play the challenger tournaments in Long Beach and San Diego, then try to qualify for San Jose in February and Indian Wells in March. We'll go up against the big boys in those two tournaments, and if we do well, we'll shoot for the Sony Ericsson Open in Florida. That way, we hit all the winter American tournaments without Roy shelling out much money for traveling expenses." Jared loomed in the back of my mind. I doubted he would go to Australia. The pain of being there without playing would devastate him, and I didn't want to leave him alone for a month.

J.D. Lambert turned on Roy. "That's a costly mistake. Australia is a golden, and I mean *golden*, opportunity."

Agents are the same the world over, I thought. Only their accents and their sports differ. In the last twenty years, they have become well dressed and professional. Most work for corporations and have become slick, savvy, suave. I couldn't help but wonder how good this little man dressed in Elvis garb could be. But I had to admit that the business end of this partnership was none of my concern. My job was to mold a champion.

Roy nodded his agreement, but before he could voice an objection, I said, "Mr. Lambert, we're here to develop Connor's career, not jump after a quick buck."

"Those tournaments you mentioned don't get the same television coverage or the national interest. They mean nothing in terms of negotiating a deal."

"If we do well in California and hopefully qualify for the Sony Ericsson," I continued, "we'll play the European clay court season. That should give us a shot at qualifying for the French Slam. I'm sure you can wait four months to become a permanent resident on Easy Street."

J.D. Lambert scowled at Roy.

Roy said, "Gentlemen, we all want Connor to succeed, and we all want to make a little money along the way. Mr. Bottega, don't you agree that the sooner we cut a clothing deal, the sooner we can pay you the lucrative salary of a pro coach?"

"I've lived on limited funds all my life. I can wait for Connor's game to mature."

"Well, I have debts!" Roy's voice grew harsh, and his face flushed. "I say we play Australia."

The room hushed except for Roy's labored breathing.

"You'll go without me," I said.

"I coached Connor before you, and I can do it again."

Grandfather Lin shuffled up and stood between Roy and myself. Stooped shoulders, thin gray hair, large gentle eyes, he reminded me of Yoda. He spoke in a soft voice. "The heart of this issue is Connor's career. Will money improve the boy's abilities? If Connor needs time, he should have it. Gambling debts have no bearing on this matter."

Grandfather Lin clutched my hand. "In China the elderly are respected, but not so in America. My voice is seldom heard. But please know that I am grateful you put the boy's needs before your own. I respect this."

Roy pulled a pack of Tums from his breast pocket, popped two into his mouth, and bit hard. I heard the crunch clearly, like snapping bones. Again, I felt his growing animosity. But to my surprise, he backed down and made a tactful retreat, turning away from me and leading J.D. to the table to load up their dinner plates.

Connor's grandmother emerged from the kitchen carrying a bowl of steamed dumplings. She crowed something in Cantonese, and everyone dug into their food, shoving forkfuls of noodles into their mouths and chewing with bulging cheeks. Everyone ate except Connor and Shar, who sat on the couch in front of the front window, whispering and giggling.

I assumed they were passing remarks about J.D. Lambert, so I strolled toward them to get Connor's take on these new developments. As I came within earshot, I heard Connor say, "I'm starving. Let's eat now." There was a grating whine to his voice that I'd not heard before.

"Darling, remember what I said before the party?" she responded.

"Fine, let's go. My sugar level is freefalling."

"Behave yourself, darling. We'll go in twenty minutes." Her voice was a whisper, but it had a governess's edge to it, as if he risked a spanking if he didn't take heed.

"Don't you love me?" he asked her, somewhat playfully. At least I'd hoped it was playful.

"Nobody loves a pain in the ass. Go munch on a wonton, for Christ's sakes, and when I'm damned good and ready, we'll go eat wherever you want."

An unusual blush colored his cheeks as he jumped up and made a beeline to the dinner table.

As I strolled up, I couldn't stop myself from saying: "You didn't answer his question. Do you love him?"

She winked at me, but it was humorless, more like a warning signal.

Grandfather Lin gripped my arm and led me toward the dining table, saying, "My wife says everybody must eat so that we can play mah-jongg. Do you play?"

"Yes, sir. My mother taught me years ago."

"Good. You play at my table so we can talk more. Now you eat. Have some crab."

I glanced at the mass of curved claws and twisted legs, covered in brown sauce. I was tempted, but it would be very messy eating with my fingers. I filled a plate with steamed dumplings and chow mein instead.

I sat in the easy chair, watching everybody take a second helping and some a third. By the time I finished my first helping, the ladies had finished pecking at the last morsels on their plates and begun carrying dishes to the kitchen. The children unfolded three card tables and twelve chairs, arranging them in a row across the living room.

Mr. Lin waved me over to the first table. "Come, sit across from me."

I stood waiting by the card table as Connor, Shar, Spencer, and Uncle Harman gathered at the front door.

"We're going dancing," Connor said. "Mr. Bottega, are you sure you won't come? I guarantee it's more fun than mah-jongg."

Connor's arm hugged Shar's waist, not letting her get even an inch away. Spencer stood close to Harman, his face glowing shyly. As a foursome, they struck a harmonious cord. *I would be an awkward addition*, I thought, *rather like a trombone player joining a string quartet.* "I've had plenty of fun today. I think I'll play a game or two before I head home."

Grandfather Lin trundled up to Connor. "You hardly ate anything," he said. "Have some noodles. Have some crab."

"We'll grab a pizza on the way to the club. I'm tired of Chinese food."

Grandfather Lin tilted his head to one side. "Tired of Chinese food?" A shameful tone resonated in the old man's voice, as if the family had let Connor down by not having a better feast. I could feel his shame from twenty feet away. Connor must have felt it too, because he glanced down, then turn toward the door. The issue, I was sure, had to do with Shar not liking Chinese food.

As they dashed out, J.D. Lambert meandered over and held out his hand. "Pleased to have met you, Mr. Bottega. I'd like to drop by your office tomorrow so we can talk more, just the two of us. I want to ensure we're both playing from the same game plan."

I shook his hand, which was clammy with perspiration. "Come at noon and I'll buy you lunch."

"Great. See you at noon sharp."

Mr. Lin escorted J.D. Lambert to the door and returned to the card table nearest the fireplace. As I sat, I could feel the pictures hanging over the mantle, as if the great-grandparents were glaring over my shoulders, waiting to see if I could hold my own in this ancient game of strategy.

Grandfather Lin poured me a tiny glass full of a clear liquid. "Drink this. It's Chinese wine."

I had never heard of Chinese wine. I sipped the fiery drink and shuddered.

"You like?" he said, smiling.

I nodded helplessly.

He drained his glass. "Like Japanese sake."

Sake? More like ammonia. Two more sips and it tasted better, enough so that I polished it off with one swallow. Grandfather Lin moved to refill my glass, but I placed my fingers over the rim.

His nod seemed unconvinced, and when I pulled my hand away and glanced about the room, my glass mysteriously became full again.

Kitty sat to my right and spilled mah-jongg tiles onto the tabletop from a black box. We all reached forward and flipped the tiles so that they all faced down and swirled them around the table with the palms of our hands to mix them up.

Grandmother Lin sat to my left, completing the foursome. The other tables filled with adults while the grandkids migrated to a bedroom to watch television.

As we stacked tiles to build four walls, I asked Grandfather Lin if he was given his name of Lincoln before coming to America.

"The America immigration people made me take a western name. They said no one could pronounce my Chinese name. I didn't know any western names, so I asked the man, 'Who was the greatest American leader?' He told me Abraham Lincoln. I could not pronounce Abraham, so I chose Lincoln as my name."

Kitty rolled the dice to determine the playing sequence. She started first, which meant I was last. She threw the dice again, lifting a tile from the right numbered spot on the wall. I arranged my tiles by the sequences of colored balls and bamboo sticks.

Grandmother Lin and Kitty exchanged small talk in Cantonese mixed with broken English. I had no idea what they were saying, but it seemed like they were not listening to one another. Both were intent on arranging their tiles.

"What year did you come to America, Mr. Lin?" I asked while waiting my turn.

He sorted his tiles, considered each one carefully. He did not answer my question, and he did not play his turn until he had arranged his hand to his satisfaction. He threw the dice and took his tile at a comfortable pace. He said, "1946. I took a cargo ship to Honolulu and then to San Francisco, one year after the war."

"Did you come to America to escape the Communists?"

He studied his tiles.

"Tell him," Kitty said. "Tell your story, Grandfather."

He continued to scrutinize his tiles, but he said, "In China, I lived with my family in Shaoguan. I was fourteen years old, too young for the army. My father was a doctor, but I fished the river. I used birds with ropes tied around their necks to catch fish. Those birds were my pride, and being on the river was my joy. All around the curving river were jagged peaks, and green moss covered the shoreline. So beautiful. So peaceful.

"The Kuomintang came and told us the town was no longer safe. We knew then that the Japanese were winning. People from all over Canton came pouring through Shaoguan ahead of the Japanese army. Peasants and bankers, storeowners and rickshaw pullers, they were all refugees carrying whatever treasures they had. Some carried boxes of gold coins, some carried babies. They were all trudging to Chungking.

"When they went, the people of Shaoguan went with them. They took everything they could carry: money, clothing, livestock, heirlooms."

I rolled the dice and picked up a flower tile, but it didn't match anything I had. I sipped more wine. My mind drifted away from the game. The old man's story held my interest.

"Bombers tore apart the town. I packed my birds and all our food and took my family to a secret cave in the hills. There were other families in other caves, but we had a cave to ourselves. The echo of bombs stopped, and we knew that the Japanese troops would come.

"We hid like animals until we forgot what the sun looked like. Our food depleted, so every night I went out searching for food. I found bodies everywhere, in the fields, the streets, the burnt-out houses. They smelled like rotting fish. The Japanese slaughtered so many people, and no one buried the dead. The birds and town dogs fed on the bodies. Terrible! Terrible! I would lay down and play dead so the dogs would come to eat me, and I grabbed them instead. But soon there were no more dogs or birds to feed on.

"I found other things too, things that people left behind: fancy silk clothes, jade pendants, gold rings, porcelain bowls. I hauled them back to the cave. Then one day I found the most precious thing of all. I found my Chew-Gen, wandering alone through the outskirts of town. I took her to the cave and made her my wife."

He paused for a moment, smiling.

"We lived in that cave for over a year. I fished with my birds for food and hunted for treasure at night. My parents both died in that cave. I buried them in the silt by the river.

"After the war, I had a whole cave full of treasure. Chew-Gen told me she was having a baby, and we both want to have our baby in America so that he will be a citizen of the gum san, the Golden Mountain. So I sold all my treasures to get enough money. We arrived in San Francisco just in time. We were still in the Angel Island Immigration Station when Harvey was born. I bought a sewing factory in Chinatown with the leftover money. The cave was a horrifying time, but from it grew my greatest joys."

"Aii-ya," Grandmother Lin said as she picked up a tile. "Pung!" and "Mah-jongg." She spread her tiles out with a satisfied laugh. We counted the points and began again. The more wine I sipped, the better I played, or so I thought, although Grandmother Lin seemed to win every game.

Grandfather Lin's cave story haunted me on the drive home. I kept wondering if I had the courage to endure such hardship, and at the same time, I felt grateful for my comfortable life.

AT HOME, I walked into a darkened living room. A shadow ran across the floor toward me, and Mr. Toa brushed my leg. I switched on the lights and found Jared stretched out on the sofa, naked and snoring softly. A half-empty bottle of Haig and Haig Scotch Whiskey sat on the coffee table beside the sofa.

I felt the urge to walk back out of the apartment, but I had nowhere else to go. No secret caves burrow under Russian Hill.

CHAPTER 10

I WOKE in the night to the sound of Jared fumbling about the apartment. I lay motionless, listening: the toilet flushed, the bathroom faucet ran, the refrigerator door opened, the cork popped. I wondered how many hours and how many drinks before he returned to bed. I slipped from the covers and tiptoed to the bathroom to pee without letting him know.

Back in bed, I lay sleepless. Light from street lamps filtered through the blinds, giving the room a silvery glow. I waited. After endless hours, he stumbled into the bedroom. In the dim light, he looked like a ghost. He fixed me with a cold stare, not bothering to speak. He looked away, turned to walk out.

"Come to bed," I whispered.

"Can't sleep." He slurred the last word.

"Hold me."

"My life is whooshing down the toilet. Everything sucks. I can't do this anymore."

"Please, Jared. Please hold me."

I felt him climb onto the end of the bed and crawl on all fours until he slipped under the cool sheets. He draped an arm over me. It felt heavy and warm on my chest. I turned to face him, into his boozy breath, and I stroked his cheek with the back of my fingers. He forced his eyelids shut and said, "Go to sleep," as if he couldn't stand to have me look at him.

I had lost him again. The world had killed him, even though his heart pumped and his lungs drew air. I felt so alone. I've read that couples need time away from each other, that no matter how deeply in love, they crave time alone and they are jealous of that in each other, but I have never once felt that way.

I have all too often experienced that gut-empty aloneness when he held me, though. We both did. During the day we were alone against the rest of the world, them against us. I didn't mind that he and I stood united against the many, but this other aloneness, the terrible kind that happened at night, with him touching me and yet not there at all, made me feel as if my guts were being yanked out one yard at a time.

When we had just started on the tour, those first four years, he had been so strong. I thought he was indestructible. But the world has no pity for strong people, and it does whatever it takes to break them. It breaks them, heals them, breaks them, and each time they grow stronger in the broken places until they are so strong that they refuse to break anymore. That's when the world kills them. It kills the good, the gentle, the strong, impartially. It kills everyone, but with weak people, it takes its own sweet time.

MORNING broke. I woke to the tap tap of rain against the windowpane. The aroma of brewing coffee permeated the room. I realized that I was not alone. Mr. Toa sat on the end of the bed. His eyes nailed me through slits. His tail brushed from side to side like a metronome measuring the passing seconds. I swung my legs over the bedside and pulled on a pair of red shorts before stumbling to the kitchen. Jared sat at the table with a half-full cup in front of him.

"How're you feeling?" I asked, not liking the look of him.

He stared at me with soulless, bloodshot eyes.

"Want some breakfast?" I asked.

He shook his head. "I couldn't hold it down. My head's throbbing, my stomach's doing somersaults. If I were a horse, they'd shoot me." His voice was raw, and so soft I had to strain to hear.

"Take some painkillers."

"I took eight. It doesn't help."

While I poured myself a cup of coffee, my mind churned with things I wanted to tell him, or more accurately, lecture him about—that drinking exacerbates the problem, that drinking on an empty stomach is beyond moronic and he deserved a hangover, that his root problem was self pity and if he didn't find a way to work through that bullshit I *would* shoot him—but there are times to speak out and times to shut up, and my venting at that moment would have benefited no one.

"They beat us," he said. "Beat us twice."

"They whipped us before we started," I replied, "before our first tournament. Just took us time to realize it. But at least we played the game, and we got to see what we could do."

He shook his head, and his eyes shone with tears.

"We grow wiser in defeat," I said. "Victory brings happiness and pride; defeat brings wisdom. It's a small consolation." I even depressed myself. *That's why it does no good to talk about those things*, I thought. *You can't work it out with words. You can only pick yourself up and keep moving to the next moment without looking back.*

RAIN fell throughout the morning, freeing me of Connor's practice. I burrowed myself in my office and organized my thoughts around Jared, sitting at my desk, looking up at the ceiling fan as it ticked away the seconds.

An idea rippled through my head: would he be better off without me? I might be a constant reminder of what he had lost, and without me, he could begin to heal. I dismissed that thought. In my heart, I knew that I was all that was keeping him from drinking himself into the gutter. Another more troublesome question crossed my mind: would I be better off without him? I dismissed that thought as well.

I stood up and hunted for something to do. The office couldn't get any more tidy, so I had nothing but the half-dozen rackets stacked by the stringing machine, but they could wait another day, or two, or three. I felt the need to walk. I slipped on my parka, zipped it up, pulled the hood over my head, and strolled to the greens, chewing up divots of grass with each long stride.

I loved the golf course when it rained. I had those fairways to myself; I could leave the world behind and hike for miles until the pain dulled. I walked until the rain stopped and the sun broke through the cloud cover. It was almost noon before I remembered that J.D. Lambert had said he'd meet me for lunch. I climbed the hill to the clubhouse and saw him through the glass, dressed in the same Elvis style suit and hairdo. A toothpick hung from his mouth. To my surprise, Shar sat beside him.

She wore the same slinky black party dress and lizard high heels that she had worn at last night's party. Her face looked rather bruised in the noontime light, and I would have bet her eyes were bloodshot, but there was no way to see beyond her thick, dark sunglasses. When she saw me, her hand tried to smooth her tousled hair, but it did little to improve her looks.

Why not? I thought, crossing the room. *Let's wash all the dirty laundry with one load.*

I shook hands with J.D. and, before I could stop myself, I said, "Hi Elv... I mean, Mr. Lambert." An uncomfortable silence settled over us as I sat down. To cover my embarrassment, I raised my arm to signal the waitress. Turning back, I noticed that J.D. was already drinking creamed coffee and she was sipping a martini.

I nodded at her drink. "Early in the day for that, isn't it?"

"Technically speaking, no. I'm still going strong from last night." She blushed and glanced away with a self-amused expression.

I assumed she had kept Connor up drinking all night too. My anger, which had taken me hours to walk off, began to simmer with new strength. "That must take some effort. Must be nice to summon up that kind of stamina."

"The trick," she slurred, "is not to pussy out in the wee hours. Once you make the dawn, it gets easy."

"Shar, why are you here?"

The question didn't embarrass her. She seemed amused at my confusion. "Just looking out for Connor's interests," she said with a toss of her head and a rather condescending grin.

"Yes, he obviously needs a lot of looking after these days."

"A disapproving tone of voice, darling? What, am I in trouble now because I keep my client happy?" Her grin spread into a smile.

My anger jumped to a rolling boil, and my hand twitched with a mind of its own, wanting to smack that smile off her face.

"That's right. I don't approve of mixing personal and professional relationships, and I want it to stop." One smack, one measly little smack, was all my hand craved. It was almost too overpowering. I stuffed both hands in my jacket pockets.

"I'm going to pretend that you didn't just butt into my personal affairs. You seem confused about who's the boss and who's the employee? That's Connor's decision, not yours."

"Oh, I'm very aware of who the employees are, and there's a name for women who fuck the boss. Let's see, it was just on the tip of my tongue...." My voice had a rising inflection that broadcast my growing contempt.

"Don't you dare go there!" Her smile faded.

It was my turn to grin, but I felt too lousy to make the effort. "Sorry," I said, and meant it. I couldn't tell if I was that angry at her or still upset over Jared or in what the English call "a muddle," a term for which there is no American equivalent.

"You'd be a damn sight sorrier if you'd hit me like you wanted to do. Oh yes, darling, I read you like a book. Men like you want to think women are stupid, that you're somehow superior, and when we push back and show our intelligence, you want to slap us down."

"Men like me? Like you somehow know me?"

"I know that you're acting very superior, even though you've done nothing that grants you that privilege. His winning one minor tournament says very little about your abilities."

"Okay, that's me: cocky without a cause. Let's get back to why you're here. What are you after?"

"Perhaps I'm just a girl who can't sit still, and a free ticket to all those exciting cities across the globe is an offer I can't refuse."

"That wouldn't explain why you're meddling into Connor's financial affairs."

"Perhaps I've fallen for your young protégé and my motherly instincts are emerging. So much so that I'm trying to protect my little chick."

"I'd say the bullshit has gone from hip deep to right under our noses."

"I'm here for the same damned reason as you are: to ride our shooting star long enough and high enough to walk away with what I call Up Yours Status."

"That's a new one on me."

"Up Yours Status is having an esteemed professional reputation and enough money in the bank so that I can tell any crass, egocentric S.O.B. that crosses my path to go stuff it." Her tone sounded a little too accusing for my taste.

"Nice to know you have such lofty aspirations."

She peeled off her dark glasses and squinted at me. "If you think you're here for a different reason, then you're up to your ears in denial, and if you ever butt into my personal affairs again, even with no reputation and no money, I'll tell you where to stick it in a heartbeat."

J.D. had sat there chewing on his toothpick, but he held up his hands and stammered, "Hold on, the both of you. I didn't come here to referee a catfight; I'm here to talk business. Do you realize that we're sitting on a gold mine? I tell you, with a little surgery to rebuild his nose, this kid can do commercials, acting, modeling, you name it."

The waitress sauntered up with menus, but none of us wanted lunch. J.D. asked for a coffee refill, I ordered tea, and Shar tapped her empty martini glass, saying, "One more, three olives." She glanced at me, her expression an obvious challenge.

J.D. slid the toothpick to the other side of his mouth, picking up where he left off. "This kid's got looks, charisma, an overpowering baseline game, and he's Chinese. Advertisers will crawl all over him. He doesn't need to win a single tournament. Look at Srichaphan, what did he win? He barely crawled in the top twenty, and in Thailand he's bigger than Tiger Woods and Michael Jordan put together. And what about Anna Kournikova? She never won a singles title, and she became the top paid woman athlete of any sport. The point is, if we play this right, get him the right exposure, he gets very, very rich and we all do swell in the fallout."

"He's not asking you to compromise Connor's training," Shar said, her smoky voice now almost a croon. "He's suggesting that you do your job and let him do his."

J.D. shifted the toothpick in his mouth again. "That means I decide which tournaments he plays and what kind of exposure he gets."

"Look," I said, "I'm trying to transform a talented athlete into a champion. That's all I'm here for. And to do that, I say when and where and how he plays. If you play along and he stays healthy, everything else—the contracts, the exposure, the fame—will come in its wake."

The waitress brought a tray of drinks and placed them in front of us. She handed me the check and walked away.

J.D. said, "I know what you think of me. You think I'm a vulture, a no-talent bum trying to cash in on some innocent kid. I see it in your face."

Silence.

"Look," he said. "I'm not such a bad guy. I have a wife and two girls, seven and twelve, and a cocker spaniel who thinks I'm pretty okay. Right now I play cello in a string quartet in order to put food on the table. You have any idea how little musicians get paid, even the talented ones? All I'm trying to do is make a little money for everybody involved, including you. What's the harm?"

"Nothing. I've got nothing against money. But Connor wants to become the best player in the world, which, as you've pointed out, is not the same as making millions. I'm trying to help him realize his dream, and I'm not letting the pursuit of money"—I looked at Shar—"or anything else, for that matter, get in the way. Connor needs to focus on his game, and he needs to take small steps. It's like climbing Everest. Every couple of thousand feet, you need to stop for a few days to acclimate, otherwise you die of High Altitude Pulmonary Edema. Connor is fragile. He needs to be brought along carefully."

"Timing is everything in this business," J.D. said, shaking his head.

"It's quite simple," I said. "You mentioned Kournikova? Yes, she made tons of money, but her career was over before she turned twenty. If we mold him into a champion, the wins will come. With wins come titles.

With titles come endorsements. If you don't work from the ground up, you end up a flash in the pan with nothing but a bank account."

"You're afraid," he blurted as his face turned a precise shade of purple. He pulled the toothpick from his mouth and pointed it at me. "You're scared shitless that if they make some real money, they'll be able to afford a better coach, not some has-been faggot that got run out of the game. Don't look so surprised. I know all about you and Jared Stoderling."

"Well, at least you said has-been instead of never-was. Thank you for that."

I pushed the check over to Shar. "You can get this, darling, since the way you make your money is so much more fun than me busting my ass on the court for six hours every day."

There wasn't much gin left in her martini glass, but what there was found its way to my face. The smolder in her eyes was coldly red as she set her glass back on the table. She lifted her chin and turned away with a posture like royalty dismissing the servants.

I rose and stalked from the dining room. As my mind calmed, I noted that the clouds were dissipating. The courts would be dry for Connor's three o'clock session.

I EXPECTED Connor to show up energized from his big win, but he was quiet and moody. *No doubt*, I thought, *the result of a hangover combined with little or no sleep.*

Spencer, on the other hand, glowed. He and Uncle Harman must have hit it off, and I couldn't help wondering if he had gotten laid. That would explain his shit-eating grin.

We began with tai chi to clear our minds. Shar sat on the veranda, watching us move through our routine. With her there, I found it difficult to let go of our earlier conversation. I forced myself to focus on the feel of my breath filling and emptying my lungs, the sound of my shoes moving over the court, the breeze flowing over my face. The exercise pulled me into silence, and the world dropped away one thought at a time.

When we began our warm-up, Connor's moodiness weighted him down. He seemed listless, distracted. I assumed he nursed a hangover. The best thing for that, I knew, was to sweat it out by driving him hard. I had him perform speed drills, running him side to side, smacking a wide forehand after racing to smack a wide backhand, again and again. He built up a sweat, but he only gave it half his normal effort.

After ten minutes of aggressive running, I called him to the net.

"What's wrong?" I asked.

"You're pushing too hard."

"Not true. We do this drill every week, and you always give me a hundred percent. Are you hung over?"

"I had one beer, so crawl off my back."

"Listen, Connor. You're running on three cylinders, so either you don't feel well, or you've got some bug up your ass, which is fine as long as we work through it. You see, this happens on tour. You'll feel like crap most of the time, but you still have to drag your ass on court and raise your game enough to win. Some days you're operating at a hundred percent and you'll play awesome tennis; other times, you're at sixty percent or worse. You need to learn how to squeeze a hundred percent effort out of a sixty percent day. It's about attitude. That's what champions do: they push themselves to the wall even when they feel like dog barf."

"Whatever."

"Let's start by showing a bit more enthusiasm."

"Get Spence on court," Connor said. "He's the one that danced his ass off with Uncle Harman and slinked off to fuck the rest of the night. He should have plenty of enthusiasm."

"We didn't have sex!"

"You were on him like white on rice."

"I'm going to pretend that you didn't just use that particular metaphor," Spencer said, grinning and trying to lighten the mood. "Besides, Harman didn't seem to mind."

"Yeah, well, maybe I do. Why pick on my family? Why can't you find somebody else to fuck?"

"Con, I thought you'd be happy for me."

"Yeah right, happy that you turned my uncle into a cradle robber? Christ, he's almost thirty. I didn't even know he was gay."

Spencer's eyes narrowed, and his face darkened. He grabbed his tennis bag, slung it over his shoulder, and stalked toward the clubhouse. After a dozen steps, he stopped and turned. Anger disfigured his face.

"I'm not giving him up. He's taking me to dinner tonight, and I plan to give him anything he wants. He likes me and I like him, so deal with it." Spencer turned and stomped away.

"Fuck!" Connor hissed, struggling within himself, no doubt trying to decide whether he should chase down his friend and apologize. I gave him a minute, until I realized he wasn't going after Spencer and I felt a twinge of disappointment.

Doing any kind of drills would have been pointless, but I knew he needed some intense physical activity to work through his emotions. I told Connor to leave his stuff on the bench and run with me. He nodded and threw his racket toward his bag. Seconds later, we were running side-by-side through the junipers at the edge of a fairway.

The dull roar of cars tumbled downhill from the highway, but I focused on the desperate quality of Connor's breathing. He seized the lead, and I followed his flowing body through the shadows made by the trees. I loved to watch him run. Even when he was boiling inside, he still moved with the grace of a gazelle.

We crossed the Great Highway and flew down the beach. The loose sand slowed our pace, but Connor worked hard to maintain a fast clip. He gave a hundred percent, and I was thankful for that. It meant he had put aside his self-pity and ran with an empty mind. He needed that; we both did.

We ran like shore birds scurrying across the wet, gray sand, but after two miles, he began to limp. We slowed to a walk and stopped. He bent over with his hands kneading his right thigh. His leg muscles quivered with tremors.

"I'm cramping," he gasped with ragged breath. Intense pain grimaced his face.

"Keep your weight off it." I drew my arm around his waist to help support him. My free hand felt his forehead, and I found that he was running a low-grade fever, a typical symptom of over training. Between the tournament, our practice sessions, and Shar's training schedule, we had over-extended him, no doubt resulting in magnesium loss, which would also account for his moodiness.

"Christ," he said, "I'm such a stupid fuck. He deserves better."

I was wrong; he was still boiling about Spencer. My instincts told me to keep my mouth shut, but against my better judgment, I said, "He's searching for what you've already found."

"I know, I know."

Still supporting him with one arm, I put my free hand on his shoulder.

He sighed. "It's just that everything's getting complicated."

"Yeah, life does that, especially when you throw sex into the mix."

We started back. He limped at first, but soon his leg muscles loosened a bit and he walked without my support. Cold gusts blew off the ocean and chilled our sweat-drenched bodies. I began to fear that he would catch cold if we didn't jog fast enough to keep warm.

"How's the leg?" I asked.

"Better. But man, it was on fire a minute ago."

I nodded. "This will happen on tour. Your body will break down; it happens to everyone. All we can do is condition your muscles to their peak and minimize the stress."

"I've never hurt him like that before."

"An apology helps to speed through these kinds of disagreements. Try to imagine what he's going through. You abandoned him when you took up with Shar. Now he's alone."

"But Harman's my uncle."

"Would it be easier if he were a stranger? Do you know why you're upset?"

"I'll bet you and Jared never had these problems."

I laughed. From deep in my belly, I laughed hard. How sweet life would be if my problems were so trivial, I mused. But I realized how condescending that sounded. I shook the thought from my head.

"Speaking of Jared. Looks like you've lost your doubles partner. Not showing for practice today means he won't be playing any more tournaments."

"That's total bullshit. He loved it. We're a great team!"

"He loved it until they cheated him out of the title. He doesn't handle discrimination all that well. Anyway, we'll need to find you a new partner." In the back of my mind, I toyed with the idea of my being his partner.

"I thought he had more spine."

A large part of me agreed with him, but that didn't stop an intense anger from burning in my head. I didn't know if it was directed at Connor or Jared—or Shar and J.D., for that matter.

"What did I say about putting yourself in the other person's shoes? You have no idea what he's been through, so leave it."

"That fucking weenie! Is that what it means to be a fag, to hide like some spineless pussy whenever anybody says 'boo'?"

I turned and slapped his face before I could stop myself. The smacking sound ricocheted off the sand dunes, and we stood glaring at each other. Tears sprang to his eyes, and he slapped me back. I saw it coming: his arm cocked and his legs braced. I felt just bad enough that I stood my ground and let it happen. He poured all his pent-up frustration into that slap, and the whole side of my face stung like a bitch. Without a word, he turned and blue-streaked up the beach.

I yelled for him to stop, chased after him. He ran all-out, and I had no chance of catching him. I pushed my anger into a compartment in my mind and focused on him running on that injured leg. He could damage it if he kept up that pace. *I'm so stupid*, I thought. *Why can't I follow my own advice?*

I slowed to a comfortable jog. All the way back, I expected to find him doubled over and holding his leg, but I made it back to the clubhouse without seeing him. Relief surged through me like a sea swell.

Shar still sat on the deck overlooking the courts. As I ran up the steps, she said, "I need a word with you!" The edge to her voice told me she wanted more that a word, she wanted a fight.

Might as well, I thought. *I'd hate to leave a stone unturned on a day I'm batting a thousand.*

"Where's Connor?" I asked.

"In the locker room. What did you say to him?"

"We need to rethink his diet and fitness training. He's cramping, probably from magnesium loss. We either pushed him too hard or he's not eating right."

"I've got a handle on his training, and I'm not overdoing anything. It must be stress triggered from whatever it was that you said to him."

"Shar, I didn't say anything until after he cramped, so instead of getting defensive and pointing fingers, you need to take some responsibility and figure out what to change."

"The thing I need," she bristled, "is for you to stop telling me how to do my job."

"You've worked with him for months, and his legs are as fragile as ever. Maybe it's time to use your brain on him instead of your other body parts."

She swung her arm, trying to slap my face, but I caught it before she made contact. "I've had my share of that today, thank you very much."

I let go of her hand, and she stepped back, eyes flashing. "So that's what's got your nuts in a wringer. You're jealous."

"I'm pissed because you're not being professional, and that's hurting everyone."

"Can't you see that he needs to be loved? He needs what I'm giving him. He sure as hell doesn't get it from you or his father, and Spencer's a piss-poor substitute."

I heard a faint call from inside the clubhouse.

"Daniel!" Connor's cry carried an urgent note. I hurried to the men's locker room. Bolting through the door, I saw Connor bent over the bench in front of his locker. His clothes were strewn on the concrete floor, and he wore his white cotton jockey shorts. His face scrunched into a teeth-gritting mask as he held his right thigh. His pain seemed monstrous. "Help!"

I knelt beside him, pushing his chest until he lay on the bench. I lifted his leg over my shoulder and kneaded his thigh from knee to crotch. The muscles under his skin were locked hard as granite. I worked the leg while his body twisted in agony.

The room was silent except for his panting, broken occasionally by sharp gasps. The muscles loosened by imperceptible degrees, and I massaged with more pressure. The cramp began to dissipate, but his body vibrated with tension, and his skin became burning hot.

I took in the vision before me. His body lay quivering, lean and golden and perfectly defined. I had not seen him undressed before, and his sculpted loveliness stunned me. I understood why Shar couldn't resist him. His burnt-coffee-colored hair cascaded toward the floor, one arm crossed over his eyes, his other foot braced on the floor. Sweat beaded on his breast and ribs, and under the glistening moisture were cool bluish veins weaving under the pale skin.

My gaze inched down his abdomen until I stared at the soft fabric of his shorts. I looked away. My fingers labored up the length of his thigh and stopped just short of that fabric. I felt more muscle tremors, and I asked, "Feel better?" My voice was husky, and I felt my face flush.

"Still burns."

Good, I thought. *He wants me to keep going.*

"I'm sorry," he said.

About what, I wondered: our argument, slapping me, running away on an injured leg, the way he treated Spencer? Could have been everything or something entirely different, but I didn't care. My concentration wouldn't be drawn away from kneading that injured leg.

His muscles turned supple under my touch. At the same time, I notice that the bulge in his cotton shorts had begun to swell. Now that his pain had retreated, it had occurred to him that we were in an intimate situation. I lowered my head and pressed my cheek to his silky inner thigh as I massaged his quadriceps. I glanced at his bulge again. It began to strain the material.

He was straight, I knew, but he was turned on regardless. *If I want him*, I thought, *I can have him here and now.* My eyes traveled over his body. My mind wavered. Should I? A thought shrieked, "Get the hell out of here," but my fingers seemed to have a mind of their own. They wouldn't break away from caressing his sumptuous skin.

As if reading my mind, he pulled his arm away from his eyes, lifted his head off the wooden bench and gazed at me. I stared back. A long stillness passed while we came to a silent understanding that the situation had pushed us both over an invisible and inappropriate line, and we needed to back away quickly. As my fingers pulled away, I think we both felt a tinge of regret—and also relief. He looked beyond me, toward the door.

I turned my head and saw Shar standing at the doorway. Her eyes were level, accusing, and furious. Her expression told me she'd been there the entire time.

CHAPTER 11

A TORRENT broke over the city sometime around midnight. Something woke me enough to hear rain lashing against the bedroom windowpanes but not enough to register in my consciousness. I was about to slip back into sleep when I heard a definite knocking, louder this time, more persistent. I sat up and looked around. I was alone. Jared had abandoned the bed without waking me.

I slipped from the covers and pulled on my grey boxer shorts. The window was cracked open an inch, and my bare feet found where the rain had puddled on the hardwood floor. I closed the window and stumbled down the hallway, moving toward the front door.

In the living room, enough city-light filtered through the bay windows for me to see Jared lying on the sofa. His breathing was heavy and regular, his body stretched and limp as a sleeping cat. His skin, taut and radiant, seemed to refract the man-made light, making him shimmer like a transparent child. A pair of jockey-shorts covered his glowing skin.

Then I noticed the whiskey bottle on the coffee table.

I felt heart-shot. My whole body sank into despair. Once again, I had been discarded for alcohol, but this time a switch had gone off in my head, and I knew we had come to the end of something. I could not, would not, go on like this. Half of me wanted to nuzzle my face into that soft valley where his neck met his shoulder and entice him back to bed, while the other part of me wanted to walk out the front door and not look back. I was still groggy from sleep, but I was thinking clearly enough to know something dramatic had to change. Waiting was no longer an option. But as I reached the sofa and began to kneel, a knock sounded again. I had forgotten someone waited outside.

I hurried to open the door and found Grandfather Lin standing on the porch. His gray hair was plastered to his head; raindrops spotted his thick glasses. He wore a tan overcoat and carried a black umbrella.

"I'm disturbing you," he said, offering the polite Chinese greeting used when calling on someone unannounced.

"Is there something wrong? Is Connor okay?"

"I couldn't sleep. It's a very serious matter. We must talk."

I glanced at Jared. He had sat up and was rubbing the sleep from his eyes. I led Grandfather Lin into the living room and removed his coat. I turned on the room lights and scrutinized Jared to ensure he was relatively sober.

"What's wrong, Mr. Lin? Is Connor in trouble?"

"No, Mr. Bottega. I'm afraid you are."

"We're fine, as you can see."

"I think not. Connor tells me that Jared will no longer play doubles with him. He says Jared has given up, has lost his will."

Jared lifted himself off the sofa and shuffled our way. Grandfather Lin showed no sign of embarrassment standing before two almost naked men. He leaned very close to Jared and peered into his eyes. "You won't play with my grandson?"

Jared shook his head.

"You make a winning team."

"You want me to help Connor become a champion, but...."

"No. I want him to earn money for college. He will become a doctor, a healer of people. Tennis is a game; healing is a profession. Please, help Connor win money for school."

"It's not worth the aggravation."

"What aggravation?" Grandfather Lin asked. "That they call you queer? That they do not play fair?"

Jared's face colored. "You don't understand."

"I live with discrimination every day of my life, but I do not let stupid people keep me from what I need. You are a coward, afraid to face life."

"Connor doesn't need me."

"Maybe this is true. Maybe you need him?"

"I don't need anybody, and I don't need a lecture from you, old-timer."

"Stop feeling sorry for yourself and become a man. You think you have it hard? You think life is unfair? You are worse than a baby, crying, crying, crying."

"Leave my house, old man," Jared growled.

"I will tell you what a hard life is: being a fourteen-year-old boy chased from your home at gunpoint, watching aunts, uncles, cousins slaughtered like hogs, hiding in a cave, never seeing daylight, searching for food at night when there is no food so you cut meat from bodies that the Japanese soldiers leave along the roadside. When the bodies go rank there is nothing but grass, but that is never enough, so you watch your family grow weak and sick. Then you marshal the courage to sneak up behind a Japanese soldier and slit his throat in order to steal his food so that your mother and father might live a few more days. I will not bother to mention the trials of raising a family in a new country where you do not know the language and everyone spits at you. You say I do not know? You are a fool."

Jared and I stood like mannequins.

"Someone cheats you out of a game and you crawl into a bottle and pity yourself. You have a life of comfort, and you act like it is a heavy burden. Your problem is that you are ashamed of what nature made you. Well, I am ashamed of you too, not because you are gay, but because you are afraid to be a man."

I was torn in two. On the one hand, I felt every iota of the pain that showed on Jared's face, making it look as hard as a morning without breakfast. I wanted to comfort him, to protect him. On the other hand, Grandfather Lin had hit the target dead center.

For him to be rude to us went against all Chinese etiquette. It showed how important it was for him to give Connor what he needed. Or could he be more interested in helping Jared work past his self-pity?

Jared's pain twisted into anger, and I wasn't sure if he was mad at Grandfather Lin or at himself, but just in case, I stepped between them, taking Grandfather Lin by the arm, leading him to the door and helping him into his coat.

I shut the door and spun back around to Jared. Was this it, the time that I should throw my two cents in as well? Should we get it all out and over with now, while he was already struggling with what had been thrown in his face? And what could I say that Grandfather Lin had not said, except that I couldn't live like this another day?

His expression seemed dull and lifeless as his mind puzzled through his emotions. A jolt of panic rifled through me, thinking that this was the moment. The support structure of our relationship had been deteriorating for years, and now it was about to collapse.

What he said, though, was, "That old man's a few cards shy of a full deck. Let's go to bed."

Everything in me resisted. But fear of ending up alone made me take his hand and lead him back to bed. Vowing to give it one last try was so much easier than losing him.

Once we slipped between the sheets, he pressed my head to his chest. His heart beat loud in my ear, and its vibration moved through my skull in waves. It beat a strong and even pace, but it skipped a beat and began to throb with a different rhythm.

CHAPTER 12

BYPASSING the Australian Open proved to be a sound decision. Connor struggled with inner demons that he refused to talk about, and those demons caused his performance to dip in November. Each week, his progress resembled a bouncing ball; one day, improvement, and the next, regression. It could have been any combination of issues: his falling out with Spencer, the growing tension between him and Shar, the fact that Shar and I had stopped speaking to each other, or Roy trying to take a stronger role in his training.

The bright spot, however, was that Grandfather Lin's midnight visit had somehow persuaded Jared to play again. He attended every afternoon practice session. I was so encouraged that I entered both him and Connor in the Long Beach singles tournament in November and, to everyone's disappointment, Connor lost in the first round.

Shar, to keep her distance from me, chose not to go along. That upset Connor, but his poor play seemed to stem from more than that. He went for too much power on every shot, and he couldn't rein it in, like a runaway train highballing down a mountainside. He seemed intent on proving to himself that he could win on his terms—that he didn't need my coaching, or Jared's support, or Spencer's love, or Shar's intimacy. He was absorbed with showing us all he didn't need us, but that self-absorption—being too concerned about the outcome—stifles silencing the mind and makes it nearly impossible for the chi to make the power-shift.

It proved a painful lesson, doubly painful because Jared won all his matches by sticking to our game plan. Connor's crushing defeat sent him free-falling into depression, and the more Jared won, the deeper he plunged. Jared fought his way into the final, winning it in a second-set tiebreak.

During Jared's matches, several line calls had gone against him, but rather than letting them upset his concentration, Jared played safer shots well inside the lines—item number one of our game plan.

I sent Connor home with orders to be a couch potato for seven days, hoping that a break would smash whatever bug had crawled under his skin. But two days later, he showed up for practice with a new attitude burning in his eyes.

In mid-December, he experienced a breakthrough, and his game elevated sharply. I had glimpsed his true potential several times, but now it began to shine through like the sun on a cloudless day. Something inside him had incinerated everything except the desire to win. In time, I came to believe that this new attitude sprang from his humiliating defeat at Long Beach coupled with having to watch Jared fight all the way to the championship. I became aware that he had set his sights on a new goal: beating Jared.

His performance boost came from more than his new attitude, though. Despite our differences, Shar had taken my criticism to heart, cutting back his workouts and increasing his protein and vitamin B intake. She weaned him down to a one-hour workout every other day.

Connor welcomed the cutback because Spencer had stopped participating, so it was no longer fun. His overstressed body began the slow process of healing itself, and the results on his physical abilities and stamina were dramatic.

The San Diego tournament in December had a different outcome. Every day, just like in the Long Beach tournament, I scouted Connor and Jared's opponents: identifying their strengths, weaknesses, patterns, favorite shots in key situations, what worked against them. All that information went into my notebook, and from those notes, I created game plans.

The plans were a roadmap to keep my players on the most effective route to the goal. There were detours along the way—the opponents sometimes came up with surprises, and my boys occasionally found themselves lost—but the basic route was established in the plan, and it kept them on course.

A plan didn't guarantee success, but it gave them a tremendous advantage. We discussed the strategies over dinner, and we practiced executing the plans during the next day's warm-up. This time, they both stuck to the program.

Connor cruised into the semifinals without dropping a set but lost a hard-fought match to Juan Gomez, a player from Mexico City who had an ATP ranking of 96. Jared beat Gomez in the final to win his second title in a row.

During the trophy ceremony, a paunchy coach sitting in the players' section yelled, "Way to swing your purse, you fucking fairy!" Snickers peppered the crowd around us, and the faces of the officials awarding the trophy all turned the same broiled shade of pink. The gossip had begun to spread.

I watched Jared's eyes for any reaction, but I found none. It was the opening volley of an arduous battle, but rather than letting it affect him, his success made him focus harder. Our new mantra became *drill, baby, drill, and drill some more*, and as long as we won, who cared what they thought or even if they thought?

Encouraged by their performance in San Diego, I sent applications for Jared and Connor to play the qualifier's tournament to compete for spots in the SAP Open tier-two tournament held in San Jose, California, during the second week in February. Three weeks went by without a word. We received a polite but firm letter explaining that they had not received the applications until after the deadline. They were, of course, very sorry, and they didn't mention the word "gay," but we all knew why we didn't get in.

Our next shot was in mid-March, the tournament in Indian Wells, California—a pleasant thirty-minute drive east from Palm Springs. This time, I sent the applications certified-mail return receipt and mailed them two weeks before the deadline. I entered them both in the singles competition and also paired them in doubles. This would be Connor's first chance to test himself against the sport's elite in a major competition.

As the tournament approached, we settled into a new routine. Jared stopped giving tennis lessons, quit drinking, and rejoined Shar and Connor for their dawn workouts. I attached a punching bag to the rafters of our living room, and for an hour every evening, Jared boxed with the bag. He enjoyed boxing as much as tennis, so I encouraged him, and although I was nervous about the possibility of him bruising his hands, I loved what it did for his footwork and balance. His body responded to the workouts, growing stronger, faster, more agile—not to mention the stress relief.

Each day, Jared arrived at my courts as Connor finished his morning practice. He always brought sandwiches, and we enjoyed a quiet bite in my office or, if the sun was shining, we'd stroll into the trees beside the ninth fairway and eat lunch picnic-style.

He always arrived ready to work. I had to slow him down during lunch because he felt so anxious to start the drills. His hands would sometimes shake while we ate, like a junkie needing a fix. I would run my fingers through his hair or along the curve of his neck to calm him. He needed that touch. He often clung to me like a man at sea clings to a life preserver.

Once we stepped onto the court, however, he relaxed and became focused, attacking each drill with tenacity. As his game improved, he relaxed more and began to enjoy himself. Often I caught him smiling to himself after nailing a difficult shot, and I occasionally heard the sonorous ring of his laughter when he managed to amaze himself.

Connor and Spencer arrived separately around three thirty, and we went right to work. Connor's new goal of besting Jared became an obsession, and nothing could hold him back. But unlike Jared, he was no longer having fun. He became serious. Also, he and Spencer often traded bitter and catty remarks. For a while, Connor referred to Spencer as "Harman's boy-toy," until Spencer retorted that at least no one was paying Harman to fuck him. After that, they lapsed into a cool silence whenever the other was near.

It saddened me that they had misplaced that playful spark of puppy love that had made me so envious that first day on the beach. I encouraged Spencer to keep coming to practice because he enjoyed the workouts and we needed a fourth for doubles practice. I also felt he was a beautiful person whom I had begun to love in a kid-brother way.

I kept hoping Spencer would stop dating Harman so he and Connor could recapture that intimacy, but as time passed, he fell into profound bliss. He often showed up with a contented glow, like a new mother, and I knew where he had spent the previous night. Even if they had split up, I'm not sure he and Connor could have recaptured what they had shared. Some things can never be rekindled.

During the first six months of training, I had worked on improving Connor's stroke production and footwork, but especially to focus his mind to make the power-shift. The Japanese call it *Mushin*: the state of mind that Samurai warriors used in battle. It means the still center. It's the ability to stay calm and read your opponent while attempting to redirect his aggression. Mushin is to remain unbiased, to have no emotional attachments, to stay open and flexible like a willow in a strong wind. If you control your mind in this way, you control your opponent as well by making him react to you rather than you reacting to him.

In February, I switched our focus to play-strategy. Each day we studied a single stroke—a kick serve, a backhand slice, an inside-out forehand—getting Connor to absorb the power that each stroke contained and what circumstances were best to use each particular weapon in his arsenal. I explained that each stroke is a chess piece: each one moves differently, moves his opponent differently, and contributes to his game in a specific way.

We discussed the mathematical aspects of the game, understanding the geometric angles and trajectories and why it is critical to control the center of the court, like the center of the chessboard, and use angle shots to keep the opponent scrambling.

After two weeks, we switched from geometry to algebra. I explained that the net is the equal sign, and to find the answer implied by the circumstance, he needed to work the equation from both sides of the equal sign. Changing something on one side of the equation means a change must occur on the other side. To find the winning solution, the unknown value of x or y, requires calm and relentless logic.

Using the principle of algebra, I taught him how to read an opponent's strengths and weaknesses. That way, he could modify his shot selection in order to change the other side of the equal sign—to make the opponent adapt to him.

Tennis is a game of tactics between two adversaries who hold clashing ideas. The one with the clearest plan for both attacking and defense will control the opponent and thereby control the match. That is why it was imperative to have a solid game plan but also be able to read the opponent and hone the game plan as the match progresses.

That is the beauty of tennis. It's a thinking person's game, like chess. A great player must read in a split-second what's happening during a point and change tactics—moving from defense, to neutral, to offense, and back to defense—all in the blink of an eye. At the pro level, the top players have all the strokes, the footwork, and the burning desire to win, but it's the players who can read the circumstances and adjust in order to control the match who consistently win.

I named each one of my strategies for gaining control of an opponent. Many of these tactics I gleaned from Miyamoto Musashi's classic book of Samurai strategy, *The Book of Five Rings*. The Double Attack from the West. The Flying over the Charging Tiger. The Flowing Water Cut. Lunge and Slash. The Chinese Monkey's Attack. Sand in the Eyes. To Cut off a Wing. To Hold down the Pillow. Use the Unseen Sword to Stab at the Heart. And the most effective of all, To Become the Enemy. Day by day, I taught Connor everything I knew, and he absorbed it all like a dry sponge.

A week before the tournament, Roy drove Connor, Jared, Shar and me to Indian Wells in his new twelve-seater van (bought, no doubt, with Connor's winnings from San Diego) to play the four-day qualifier event leading into the Open.

We stayed at a seedy Motel 6, a ten-minute drive from the courts, and ate at a greasy-spoon called John's, where we could get three eggs and a short stack for a couple of bucks.

The desert climate in March was sunny, mid-eighties days and frigid nights.

Thirty-two players, ranked from 80 to 200 in the world, competed for the eight open slots in the main-draw tournament. Connor and Jared needed to win at least three matches to qualify for a slot. It was a diverse group of players: teenagers on the rise, journeymen still chasing the dream, stars battling back from injuries. Most of the qualie players were talented, hungry to prove themselves, and unknown. Connor fit right in.

A huge pressure weighs on a player during a qualifier event. It's all or nothing. You either make it to the big dance or you thumb a ride back home. The lucky eight players get a decent paycheck (a first-round loss in the main draw earns $2,000), chauffeured cars, and a free hotel room for the week. The losers get nada.

Every morning we were up at dawn for a carb-packing breakfast at John's followed by a two-hour workout where we practiced the day's game plan. Jared and Connor downed energy bars at nine thirty, played their matches at ten, and we were back at John's for lunch by twelve thirty.

Jared won three matches before falling to Justin Greer, the highest ranked player. Connor breezed through the draw, winning every match. He was firing on all cylinders, and, although I was pleased, a stab of anxiety had me worried that he would peak before the real tournament began. But both my boys had made it into the main draw of a Masters Series event, and my glow of happiness out-shone my fears.

On Thursday, we drove back to San Francisco. It seemed crazy to drive ten hours to stay just two days before returning to Indian Wells, but it proved beneficial. As Roy's van pulled into our driveway, I saw Spencer sitting on a bulging suitcase by our front door. His face was shaded with gloom.

While we were gone, he explained as we stood in our living room, he had received notice that Stanford University had granted him a four-year scholarship for his pre-med studies with the stipulation that he play on the prestigious Stanford tennis team. His family gushed with pride, so he thought there would never be a better time to come out. He mustered his courage and announced that he was having an affair with a Chinese man ten years older than himself.

Connor gave him a warm hug, the first intimate gesture I'd seen between them since Spencer started dating Harman.

"I'm so proud of you," Connor said. "I'm sorry I wasn't here for you."

A look of pure shock flashed on Roy Lin's face. He seemed incredulous, livid. He didn't say a word, but only because his jaw locked so tight that he couldn't have spoken if he'd wanted to.

Shar hugged Spencer. "You brave, sweet boy. What did your father say, actually?"

"He demanded to know who I was seeing. He said something about ripping off his head and stuffing it up his stink hole. When I wouldn't tell, he ordered me out of his house. He's always been a hard-ass conservative. So I packed a bag and hitched a ride over to"—he paused and glanced in Roy's direction—"you know who's apartment. I thought we could live together, but he is not ready for that kind of commitment. We had a big fight. I guess it's hard to come out when you're that deep in the closet. I think he is also a little afraid of my father. I don't blame him. Dad will put him in the hospital if he finds him. So now I don't have parents, a boyfriend, or place to live."

Connor glanced at his father with his eyebrows arched in a silent question, but Roy's expression made it obvious that Spencer was no longer welcome at his house either. Connor stepped closer to Shar, wrapped his arm around her waist, and drew her near, as if to show Roy that he was straight.

"I say fuck him," Spencer said, but his voice carried a tone of sadness instead of the anger that he must have intended. "I have my scholarship. I only need a place to live until the fall. This summer I'll get a job to make some spending money."

Jared took Spencer into his arms, gave him a firm hug. "Put your suitcase in the guest bedroom. You're staying with us for as long as you need."

It seems funny when I think back on those things that make me proud of Jared. Of course we would take Spencer in, no question. We couldn't stand by and not help. But Jared handled the situation with no discussion, no hesitation. He reached out with compassion, which somehow made me feel grateful.

Spencer's puppy eyes peered at me. I grinned and nodded. He flew into my arms to hug me, and, feeling his tears dripping onto my neck, the kid-brother love I felt for him now seemed startlingly intimate.

CHAPTER 13

BEFORE we drove back to Indian Wells, I met Carrie Bennett in the Windsor Club dining room to explain that my conscience wouldn't let me keep taking a salary and health benefits from the club. For the past several months, I had devoted myself to two players, which meant that I hadn't performed the job they had hired me to do. And now that I would be touring, I wouldn't be there at all. It wasn't fair to the hundreds of members who needed coaching and were being left to fend for themselves. I told her if she wanted two weeks' notice, it would have to wait until I got back from the Sony Ericsson tournament in Miami, which was two weeks away.

She reached out and held my hand, telling me she didn't need any notice and it would be best for me to make a clean break. She must have seen the fear in my eyes, because she winked and said, "You'll do fine. As usual, you're playing the percentage shot."

We strolled to my office, and she watched as I stuffed my belongings into a cardboard box. As I took down my six autographed pictures, I heard the paddle-bladed ceiling-fan wheeling above, announcing the passing seconds with each rotation.

When I had everything packed, I garnered a last look at the tobacco-spit-colored walls and ambled to the veranda to gaze at my pristine fleet of green and white courts. Two courts were occupied by people I had taught how to hold a racket and play the game. I heard the wind flowing through the trees and the pop of the ball striking the strings, a soothing, familiar rush of sounds.

Carrie gave me a prolonged hug and wished me well. I climbed the hill to the parking lot for the last time. Those familiar sounds grew faint, dissolving into silence. I jumped into Slug and drove home with a heavy foot.

ON THE Saturday before the tournament began, we all trooped back to Indian Wells in Roy Lin's van. This time, J.D. Lambert joined us. It rained all the way down Interstate 5, a gray and gloomy ride through the green squares of Central Valley cropland. At Bakersfield, to escape the rain, we turned due east and climbed over the mountains on Highway 58, which dropped us down onto the baked-brown plains of the Mojave. We cut due south for the last leg of the drive.

The dry weather didn't improve our mood. The draws had been published the day before, and Connor's first match was against the second seed, Alec Gardener, the highest-ranked American player. It would take a miracle for Connor to beat him, so the glum certainty that Connor would go down in the first round hung over everybody except J.D. Lambert.

Lambert crowed that Connor's match would be on the stadium court and televised. Hundreds of thousands, perhaps millions, of viewers would watch him play. If he played well, the sponsors would take notice. A dream come true, by his reckoning. And if by some impossible stroke of fate Connor beat Gardener, we'd be in high cotton regardless of what else happened.

I agreed that we were lucky, but for a different reason: if Connor gave Gardener a good fight, that would boost his self-confidence and catapult his game to a higher level.

The tournament fell on the same week as Spencer's spring break, so he tagged along without missing any school. This time, since each player was guaranteed a free room and a minimum two-thousand dollar paycheck, we all checked into the players' hotel.

As we drove past the Motel 6 on our way to the Hilton Village, Jared and I exchanged smiles; our slumming days were over. Roy Lin and J.D. Lambert shared a room, as did Connor and Shar, and Jared and I upgraded to a suite with two bedrooms, one for us and one for Spencer.

We checked in just before midnight, and everyone went straight to bed. At seven the next morning, we stopped at John's greasy spoon before hitting the practice courts. Both Jared and Connor ordered the huevos rancheros special. They gorged on eggs and rice and beans and tortillas, then made a grab for my toast to wipe their plates clean. I was happy to see them packing in the carbs, because I had planned a long and grueling practice session.

We arrived early because both my players had to submit urine samples for drug testing. I ensured that the urine bottles went from my players into the hands of the independent testing agency to guarantee no shenanigans by the ATP. I planned to do this at every tournament. I was also prepared to hire a separate testing firm if I suspected any tampering.

After the testing, we had an hour to kill before our practice court became available. Roy and J.D. wandered off in search of sponsors. The rest of us roamed around the grounds.

It had always amazed me that this place had once been barren desert. Lush green lawns and manicured flowerbeds surrounded the stadium and the twelve outer courts. Bordering the complex were miles of tract homes sprawling over the hazy plain, and beyond them stood the rugged, wind-sharpened mountains. They rose and rose to meet the sky like towering fortress walls, pale gold and sunburned red in the morning light. The thin air felt dry, and the temperature soared into the eighties, causing waves of heat to radiate off the tract home rooftops.

I couldn't contain my excitement at playing a tier-one tournament again: mingling with the elite players, comparing notes with other coaches, hobnobbing with the magnates who organize professional tennis. I was overwhelmed.

Jared glowed like the desert sun. He had that old swagger in his step, and no matter what happened, no matter how ugly it got, it was worth all the months of work just to see him like that again.

As we strutted toward our practice court, Jared draped an arm over my shoulder and pulled me close. I was too surprised to pull away. Besides, I welcomed the affection. Connor did the same with Shar.

We strolled in silence, each person wrestling with those stomach butterflies that were as big as elephants. We passed other courts where the stars, coaches, and wannabes all argued about strategy and stroke techniques in a dozen different languages. We stopped to exchange pleasantries with a few coaches and players who welcomed us back in the game. *This is it*, I thought, *what we had dreamed about*. We were all afraid to say anything that might diminish the experience.

We stripped off our warm-ups and performed tai chi. Most players stretch their muscles to warm up, but I wanted to slow them down, to have them breathing right, quieting their minds and expanding their chi.

Roy and J.D. came scurrying toward our court towing two men whom J.D. introduced as John Sikes and Louis Wang, marketing representatives from Nike who were interested in seeing Connor work out. Roy sported a wide, toothy smile and dollar signs in his eyes. As we took to the court, Roy told them in a loud voice how he had trained Connor to get him to this point and that now he supervised all Connor's practice sessions. Shar jumped in to describe Connor's diet and workout program.

Connor shot me an embarrassed, sideways glance, but I smiled and tuned everything out. I focused on the boys warming up like we'd done a hundred times before: slow, steady, controlled strokes until a sheen of sweat glistened across our foreheads. I nodded at their solid follow-through, and I paid particular attention to their faces to ensure they were in that Mushin mind-space of controlled emptiness.

After the warm-up, we focused on the business of preparing Connor for his match with Alec Gardener. Alec possessed the fastest serve in tennis and a powerful forehand that could smack winners from anywhere on the court, but Connor had a superior backhand, return of serve, and better movement.

Connor's first key to the match was attacking Alec's backhand, forcing Gardener into a backhand-to-backhand rally, waiting for a short ball to drill down the line or come to the net for a put-away volley. We practiced that strategy again and again.

The second key was holding serve. Connor would get precious few chances to break Gardener's serve, so it was imperative that he always hold his own serve. He didn't possess a powerful serve, so he had to compensate by using variety and pinpoint accuracy. We spent half an hour on serves: hard and flat down the centerline, spinning into the body, kickers out wide, serve and volley.

The last key was returning Gardener's humongous serve. Connor needed to bunt enough big bombs back in play to frustrate Gardener. Gardener always expected to win a heap of cheap points on his serve, and he got frustrated with anyone who made him play long rallies. If Connor could return several missile serves early on, Alec could begin going for too much on his first serve, giving Connor a look at a lot of weaker second serves. We practiced returning serves with Jared standing halfway to the net drilling balls at Connor. He stood closer to give Connor less time to react, simulating the 150 mile-per-hour Gardener rockets.

To my surprise, Connor bunted a dozen of those serves back into play, which raised my hopes the width of an eyelash.

During our first rest period, our shirts came off, and we downed quarts of water. The air had turned hot, and the intense workout had us all smiling.

A crowd of twenty spectators gathered at courtside to watch four shirtless, sweat-soaked men play tennis. Some even took pictures. A few coaches and players were sprinkled among the fans, sizing us up. They affected Connor. The fact that pros were watching had him showboating.

I assumed his concentration would lapse, but they had the opposite effect. Intent on impressing them, he honed his focus so that his performance surprised even me. I glanced over at John Sikes, and I saw that he was even more impressed than I was.

When we called it quits, Jared ambled over and hugged me. He radiated happiness. He hugged Connor as well and wished him luck.

John Sikes, who had stayed to watch the entire workout, shook his head and said, "I come from Nebraska, and back there men shake hands. They wouldn't know what to make of men hugging each other." He chuckled and glanced at Roy.

"Says a lot about Nebraska," Jared said.

A few spectators gave off a nervous, sniggering kind of laugh.

"Well, hell, what's next," Sikes said, "players kissing?"

"Let's give it a try and see," Jared said. He seized the back of my neck and drew me to him, kissing me on the mouth. The move surprised me so much it took me a moment to pull away.

The crowd fell silent. John Sikes's and Roy Lin's faces turned to stone. Sikes walked away. I gave Jared a cold stare and shook my head.

"Hell," Jared said, "I want everyone to know. Don't you?"

"What's the point of broadcasting it?" I made no attempt to hide my anger.

"The first time," Jared said, "everything happened behind closet doors. That's how they beat us, by keeping us afraid and in hiding. This time we'll flaunt it. They'll probably still beat us, but at least everyone will know why."

Spencer slid up beside me and wrapped an arm around my waist, squeezing affectionately. His gentleness soothed me somewhat. Since moving in with us, he'd become more intimate, altering the dynamics of our household from couple to family. He never strayed far, like a puppy craving its mother's warmth. "Jared's right," he whispered. "People should know."

"You wacko bastard!" J.D. hissed through clenched teeth. "You just blew a two-million-dollar deal. You want to fuck your career, be my guest. But you have no right to pull Connor down with you."

Roy's face grew ashen, as if he needed a blood transfusion. I told him he had better sit down before he fell down, but he ignored my suggestion and pointed a stubby finger in my face.

"What's been going on behind my back?" His eyes squinted to slits, darting from me, to Spencer, to Jared, back to me.

Spencer nuzzled closer, as if to protect me. Connor held his eyes with a steely stare.

"Just what are you asking, Mr. Lin?" I said. It took every iota of self-control I possessed to steady my voice.

"If you've seduced my son, I'll, I'll...."

"Chill, dad," Connor interrupted. "Nobody seduced anybody."

"Mr. Lin, we haven't done anything improper," I said, glancing at Shar. She looked away, unable to hold my eye.

"Nothing improper? You just cost me two million bucks. I'll sue you!"

"Sue me because a Nike representative is homophobic? Good luck!"

"You're fired. I won't have my son associating with a pack of queers. And that goes for you too," he said, shaking a finger at Spencer. "You stay the hell away from Connor."

"Who the fuck needs you?" Jared sneered. "You're the one who came begging for help, not us. We can make it on our own."

I whirled around to face Jared. "Hit the showers. You've done quite enough for one day."

A huge smile split his face in two. He snatched his tennis bag and gave me a peck on the cheek before strutting off toward the showers with Spencer in tow. Before they walked a dozen steps, they were surrounded by fans who had watched the workout. Jared signed a few autographs and chatted with the fans.

The spectators drifted away in twos and threes, and the warm desert air was peppered with their ringing laughter. My legs felt weak. I glanced around our circle and at Jared and Spencer shuffling off. These six people with opposing views had been brought together for one purpose, and I realized that to achieve that purpose, my role must be to bridge the chasm that separated each one of us from the others. *I am the bridge*, I thought, although at that moment I felt more like the chasm. The experiences and achievements that I assumed defined me were lost in the past, and it seemed as though I was treading over an ice field of continually changing shapes, my personal *March Of The Penguins*. And it felt like very thin ice indeed.

Connor, who stood beside Shar with his eyebrows lifted, chimed in, "Dad, nobody's firing anybody. It's none of our business what they do in their bedroom."

"You're wrong," J.D. hissed. "Everybody on tour will make it their business whether you like it or not. And they'll assume that you're one of them. They travel in packs."

His "packs" slur stuck in my craw, but he was right about one thing: pro tennis is made up of three or four hundred people all migrating from one event to the next, like a nomadic tribe following the herd, and there are no secrets in a tribe. Sneeze at breakfast, and everybody says "Gesundheit" by lunch.

Shar spoke for the first time. "We'll show them that it's not true," and she put her arm around Connor's waist and drew him closer. I smiled at her as a way of saying thank you, and she winked at me, a long, slow whiplash of her eyelid. I read a lot into that wink. I read that she and I were becoming friends again. There is nothing like a common enemy to bring people together, and she had despised Roy from day one.

"You can't be serious," Roy screamed. "They'll ruin us. Even they know that. That's why they kept it secret."

"Dad, they haven't kept anything secret. Daniel told me the first day. Everybody knew except you. Even Mr. Lambert knew."

Roy became stock-still and stone-cold silent. Finally, his lips began to twitch, as if he were holding back something he wanted to shout. His breathing grew loud. Before he could voice whatever was on the tip of his tongue, Connor said, "Jared is right. If we don't hide anything, it will blow over. I'm willing to take that chance, so please, Dad, I'm asking you to deal with it."

"You will do as I say. I'm your father, and I know what's best."

"And I'm the one who steps onto that court and jumps through hoops, and I'm telling you I can't do it without them. I wouldn't even want to try." Connor's voice went soft. "Please, Dad, it's not cool to make me beg like a dog."

"We'll find a better coach."

"I don't want better. I like them."

J.D. grabbed Roy's arm. "Listen, Roy, we don't have to decide now. Let's go find the Nike people. Maybe we can patch this up. Those bastards are so greedy for new talent they'd peddle their own grandmothers on the white-slave market if it would sell their damned shoes."

Roy glared at me. His face seemed to droop around his eyes, giving the impression of intense sadness. The steam ran out of him like a punctured pressure cooker. He said, "Have you ever thought about seeing a psychiatrist?"

"I'm happy with my husband. If you have a problem with it, Roy, perhaps you should seek professional help."

With a visible surrender, he allowed J.D. to lead him off toward the Nike exhibit booth.

As they walked away, Shar gave Connor a warm hug.

"That took guts, darling. I'm proud of you, and Jared is my hero. But there's only so far you can push before they push back, and I'm not talking about Roy and J.D.!" She leaned my way and hugged me. "All in all, that went better than I expected. Don't you think?"

"At least you and I are talking again," I said. "Sorry I've been such a shit."

"You were right, about the over-training and about my professionalism. That's why I got so damned mad. How about I buy you a cup of tea while this stud hits the showers?" She patted Connor's butt. Connor grabbed his tennis bag. As he headed for the locker room, she called after him, "No horsing around in the shower, and don't bend over to pick up the soap."

CHAPTER 14

JARED, Spencer and I had a quiet dinner at the hotel and hit the sack early. The others ate at John's greasy spoon. I know Roy and J.D. were pressuring Connor to fire me. I hated causing a rift between father and son, but I didn't want to lose Connor. There was so much more I could teach him. I knew I could help him achieve his dreams, but I felt my chances slipping away.

That night in bed, with Spencer asleep in the next room, Jared propped himself on his elbow with his body stretched out against mine. I felt his warmth all the way down to my soles. He ran a hand down my flank, and I shivered. I wondered if he was trying to get me in the mood or just comfort me.

"What's bothering you?" he asked.

I shook my head.

"We have another chance here," he said. "So let's do it right this time. If we make it, we make it. If we don't, we go down swinging. Somebody's got to be the sacrificial lambs if this sport is ever going to change."

"I don't want to hurt Connor's chances. He has what it takes, I'm sure of it."

"He's smart enough to make his own decisions. If things get too rough, he'll know when to back away."

I cuddled into that hollow space between his arms and fell in sync with his breathing before drifting off to sleep.

I woke in the night to find that we were not alone. Jared pressed against me and slept peacefully. Spencer had slipped into the other side of our bed and was snuggled up to Jared. It had the feel of a little boy slipping into bed with his parents on a stormy night. Deciding not to make a scene, I drifted back to sleep.

The next morning, Spencer was still in our bed, but he'd somehow wormed his way between us. He nuzzled against me while Jared nuzzled against him. Waking, I felt his warmth and his soft, boy-sweet breath on my face. He lay wide-awake, and when I opened my eyes, he kissed me while his hands caressed my morning woody. His lips pulled me into full consciousness, and my warning buzzer went off. I jerked back and shook my head, even though my entire body sizzled at the possibilities of sharing this beautiful boy with Jared.

"Go back to your room, now," I whispered.

"I'm so lonely," he said, trying to kiss me again.

I pressed my fingers to his lips with one hand and pointed to the door with the other. Without another protest, he crawled over me, getting out of bed, and left the room. I snuggled into that space between Jared's arms and tried to drift back to sleep, but my mind, caught in a vise between desire and fear, refused to calm. Thirty excruciating minutes passed before Jared woke and we started our day.

We showered, had breakfast at John's, and made a beeline to the courts. I didn't think Connor would be there, but when we arrived at the site, he, Shar, and Roy were waiting for us. Roy and I fell into an uncomfortable truce, at least for the time being. How long it would last was anybody's guess.

We had a forty-five minute warm-up on the stadium court before settling into our seats in the players' section to watch the first match up. Roy fiddled with a new top-of-the-line Canon digital camera. He planned to immortalize all of Connor's matches in snapshots. He opened a little notebook of directions on how to focus, zoom, store and retrieve pictures, but he chose to ignore the instructions and bumble his way through it.

A few minutes later, Gardener strutted onto the court with Connor on his heels. Gardener wore all white. He exuded confidence, acting as if the court was his living room and Connor an unwelcome guest.

Connor sported a powder blue collared shirt and white shorts. Embroidered on the back of his shirt was a red and yellow Chinese dragon, for courage and luck. I hadn't seen it before, and I wondered if Grandmother Lin had made it. *He needs both luck and courage*, I thought. Judging from the expression on his face, it looked like he was preparing for a root canal instead of a tennis match.

The chair umpire waved them over, and Connor won the coin toss, electing to serve. As the players warmed up, an announcer introduced them over the P.A. system. A cheer soared for Gardener, then polite, sympathetic clapping for Connor. The clicking of Roy's new camera had already become irritating. I began to hope that he would soon run out of memory.

The fans were eager. The stadium echoed with the sounds of phlegmy coughs and squeaking seats from people adjusting their sitting positions. Roy sat on my left under a broad-brimmed hat, crunching on Tums and clicking away. Shar sat to my right, the others one row behind us.

Roy wore a purple warm-up suit with red stripes running down both sides, even though the temperature had already topped ninety. Stuffed into one of his pants pockets was a massive white handkerchief. Now and again he ripped it from his pocket and swept it across his forehead with a flourish.

I knew Gardener would dominate the match with his blistering serve and powerful forehand groundstrokes, so as they warmed up, I calculated Connor's chance of winning at roughly zero, nada, nil. Still, my hands trembled. I hoped that he would put in a good fight, winning two or perhaps three games each set.

The stadium had a party-like atmosphere. American tennis fans idolized Gardener, and they were anxious to see him crush this unknown qualifier.

Connor won a nervous-looking first-service game. My hopes raised an iota.

For the first point on his own serve, Gardener stepped to the baseline and blasted a 143 mile-per-hour ace up the centerline. The crowd roared.

The first seven games flew by with Gardener seemingly winning every point, breaking Connor twice for a 5-2 lead. Gardener cruised in his service games, and Connor hadn't gotten a sniff at a break point. Connor played passively, seemed emotionless. He stayed relaxed and kept his Mushin mentality, but he needed to light a fire in his belly and play with controlled aggression.

Roy squirmed on the edge of his seat and bled with every point that Connor lost. "Wake up, for God's sake," Roy yelled. "That's his ninth forehand winner. You need a fucking neon sign to tell you to hit to his backhand?"

"Shhh," I hissed. "No coaching. You'll get us thrown out."

Roy sucked in his lips, ripped the handkerchief from his pocket, and swabbed his forehead. His face scrunched up like a prune, and I imagined that he was trying to send advice to Connor telepathically. Gardener served for the set, and during the first point of that game, Roy jumped to his feet, screaming, "Lob him, for Christ's sake. Use your head!" I pulled him back into his seat and silenced him with a glance.

I noticed tightness creeping into Gardener's ball toss. Under the pressure of serving out the set, he began to spray his first serves a few inches long, giving Connor a chance to smack his second serves back into play.

With the set all but lost, Connor went for broke and spanked a few winners, upping his level of aggression. He fought off two set points to break Gardener, and that momentum helped him hold his own serve. But Gardener closed out the set on his next service game, fending off three breakpoints.

Gardener had won the first set, but Connor had stepped up his play with the right amount of intensity. It looked like he might make a match of it, which caused goose bumps to chill my shoulders. Roy pulled a roll of Tums from his pocket and popped two in his mouth, biting down with force.

Breaking Gardener in the first set allowed Connor to believe he could beat the world-number-three, and belief blossomed into determination. He began to out-scramble, out-hit, and out-think the veteran. Gardener's huge serve kept him winning his service games, but Connor won the lion's share of rallies.

Roy settled into his seat with his lips sealed tight as a drum. Each time Connor won a hard-fought game, an emphatic "Hmmmmph" escaped Roy's lips. At four-all, Connor broke Gardener and served out the second set to even the match. When he won set point, a triumphant "Hummmmph!" flew from Roy.

Connor's determination intensified with every game. He fought toe-to-toe with the veteran, proving he had world-class talent. I became dizzy. He had surpassed all my hopes. It felt like all the planets had aligned. Even Roy's annoying clicking had stopped. He had maxed his camera's memory, and although he had a spare memory chip, he couldn't figure out how to install it. He scrambled to find the directions.

The third set turned into an edge-of-your-seat thrill ride. Both players elevated their intensity. Neither man could break the other. The fans cheered every point, urging both men on.

The red and yellow Chinese dragon embroidered on Connors back seemed to swell with vehemence. The goose bumps on my shoulders spread, shivering up my neck and spilling across my scalp.

But I saw something creep into Connor's game. He became too confident and began to showboat. On several of his backhand groundstrokes, instead of planting his feet in a balanced stance for a solid shot, he took the ball early at shoulder height by jumping off the court and striking the ball at the top of his jump. It's a shot that former world number one Marcelo Rios introduced and top players like Mark Nicholas and Sebastian Seaborne continue to use. It allows you to get more power into the shot and create sharper angles, but it's risky. I was overjoyed to see him feeling so confident, but I now believed he could win the match, and I didn't want him throwing it away by trying flashy, low-percentage shots.

In the third set tiebreaker, Connor bunted every one of Gardener's bullet serves back into play, making the veteran come up with the goods. A twenty-eight-stroke rally at four-all clinched it for Connor when he drew Gardener to the net with a drop shot and nailed a topspin lob. The final two points, both on Connor's serve, were a formality. He served and volleyed the first for a winner, his first serve and volley of the match. On match point, he smashed an ace up the centerline. His racket sailed thirty feet into the air, and he flashed a triumphant smile across the net at Gardener for good measure.

I leaned toward Roy and said, "This time next year, the whole world will sit up and take notice. Connor has a reservoir of determination that he's just beginning to tap."

He grunted with satisfaction. I assumed he was agreeing with me, but I realized that he had just replaced the memory chip in his camera so that he could capture the handshake. As Connor approached the net, Roy began rapid-fire shooting.

Connor and Gardener shook hands. Gardener almost ran off the court, while Connor took his time, signing autographs to hordes of kids.

Roy and I hurried to the pressroom to hear the post-match interviews. Gardener sat at a table half-surrounded by two dozen reporters and an ESPN camera crew. I saw at a glance how the loss had demoralized him.

The reporters fired questions like a machine gun. Gardener blamed a cramping muscle in his back that kept him from serving well and the fact that he felt exhausted from winning his previous tournament the week before—the usual excuses. All his answers emphasized how he had lost the match rather than how Connor had won it. When the questions petered out, he slinked to the showers looking like a whipped dog. My old feelings of sympathy surfaced. Gardener hadn't played a poor match, and he was the better player, but I knew how this loss would mess with his self-esteem. Connor had played the match of his life. It happens with the same regularity as blue moons.

Connor cut through the crowd and sat at the interview desk. He flaunted a nervous smile and, even though this was his hardest-fought victory, he radiated energy. Reporters crowded around him to pat him on the back and congratulate him. Several people patted him right on his embroidered dragon, as if they were hopeful that some of his luck would rub off on them.

Once Connor sat in front of the cameras, with all the lights blazing and everybody staring, he seemed to deflate. He was uncomfortable. His eyes grew large as he glanced around the room as if he were searching for an escape route.

Roy rushed over and sat next to him as the reporters blasted Connor with questions. I tried to stop him because only players are allowed to give the post-match interview, but he was too quick for me. Everyone in the room gave a glance at the person sitting next to him.

Before anyone could object, Connor introduced Roy and congratulated Gardener on a well-played match. He explained how our game plan had won him a few pivotal points, then responded to each question with a nervous hesitation.

His timid charisma seemed to charm everyone. The reporters ate it up and drooled for more. They all had the tangible hope that Connor was the next big thing, and they were there to record its birth. Excitement electrified the room.

A reporter asked if his embroidered dragon held any significance. Connor stated that his grandmother had embroidered it for luck and to show his pride in their heritage.

The excitement level vaulted over the moon. The fact that this kid's grandmother played a part in his tennis gave him a hometown, family-oriented air that was unheard of in the polished world of professional tennis. The room sizzled.

One reporter asked the question I had been dreading: "Connor, the rumor mill is saying that your coach is gay. Is that true?"

The background buzz hushed. More than a few eyebrows lifted while everyone leaned forward.

"I'm his coach," Roy said, "and I can assure you I'm quite normal."

"It's no secret you've been working with Daniel Bottega and Jared Stoderling, and the rumor is that they're lovers. Can you comment?"

Roy cleared his throat. "Yes, we've worked with Daniel, and Jared is my boy's doubles partner for this tournament, but our relationship with them is strictly a professional one. We have never discussed their personal lives with them or anybody else. If you wish to pry into their affairs, I suggest that you ask them directly."

"Connor, are you gay?"

Roy began to answer, but Connor laid his hand on Roy's arm to quiet him. He tilted his head to one side and frowned, silent for a moment, as if to summon up his courage. He said, "You seem to be an educated man. I'm sure you can find a more dignified question to ask, perhaps one pertaining to tennis?"

Silence blanketed the room.

The tournament director, David Salinger, stepped in front of the table and said that if there were no other tennis-related questions, we should let the hero of the hour retire to the showers. His eyes rested on me, and if looks could kill, my story would have ended right there.

As Connor slipped off to the shower room, everybody stood and applauded, and the smile reappeared on Connor's face. I wondered if they were clapping because of his win or the classy way that he had handled a touchy situation. I felt the urge to rush over and hug him, but that, of course, was the last thing we needed.

UNLIKE Connor's dramatic match, Jared's first round was a stroll in the park. He played another qualifier out on court six. He kept the ball well inside the lines so that the umpire had no chance to overrule any line calls.

Only a handful of spectators sat in the bleachers, and nobody grew excited as Jared mauled his opponent in straight-sets. But after the match, a mob of reporters and an ESPN camera crew stampeded into the pressroom to get an interview. I knew what was coming. They never bothered to interview players ranked outside the top twenty unless they sniffed blood, and Jared had those jackals licking their chops.

My stomach folded in on itself. Jared shot me his best what-the-fuck smile as he sat at the interview table. Ralph Carter, the ESPN reporter, brushed past all the tennis-related issues by congratulating Jared on his return to pro-tennis and on his win today.

Jared nodded his head; his smile widened.

"A rumor is going round," Carter continued, "that you and your coach, Daniel Bottega, are lovers. Will you comment on that?"

A roar erupted from the stadium court, and it seemed deafening compared to the hush in the pressroom. Everybody went rigid.

Jared gazed at the reporter. "Daniel and I have been life-partners for over ten years. It's no secret that we love each other. Is that some kind of news? I can assure you that we're not the only gay men on the tour, just the only ones who are out."

Surprisingly, that tight feeling in the pit of my stomach began to relax. The hush turned into silence. Nobody had expected to hear the truth, and they didn't know what else to say. Carter cleared his throat and asked, "Jared, have you or Daniel had sexual relations with any of these other closeted players?"

Jared shook his head. "Sex with other players? My goodness, no," he said, appropriately shocked. "Like I said, Daniel and I are life-partners. To us, that means a loving, monogamous relationship. There is nobody else I'm interested in."

I felt myself glowing. A murmur rose from the press corps. Several reporters seemed to swing on to Jared's side.

"So neither of you have had sexual relations with Connor Lin?"

Jared's eyes widened. "Of course not. Connor's girlfriend would roast us alive if we got cute with him."

A roar of laughter swept through the reporters, who now swung behind Jared. They jotted notes. Ralph Carter ran out of steam, having nowhere else to take his line of questioning. Jared didn't give him a chance to recover. He said, "I fear, Mr. Carter, that you have no intention of discussing tennis, but rather are attempting to draw me into a discussion on morals. Do you represent ESPN or the Christian channel?"

Applause.

"Jared," a voice from the back cried as the noise faded, "are you willing to disclose the names of other gay players?"

"Their personal lives are none of my business and none of yours."

"Jared," another voice said. "Does your being gay have anything to do with your four year absence from the tour? And if so, what brought you back?"

Jared shook his head. "I prefer not to comment on my reasons for leaving the tour. What brought me back was my love for the game."

"Would you consider playing mixed doubles with Martina or Amelie?"

"I'll be happy to play mixed doubles with any woman on the tour."

My heart beat so fast that I felt the blood surging through my veins. Jared stayed icy cool under fire. His eyes held the frightened stare of a cornered animal, but his voice and body showed no sign of tension. I had a hard time believing this was happening. I knew it had to happen at some point—a male player coming out—but I never dreamed it would be us.

A pause gave Jared an opportunity to stand, wave, and head for the showers. The reporters were so stunned that no one tried to ask more questions. I was half-afraid they would turn on me with their questions, but to my relief, they finished writing their notes and left the room in twos and threes, discussing the interview in excited tones.

David Salinger sauntered over to me. He shook my hand and said, "Personally, I think you're loony. This is not San Francisco, ya know," he said. "Coming out on national TV is huge. I hope ya know what you're doing."

"No," I said, showing a sheepish grin. "We don't have a clue."

That afternoon, my boys played their first doubles match and won in straight sets, 6-3, 6-4. It was an impressive win considering they were both still flying high from their singles wins. They proved they could put their excitement aside and concentrate like I had taught them. After a clean sweep on day one, a taste of fear soured the sweetness of our wins—my fear that things were going too smoothly. *It can't last*, I thought. *Can it?*

CONNOR'S win over Gardener gave the Nike representatives a change of heart. They insisted on taking us to dinner at a restaurant called The Chicago Steakhouse, which seemed gay-friendly. At least the male waiters were stylish, and both women bartenders were slinky and pretty, but they looked like the kind of women who didn't take crap from anyone.

Connor and Jared both ordered the porterhouse steak ($75 each) and a green salad ($18 each). Roy and J.D. both had the Maine Lobster ($86 each) and baked potato ($12 each), Shar and Spencer had the Caribbean shrimp and scallop ceviche ($44 each), and I had the New Bedford bay scallops with orange-miso vinaigrette ($58.75). J.D. topped it off by ordering two bottles of Black Hawk Creek Cabernet ($115 each).

We had so much to celebrate, but I couldn't shake the nagging feeling that we were spiraling into trouble. Jared and Connor stuffed their mouths with bloody rare prime, salad, and sourdough rolls. They chewed with bulging cheeks. Roy and J.D. hardly ate a bite. They were too busy sucking up to the Nike reps—industrial-strength Hoover vacuum sucking.

Connor sat to my immediate left. He leaned toward me and asked in a low voice if he should take the Nike deal or shop around.

"Depends on your life goals," I said. "Nike will probably deliver the most profitable deal, so if you want a tennis career, it's a sound move. But the day we met, you said that tennis was a way to make money to attend a medical school. If you sign that contract, you're committing to play tennis for the next five or ten years. Bye-bye, Dr. Lin."

Connor grew silent. A minute later, he said, "If I don't sign, my dad will go ballistic. He and Mom have sacrificed so much."

I reached up and patted his shoulder. "Who said life is fair? Besides, you think they'll stop loving you if you become a doctor?"

He dropped his head.

"You know," I said, "at eighteen, Johnny Mac was the number one junior in the world. After that he reached number twenty-one on the pro tour. You know what he did then? He quit the tour and went to Stanford, spent a year studying and playing the NCAA circuit, and when he was damned good and ready, he when back on tour. The rest is history. My point is, you have options."

"But if I sign the contracts...."

"You don't need to decide right now," I said. "As long as you keep winning, these vultures will keep circling. The more you win, the bigger their offer grows. So if you're not sure, give it time. Focus on your tennis and forget about contracts. Stay in the now, and right now you need to prepare for your match tomorrow, so finish that steak."

He nodded, but he didn't say another word during the rest of dinner. I was lost in thought myself. I wanted him to realize his dream, wherever that led, but for selfish reasons, I wanted him to sign that contract. That way, I could coach him for the next five years and be paid the going rate for my work, which was triple my present salary.

I knew that torn-in-two feeling that showed on Connor's face.

CHAPTER 15

THE next morning, we hit the gym, then drove to John's for breakfast. Over coffee and before the food arrived, we found ourselves splattered across the morning papers: "Gay Tennis Star Comes Out on ESPN." We were not the feature story, but we did make the front page with pictures of Jared, me, and Connor. We later learned that the story received nation-wide coverage.

As Roy read the article, his face blushed a poached-salmon color. We ignored him as we discussed the day's schedule in low voices.

A gay couple in the corner booth kept glancing our way. After paying their check, they sauntered over and asked for our autographs. They gushed about how proud they were of what we were doing. Roy turned to stare out the front window while chewing his pancakes. After the couple left, I asked, "Something wrong, Roy? You got quiet all of the sudden."

"I don't want to talk about it," he said.

"Good," Shar snapped, "because nobody wants to hear it."

Jared and I exchanged looks. I could read his mind, and it mirrored my own: it was either her time of the month, or someone didn't get any nookie last night. We both smiled. Her comment brought about a silence that lasted for the rest of our meal.

When we arrived at the tennis facility, we found it mobbed with several hundred gay men who seemed to be waiting for our arrival. Most of the crowd seemed young and athletic. Many of them probably played tennis themselves. There was also a smattering of older gay couples walking arm-in-arm and three drag queens dressed in wigs and women's tennis outfits—looking like Amelie, Serena, and Maria. Five shirtless gay teens wore rainbow flags as capes. Each one had a large red block letter printed on his chest. When they stood together, the letters spelled out Jared's name.

The entire group gathered around our practice court, pushing, shoving, and scratching their way to the front for a snapshot. They were beyond a doubt the most enthusiastic fans I'd seen anywhere in the world.

In our first match up, Jared would play the serve-and-volleyer James Holden from Great Britain. Holden rarely went for power shots. He used superb ball control to work his way to net for a volley put-away. I had Connor serve and volley against Jared, getting him used to having the opponent charging the net. Jared passed Connor two out of three attempts, which made me hopeful. Jared also practiced moving forward as a way to take the net first and force Holden to play the backcourt.

By nine thirty, the temperature had nudged toward ninety degrees. Jared peeled off his sweat-soaked shirt, and a collective gasp ricocheted through the crowd. Cameras clicked nonstop, sounding like a swarm of crickets. Not to be out-done, as soon as Connor realized the crowd's reaction, he pulled off his own shirt. The fans cheered. Shyness kept Spencer from following their example.

Cries of, "We love you," soared over the court, and it became impossible to keep Connor and Jared focused, because they both kept smacking the beans out of the ball to impress their audience. We practiced for forty-five minutes, followed by fifteen minutes of signing autographs. We had to hurry to the locker room to get Jared ready for his second-round match. The crowd followed us like legions trailing Hannibal across the Alps.

Because of the vast numbers of fans that had come to watch my boys, the tournament organizers did some schedule reshuffling, putting us on the main stadium court, the only court with enough seats. Jared would play at eleven o'clock, Connor at three. By match time, the cheap seats were packed with gay fans, and a roar went up as Jared stepped on to the court.

James Holden had fallen to number twenty-eight in the rankings, but he still had enough game to beat anybody on any given day. *But if Jared stays focused*, I thought, *he can win.*

From the get-go, Jared controlled the match with his forehand groundstrokes, keeping Holden nailed to the baseline until he could unleash a winner. Every time he hit one of his bullets, the gay fans went wild. It sounded like Carnival. Rainbow flags soared through the air like battle banners. The wave went around the stadium every time Jared won a game.

Jared rushed the net on several critical points to keep Holden back and won the point nearly every time. Twice the chair umpire overruled a line call in Holden's favor, and each time the gay fans booed so loud and for so long that I thought they would stop the match. Fortunately, being on center court, they had the Shot Spot verification system, which allowed Jared to challenge the calls. Both times they confirmed that Jared had indeed won the point, and the fans shrieked. I felt sorry for Holden. He not only had to battle against Jared's huge groundstrokes but also maintain his concentration while several hundred fans jeered at him.

When Jared stepped to the baseline to serve for the match, the cheers were deafening. As he won match point, the jubilant crowd erupted. I had to cover my ears.

In the post-match press conference, Holden voiced remarks about the noise level from the more "flamboyant" fans. Afterwards, the reporters peppered Jared with questions about the fans, about being gay in a straight-dominated sport, and about our relationship. He handled each question with dignity, and once again, he had me glowing.

While we waited for Jared in the players' lounge, David Salinger informed me that Karl Diefenbach, president of the ATP, had flown into town that morning and wanted to take Jared and me to lunch. It was like being summoned by royalty. We couldn't refuse.

I informed Roy and Connor about the luncheon, adding that if we weren't back in time to prepare Connor for his match, Spencer would need to warm him up forty-five minutes before play time. We reviewed the game plan, and I told them to ensure that Connor stayed warm and limber with stretching exercises right up until match time.

A limo chauffeured us to an exclusive club in Indian Wells. We walked from the desert sunshine, past wooden doors, into a cool, dim entry hall with oil paintings set between curtained windows and lit by chandeliers.

Before I could give our names to the headwaiter, Diefenbach glided across the plush carpet as quiet as a mouse. He wore his good-old-boy smile and called out, "They're with me, Thomas." He shook my hand with slim, polished fingers and flung his arm over Jared's shoulder in an unconvincing gesture of friendship. "Congratulations on an impressive win against James. I hope you're both hungry; the food here is superlative. I've booked a quiet table so we can talk."

He had a regal face, lean, with a stubborn line to his mouth. His eyes were hazel and small. His Brioni suit, linen shirt, and silk tie were all the same shade of black. The only other color on him was his silver hair and his pale skin, which seemed devoid of color altogether. He looked like an undertaker.

Thomas led us through a dining room done in red velvet drapes and mahogany furniture. We passed tables of white-haired men dressed in leisurewear to a corner table protected by a marble pillar and two potted dracaena palms. No one sat within earshot. From a white Steinway Grand by the bar came the tinkle of a Chopin nocturne. Jared and I had never before experienced this kind of world; it made the Chicago Steakhouse seem like a Dunkin Donuts. We glanced at each other with a slight apprehension of what was to come.

"Marvelous, simply marvelous that you two are back on the tour. The sport needs talented people like you."

An African-American waiter in a mauve dinner jacket handed us menus and stood waiting for drink orders.

"Thank you, Mr. Diefenbach," I said.

"I shall be insulted if you don't call me Karl. Now, shall I order champagne, or would you prefer cocktails?"

"Sparkling water for us," I said.

"Of course. How silly of me. Well, some time when you're not playing a tournament, we'll have to tie one on." He turned to the waiter. "Bernard, a bottle of San Pelegrino and champagne for me, if you please."

We opened our menus, and Jared and I shot each other a stare. I had heard about places where the menus didn't include the prices, of course, but until that moment I'd never seen such a menu.

"The trout amandine is superb, and they do an excellent job with the Beef Wellington. Which shall you have, fish or beef?"

"The fish," I said.

"And I'll have the seafood pasta," Jared said. His voice carried a hint of caution.

"I've asked you here to talk about all this publicity you've provoked in the last few days. Your comeback has made a sizeable splash, not only in the newspapers and on television, but by having those sissies coming to the tournament dressed as women." He shook his head and made a clucking sound.

"I only saw three people in drag," I said. "I hardly see that as an overwhelming problem. Besides, we didn't ask for publicity. We wanted to keep our relationship private."

"Fucking deplorable, actually. Journalist are whores," Diefenbach declared, his voice deep with understanding. "They'll screw their own grandmothers for a headline."

A few moments of silence passed before Bernard returned with our drinks. He poured our water and set a flute of champagne in front of Diefenbach.

"Bernard, we'll start with shrimp cocktails, and for the main course, we'll have two trouts and the Beef Wellington for my other guest," Diefenbach said, waving a hand in Jared's direction. "And we'll all have your magnificent soufflé for dessert."

Jared raised an eyebrow but shook his head to indicate that the order mix-up didn't matter.

Turning back to us, Diefenbach said, "Your announcement on ESPN has generated an avalanche of emails to the ATP. I've read some of them myself. Some, understandably, are very supportive. A high percentage, however, is pure hate mail. A few are truly frightening. This tournament has even received threatening phone calls. There are people out there who want to hurt you. We've had to double security, and that's costing a fortune."

I glanced into Jared's eyes, wishing he had not come along. This information would no doubt create emotional stress, which causes the blood lactate level to rise, which produces fatigue. This could only hurt his game, even for a tough competitor like Jared. I needed to protect him from this kind of stress.

"For your own safety, I advise you to pull out of this tournament," Diefenbach continued. "You see, I'm not altogether sure we can protect you from these fanatics. We don't want another Seles incident."

Before I could respond, Jared said, "We'll take our chances."

"We can force you out, for your own protection of course, and we can bar you from other tournaments, next week's Sony Ericsson, for instance. The ATP Governing Board members were all appalled at your coming out so blatantly at a time when we're trying to grow this sport by using wholesome publicity."

Bernard glided up and set a tray on a stand beside our table. One by one, he lifted plates holding glass bowls full of shrimp and cocktail sauce and placed one in front of each of us.

"We've experienced those kinds of tactics before," I continued, "but don't try that again."

Diefenbach measured me for a moment, smiled. He smiled again, a full-beamed smile. I remembered that double smile all too well. I saw it on all the tournament officials' faces as they wrecked our careers the first time. The same thin lips, the same duration, the same degree of forced compassion.

"Trust me, gentlemen. Any action we take will be to guarantee your safety."

Jared began eating his shrimp. I wondered how he could still have an appetite. Diefenbach ate cautiously, as if the discussion were closed. That spurred my anger, and I decided to bluff.

"We have lawyers. If you bar us from the Sony Ericsson or any other tournament, we'll have the U.S. Federal Court in California issue a court injunction, which will shut the tournament down, pending a hearing. The California courts frown on discrimination based on sexual orientation. And believe me, we'll be asking for huge, I mean astronomical, damages. If you think coming out on ESPN is bad publicity, wait until we stop a Masters Cup tournament while we haul the ATP into federal court for discriminatory treatment based on sexual orientation."

"And those 'sissies' you mentioned," Jared chimed in. "Picture them and hundreds more carrying signs in a protest march outside the front gates of the Sony Ericsson, Cincinnati, and the U.S. Open. The media will have a field day, and sponsors will run for the hills."

Diefenbach became a wall of silence.

"Naturally," I continued, "you'll want to check with your own lawyers to verify that we can persuade the federal court in California to stop a Florida tournament, but I think we both know they can and will. The question is whether we stand a chance of winning damages. What I think is, it doesn't make a damn bit of difference whether we win or lose. Either way, the ATP will hemorrhage big time."

Diefenbach cleared his throat, shifted in his chair. "You're prepared to damage professional tennis worldwide?"

"We'll do whatever it takes to ensure we get the same treatment as every other player. If that hurts the sport, then the sport needs to bleed."

A few silent minutes passed as Bernard whisked away the shrimp plates and brought our entrees. My plate held a twelve-inch trout staring at me with an eye as dark and blank as Diefenbach's at that moment. I didn't touch my silverware, having lost my appetite. Jared, on the other hand, dug into his beef and chewed while grinning.

Diefenbach stared at me with candid earnestness. *For the first time*, I thought, *I am seeing the real man, stripped of all facades*. In a kind of lost-boy voice, he said, "I don't know what can be done. We can't go to court, and we can't keep having this kind of publicity. I'm at a loss."

"Mr. Diefenbach," I said, realizing this was the time to compromise, "we don't want publicity either. It's a nuisance for everybody. But we can't control the media. The one thing I know is, we're not backing down, and the more we fight each other, the more those bloodsucking reporters froth at the mouth."

"Yes," he said. "I see your point." He adjusted the napkin at this throat.

"The question is, can the ATP pressure the media to back off?" I asked, knowing that the answer was assuredly yes.

He frowned, chewed a bite of fish, cuffed his mouth with a corner of his napkin. "I imagine you think you're rather clever," he said, resuming his composed facade. "Well, I suppose you are," he said, after I failed to respond. "If we allow you to play whichever tournaments you can qualify for, will you guarantee to maintain a low profile and avoid the topic of being gay?"

"We can't control the media. That's a battle you'll have to wage. But I guarantee that we'll keep our mouths shut and focus on tennis."

"Very well, that's how we'll play it. I'll draft a memo to the Governing Board this afternoon."

Diefenbach was too busy cutting his fish to notice my astonishment.

"We can play the Sony Ericsson?" Jared asked.

"Yes, of course. I've said so. You'll have to win enough matches here in order to qualify, just like everyone else, but assuming you can do that, yes." He turned to me. "How's your fish?"

"Marvelous," I mumbled, even though I had not eaten a bite.

"And no more bad overrules from redneck chair umpires." Jared's voice rose well above the club's allowed decibel level.

Diefenbach glared at him. "Of course. I'll include that in the memo." He smiled and stacked his mouth with fish and peas and crusty bread.

We ate in silence. The piano player switched from Chopin to Mozart. My heart pounded to the livelier melodies.

"Mind if I give you a word of advice?" Diefenbach asked.

"Please do."

"Don't push me too far. I'm a stalk of bamboo: I bend with the wind, but I also snap back with stinging force." He said this with a glint of steel in his eyes.

"You've been both kind and fair, Karl," I said. "Thank you."

He signaled Bernard for coffee and dessert, then glanced at his watch and said, "I'm afraid that I'm late for an appointment, gentlemen. I'll have to leave you to the dessert. No, please don't leave. The soufflé is ambrosial. Stay and enjoy it." He tore the napkin from his neck. "We must do this again. Next time, bring your protégé—what's his name, Connor?"

Before I could answer, he had risen from the table and sailed across the dining room, signing the check on his way out.

Bernard glided to our table carrying a silver coffeepot. He asked me a question, but I couldn't hear him over the cheering voices echoing in my head.

BY THE time we returned to the stadium, Connor's match with Michael Duras was already deep into the second set. Down a set and a break, Connor fought for his life, but Duras would serve for the match in the next game.

I sat where Connor could see me on the changeover and yelled, "It's not how you start; it's how you finish." He scowled, eyes blazing. I pointed at my head, signaling him to focus. He turned his back on me. The dragon on his shirt glowered at me with cold yellow eyes.

In the next game, he threw himself at the ball with new energy. It seemed that my being there gave him a boost of determination, or maybe fury. Whichever it was, it lifted his game. He broke Duras at love, then held his own service game to go up 6-5. On game point, I leaped to my feet and pounded my heart with a fist. Connor poured all his ferocity into winning the second set tiebreaker. It was a gutsy performance. Duras's confidence crumbled. He played conservatively, which gave Connor the edge he needed to roll over Duras in the third set.

When Connor stormed off the court, steam seemed to spew from his eyeballs. I met him in the hallway leading to the pressroom. Before I could congratulate him on lifting his game at a critical time, he yelled, "Where the fuck were you?"

"I told you. We were summoned by his majesty."

"Fuck that! You left me hanging. He wiped the floor with me while you were hobnobbing."

"Connor, I'm sorry. But I couldn't leave in the middle of negotiations. I did it for you and Jared. They were threatening to bar Jared from playing."

"You're here for me. Comprende? Everything else comes second. Don't ever do that again!"

He tramped away, leaving me aching to smack his face. I took deep breaths, reminded myself that it was fear talking. He was still so fragile to be burdened by all this pressure.

At the interview desk, his whole demeanor transformed. He smiled, and it seemed genuine enough. He timidly accepted their praise. Roy sat beside him, and he discussed how they had prepared for the match. When asked what went through his head when he turned the match around, he said that he felt the adrenaline of anger flowing through him, and he channeled that anger into seeing the ball. "The shots came out of nowhere," he added.

Roy talked at length about their strategy for the match. Reporters directed questions at Connor, and each time, Roy cut in to answer. I stood watching flames dancing in Connor's eyes. Was he still mad at me, I wondered, or was this a new anger bubbling up?

Nobody mentioned the gay issue, so I began to hope that that storm had already blown over.

CHAPTER 16

THE next morning, we found thousands of gay fans milling around the tennis facility. The Palm Springs gay fans had showed up in force. They were joined by several hundred others who had made the two-hour drive from L.A. The place pulsed with a circuit-party-like atmosphere.

The tournament organizers were elated by the increased ticket sales, but I detected an edge in their smiles. They insisted that we perform our warm-up on the stadium court because there wasn't enough room around the outer courts for the mob that had come to watch us work out; stadium tickets were twice the price of grounds passes for the outer courts. They packed into the upper-tier cheap seats, holding signs with glittering letters: "Poof the Magic Dragon" and "We Love You, Jared."

The noise level intensified, and Jared had difficulty concentrating. He had flung open Pandora's closet, and now he had to find a way to close the door.

Connor, on the other hand, was spurred on by the attention. It energized him. The gays became aware of their effect on him, and they grew louder, chanting his name. They adored him, and he sparkled under the glow of their adoration.

Jared played against Timothy McEwan, another hard-hitting American. Jared seemed nervous, like someone aware of being stared at but not knowing from where. The match became a display of power tennis. All too often, however, Jared was a step slow getting to the ball. As the match wore on, the gay fans' encouraging shrieks grew thunderous, but it didn't help. Jared fell in straight sets.

The crowd deflated. It was disappointing, because a third-round loss meant that Jared wouldn't earn enough points for an entry into the singles draw of the Sony Ericsson tournament. His only chance now was in doubles. The good news was that his ranking improved nearly five hundred spots to number 220 in the world. If he continued with the same determination, he would move into the top one hundred in time for the U.S. Open in September.

He fast-talked through a brief interview where he praised McEwan's high level of play. No sexual-orientation questions came up, although one reporter mentioned the huge number of vocal supporters pulling for Jared. It seemed that Diefenbach did indeed have influence over the media.

I intercepted Jared on his way to the locker room, telling him how well he played. It didn't help, didn't hurt either. I trailed him all the way to the showers, where he stood under a hot spray. Steam boiled around him as he labored through his disappointment. It was his first singles loss since his comeback. He stood there a long time. There was nothing to do but let him work it out internally.

I felt helpless. I was about to drag him out when he reached up and turned off the water. I threw him a towel. He dried and dressed. We dawdled back to watch Connor's match.

By the time we reached our seats, Connor and his opponent, Nicolas Marakov from Russia, had finished their warm-up and were about to start. Connor bolted out of the blocks on fire. A stunned Marakov dropped the first set at love as Connor cracked numerous winners off both wings. He smacked the ball as hard as he could and with so much topspin that his shots kept dropping in. He was in his zone, whipping the fans into a frenzy.

During that first brief set, I noticed that the television cameraman across from us kept zeroing in on Shar and Roy between points, as if he were deliberately trying to show the television audience that Connor had a girlfriend. I had to smile.

In the second set, Connor's confidence sailed over the moon. He attempted impossible shots. He made a handful of flashy winners, but he missed enough to let Marakov back in the match. Marakov won the second set, 6-4.

The third set produced several momentum shifts. Connor tried to control the points and revive his crumpled confidence. They both held serve until Connor broke Marakov at 5-5. Then Connor blasted four unreturnable serves in a row, winning the match.

He had fought his way through that last set with some shaky tennis—battling nerves and lost focus—and won by sheer determination. Jared raised his eyebrows and nodded, no doubt kicking himself for not doing the same thing.

We trooped to the pressroom. Again, Roy joined Connor at the interview desk and fielded most of the questions. He used an authoritative voice, giving the impression that he was Connor's sole coach. No one mentioned the gay issue, but one reporter said, "Connor, ESPN conducted a poll today, and the fans voted you the sexiest male player at this tournament. Care to comment on that?"

Connor's grin faded. Before he could respond, Roy cut in, "He's eighteen, so I guess there must be an abundance of teenaged girls in the stadium, or a lot of pedophiles." He glared in my direction as he said it. I glanced around; no, he was looking at me. I lifted a hand and wagged a finger—a warning not to push too far.

Roy's comment raised a laugh from everyone except David Salinger, who stepped in to halt the interview before it progressed any further down that road.

When Connor emerged from the locker room, Roy threw a proud arm over his shoulder. As we ambled toward the cafeteria, I heard Connor say under his breath, "I wish you wouldn't do that. You're not my coach."

Roy jerked to a halt and yanked his arm from Connor's shoulder. The rest of us froze.

Connor stammered, "Besides, how many other players have their parents help them with the interviews?"

"Aii-ya," Roy howled. "So now I'm an embarrassment?"

Connor dropped his head. "I didn't say that. It's just that you're not my coach. What you're doing is so obvious."

"How many years have I sacrificed so you could become a star? How many hours did I spend drilling balls at you?" His voice cracked. "Now you win a few matches and you're ashamed of me?"

"You're putting words in my mouth. Look, just forget it, okay?"

"No. I want to know. What did you mean?"

Anger flashed in Connor's eyes. I wanted to help, but he had to fight this battle himself.

"You're using me!" Connor said. "If you want to be a big-time coach, then find somebody to coach instead of taking credit for Daniel's work."

Roy's eyes squinted into slits. He gathered his dignity around him like a blanket and stomped off in the other direction.

"Dad," Connor yelled after him. "Don't be mad. I only meant...." But Roy had already charged out of hearing distance.

I patted Connor's back. "You know," I said, "he did a hell of a lot of work with you before I came along. Wouldn't hurt to cut him some slack."

CONNOR and Jared won their doubles match that afternoon. Roy joined us after the warm-up had begun. He had regained his usual humor and seemed to enjoy the match. They played on court three. The bleachers were packed with riotous fans. Their opponents were noticeably annoyed at having to play before such a boisterous crowd.

We arrived back at the Hilton around six thirty and found Uncle Harman waiting in the lobby. I assumed he had come to spend time with Spencer, whose eyes grew to twice their normal size while a grin creased his lips. They ogled each other until Roy yelled, "Surprise! Connor, meet our new manager. I hired him this morning, and he took the first flight down. He'll manage our financial affairs, reservations, scheduling, transportation, whatever. He'll even turn us into a corporation and handle all the money so that the government doesn't steal it all in taxes. We'll need that before we sign the Nike contract, and having him here will give me more time to help with your training."

Everyone gawked at Roy until the silence grew awkward. Roy slapped Harman on the back. "Might as well keep it in the family. Have you checked in?"

"Tried to," Harman said. "They're full up because of the tournament. They suggested the Ramada Inn."

"There's an extra bed in my room." Spencer's voice trembled slightly.

The way Roy eyed Spencer, I could see the wheels turning in his head, weighing the cost of an additional motel room against having his brother share a room with a gay boy. My interest perked up to see which would win him over, money or morals.

"That's fine with me," Harman said, and he smiled.

"Good," Roy snapped, closing the issue. "Saves ninety bucks a night. Let's all meet down here in an hour. We'll find a Chinese restaurant tonight."

Jared said, "Roy, I need a long soak." He winked at Spencer. "Maybe Daniel and I should have dinner in our room."

"I second that," Shar said, also winking at Spencer. "Connor and I could use some alone time, right honey?"

Connor frowned but said, "Whatever."

"Me too," Spencer said. He and Harman peered at each until Harman nodded.

"Okay," Roy said. "We'll all stay in and go out tomorrow night."

Jared and I strolled to the elevators. I could hear their footsteps right behind us.

Once we were alone, Jared grew moody. At first, I thought he might be envious of what must be going on in the next room, but I realized that he still agonized over his loss.

I found it interesting that following his loss, under the shower, his pain seemed sharp, and it was no problem. That kind of disappointment is natural. But once alone, I knew his mind was replaying the points he could have won but didn't, like the four squandered breakpoints in the second set. Now his disappointment mutated into suffering, which gave birth to bitterness.

The foundation of Buddhism and the first of the four Noble Truths taught by the Buddha states that life is suffering. It is human to suffer, unavoidable, but I believe there is constructive suffering and destructive suffering. That immediate, sharp disappointment helps spur a player to train harder and perform better the next time, whereas lingering bitterness drags a player's energy down and eats away at his confidence.

I ran a hot bath, and we crawled in together. I folded my arms around him. The heat relaxed me, but Jared stayed tight as a bowstring. I said, "You're fighting something that can't be undone."

"You want me to forget what happened?"

"I want you to feel that disappointment. Feel every nuance of it, accept it, and let it go. Fighting against it keeps the pain alive. If you feel it instead of thinking about it, it burns itself out and you can move on."

He murmured, "First you teach me how to win, now you tell me how to lose."

"No, honey. I'm reminding you not to let your mind spin out of control. That's what we do on court in order to play our best."

He kissed me, and I could feel his body relaxing into mine.

"I love you," he said. "Hand me the shampoo. I'll wash your hair."

I knew he'd be fine for tomorrow's match. While he scrubbed my scalp, I wondered how Connor would react to his first loss in a major tournament.

THE next four days were a blur. We stuck to a daily routine of a brisk workout, tai chi, breakfast, an hour on the practice courts with hundreds of adoring fans in attendance. Connor would play his singles match, and after lunch they would play doubles. They kept winning.

Connor experienced another breakthrough, the kind that coaches and players dream about but seldom see. With every win, Connor became more confident, more determined. He wanted to take on everyone at once. He couldn't wait for his next match to see what new level he could push his game to. With each new match, the players were better, the matches tougher, and both Connor and Jared answered the challenge.

Connor attained respect in the locker room. Players and media people began calling him "The Magic Dragon," because of his trademark embroidered shirt, which he wore at every match. The homophobes called him "Poof," but even they said it with a somewhat respectful tone.

Most of Connor's matches were drawn-out battles. We all rode the crest of a wave, and everyone stayed in a constant state of wonder.

Everyone, that is, except Spencer and Harman. As it turned out, even though they shared a bedroom, they didn't share the same bed. Harman's fear of forming a committed relationship continued to be an obstacle, so they followed the rest of us around looking like sick puppies.

I often became angry at their situation, and I had to keep reminding myself that it would only last a few days. Soon, Spencer would drive back to San Francisco for school and Harman would fly with us to Florida for the Sony Ericsson tournament—end of story as far as they were concerned.

Harman blossomed into the role of manager. He took charge of planning everything: picking up and delivering laundry, making dinner reservations, arranging for ATP cars, chauffeuring us around, paying all the bills, and making the travel and hotel arrangements for the Sony Ericsson. He became indispensable.

Spencer used Harman's laptop to create two web sites, one for Connor and one for Jared, where fans could see their pictures, uploaded from Roy's digital camera, and check on the latest scores and stats. By the end of the week, both sites were getting fifteen thousand hits a day.

He also set up two separate email addresses where people could email us. He spent four hours each evening managing the influx of email. Most of it came from gay men cheering us on, but Spencer showed me several examples of hate mail that he received on a daily basis. One showed a picture of a man wearing a wig and makeup. His throat had been cut, and he lay in a pool of his own blood. The caption at the bottom read: Welcome to Florida!

Over Spencer's protests, I decided not to show those emails to the others. There was no reason to upset Connor and Jared when they needed to perform at their peak, and why give Roy any more ammunition than he already had?

Harman's efforts freed up all of Roy's time. Now he attended every practice session, but luckily, he never tried to influence my work. He sat at the sidelines—watching, listening, studying—with the concentration of a tiger stalking its prey. He also accompanied me when I scrutinized Connor's upcoming opponents. We discussed the strengths and weaknesses of each player and formulated a game plan together.

On Saturday morning, Connor played a spectacular semifinal match, beating Germany's Thomas Schindler in a three-setter. The press pounced on Connor after the match. Not only had he beaten a veteran player ranked number sixteen on the ATP tour rankings, but he was also the first ever qualifier to reach this tournament's final.

Connor enchanted them and handled every question. Roy no longer joined him at the interviews. Watching Connor alone in front of the camera, lustrous with charm, I could only hope that he would handle the media as well after losing a match. But at that moment, losing was the furthermost thing from his mind.

That afternoon, the Australian player, Joshua McEwan, pulverized David Madison to become the other finalist. In the post-match interview, a reporter asked McEwan if he was pleased to be playing a qualifier in the final. McEwan, known for sharing his unvarnished opinions of other players, said some unsavory things about "having to share the locker room with poofs" and "playing against the star fairy." He boasted that he would thrash Connor in pretty quick order.

Only a few players were vocal about their aversion for us, but McEwan's remarks established him as the macho defender of heterosexual sports, and the press egged him on.

SUNDAY gave us a cloudless sky and air as crystal clear as only the desert air can be. It grew hot, like true summer, and the gay fans came out in force. I counted no fewer than twelve men in tennis drag. There were, of course, an equal number of old guard straight tennis fans there to cheer McEwan on. This match had all the trappings of Billie Jean King's Battle of the Sexes, but this time, to my amusement, it was two straight men playing each other.

When Connor followed McEwan onto stadium court, a lump wedged in my throat. In place of his blue shirt with the embroidered dragon was a black silk muscle shirt with a sequined red dragon blazing on the back. The dragon's eyes sparkled a piercing yellow, and the whole image shimmered with life as he moved.

Shar leaned toward me to say, "Some Hollywood clothing designer named Soochow made that. He dropped it by the hotel last night, and Con fell in love with it."

"Hollywood, my ass," I said. "It's pure Las Vegas."

I felt a little stab thinking that Connor's grandmother would be watching on television. How would she feel seeing him play without the shirt she had made? Roy's thoughts must have mirrored my own, because he became visibly agitated. A few minutes later, he recovered himself and lifted his camera, snapping the first pictures of the day.

A party-like atmosphere infused the crowd. During the five-minute warm-up, several exchanges between the gays and the old guard fans put everyone on edge. The air crackled with tension.

Connor served first, playing our strategy to perfection. McEwan loved to run side to side. He played the angles better than anyone. Hit a ball out wide and he would respond with a more drastic crosscourt angle, pulling his opponent off the court so that his next shot was a winner into the open court. But Connor blasted all his balls right down the middle with enough pace that McEwan couldn't generate the kind of angles that allowed him to control the point. They kept pounding balls right at each other until someone made an error, and that was usually McEwan. Our plan had nullified McEwan's strengths.

Both players held serve until McEwan served to stay in the first set at 4-5. Connor stepped up his aggression and broke him, winning the first set with a down-the-line backhand. The crowd erupted. The gays cheered Connor, and the straights booed McEwan.

McEwan was stunned. Spectators had booed him plenty of times, but never half the crowd. He had lost a set to someone suspected of being gay, and that must have felt like a very public castration.

But the match was far from over, and McEwan knew it. At the changeover, I saw the anger boiling in his eyes. He became very calm as the wheels turned. He was determining what he needed to change to make Connor play to his advantage.

Seeing that calm deliberation come over McEwan's face, I began to worry. Connor had played magnificently, but this was his first singles final in a tier one event. Those butterflies in his stomach would mutate into dive-bombers when he got into the homestretch. My palms poured sweat. I kept wringing a towel to keep them dry. Roy kept popping Tums and crunching so loud that I found it more irritating than his clicking camera.

As the second set began, McEwan's plan became clear. He aimed for the sidelines no matter what came to him. It worked. He lured Connor into crosscourt rallies, using his speed and angles to control Connor.

I lost heart and grew angry at Connor for not sticking to our game plan, a plan that had worked. But as the set drew on, I realized that Connor was holding his own playing to McEwan's advantage. In the fourth game, Connor began creating the angles before McEwan could, luring the Australian into a crosscourt exchange and drilling the ball down the line before McEwan could. He out-McEwan-ed McEwan.

Once Connor established his dominance playing the angles, he won every game after that, winning the championship 6-4, 6-2.

This is it, I thought. This tournament took his ranking from number 714 to 77, enough to get him into the Sony Ericsson. Assuming he continued to play well, he would never have to play the challenger circuit again, never have to fight his way into the main draw, never be the unknown that nobody had heard of. This win catapulted him into prime time. It established his credentials as an elite player and placed him on a pedestal with one hundred other athletes.

I was so dazed that I didn't hear the fans screaming their lungs out. But I did hear Roy Lin as he leaned close to my ear and yelled, "You say in another year he'll be a top player? I say, fuck you! He's there now."

I nodded my head even though I still wasn't convinced. I thought about the difference between arrival and establishing yourself. Arrival is an immediate physical event: a plane touches down, a train pulls into a station, you step from a bus, you walk down a street or two, take pictures, see the sites, have lunch, and over coffee, wonder what's happening back home.

Establishing yourself takes time; you get to know where the locals eat, where the best jazz clubs are, where to get your shirts pressed. Then, one day, you stop thinking of home as being somewhere else. Had Connor arrived? Perhaps. But there was plenty of work in front of us.

I gave Jared and Shar and Spencer big, joyous hugs. I would have given J.D. Lambert a hug had he not raced off to find the Nike representatives.

Ten minutes later, during the trophy ceremony, my heart still pounded like a jackhammer. David Salinger interviewed Connor. He asked, "There was some trash-talk before this match. How good does it feel to win after hearing that?"

"You didn't hear any trash-talk from me," Connor said. "I was too overjoyed to be playing at this point in the tournament. Besides, when it comes to tennis, I let my racket do the talking. But I will say that winning this awesome tournament is the most thrilling thing that's ever happened to me. I've played some hard-fought matches this week, and I hope that my winning so easily today didn't disappoint the fans."

McEwan reddened. He stayed that way as Connor went on to thank the organizers, the sponsors, and the ball kids. He thanked fans who had cheered him on. He was delighted with himself, and I think that little covert dig at McEwan was the cherry on the cake.

In a sport where most athletes stammered out the same boring clichés, Connor gave a fresh, articulate interview. At the end, he waved to the crowd and shouted, "I love you all!" The organizers and the press returned his affection. The gay men leaped to their feet, screaming and waving their arms.

The crowd had thirty minutes to rest their vocal cords while workers prepared the court for the doubles final. Jared and Connor appeared on court leading their opponents, the Richardson brothers from Southern California. A lump wedged in my throat from the first ball hit in the warm-up until Jared won match point with a down-the-line smash that landed an inch inside the baseline.

The cheers could be heard on Jupiter. I'd never seen a crowd go that wild at a tennis event. As everyone else bounded to their feet, I put my head between my knees and tried to hold back the tears.

That exquisite, spine-tingling moment became something Jared and I would both take to our graves. No matter what else happened, we would own that Masters title, and at that moment, it was worth every heartache along the way and to come.

Jared climbed into the stands and took me in his arms. ESPN broadcasted every intimate moment of our championship hug and kiss. The fans went Times-Square-at-New-Year's ballistic.

WE WERE invited to a gay party that night by one of the tournament board of directors who was secretly gay. Roy and J.D. dined with the Nike people, and they planned to have an after dinner nightcap with the Adidas representative, so we didn't see them for the rest of the night. Spencer and Harman elected to have dinner in their hotel room—no big surprise. So Connor, Jared, Shar, and I trooped off in Roy's van to dine at a gay-friendly restaurant in Palm Springs for some elegant French food.

The gay waiters fawned over us. We felt shocked to find ourselves the center of attention even off the court.

After dinner, we drove to the party, which took place at a villa on a rise overlooking Palm Desert. The expansive patio had hundreds of gay men milling about a cobalt pool. Many of them were well-to-do seniors with younger men at their sides. Several men wore military uniforms. I counted three Naval officers, an army Colonel, and a marine sergeant. A dozen men played volleyball in the pool.

A five-piece band of musicians, whose taste ran in the direction of twangy Hawaiian jazz, pounded out tunes. They were shirtless and wore coconut shell brassieres, grass skirts, flower leis, and leafy headdresses. The drummer had a huge round belly and flaccid arms and was covered with tattoos. He wore a hat piled high with fruit a la Carmen Miranda.

The whole place seemed to detonate when we arrived. We elbowed our way through a mob while being hugged, kissed, squeezed, and groped. The entire party lionized us three men. Poor Shar was ignored. In their eyes, young and old alike, we were sex gods.

As we mingled, Jared kept staring at me with an astonished grin. A number of men made passes at Connor even though Shar stayed glued to him. He was not interested in them sexually, but he didn't shy away from them either. He was the star of the show, and he played the part beautifully. He even led them on, toying with those hopeful men to see how far they would go.

I shone my attention on the older couples. One couple became prominent: balding men who appeared never to have lost their baby fat. Their bodies squeezed into matching Hawaiian shirts, pressed slacks, and sandals. With their round, pale faces, they each resembled a miniature man on the moon. They were very dignified, however, and fit comfortably around one another—that relaxed intimacy that comes from being together for decades.

"Hello, handsome," one of them greeted me. "I'm Fred and this is Jim, but our friends call us Fred and Ethel."

"Waiter, our gorgeous friend needs a drink, if you please," they both said at the same time.

A martini glass slipped into my fingers and, with a hand on each of my arms, they escorted me around the grounds. As it turned out, they were our hosts. They took possession of me, dangling me in front of their other guests like a new diamond bracelet. In their older, somewhat frumpy way, they were cool—and obviously still in love. I found myself looking forward to the time when Jared and I would enjoy their kind of intimacy, hardly needing to speak because we shared the same thoughts.

The crowd devoured Connor and Jared. Fred, Ethel and I made a pass at the buffet table. We migrated from one couple to another, meeting people and chatting easily. As soon as I'd take two sips of my martini, one or the other would snatch it from my hand, and a fresh one would replace it. It was dream-like, being the center of everybody's radar. But I had the feeling that something was wrong, that we didn't deserve their adoration. At the same time, I felt it had been a long time coming, and I kept telling myself to enjoy it.

At the stroke of ten, to Fred and Ethel's vast disappointment, I gathered my chicks and herded them back to the van. They all groaned, but I reminded them that we had an early flight and they had to be ready to play a first-round match on Tuesday. We basked in a boozy glow on the ride to the hotel. When Jared and I arrived at our room, Spencer and Harman's bedroom lights were already out.

The following morning, the Palm Springs newspaper hit the newsstands. We bought a copy at the airport. They ran a photo of Connor on page one with a quote from David Salinger touting Connor as the next American hope, a prodigy, and the first Chinese-American since Michael Chang to have a shot at the number one ranking.

I was hopeful as we flew to the Sony Ericsson tournament, the toughest draw outside the four Grand Slams. We were all anxious to show what we could do. We had fought our way into the big dance. We had arrived—I had arrived—and nothing could stop us now.

CHAPTER 17

SPENCER dropped us at the airport, pointed the nose of Roy's van west, and drove back to San Francisco. We flew east as the sun rose above the curve of the earth. A van met us at the Miami airport and sped us to the hotel, where we spent a quiet day recovering from the flight.

The next morning, the same van sped us to the tennis facility for our first round matches. Arriving at the stadium, we were pitched into bewilderment. Hundreds of protesters held signs and chanted while marching in two large circles in front of the main gates. One circle displayed anti-gay signs: "God Hates Fags" and "Keep Our Sport for Real Men." The other had pro-gay signs: "Gay Tennis Rocks" and "We Love Connor and Jared." Police were on hand to keep a lid on the hostilities, but as we passed on our way to the player's entrance, I heard the two groups hurling insults at each other.

"This is insane," I mumbled to no one in particular. The day was windy, and I noticed that the protesters were having trouble keeping their signs held high. I looked up. The flags rising above the front gates were snapping toward the west. My mind turned to thoughts of what the wind would do to my players that afternoon.

Armed security guards ushered our van through the players' entrance and escorted us through a mob of protesters milling inside the grounds. An egg smashed against my door window. There were shouts. Eggs, tomatoes, and even rocks pelted our van. Security guards surrounded us as we crawled toward the players' lounge.

Security pushed the mob back thirty yards. Violence hung in the air. I looked up to see Karl Diefenbach standing beside a red-faced Dan Pope, the tournament director.

"You're to blame," Diefenbach hissed as I stepped from the van.

"Me? I had nothing to do with this," I said.

"You had to do it, didn't you? You had to kiss each other on nationally televised ES-fucking-PN. We had a deal."

"That's right," I said. "And we're sticking to that deal. We haven't mentioned being gay."

Dan Pope spoke up. "How the hell am I supposed to run a tournament with this mob running wild? This isn't California. Things are different down here. We take our Bible to heart."

"If that were true," I said, "there wouldn't be a problem."

"I can't let you play," Pope said, "because I can't protect you from these fanatics."

Roy looked ready to explode. "Are you searching bags and making everybody go through a metal detector?"

"Of course," Pope snapped. "That's standard procedure, but it's no guarantee."

Roy pointed a finger in Pope's face. "We earned the right to play this tournament, and it's your responsibility to insure that every player, including my son, gets adequate protection."

Pope held up his hands. "That's what I intend to do: protect you. And that means I don't expose you to thousands of hostile fans."

I looked around the grounds, at the straights and the gays holding signs and jeering at each other. I shook my head. "Mr. Pope, Mr. Diefenbach, you have to let us play. At least half these protesters are gay. If you rob them of the chance to watch us, they'll tear the place apart."

"Just what the hell do you suggest I do?" Pope almost screamed.

"Gentlemen," I said. "My boys are exhausted and jet-lagged. Chances are they'll go out in the first round. This problem might solve itself by the end of the day if you let us play."

"You don't understand, Daniel," Diefenbach said. "We've had a number of death threats. The people down here are pretty simple. They see something they don't like, they get rid of it. It's too great a risk."

I glanced at Jared as my stomach tightened into a knot. He seemed shell-shocked, but I saw a glint of defiance in his eyes. The vision of that email, the drag queen with his throat cut, flashed into my mind. I wanted to back away, but I could feel Jared's resistance gelling. He would insist I was being paranoid, and I admit I was afraid. *Relax*, I told myself. *Think clearly.*

"We either play," Jared spoke for the first time, "or I walk over to that camera crew and spill my guts. From the looks of things, that's what this powder keg needs to ignite."

The blood drained from Pope's face. Diefenbach held up his hands. "Now, now, boys, let's not fly off the handle and do something we'll all regret."

Jared began to walk toward the camera crew. Diefenbach grabbed his shoulder and shouted, "Wait!"

"Dan," Diefenbach said to Pope. "Have security cordon off practice court sixteen and let these men do a warm-up. We'll move their matches to the earliest possible start times, put them on the stadium court, and ring the court with officers. It'll be a zoo, so we'll need extra security. Can you handle that?"

"I'll do my best, Karl."

Diefenbach turned to me and Roy. "I suggest that you not stay at the players' hotel. We should find you a low-key motel close to the airport and check you in under assumed names. If that's agreeable, I'll make the arrangements while you warm up."

Harman stepped forward. "No need to trouble yourself, Mr. Diefenbach. I'll find a quiet place and check us in."

"Excellent," Diefenbach said. "And I'm assigning you two bodyguards while you're here at the facilities." He waved a hand at two men who both stood over six feet, two inches tall and sported bellies hanging over their gun belts. They sauntered over with a swagger that seemed stylized from John Wayne westerns.

Diefenbach turned to me. "I'm already regretting this decision. Let me warn you, any display of affection, on camera or off, and I will escort you from these facilities and bar you from ever playing again. Understood?"

THE sun had climbed halfway to its zenith by the time we began our warm-up. The hot and humid air seemed to smother us, but nobody noticed. We were dazed, but the warm-up routine focused us on the task at hand. The pop of the ball made a soothing sound, and soon we were running, sweating, and able to achieve the Mushin mind-space.

Connor's first round opponent was Prong Ananda, an eighteen-year-old qualifier from Thailand. Ananda was a hard-hitting, all-out competitor who loved to smash winners. In our workout, we focused on using Ananda's pace against him. The key would be to make Ananda hit a lot of balls. With his all-out style, he'd make a ton of errors if he were forced to hit several balls on every point. So we worked on that; Jared smashed balls and Connor looped them back, over and over.

The fans were kept well away from court sixteen, but we heard their chanting. After a forty-five-minute workout, I felt better; however, I prayed for easy first rounds, because my boys were a bit sluggish during the warm-up. I could only hope that the adrenaline rush of competing would energize them. I even felt better about the crowd. *By tomorrow*, I thought, *everything will settle down, and we'll be yesterday's news.*

We had barely enough time to eat before Connor's singles match, so we packed our gear and hurried toward the players' cafeteria, led by our two armed guards.

I could tell that Jared was looking forward to playing his doubles match. Their opponents were lower-ranked players that my boys could beat as long as they stuck to our game plan. I stayed as close to him as possible as we walked, hoping to soak up some of his enthusiasm.

We were fifty yards from the cafeteria doors when someone in the nearby crowd shouted our names. Thirty or forty people ran toward us. Some had TV cameras perched on their shoulders. They were intercepted by a dozen security guards, but a few broke free and kept coming.

We hurried past a security car and were almost to the cafeteria door when I noticed something out of the corner of my eye, a flicker to my left. My head swiveled toward it. Sunlight reflected off metal in a man's hand. The man stuck out his right arm, Moses-like, pointing at me with an accusing shiver.

I saw a flash, and the universe shifted off balance. Goose bumps spread over my scalp, and something had a grip on my throat. It seemed to take an ungodly amount of time before I felt a pain slam into my back. I gazed into the gunman's eyes. They seemed as big as baseballs. His mouth turned up at the ends, smiling. This man had no fear, no remorse.

Until that moment, I had always thought of evil as a shadowy form, but the obscene whiteness of the gunman's toothy smile as he squeezed off another round made me realize that evil comes in every color.

As I turned to protect Jared, my mind vaulted beyond the pain, and I could do nothing but witness the chaos around me. It happened in slow motion. No time and no pain, only people screaming. I surrendered to my terror.

Over the chaotic sound of voices, I heard another pop, like the strike of lightning overhead. Something slammed into my back again. Every muscle in my body let go. My hips snapped to the right, and both knees liquefied. Another pop. Something smacked my head, and I heard my skull crack.

A tension gripped my upper body, as if I were locked in a vise.

I saw blood spatter Jared's face. We fell, eyeball to eyeball, all the way to the pavement. We hit the ground with a thud and rolled sideways, coming to rest with him over me. His legs continued to kick out like a runner, as if he were trying to cross some invisible finish line.

I called his name. The sound of it ricocheted in my head, and I felt a closing-down in my chest. My vision turned red, and a ringing in my head drowned out all other sounds.

Jared smiled at me. He seemed unconcerned, as if we were tumbling into bed, and he smiled at me. His smile made me feel resentful.

The burning sensation in my chest grew. *My God*, a thought floated up through the pain, *I'm going to die*. I opened my mouth to scream, but I couldn't utter a sound. My head flopped to one side, and I saw with clarity Roy Lin hauling Connor and Shar to the ground while J.D. Lambert tackled the gunman.

People scattered, and a heartbeat later, several officers pounced on J.D. and the gunman. Before I could grasp what had happened, they handcuffed the gunman and hauled him to his feet.

Jared's face hovered above me as an icy wind blew though my center. I coughed, spraying blood across his lips. He no longer smiled. He lay on the asphalt gasping for breath. His eyes were riveted wide open, as if he were staring into an abyss. He stumbled to his knees, tore the T-shirt from his back, bundled it up, and pressed it to my head.

Shar's voice pierced the pandemonium. "For Christ's sake, somebody call an ambulance!"

I lay still, eyes unblinking. In that tropical heat, I felt cold. Seconds ticked away like months. I wanted to move, to pull myself to a sitting position, but I couldn't. It felt as if great rifts had opened in various parts of my body—back, chest, skull—and my life-force seemed to hemorrhage through them.

I felt a tear drip onto my cheek—Jared's tear. There was something comical about his helpless expression. Connor appeared on the other side of me, staring down with wide, round eyes. He ripped his shirt off and lifted me enough to press the shirt against my back.

Roy tried to pull Connor to his feet and spirit him away, but he shook off Roy's hands. He stayed with me, pressing his cheek to my chest to listen, saying I would be okay, that my heartbeat was strong, that he was there, that he would care for me. *He would make a fine doctor*, I thought, *given the chance*. I wanted to tell Connor and Jared that it was okay, that the pain was bearable, but I couldn't speak. Jared curled an arm under my head and across my shoulders.

"Christ, he's dead." I recognized J.D. Lambert's voice.

Jared shook his head. He still held that comical expression. "You'll be okay," he croaked. "Don't leave me," he whispered. "For God's sake, don't leave me."

An eternity later, I heard sirens, but by then I couldn't see anything, only a cold blackness. I felt myself being lifted—ascending to heaven? The sudden movement caused what was left of my consciousness to tumble through a vast nothingness, falling, falling, with no place to land.

CHAPTER 18

I CAME awake. Minutes passed. I could not remember who I was. Everything felt alien, as if the familiar parts of me had disintegrated and the rest were dissolving. I lay suspended in a vacuous inner space, a sphere of unbroken silence. I peeked out at an unfamiliar world with an unblinking stare.

After what seemed a millions years, a gray light bled through windows. When the sun, a blurry spot of weak yellow, edged between the horizon and a thick cloud cover, I realized that I lay in a hospital bed.

The top half of my bed was tilted upward at a twenty-degree angle, giving me a view of tile walls, televisions hung from the ceiling, a bed-table crowded with flowers—all sterile and dreamlike. The air had an antiseptic stench, reminiscent of grappa and so strong I seemed to ingest it rather than inhale it. Six beds filled the room, with curtains that could separate one bed from another, three against one wall and three against the opposite wall.

I lay on my back in a middle bed. The beds on either side of me were unoccupied, but an old man slept across the room from me. He huddled in a fetal position with one arm dangling over the side of his bed.

Coils of tubes assaulted my body: a respirator in my mouth, feeding tube up my nose, and other IV tubes fastened to my neck and arm. A flurry of wires attached to electrodes were stuck to my skin with flesh-colored tape, feeding impulses to a bank of monitors that stood beside my bed, recording my heartbeat, brain activity, blood pressure. I felt like a butterfly pinned to a spreading board.

I had vague memories of waking in a different room: intense lights, beeping machines, that same grappa stench, white coats with human heads wearing green masks all bobbing around. It must have been the intensive care unit, but I couldn't be sure. The white coats would appear like apparitions, surround me, prod me, take my numbers, ask questions I couldn't answer, and vanish without any kind of acknowledgement or encouragement. I was never sure if they were real.

I heard muffled sounds. I shifted my head, and shapes came into focus. On the other side of a glass door, Jared argued with a woman dressed in a lab coat covering her green scrubs. An ID tag hung from her front pocket. Her back was straight, her shoulders delicate. She held up an X-ray sheet and pointed to a spot as they both studied it.

She held up another, and another. I was touched by how vulnerable Jared appeared. His face grew pale and translucent. It mirrored the white blurs on the black X-ray sheets.

I heard his voice, though I couldn't make out his words. Yet I knew that tone; I know all of his voices. That tone meant that Jared was terrified. I watched the woman shake her head as her face molded into an expression of despair. Then she walked way.

Testing myself, I found I could move both arms and all my fingers, but my legs felt wooden. I tried to wiggle my toes, but nothing happened. *Probably the sedatives they have me on*, I thought. Bandages swathed my head, waist, and chest. A tube pumped oxygen into my mouth.

Pain began to seep through the side of my head, blinding me. My brain tissue sizzled. I closed my eyes against the pain, and a few moments later, I felt something squeeze my hand. Opening my eyes, I watched Jared sit on the side of my bed. He wore jeans, a polo shirt, a black and orange Giants ball-cap, and a wounded smile. He had lost weight in his face. He now seemed shrunken, and sitting beside me in the almost polar bleakness of this impersonal setting, he seemed like a lost child. He lifted my hand—the one with the intravenous drip joined to a vein in my wrist— and kissed it.

I tried to move, and it hit me: fire in my right side. Worse than fire— lava dripping on my skin from the inside out. Pain shot up my spine. I tried to ask Jared what happened, but I only managed a groan.

Jared leaned forward and held me while he placed another pillow behind my head. His unshaven face burned my cheek.

"Hey, lover man," he said. "You look like a ghost come back to life."

I tried to speak but the respirator tube in my throat prevented it. I reached up and pulled it out. "The others?" I croaked.

"We were lucky. Everybody's great except for you, of course. But even you're lucky. If that bullet had been half an inch higher, we wouldn't be having this conversation on such a drizzly morning."

"How long...." My voice trailed off before I could finish my question.

"Seven days in intensive care, two days here." His chin trembled. He buried his face in my shoulder and hugged me. Every place he touched hurt.

"Oh God, I've been so scared," he groaned.

"I can't feel my feet."

Jared reached for words but came up empty. He smiled that wounded smile again and turned to stare out the window at the oncoming storm. "Everything's fine. We just need to get you home."

My teeth began to chatter. I felt like my capillaries were carrying ice to all the tissues of my system. Nine days? I heard a pattering at the windowpane. Droplets smattered the glass, sounding like a continuous moan. A shiver rattled the base of my spine, transcending the pain in my side.

Jared ran his hand through my hair while bending to kiss my brow. "I'll get you another blanket."

He slipped off the bed. From a closet on the far wall, he pulled a blanket from the top shelf. "You've been in and out of consciousness for the last three days, and you've had a fever." He spread the blanket across me. "Doc Galloway was worried that you would slip back into a coma, but now that you're awake, you'll be out of here in no time."

He pulled the blanket up to my chin and tucked its edges under the mattress. Snatching a handkerchief from his pocket, he wiped some dribble off my chin. "Now that you're conscious, we won't need the feeding tube up your nose. They have some chicken soup in the cafeteria.

It's bland, but it's hot, and thick enough to grow hair on your balls. Would you like some?"

I nodded.

"I'll get some while the nurse pulls that tube out. Don't go anywhere."

Outside, the wind began to howl, sounding ominous. A crow, trying to escape the oncoming storm, crashed into the windowpane. The sound startled me, and I watched the bird fall to the ledge, struggle to stand, and tumble out of sight. The windowpane flashed. A few seconds later, thunder rumbled through the room.

My mother used to tell me that in China, they believe that thunder is a dragon. My fingers clasped the bed frame as the dragon approached. I envisioned the dragon embroidered on Connor's shirt, remembering how it seemed to lunge up his spine as he swung his racket. The thunder became sharper, closer, until it hovered above me, breaking open the room and shaking the bed. Everything went white, thunder cracked, rain hurled against the windows. I clung to the bed as if it were a life raft on a stormy sea.

A nurse shuffled in, thin as a pencil, with bright red hair that had to be a bad dye job. She seemed very businesslike, which had a calming effect. Her nametag read Sara Walker. She asked if I thought I could eat solid food. I assured her I'd eat a horse if she'd take the fucking tube out of my nose. She managed a grin as she proceeded to remove it. She took the respirator from my mouth and set me up with yet another tube that hung beneath the end of my nose and sprayed oxygen up my nostrils. Between bouts of thunder, she asked if I was feeling any unusual pain. I gave her the rundown. She nodded and told me the doctor would see me soon.

The rain's tempo increased, which underscored the sound of my chattering teeth. I glanced at the nightstand crammed with flowers. The most striking one was a sea-blue vase that held roses bursting through a cloud of baby's breath. The roses, tall and proud, were the color of blood and were arranged in a bouquet style. A cream-colored card with handwriting on it leaned against the vase. I squinted to read the print, but it was too far away.

"Those are from your mother." Jared strolled into the room carrying a tray. "The card says, 'Get well, son'."

"Always a woman of few words."

He placed the tray on a table and wheeled it toward me. The tray held a deep bowl, a spoon, and a napkin. A savory aroma infiltrated the room, causing my stomach to knot. I realized that under my pain raged a ravenous hunger.

"She's been here every day; your dad, too." Jared draped the napkin over my chest. He sat on the edge of the bed and picked up the spoon. "He's been giving me hell every visit." He dipped the spoon into the tawny-colored liquid.

With Jared so close to me, I caught the scent of whiskey on his breath and realized that he had taken a shot or two while he was getting the soup. Needing a stiff belt to brace his courage was a bad sign. I began to pity him, thinking that he had already fallen back into his old drinking habits. Pity spun into sadness, washing through my center with a frosty air.

I took the spoon in my mouth and swallowed. The heat felt glorious, but the broth was tasteless. "Why was he giving you hell?"

Jared drew another spoonful, blew on it, fed me.

"For not backing down when they told us about the death threats. He's right. I can't believe I did something so profoundly stupid. I just didn't believe that sleazebag Diefenbach." Jared loaded the spoon again and held it for me. "Honey, I'm so sorry."

As Jared filled the spoon, I asked, "Did Lambert tackle the gunman, or did I dream that?"

"We owe him our lives. Who would have thought?"

The room snapped white. I swallowed broth as a clap of thunder shivered my bed.

"There's something else," Jared said.

He hesitated, so I knew it was bad news. "I know," I said, helping him out. "This was what Roy needed to bounce me. He's taking full charge of coaching Connor."

Jared looked away, so I knew I was right. "Doesn't matter," I said. "We'll do it on our own."

He dropped the spoon and gave my hand a squeeze. "We'll talk about that later. Right now you need to get your strength back so we can get you home."

His touch intoxicated me, but the pain was still present.

"Can I have some of that whiskey you've been hoarding?"

"Now you're talking," Shar's voice echoed from the doorway. "I'll make a liquor run and pick up a bottle of Jamaican rum."

"Hold on, Shar," Jared said. "No booze until Doc Galloway says so."

Connor and J.D. Lambert followed Shar into the room. J.D., in a T-shirt and black leather jacket, wore his Elvis drag. Under other circumstances, I would have had to suppress a grin.

Everybody smiled and touched me, but the smiling faces were obviously façades. Shar gave me a long hug. Her hair fell over my face, and her perfume tickled my nose until I had to stifle a sneeze. Looking past her straight into J.D.'s eyes, I thanked him for saving our lives.

"Sorry I didn't get there a split second sooner."

I couldn't resist the kindness in his voice. For the first time, I felt him reach out to me in friendship. "Doesn't matter," I croaked. "Once I'm on my feet, we can all put this behind us. I'm just glad nobody else was hurt."

A silence grew loud. Everyone stared at Jared. There was something cowardly about that silence.

I turned to see my mother and father standing at the doorway. They seemed to be holding each other up, and when they moved to my bedside, they moved as one. Mother bent and kissed me on the forehead. Dad took my hand in his big paw, not letting go.

Mother shook her head while trying to hold back her tears.

"Son," Dad said in a gentle voice, "I still don't understand this thing you have with Jared, but that doesn't matter anymore. I want you to know, we're here for you. Whatever it takes, we're going to lick this thing together."

I wanted to tell him that I didn't understand why I loved Jared either and how much I appreciated their being there for me, but I knew I couldn't keep my voice steady. I nodded as I took deep breaths, fighting back tears. I needed to focus on something else to keep my feelings from erupting.

I turned to Jared and asked, "How did he get the gun past security?"

"He didn't pass through security. He's a right-wing Christian fundamentalist who accompanied an advisor to the Governor's office, so their limo entered without being inspected."

I grappled with the realization that someone involved in government could do such a thing.

"Well, forget about all that," Shar said. "As soon as Doc Galloway lets you out of here, you and I are going to get to know each other. You're my new thesis project. I'll be cracking the whip to get you into some kind of shape, so be prepared."

I stared at her, hoping that she was kidding but knowing from her tone that she was not.

"I'll need intense physical therapy?"

Jared snipped off a tiny white bloom of the baby's breath from the bouquet at my bedside. He held it in his palm, as if gauging its weight. The frown lines cutting across his forehead conveyed the message even before he said, "Things are different now."

Connor turned away to hide his tears. A cloud of panic grew in my stomach.

"So what you're telling me, in your tactful way, is there are more tests to do before anybody knows how bad it is, but I will most likely never walk again." My voice went harsh, and I hoped beyond reason that he would say no, that it was something different, something trivial.

He hesitated for a heartbeat, giving the earnest impression that he didn't know where to begin. He lowered his eyes, dropped his head. "Yes."

I had never heard that tone in his voice before. It made the shock even more terrifying. He crushed the flower in his palm and dropped it on the floor, snuffing the life out of it with the toe of his shoe like I've seen so many people do with cigarette butts.

My mother shifted impatiently. Father gave me a gritty smile that seemed to say, "Things will turn out fine, you'll see." When that failed to have its intended affect, he said, "The good news is that, other than the damage to the spinal cord, the rest of your body was hardly injured. Superficial wounds. Rest assured these doctors will do everything they can."

"Which right now doesn't sound like much," I said, more bitterly than I intended. "Does it?"

It was an unfair thing to say to a man who had come three thousand miles to hold my hand, but I think he understood. At any rate, his voice went soft. "No, I'm afraid it doesn't. Nevertheless, there is hope...."

"Thank you," I said, using a voice that seemed to come from far away. I wasn't sure what I was thanking him for, but I said it again. "Thank you."

The room went silent. The man in the bed across the way began to rave and fling his arms about as though he were quarreling with someone. I gazed at the figure in the hospital nightgown staring back at me with senseless eyes and voicing an endless parade of crazy words.

I had a moment of mental paralysis. When I woke from it, I heard Jared say, "Yes," and he began to explain about the lower spinal cord and motor functions, so I must have asked him a question, although I hadn't realized it.

I closed my eyes and tumbled into that silent void once again.

CHAPTER 19

A SINGLE nightmare punctured my sleep. I woke several times, drifting on the edge of consciousness for an hour or so, only to sink back into the same ordeal.

In my dream, I crawled on my belly through blackness dense as chowder, groping along an uneven tunnel that seemed to zigzag through the base of a mountain. At least it felt like the weight of a mountain pressing on me. I slithered over damp, jagged stones without any idea of where I crawled. I knew that I had to keep moving. Heat, rising from what must have been an underground lava stream deep under the mountain, bathed me in sweat, but I shivered anyway. The cave began to ascend. I heard the sound of water dripping into a pool slowly, one drop at a time. I inched toward it. As the sound grew louder, I began to smell the stench of dampness and excrement and rotting flesh. That's when I realized that I was lost in Grandfather Lin's WWII cave.

I stopped, panting. My fingers found a pool of liquid, and I wanted to drink, but fear turned me away. It felt like water, but it had the sour reek of stagnant blood. I had to find Grandfather Lin. He alone could lead me out. Was I going the right way, or did this direction take me deeper under the mountain? I had no idea. I kept going. To lie still was to die. This, then, was my path. I realized that there are no choices in life, only the illusion of choice, and beyond the illusion, there is destiny.

I heard a whisper begging for food, for water. I inched toward the sound. As I edged over sweaty rock, my eyes adjusted to the darkness, and I saw shadowy images solidify into human bodies. Around me lay rotting corpses with maggots crawling under their skin, frothing their open wounds, burrowing into their flesh. Their bodies looked like phantoms staring wide-eyed into the void.

I crept closer and saw movement in their eyes, and I thought that they were still alive, but I realized that the movement was maggots swarming in the corpses' eye-sockets. I heard them, heard the minuscule chomping sound of gorging maggots. I stifled the bile rising in my throat, forced myself to crawl toward the voice. My skin burned as I slithered over the bodies.

The path climbed upwards as I drew closer to the voice. It belonged to Grandfather Lin, his boy voice, but he spoke in a fatherly way. Then I saw him: flesh melted away, colorless skin stretched over bone, huge eyes protruding from his skull like a nocturnal animal. His body lay still, but his eyes moved relentlessly as he babbled. He repeated over and over that he had no choice. He begged for forgiveness. I crawled by him, beyond the putrid stench of death and beyond the madness that shrouded him like a cocoon.

The cave tunnel split, one side continuing to ascend and the other leveling off. I chose the level path because I felt too weak to continue lifting my body upwards. I had to keep moving or else become the maggots' feast.

A dim blue light appeared at the mouth of the tunnel. I edged closer, but it didn't get any brighter. Suddenly, red flashed within the blue. I heard a deafening bang, and a bullet slammed into my shoulder. A gunman had me in his sights. Another flash… another… another. Each time, a bullet ripped into me, severing me in two.

I tried to stand and run, but I could only scream. The terror in my voice sounded hideous as it ricocheted in my skull. I felt maggots munching on my toes. I wanted out, wanted to go home, to my quiet life. I wanted to live. I'm such a coward.

I woke in the night, alone and drenched in sweat. I thought about Grandfather Lin's cave: never seeing light, loved ones starving, desperate to save them but overwhelmed with the feelings of helplessness until, one by one, they passed into the void.

I glanced out the windows and saw that it was that blackest part of the night, that hour just before it starts to lighten. I'd become familiar with this turning point. I listened carefully. The storm had blown itself out. I heard the light tap of raindrops on the windowpanes and Jared's deep breathing. He slept in a chair at my bedside. I couldn't recall how many days I'd lain in bed, but this was the first night I hadn't awakened to the shriek of wind.

During these days—or were they weeks?—of recuperation, I'd noticed little difference in the way I felt. I still couldn't get warm. The coldness crept all the way to my marrow, and nothing curbed its icy grip. The only way to relieve the pain was to dull it with morphine. Thankfully, the nurses kept a steady drip coming. The drug also helped me sleep for hours at a time without having my cave dream—or any other dream, for that matter. Enough morphine sent me adrift in black emptiness. What a comfort drugs are. I needed more, but I didn't wake Jared, not yet. I would tolerate the pain a little longer to let him sleep. It was a small comfort to hear his breathing in the darkness.

I felt my new adversary, intense pain, drawing nearer. It lurked in the shadows, stalking me, waiting for the opportunity to consume me. Once it took me over, it came in waves, like long ocean rollers. I couldn't get past it. The waves kept thrashing no matter which way I turned. This adversary was the pop of the gunshot, the emptiness of the night, the frustration of a twice-failed career. During my dream, the adversary took on additional features: the moist density of air that reeked of rotting flesh, the pitiful pleading for forgiveness, the munching maggots. All these things combined to form the specter of my adversary. The fear it created in my heart felt lethal.

I drifted in darkness for a long time, fondling my thoughts while waiting for the nurse to come and increase the drip. I thought about my worst fear: of going beyond the protection of this room, away from the comforting needle in my arm. What would happen when I returned to the world? How would I deal with living in a chair, with the looks of pity from strangers? How would I do any niggling thing, like take a shower?

Fear shut down large parts of me, like a museum at night when all the rooms full of colorful art are steeped in blackness, doors closed, curtains drawn, and alarms set to blare with the slightest disturbance. What was left of me huddled in a corner, clinging to the drip.

Sooner or later I would have to fling open the doors, turn on the lights, and pull back the curtains. But I didn't have the courage for that, not yet. All I could deal with at that moment was the drip, and I needed it increased.

A sharp noise made me realize that I had fallen asleep and that it was morning. I listened. Someone placed something on the table over my bed, and the smell of coffee filled my nostrils. I opened my eyes to see Connor at the window. He brushed open the curtains to let a flood of painful light into the room. I winced and covered my eyes with both hands.

"Hey, what's the big idea? Close those damn curtains."

"Drink your coffee." Connor's voice was authoritative. "We're getting you out of here."

"Call the nurse. I need my shot; my head is on fire. Where the hell is Jared?"

"He's eating breakfast," Shar said. She stood by the door wearing her Homburg hat, jeans, lavender T-shirt, leather sandals. Her outfit gave her a boyish look that suited her. Only the faint outline of her breasts and her hair pulled back into a ponytail gave her sex away. "He'll be back any minute, so we don't have much time."

"Are you kidding? Time is all I have."

"Daniel, how many more weeks do you plan to lay there? Doc Galloway said that you were ready to travel. All the additional tests can be done in San Francisco."

"She doesn't have a clue of what I'm feeling, and neither do you. Nobody's getting me out of this bed until I'm damn good and ready."

Connor stared out the window at the changing cloud formations. "They've offered Jared a wildcard in Barcelona, singles and doubles. It starts in six days. If he does well, he can play the rest of the clay court events leading up to the French Open. He wants to go, needs to go, but he's not leaving you in a hospital alone. So you're not only keeping yourself prisoner here, you're holding him hostage."

"He's crazy. They took my legs. Next time they'll kill him."

Shar strolled over and took my hand, giving it a gentle squeeze. "You can't imagine what's come over our darling Jared. He's turned into the Michael Corleone of tennis. They've hurt his family, and now he wants to crawl right in their faces and make them all eat shit."

"Why not just put him in a fucking shooting gallery and give the winner a Kewpie-doll?"

"That might be," Connor said. "But one thing is certain. If he has to keep babysitting you while you lay there feeling sorry for yourself, he'll crawl back into a bottle for the rest of his life. Avenging you is his only chance."

"I get it. You need a doubles partner."

"That's right," Connor said. "We make a great team. What the hell's wrong with that? You expect him to spend his life at your sickbed wiping your ass?"

"Our careers are over. Everything is over."

"Not for Jared. The shooting has made him a celebrity. Lambert says that if Jared continues to play, he can get a two-million dollar contract with Nike."

"We don't need handouts."

"You do," Connor said, and his voice grew harsh. He tapped the side of his head with his finger. "Think. You quit your job. You don't have medical insurance. The operations have cost over $400,000, and this room is running you $2,500 a day. I was going to set up a website so people could send in donations, but Jared doesn't want charity. He wants to earn the money."

"The tournament has insurance. They'll cover the medical costs and living expenses going forward," I said, trying hard to sound convincing.

"Right," Connor sneered, "and while you were in a coma, your dear old dad got a Florida judge to appoint a redneck conservator. He could do that because you and Jared never registered as domestic partners. Well guess what, buddy, he let the insurance company settle for a measly half-million. That sounds like a lot, but you blew past that price tag last week. Now the meter is running on your dime. Now those bastards at the insurance company are backpedaling to beat sixty, and you'll have to sue them to get another penny."

When the puzzle pieces fell into place, I whispered, "I couldn't help him. Not like this."

"You bet!" Connor said, almost cheerily. "You'll never be any damned good. You're destined to lie there being useless until hell freezes over. Yep, just one more pathetic cripple taking up space."

Amazement. Suspicion. Then, more slowly, comprehension and a knowing smile. "You sure had me going for a second, you little smartass."

Connor approached the side of my bed, head bent, shadows falling over his face. He held my hand. "Do you think that you need legs to help Jared?" He glared at me with those beautiful almond-shaped eyes. "Because if that's what you think, then you're beat, kaput. But it's not too late to change your mind."

I realized those were my words, words I had used on him. We had come full circle. I glanced at the needle in my arm, craving more.

"The first time I played Jared, you told me not to be impressed with him until after the match. I guess you're the kind of coach that only talks a good game."

"Fuck off."

"You're a phony."

"The hell I am. I'm a cripple, but I'm no phony." But why was I so damned mad at Connor? He was right. I was letting this beat me.

The fist holding my chest unclenched. I breathed deeply for the first time since the shooting. One, two, three gulps of air. That somehow gave me the courage to bundle my fear, compress it into a dense stone, and drop it into the murky water of my unconscious. I watched it grow smaller until it vanished. I took another breath. Somehow, it hurt less.

I pulled the oxygen tube from my nose and ripped away the electronic sensors tapped to my temples and chest. The rack of monitors began buzzing. I heard the alarms go off at the nurses' station down the hall and the sound of quick footsteps. A white-clad nurse rushed into the room.

Okay, I thought. *I can do this.*

Jared stood silhouetted in the doorway. He glared at me, at Connor, back at me. He began to speak, but I cut him off.

"Honey, bring my clothes. We're going home."

CHAPTER 20

VIBRANT sunlight slanted through the storm-washed windows, catching itself on particles of dust suspended in the air. I sat on the bed with my legs hanging like dead weights over the side, dressed in jeans, a gray polo shirt, and worn tennis shoes. I gazed at the floating particles glistening like diamonds, wondering about the old man across from me, who had vanished in the night, whisked away by the white-clad apparitions. We had never exchanged a word, yet I felt a sense of loss. Not knowing what had happened to him stirred my fears, as if our destinies were linked.

Jared wheeled a chair into the room and stood facing me, mute, eyes downcast. To me, the chair looked like some hideous torture device from a Kafka story. He started toward me, but I shook my head. I couldn't endure the idea of him placing me in that chair. I sat staring at it for a long time, loathing it, loathing Jared for his fumbling attempt to pretend that everything would be fine, nothing we couldn't overcome. We were now strangers, not knowing how the other would react given these new circumstances.

I couldn't look at it any longer. I turned to stare out the window, into the glistening Florida sunlight. Through the hard-edged radiance, I saw speedboats racing out of the harbor and white sailing yachts riding the wind. Gulls performed lazy loops in the sky behind fishing boats. Everything out there spun in graceful, pulsating indifference.

At last he wheeled the chair to my bedside, averting his gaze as I lowered myself onto the unfamiliar seat. He stepped to the middle of the room, hands on his hips, gazing out the window, his shadow falling over me.

"It should have been me," he said.

I eyed his healthy legs, locked with tension and so close I could reach out and caress them like a trainer might stroke the legs of a racehorse. I knew what he meant. I was the counter-puncher, the one who always played the percentage shots. This was not supposed to happen to me. I had the safe life, the guy in the background pulling the strings. Jared, the intrepid one, loved taking chances, loved being on center court battling the world. He was the perfect target.

But life seldom plays it straight up. Hardship, illness, untimely death—they happen to humble people too, the ones who play it safe, the salt of the earth, people like me—but not to Jared.

Almost absentmindedly, I grabbed the chrome runners on the wheels and spun around to the doorway. Jared bent to embrace me, but I drew back sharply. I wanted to blame him—if only he hadn't made such a public spectacle of our relationship—but I couldn't. He had exposed what was going on. We were all to blame, everybody, society.

"Don't!" I snapped. "Don't treat me like a cripple."

He stood there dazed, not knowing how to respond. I wanted him to react, wanted him to slap my face, hard, knowing that would somehow ease my pain. It dawned on me that this pain was born from our resentment. Society not only beat us, they had broken us. Jared felt it too, I was sure. Broken us to the point where we both felt a panic-stricken sense of not knowing what to say, how to act, or even what to think. An angry resentment simmered deep in our hearts, bringing the humiliation of our defeat to a boil. Resentment at our life, our potential, our dreams, being stripped away by the squeeze of a trigger. We couldn't tolerate this indignity. But how could we break free of it, or from each other? From that day forward, my life would be based on resentment.

I tilted my head so that I could stare into his eyes. He extended his hand and grasped mine. The warmth of his touch shocked me.

"Okay," I said. "What now?"

SOMEONE on staff must have tipped off the press. We fought through a scrum of shouting reporters and TV cameras in the hospital lobby and again at the airport. It became a free-for-all. I felt the overwhelming urge to rush back to my hospital room and slam the door shut.

We were assaulted in San Francisco by the same frenzied throng. I'm sure another group waited at St. Frances Hospital—our planned destination—but we drove home instead, locking the damn door behind us. The phone rang. Jared took three different calls in succession from reporters, refusing comment, before unplugging the phone.

The room plunged into silence. I echoed my same question as before, "What now?"

Jared cleared his throat, the way he did when he had something difficult to say. "We find a nurse to care for you while I'm gone."

"Gone?"

THE clay court season starts in mid-April with three consecutive tournaments: Houston, Monte Carlo, and Barcelona. The Monte Carlo tournament is a Masters Series event and is the most prestigious, which means the top clay court players competed there. Barcelona is less prestigious and a much smaller purse, so it draws the second-tier European and South American players. Only the American players choose to start off the season in Houston.

Connor was granted entry into all three tournaments. He chose to start in Barcelona because the competition would be easier for his first clay court tournament and it was the only tournament that had granted Jared a wildcard entry. It was also safer than playing in an American tournament, as the Europeans tend to be more liberal, especially in Spain, where equal rights is not merely a campaign slogan and gay marriage is legal.

After Barcelona, if all went according to Hoyle, they would play Munich, followed by the Italia Masters in Rome and the Madrid Open. They would have a week of rest before finishing with the French Open in Paris.

If Jared played deep into each tournament, it would be a grueling schedule by the time he arrived in Paris, but I expected him to lose early in at least one or two of these tournaments, so he would have plenty of rest time.

Jared and Spencer flew to Spain the second week of April. I knew he hated to leave me, and I fought against his going, but two days after we returned home, Jared and Spencer labeled their clothes, packed their bags, and took a Yellow Cab to the airport.

Roy, Connor, Harman, and J.D. boarded the same flight a day later. To Connor's dismay, Shar stayed in San Francisco to take charge of my rehabilitation. Roy had agreed to let Connor play doubles with Jared, but he refused to let them go near each other any time they were not playing a match.

Spencer became Jared's practice partner, and Roy coached Connor. I didn't give them much of a chance at doubles if Roy didn't allow them to practice together, but I had no say in the matter. It took some doing to convince Jared even to play with Connor. Jared fumed over the fact that Roy never visited me in the hospital. But no one else would play with him, and we felt that he could earn some extra money if they won a round or two in each of the tournaments.

As it turned out, we needed that money. The hospital bill astounded both of us. They charged for every cotton ball, every pill, each drop of morphine. I could have stayed in the penthouse at the Ritz for what they charged. My morphine bill alone could have fed a family of eight in Bangladesh for five years. The half-million dollar insurance settlement would cover the lion's share, but there was still a sizable price tag left on our shoulders.

For the first time in my life, I realized what a shameful crime the U.S. medical system is for people who can't afford insurance. The doctors wanted to perform more tests, but how many hundreds of thousands of dollars could I pour into a hope and a prayer, especially since the tournament insurance company refused to pay another dime?

I didn't see them off. The journey from Florida to San Francisco had been too emotional. Wheeling through those airports, I saw too many looks of pity and curiosity on the passing faces. It sickened me. Reduced to something to be stared at, I felt small and helpless. Once at home, I refused to leave.

Alone, from the new prospective of my chair, I felt overwhelmed by the number of useless things in my apartment—the Gauguin painting, statues of the Buddha, Chinese porcelain, Tibetan carpets, mirrors, plants—all reminders of a past life. I'd always thought that I kept my home monkishly bare, but every direction I gazed, something stared back at me. My thoughts were drawn to objects. I wanted to throw them all out, everything useless. Anything with no function had to go. I longed to turn my home into a Zen master's cell.

The only thing I could tolerate was Mr. Toa, my orange tabby cat. But any time I sat in my chair, he kept his distance. While I lay in bed or lounged on the couch, he nuzzled me, demanding a scratch behind the ears, but never while I sat in my chair.

Before J.D. Lambert flew to Spain, he delivered a widescreen television and a satellite dish. He set it up himself and demonstrated how the remote worked. The reason he brought it, he explained, was so that I could watch the tournaments. The Tennis Channel broadcasts all the clay court events, including the French Open, and ESPN also covered the French. Both of which, he assured me, this setup had.

I hated it even before he fished it out of the box. I knew the real reason behind it. It would keep me occupied while I sat in my chair, my new Cyclops babysitter. I tried to say no, that I couldn't accept such a generous gift, but he failed to hear the anger singeing my voice. He said it was no problem, a loan until they returned. His house already had one in every room. They could spare one.

When he clicked it on, the images tumbled out at an alarming speed, flicking from one scene to another to another with each blink of my eye. It was exhausting trying to keep up. After a few minutes, my head began to hurt. He showed me how to surf the channels, stopping a millisecond on each station before deciding it was no good. "Three hundred channels and nothing to watch," he said, but he didn't turn it off. He settled for some program where people competed to see who could eat the most disgusting things.

It is incomprehensible how the greatest educational tool invented since language itself could transmit so much trash, all in the name of entertainment. What is so damned entertaining about watching nitwits feasting on banana slugs? I'd heard so much about the dumbing-down of America, and for the first time, I realized what that meant.

As soon as J.D. left, I wheeled to the remote and clicked it off. Of all the things filling my apartment, that television was by far the most useless. But staring at that flat screen, it seemed to wink at me as it went black, and I realized that it held my future. I was a prisoner within these apartment walls. Sooner or later, I would tire of reading books, listening to music, and surfing the web. Boredom would draw me to it, at first just to watch tennis, followed by movies, game shows, and finally the soaps. Yes, once it sucks you in, you live your life through it. I sat glaring at my future, and I felt the urge to vomit.

I spun around to gaze out the windows, opening one to let in the city sounds and smells. I positioned my chair so that I could lean my head out, to get nearer to all that life out there.

Trapped within my cell, I was appalled at the speed of movement I saw below me. Cars jammed the streets, buses zipped up hills packed like sardine cans, pedestrians bumped and shifted and jabbed their way along the crowded sidewalks. They rushed to get as much as they could while they could. Watching them exhausted me even more than the television, but as least they were real.

My first day alone could hardly be considered being alone. A stream of people dropped in: friends I hadn't seen in years and family making the obligatory visit. Carrie Bennett called, and I told her not to come. Too many well-wishers had already brought food, cleaned up after me, kept me company. My mother called, and I told her not to come either. I was still angry at them for signing off with the insurance company.

Our landlord presented me with a stack of articles covering my shooting that he had cut from the New York Times, the L.A. Times, the San Francisco Chronicle, and several other publications. Like so many of my visitors, he had that placating smile and cheerful don't-worry-dear-everything-is-for-the-best façade. It was maddening. I grew sick of being stared at, sympathized with, and babysat. I yearned for Jared, and no substitution would do.

The night before he left, he took me in his arms and made tender love to me. I had not retained much feeling in my groin area, but it didn't matter. I felt immense pleasure in his lavish caresses, his sensual kisses, his formidable body consuming mine. I held him to me, felt his warmth. He whispered my name in my ear while he made slow love to me. I wept.

I craved his love—like I craved the morphine shots and the painkillers that I ate by the handful—and he gave it copiously, long into the night.

That first night alone, he called. We didn't talk long. He described his flight and his charming hotel, and I listed all the well-wishers who had dropped by. I jokingly asked if he and Spencer were behaving themselves, but we both knew it was no joke; it was already an issue. He assured me that I had no reason to worry, but the issue remained lodged in the back of my mind.

I reminded him not to let any ATP officials handle his urine samples the next day when they tested him. "Make sure," I told him, "to hand the bottle to the independent testing agents and have Spencer on hand as a witness." I was less worried about shenanigans after the shooting, thinking that they wouldn't dare pile that on top of what happened, but you never knew.

When we said our I-love-yous and hung up, the warmth inside me cooled until I felt nothing but unmitigated emptiness. I glanced at the television, tempted to let it lull me for a few hours, but I wheeled away. *It may hold my future*, I thought, *but I'll resist it for another day.*

I slipped Beethoven's sixth symphony, the Pastoral, into the disk player and listened to Von Karajan conducting the Berlin Philharmonic. I snatched up the stack of articles covering my shooting, wheeled into the bedroom, curled up between the sheets, and began to read.

"Gay Tennis Coach Gunned Down," and "Right-wing Christian Zealot Goes on Shooting Rampage" and "Governor Denies Any Prior Knowledge" were on the top of the stack. All the articles provided a comprehensive history of the attacker, Peter Mann, including several comments he shouted to the press that God had ordered him to rid the world of homosexuals, but there was precious little information about me. The focus centered on Mann's motives, and nobody seemed too concerned about the victim.

To my surprise, after just three days' coverage, it stopped. The tabloids ran articles for another week about the conversations God had with Peter Mann and how the shooting could herald the beginning of the Second Coming, but even they stopped after a week.

Where were the follow-up articles spotlighting hate crimes and the growing violence against gays? Where were the stinging editorials chastising professional sports for not providing adequate security to protect both athletes and spectators? Where were the quotes from politicians stating we needed more stringent gun laws?

I had always viewed the majority of the media as sleazeballs who would go to any length to build a grain of sand into Mount Everest, but I began to realize how equally talented they are at transforming important issues into thin air. My life came down to a three-day blip, less than fifteen minutes' reading time, and the world moved on. I knew, of course, that gay-friendly web sites and gay bloggers were still, after these many weeks, shouting my name and turning me into their poster-boy against hate crimes, but the mainstream media had swept the incident under the rug.

I WOKE several times to down painkillers before drifting back into unconsciousness. But by the time morning's blush had turned into daylight, I felt myself being shaken. I opened my eyes to find Shar bent over me, her eyes glowing in the light. She unzipped a black leather bag and pulled out a plastic-wrapped syringe and a vial of clear liquid. A smile creased her mouth.

"Mama's got some candy," she said with a mischievous tone. "Turn over and I'll stick you where you need it most." She held the vial up to the window to check the level and tore the plastic away from the syringe.

I turned onto my stomach and there, on the side of the bed, was Mr. Tao. His tail swished back and forth. He leaned his head to one side, as if he were scrutinizing me.

Shar's voice went soft. "How did you sleep?"

"Off and on. Mostly off."

She held the vial of morphine up to the window with the needle stuck through the rubber stopper. "Did you have your cave dream again?" She drew the plunger back, almost filling the syringe, and thumbed the plunger back to the proper dose.

"I dreamed I was sitting on a beach, watching the sunset as cool waves washed over me. Where the hell did you manage to get morphine?"

"Darling, there is a black market for everything. We have to be careful with this, no more than two shots a day. The reason the doctors didn't give you a prescription was that you're already hooked. So, one in the morning to help you out of bed, and one in the evening to help you sleep. During the day, you use the painkillers the doctor prescribed."

"Hurry up and give me the damned shot."

"Tell me, what was sitting on the beach like?"

She set the needle on the nightstand and tucked back the blanket and sheet. She smiled when she saw that I slept in the raw. She plucked a bottle of rubbing alcohol from her bag and unscrewed the cap, turning the bottle's mouth against a cotton ball.

"Like making love, because Jared was the sea. He kept rushing up the sand, covering me, swirling over my skin. I felt his caresses bringing my legs back to life. I can still smell the salt air, feel his mist on my face."

She patted my bum with the cotton ball and stuck the needle with a flick of her wrist. She pushed the plunger down and pressed the cotton ball over the puncture. A moment later, she capped the needle and dropped it into her bag.

I could already feel the tension in my body letting go.

"I hear they've got morphine drops," I said. "You just squeeze a drop under your tongue when the pain gets bad. Think you can get some of those on the black market? I mean, that way I could take care of myself."

"Like I said, you're an addict. You want to get like Jared was with booze?"

"I'm not Jared."

"No, you're not. If he's the sea, then you're the sand." She pulled a plastic bottle from her bag and squeezed a puddle of gel onto her palm. "I'm going rub you down with liniment. It'll help keep you from getting bed sores." She rubbed her hands together and spread the gel over the ribbons of scar tissue on my back, working her fingers and thumbs into the non-injured flesh and gently, almost lovingly, massaging the scars.

I groaned with every breath. The pain of it brought so much pleasure. She spilled more liniment onto her hands and worked the flesh of my butt cheeks and useless thighs. I began to wonder if she planned to do my front as well, and the thought already had me feeling the warmth of a blush on my face.

"Is the pain still bad, I mean, constantly?" She rotated my left shoulder, beginning to stretch as well as rub.

"The morphine turns the flame down to a simmer, but it never shuts off."

"Tell me more about the beach. How did Jared feel?" She began to work the right shoulder, digging her thumbs deep into the joints, bringing more pain and, consequently, more pleasure.

"His waves splashed over my legs and crotch, pulling at me when he rushed back out, as though he were trying to consume me."

"Sounds very sexual." She wiped her hands on a white towel she pulled from her bag. She arranged the pillows at the headboard, and I hoisted myself to a sitting position.

My face blushed as she pulled the coverings all the way off. But she draped her towel over my groin area before lifting my left leg, moving it this way and that, stretching and massaging.

"That's a very good sign," she said, working the leg while seeming not to notice she was mauling a nude man. "Your sexual appetite is returning. That means your mind is recovering from the trauma. In fact, I'm shocked it's happening so soon."

"What are you doing now?" I asked, changing the subject because thinking of Jared had begun to have an embarrassing result.

"We need to exercise your leg muscles every day, move and stretch them like this. Also, the muscles in your upper body have become weak. We need to work them as well. I brought some hand weights so you can start building up your upper body again. I've written down a workout routine. It's the old 'use it or lose it' number, I'm afraid."

I nodded.

"Now that your sexual appetite is recuperating, have you and Jared done anything?"

I smiled, which made her laugh.

It was her turn to blush. "Boys are so bad. Your priorities are so off-kilter. You're aware of that, yes?"

I smiled.

"So tell Mama. Were you able to…."

"It was sensual and loving and I was able to make him happy. On my all-time list of emotional experiences, it rated in the top five."

"Now you sound like a chick!" She lifted the towel and peeked at my exposed crotch. "Yes, you've still got your balls, but you're not acting like it." She laid my leg flat on the mattress and lifted the other leg, beginning the same routine. "Can you do me a tremendous favor, darling? Can you repeat what you just said to Connor? If he approached love-making with that attitude, I'd be the happiest woman on the planet."

"There are some things that can't be coached. But before this chick mood passes, I'd like to say I'm sorry about the fight we had last fall. I was a total ass. I'm grateful for what you've done for Connor and for what you're doing for me. It's wonderful having you as a friend."

"Christ, I'd better finish this up fast before you begin your time of the month."

SHAR left with a cheerful "Bye" and a fluttering of fingers on her raised hand. I lounged in bed, drifting to sleep. An hour later, I opened my eyes and gazed around the room with no ambition to rise. I was still curled under the covers, watching the late morning light make figures on the wall, when Carrie dropped by. Two other visitors had come and, when I didn't answer the door, had gone. But Jared had given Carrie a key so that she could check on me.

"Still in bed?" she said. She wore a lavender summer dress that looked cool and comfortable and showed off her honey-colored cleavage.

"Go away."

"Not until you've made me coffee."

"Throw me my robe and help me into my chair."

"No way, lazybones. I'll wait in the kitchen."

Anger surged through me. But I thought, *Who needs her? I put myself into bed, so I can get myself out. And helping me with something so trivial would be just another form of pity, right?*

Okay, first the robe, followed by the chair, painkillers, and a razor over my face.

When I wheeled into the kitchen, I expected the coffee to be poured already, but she had not lifted a finger to make it. She sat at the table reading the morning paper. I glanced at the counter. Both the coffee and the pot were out of my reach.

"You smell like a musty bottle of multivitamins gone sour," she said.

"Pain medications ooze out my pores. I'm beginning to think that that's why Jared flew out of here so fast—he couldn't stand the smell. No kidding, I eat them by the handful: morphine, codeine, Percodan, Valium, Darvon. When you think about it, I'm a pharmacy on wheels."

Her left eyebrow lifted. "And do you always entertain guests wearing a bathrobe?"

"You're lucky I got up."

She folded the paper and laid it on the table. "Maybe I should wheel that big screen TV into your bedroom so you can call out for pizza and never leave your bed."

I struggled to think of a clever retort, but nothing came to mind. I said, "If you want coffee, you're going to have to make it. I can't reach anything."

"What would you do if I weren't here?"

"I'd still be asleep."

"Going without only works for so long, then you die."

"Jared tried to find some domestic help before he left, but there wasn't enough time."

She nodded. "Okay, I'll help you this once." She reached behind her and brought out a yard-long pole with a large, grey rubber clamp on one end that could be operated by squeezing the handle on the other end. It was modeled after the devices people use to pick up rattlesnakes from a safe distance. She said, "Now you can reach everything in the house."

My eyes narrowed to slits as I glared at her. But I took the pole and maneuvered to where I could get a grip on the coffee can. I lifted the can off the counter, but it slipped out of the clamp and, the next thing I knew, a mass of coffee grounds cascaded onto my lap.

Carrie laughed, a loud and unladylike sound. Recovering herself, she pointed at my lap and said, "There's no way I'm cleaning that up, so don't even ask."

With a clenched jaw, I wheeled to the coffeemaker, snatched it with the pole clamp, filled the pot with water, dug for a filter in the cabinet drawer, and filled it with grounds that I scooped from the heap on my lap. It took thirty-five minutes before I had it ready to go. While it brewed, I swept up the spilt grounds. Before I served Carrie her coffee, I wheeled into the bedroom and pulled on Levis and a T-shirt. Dressing when your legs don't move and your body throbs with pain is the hardest task of all. Twice the call for help hung on my lips, but I held back, remembering her unladylike laugh. I would not give her the satisfaction of laughing at me again.

I lay on the bed, overcome by an intense suffusion of frustration and self-pity and anger that Jared had left me alone. Those swirling emotions felt like a candle-flame shivering in its own consuming heat. They grew and grew until I began to cry: deep, breathless sobs beyond my control.

Carrie ran down the hall and flung open the door. Her eyes grew large as she took a few helpless steps toward me. She said nothing, uncharacteristically, and I waved her away. She turned and closed the door on her way out.

A half-hour later, I had recovered myself and finished dressing (including shoes and socks), and I served her coffee. The coffee turned out better than I had expected. Even Carrie smiled.

"What are your plans for today?" she asked.

"I thought I'd sneak past the paparazzi still lurking outside my door, point my chair straight down the hill, and, if no one runs me down as I speed through all those intersections, I'll fly right off pier thirty-nine and swim out to Treasure Island."

"Very amusing."

"Well, don't ask lame questions. I'm trapped. What plans could I have? Funny, how I used to love this place. Now it's a prison."

"The front door is right over there," she said with a toss of her head.

"This city is built on hills. Everything is either climbing or falling. I might make it down this hill without breaking my neck, but I would need a V8 Hemi on this chair to climb back up."

"You could hire some handsome muscle-mutt to fight off the paparazzi and wheel you around the city."

"I'm not ready for that. Shar comes twice a day for my torture sessions, and that's all I can handle right now. Next week I start working with a therapist, the mental kind. Shar is hooking me up with someone at Stanford."

"Speaking of Shar, how are you two getting along?"

"We grew closer in Palm Springs, and she's been marvelous since the shooting. I still feel that she's using Connor, but when it comes down to it, we all were. I was shocked when she stayed here to handle my therapy. That somehow didn't ring true with her, but I guess I didn't give her enough credit."

"She has a history of using people, me included, but considering her background, you can hardly blame her. You see, she came from the gutter. Her family had nothing but nine mouths to feed. When she turned fourteen, her father married her, which is to say, sold her, to an American whose wife had left him because he beat her half to death. That's how she came to New Orleans. He put Shar in the hospital six times. She put up with that bastard until she graduated high school, then thumbed her way out west. She found me, and I found…." She smiled tenderly. "Well, I found her. I covered her expenses through her undergraduate degree. An older man put her through Stanford. Like Connor, we were all stepping-stones on her rags-to-riches ascent. She has faults, don't we all, but you have to admire someone with her kind of determination."

"No wonder she wants her Up Yours Status."

"Her what?"

"Nothing. Just something she mentioned." Carrie persisted, and I parroted what Shar had told me about getting her nest egg.

"That's all she told you? Well, let me shed a little more light on that topic. She is doing anything she can to support her mother and seven sisters. Eventually she'll pull them out of that slum and bring them here to live. She'll do whatever it takes to keep her siblings from being strapped with a pig like her husband. She'll use her brains and any other body part to save those girls. And to be honest, I'm not sure it stops with her family. I think she intends to save every girl on the planet, one at a time if need be."

Yes, I thought, *you do have to admire her.*

"You know, you're right," she said, changing the subject. "These hills are too steep. You should move to a wheelchair-friendly city."

Of course, I thought. I had begun to think of this apartment as a prison, but nothing was keeping us in San Francisco. With Jared playing the pro circuit, he'd be traveling most of the time anyway. We could move somewhere small and flat, where I could be mobile. Palm Springs? It's flat, has a sizable gay population, and I knew a real estate agent in Palm Desert.

I grabbed the real estate section of the paper and checked property values in Palm Springs. There were only a few listings. I made a mental note to surf the Internet as soon as she left. I could have us moved before Jared came home. I smiled, wanting to kiss her.

The thought of leaving this reminder of my old life and making myself more self-sufficient sent a tingle across my scalp. I glanced at the calendar by the refrigerator, counting the weeks I had before Jared returned. Just eight, but eight was enough.

CHAPTER 21

THE first day of the Barcelona tournament, the Lin family gathered at my house to cook dinner and watch tennis. They selected my apartment because only I had the Tennis Channel coverage on J.D. Lambert's television setup. Besides, caravanning food to my house seemed easier than lugging me across town.

Shar arrived earlier that afternoon to supply me with my comfort shot, rubdown, and stretches. Then she busied herself in the kitchen making beignets, a French-Cajun pastry. She sang while she worked, softly serenading me while I prepared for my guests. She wore jeans and a T-shirt, but she also had brought a simple black dress to change into when the guests arrived.

I spent the better part of an hour donning my best casual jeans and polo shirt. I splashed water all over the bathroom floor while pulling myself into and out of the tub. *Lesson learned: lower myself into the tub before filling it and drain it before pulling myself out again.* That would save me from floundering on the cold tile floor like a beached whale to soak up water with my bath towel.

I heard the party chatter tumbling down the hill long before the doorbell rang. When the front door opened, the pungent odor of Chinese cooking reached through the doorway, saturating the living room all at once. Everybody carried a platter or bowl or pot as they paraded from the front door into the kitchen. Connor's grandmother commandeered the kitchen, five-star-general-like, and the aunties became her administrative staff. The air became heavy with grease and ginger and sweet spices.

Teenagers sprawled on the sofas, and grade-school kids sat on the carpet watching a basketball game on J.D.'s television. The men sat around the dining table sipping hot tea or cold beer. The women jammed into my kitchen, where a volcano of cooking erupted. A loud cackle of laughter floated through the doorway as they literally chased Shar into the living room. When I asked her what they were laughing at, she blushed and said they were joking about how nobody could possibly cook in such a bare kitchen.

"They compared it to making love to a man that only has an inch-long penis." Even she laughed at that, although I failed to see the humor in it.

Grandfather Lin wore a gray Mao jacket buttoned to the neck and dark slacks. He bent close to me and grasped my hand, smiling. It was a genuine smile—not a be-brave smile and not a smile that was forced, but a smile of pure delight at seeing me again.

"Thank you for coming," I said.

"I wanted to see how you are feeling. I've been heartbroken over you."

"I'm better. Enough morphine and I can tolerate the fires of hell. And how are you feeling? You look well."

"I am old. I know this because I detect signs of age. For instance, it is easier for me to talk Chinese these days. I discipline myself to speak American, but when I get tired, I speak Chinese."

"I'm sorry that I don't speak Chinese. Are you tired now?"

"Not so much. It is a wonderful language, but we will speak American."

"How old are you?"

"I don't know. Our family papers were lost in the war. I never expected to live forever, but I very nearly have, long enough to realize that the world is a peculiar place and that I know so very little about it."

"That sounds very wise."

"The wisdom of old men is a sad fallacy. Men do not grow wiser, they grow more careful. Tell me, what do you value most in life?"

"The person I love."

"Yes, I am so sorry that I did not see him before he left for Spain. I wanted to wish him luck."

The old man's eyes sparkled, and I wondered whether he had figured things out himself or Connor had told him.

"I hope you do live forever. We need your kind of careful thinking."

He laughed and patted my shoulder. He had a beautiful ring in his voice, and I laughed with him from the sound of it. My own laughter surprised me. It was the first time since the shooting.

Connor's grandmother came out of the kitchen with a scowl. She folded her arms over her chest as she examined every detail of the living room. She began to chatter in bouts of Cantonese, sounding like the quick bursts of a machine gun.

Grandfather Lin nodded in agreement and turned to me. "My wife say, your house is lopsided and everything is pointed in a straight line out the windows. This means all your joss, your luck and worth, pours out the windows and down the hill like a waterfall. This is very bad. When your home flows wrong, your equilibrium wobbles. This house is beautiful, but its symmetry keeps you from becoming balanced. She is surprised you are not dead."

My mother had taught me about Feng Shui, but I'd never learned enough to know how to apply it. According to her, chi flows though the earth just as it does with people. It links humans to the land and so to the entire cosmos. The chi energy that we take in from our surroundings influences our moods and actions. It is a positive force as long as it is allowed to flow unimpeded. It should meander, like a stream rambling through a valley.

I asked Grandmother Lin what I could change to make it flow better. She rattled off a series of Cantonese sentences while her arms waved at this and that. All at once, the uncles jumped up and began moving the sofa, chairs, end tables, and even the piano. They repositioned the angles of the rugs, took a mirror off the wall and placed it in the hall closet. In the kitchen, the aunties rearranged the things on the counters and even shuffled the contents of the cabinets.

"My wife say, this room has not enough Yin to balance the Yang. You should consider painting the walls green or blue for better harmony."

Once the furniture had been repositioned and several items swapped or tilted to different angles, Grandmother Lin surveyed the results. She nodded, but she pointed at the television and, shaking her head, spoke again. I noted the distress in her voice. Grandfather Lin said, "This TV constricts the room's energy, but there is no better place for it. She has done her best."

I explained that the television was temporary, and as soon as J.D. Lambert returned, he would take it away. She grunted her approval and charged back into the kitchen to oversee the cooking.

I looked around the apartment, thinking that everything looked different and yet the same. I felt suddenly happy, not because the room felt balanced, but simply because it had changed, and I welcomed any change. They could have thrown it all out the windows, and I would have cheered.

"Come and eat," Grandfather Lin said. He lowered his voice and whispered, "We have shrimp and snow peas. My wife is very proud of this dish. You eat." He wheeled me across the room to the dining table, which the aunties had crammed with food.

As we wheeled past the children, I said, "I often think about the hardships you faced during the war. In the hospital, I even dreamed about crawling through your cave. Every night I had that same horrifying dream. How did you endure it?"

"The thing that I have learned over my life is that your world is a reflection of your mind. During the war, I lived in darkness, not knowing what lay ahead, seeing nothing, feeling my way through life with my fingertips, always afraid of what I couldn't see. That is true for you now. You see the world through the hardship of no legs, and you can not see how to move forward."

"You mean I must sit in the dark while the world passes me by, unable to participate?"

"Not at all! How you experience that chair depends on your nature. You see, when a creature is threatened, it reacts in one of three ways— tiger, deer, or tortoise. Tiger fights, deer runs, and tortoise pulls its head in its shell until the problem goes away. Jared is tiger. That's why he goes to Europe. They threaten his family, so he fights, maybe to the death. He is like the bird who leads the fox away from the nest before turning to fight. I think you are a tortoise." He made a fist and rapped his knuckles against my skull. "You see, very hard shell." He chuckled. "That is why you worked at the Windsor Club instead of being a tennis pro."

I opened my mouth to object but stopped. Yes, I had to admit, I spent four safe years wrapped in that shell.

"If your chi is the tortoise, you will sit in that chair, like you say, watching the world pass you by. But if your chi is tiger, you have created the most formidable obstacles for yourself."

I sat for a moment, staring into his eyes, which seemed to glow from deep within his black pupils. I said, "That sounds more like wisdom than being careful."

"No, that is simple. Wisdom is knowing that you can choose. If your chi is one way, you can make it go the other way. It is all up to you." Grandfather Lin smiled a wide, toothy smile and slapped me on the shoulder. "That is my only wisdom. We all choose our nature."

I sat at the table, flanked by Grandfather Lin and Shar. I remembered from the first Lin gathering that Shar disliked Chinese food, but she filled her plate without complaining.

I took a polite spoonful of each dish until everybody had filled their plate. I added small portions of seconds, even thirds, saying that I was already full, but I couldn't resist another bite. My mother had said that you don't feast at Chinese dinners, you graze. That ensures everyone has a chance to taste everything.

When Aunt Kitty brought out a curry dish, Grandfather Lin explained that this Thai delicacy—pork cooked in coconut-chili paste with peanuts, potatoes, onions, and chilies—stimulates blood circulation and improves digestion.

Kitty said, "It turned out too hot. It's so hard to gauge when you use fresh chili peppers. Have something else instead."

I assumed she was being modest—my mother would hide her pride in the same way—so I took a heaping spoonful. My mouth instantly turned into a blast furnace, a burn that grew progressively hotter. My first instinct was to lunge for my water glass, but I held back, smiled, and through teary eyes, declared it the best I'd ever eaten. I spooned more onto my plate.

As my mouth cooled, Grandmother Lin brought out the roasted crab, cut in sections and coated in a black bean sauce. I picked out two legs.

"No!" Grandfather Lin scolded. "Take a claw and a body."

I smiled and politely refused, saying I had already eaten too much. The black bean sauce tasted delightful. I was a little surprised that I still had taste buds after the curry.

All talking stopped, replaced by the sounds of cracking shells and the sucking of crabmeat.

The men and children finished their meals and migrated to the sofa and chairs facing the television. The ladies gossiped and picked the last few crab morsels from the spongy brain, the part I've never been able to stomach.

The delayed broadcast meant I could have checked the results online, but I didn't. Knowing the result ahead of time ruins the thrill.

When the first match started, everybody became very excited. We watched Felix Costa thrash a Spanish qualifier, which turned into a boring match to watch. Still, the Lin family stayed glued to the screen. After the match, they all smiled and nodded as if they had predicted the result from the onset.

A few minutes later, Connor's match against Fernando Salvedra began. Salvedra was a talented Spanish player and a crowd favorite. The fans screamed every time Salvedra won a point. The Lin family cheered Connor on but went stone silent every time he lost a point, which happened more often than not. I couldn't tell whether the crowd had gotten under his skin or he simply had jittery nerves, but Connor struggled. His body was as tense as his racket strings, and that tension killed his footwork. His feet stuck to the court like Velcro, making his normally fluid steps look like slow lunges. Because he got to the ball late, his contact was poor.

I saw his confidence evaporate during the first four games. After he lost the first set, the Lin family stopped cheering the few times he won a point. They saw the outcome as clearly as I did.

Watching Connor made envy rear its ugly head for the second time in my life, only a hundred times more powerful than that time on the beach. I felt acid surging through my capillaries, burning every muscle, organ, and hair follicle. It consumed me. I knew that if I had Connor's legs, I could crush Salvedra's assault. I saw his weaknesses as plainly as white clouds against a cobalt sky, and I knew exactly how to exploit those shortcomings. I could have made mincemeat of him, if I had had legs.

Connor should have recognized those weaknesses—should have known to pull him in with a short slice and pass him cross court, to chip and charge that weak second serve, to play the ball out wide to the forehand wing to bait him into going for a huge low-percentage shot—but Connor was experiencing a brain cramp.

And I knew exactly why. Winning in Indian Wells had raised his expectations. High expectations create pressure, and pressure cramps the brain. A causes B causes C—simple. He needed to put his achievements and expectations aside and focus on executing his game plan, but that was clearly not happening.

As he was about to drop another game, down 1-4 in the second set, a miracle happened: Salvedra rolled his ankle. The room went utterly still while we waited for the trainer. Long minutes crawled by as the trainer hustled onto the court and taped Salvedra's foot. Salvedra stood to put weight on the leg, gingerly testing it. When Salvedra called Connor over to shake hands, giving Connor the match, a sea surge of relief swept through my living room. Everybody but Shar and I was elated.

Uncle Harvey said, "You know what they say, better lucky than good."

"Looks like Connor needs a lotta practice before his next match," Uncle Martin scoffed. The whole gathering laughed and nodded their heads.

In the post-match interview, Connor finally confronted the other side of fame. The reporters hammered him with questions that sounded like sneers. Why hadn't he moved better; why had he played so defensively; what was going through his head as Salvedra's assault pummeled him like a pit bull mauling a rag doll; what would he change in order to play better in his next match; why is it that Americans can't perform on clay?

For the first time, the press had swung against him, and he didn't know how to respond. He stumbled through half-hearted excuses. I couldn't help but wonder if he was sorry for pushing his father away from the interviews. I'd have bet a million bucks that at that moment he would have welcomed Roy's presence to take the heat off his shoulders.

They broadcast Jared's match next, and I was eager to watch it, but everyone else had lost interest. The uncles set up card tables while the aunties packed away the leftovers and cleaned the dishes. Grandfather Lin jabbed a toothpick into his mouth, then leaned close to me to ask, "Why did Connor play so poorly?"

I told him that I wasn't sure, but I thought that he was confused. When I coached him, I made sure he never stepped on court without a meticulous game plan. That gives a player confidence and also gives them something to concentrate on when things aren't going well.

"Roy is a fool to think he can coach the boy," he mumbled. He pulled the toothpick from his mouth and pointed to a crab carcass on the serving platter. "Roy is like the crab. He can only move sideways, walking crooked." He leaned closer to me. "Connor needs you."

"He needs a professional coach."

"I don't care if Connor becomes a champion," the old man murmured. "But he must make enough money to attend medical school and become the first doctor in our family. That is his dream, and mine."

Connor hadn't mentioned medical school since the first day I met him. After his championship win at Indian Wells, he went from an unproven player to a champion, from pauper to prince in one week. He seemed to enjoy the limelight, being fawned over by fans, signing autographs, and he had given me little indication that he still considered giving up tennis for medical school. *No*, I thought, *Connor has abandoned his dream of becoming a doctor.*

"School doesn't interest Connor anymore," I explained. "He wants a tennis career."

The old man suddenly seemed irritated. "Some dreams are so precious you hide them deep in your heart to keep them safe, and you forget they are buried in there. You know his head, but I know his heart."

The adults spilled mah-jongg tiles onto the card tables and began to mix them. The kids set up a Monopoly game on the coffee table. Grandmother Lin served a plate of orange wedges and a mango-swirl cheesecake. Grandfather Lin ate an orange slice and smiled at its sweetness. He cleared his throat twice and patted my hand. He asked me to join his table for mah-jongg, but I said that I would rather watch Jared's match.

I could not concentrate with all the chatter and cackling. The ladies especially were having a grand time. Only Shar and I watched the match.

To our surprise, Jared strutted onto court with two diagonal red lines painted on each cheek and a red bandana wrapped around his head. He vaguely resembled a Comanche warrior. At the net, waiting for the coin toss, he bounced on the balls of his feet like a prizefighter ready to brawl, as if he couldn't contain all the energy burning inside him. After winning the toss, he sprinted to the baseline and continued to bounce, visibly informing his opponent that this match would be a street fight that could get bloody.

It was no surprise when he launched an all-out assault on fellow American Greg Trout. He simply took the ball early and annihilated it with every swing of his racket, smashing winner after winner. Every time he hit the ball, I could almost hear it scream. The ball rocketed back at Trout even before he could finish his follow-through.

I'd never seen Jared play so fearlessly. He struck dead center into his zone like an arrow to a bulls-eye. I prayed it would last the whole match. His awesome display of precision and power left me stunned. I couldn't even feel that envy I'd felt watching Connor.

Jared exhibited tremendous presence. A pure athletic aura surrounded him, and his body language displayed the utmost arrogance. Even when the chair overruled a line-call against him, he didn't flinch. He simply aimed further inside the lines and poured on the gas. Trout couldn't marshal any kind of rhythm. As the match progressed, Trout's confidence crumbled.

Jared won the match in fifty-five minutes, leaving me in a cold sweat. I glanced at the kitchen clock. He wouldn't call for another hour, but the anticipation gave me goose bumps.

A sharp whoop drew my attention to the Monopoly game. Christopher sported a cocky smile as he held out his upturned hand to Curtis, who had just landed on Park Place. Curtis counted out hundred-dollar bills while the others howled with delight, saying, "About time!"

Thirty minutes later, the phone rang. The mah-jongg and Monopoly games were still in full swing, and the aunties had carried out a second round of desserts. I wheeled to the phone, breathless, but Connor's voice came through the receiver.

I asked him to wait while I called Shar to the phone, but he said no, he had called to talk to me, and he didn't want his family knowing. I detected a note of fear in his voice. He said he had played poorly because he felt lost without me. Could I please help him with his next opponent, Tommy Bolton?

I'd never seen Bolton play, so I didn't know his game. I asked if Roy had scouted Bolton, and Connor explained that Roy didn't bother scouting. Roy felt that if Connor played his A-game, he would beat anybody, so it didn't matter how the opponent played.

I paused for a second, silent, my anger rising. I asked him what his game plan had been against Salvedra. He said, "To hit everything to Salvedra's weaker wing, his backhand."

"That's all?" My voice rose for the first time. Everybody at the card tables stared.

"Listen," I snapped. I wanted to scream that Roy was the problem, that he needed to find a professional coach, but he knew that already, and I hated to undermine Roy behind his back. "You got scared under pressure. When you feel great and everybody's on your side, you're unbeatable, but a little pressure slithers into the picture, and you panic." I paused to let that sink in. "Connor, to compete at that level, you must love the pressure. More pressure means more glory. You have to crave the big matches, the way you did at Indian Wells. That's what makes a champion."

I spent an hour giving him a general game plan that would be effective against most clay-court players. We went over everything twice. I stared at the kitchen clock the whole time, knowing that Jared was trying to get through and wanting desperately to talk to him.

Grandfather Lin watched me from his place at the mah-jongg table. I kept my voice low, but I know he heard enough to realize what was happening. At last I told Connor that he would need to scout his opponents himself. He knew what to look for. We had gone over it a hundred times.

By the time I finished, the Lin family had packed up and were about to leave. I handed the phone to Shar so that I could say good-bye to the Lin family. She took it into the bedroom for privacy.

Grandfather Lin shuffled over to shake my hand. Then, as if he had just remembered, he unclasped a silver necklace from his neck. It held a jade pendant the size if a silver dollar. He wadded the pendant and chain in his right fist so that when he shook my hand, he placed the pendant in my palm and wrapped my fingers around it.

"I can't take this," I protested.

"This is the last of my cave treasure," he said, using a coaxing tone of voice. "It brings joss, luck. Give it to Connor when you see him."

I began to tell him I wouldn't see Connor again, but he stopped me short. "Nala, nala"—*take it, take it*—he commanded, then patted me on the head like I was a good dog.

I stared down at the pendant. It smoldered with beautiful verdant hues.

"The color is very dark because this is old jade," he said matter-of-factly. "Old jade is strongest with joss. The more Connor wears it, the darker it grows, the more formidable his luck."

The old man trundled to my front door and waved just as I clasped the necklaces around my own neck. The door shut, and the room fell silent except for the barely perceptible purring of Mr. Toa. I turned to see him perched on the windowsill, staring at me with his eyes narrowed and ears flattened.

After Shar left, I switched off the lights and gazed out at the shimmering city below, waiting for Jared to call. When he did, we talked about his fierce style of play, about Connor's phone call, about how I was coping. I lied, saying that I was fine. I felt horrible about the lie, but I wanted him focused on his tennis, not worrying about me.

Before he hung up, he shared the good news. He had received responses to his emails from organizers of the Munich tournament, the Italia Masters, the Madrid Open, and the French Open tournaments. Each one granted him a wild card entry. He was set for the whole clay-court season.

I could not contain my excitement. I longed to hug him, but I could only sit there, drenched in the city light filtering through the windows. I gazed at those lights long into the night. Every hour or so, a word of thanks passed my lips.

I sat there until the sky paled beyond the Oakland hills.

FOR the next five days, Carrie arrived at about the time Shar finished our evening therapy session. The three of us would prepare dinner and eat while enjoying the tennis. Most often we watched other matches while waiting for them to broadcast either Connor's or Jared's match. Some days they showed one or both, some days neither.

Each evening, after the ladies' departure, I waited by the phone. Connor always called before Jared. We chatted about his next match, which combinations of shots to practice, how to treat those nagging aches and pains. We never talked for long, just enough to share our voices. I followed up with emails, where I went into lengthy detail on each topic. I seldom talked about me, on the phone or in the emails, except to say how proud they made me.

Jared continued to wear his war paint and play his new all-out-assault style. He told me the other players had begun to call him Tonto, the slur being that the famous Indian was said by some to be the Lone Ranger's closeted lover. They said it with tones of respect, he assured me, because they were awed by his ferocious level of play.

Connor, on the other hand, struggled constantly. At first I thought his issues stemmed from being without Shar, which was clearly part of the problem. He needed her to calm and relax him. But I soon realized that he struggled from hiding our daily coaching sessions from his father.

I began to regret that I'd come between them, but Connor felt it was the only way to keep winning and, given the situation, I had to agree. I also got the impression that the pressure was weighing more heavily on him and the bouts of throwing up before his matches had returned with a vengeance, although we never discussed that.

They won their singles matches until they faced each other in the quarterfinals. Jared overpowered Connor in that match with a barrage of heavy baseline bullets, winning easily in straight sets. In doubles, they were awesome. Nobody could break their serves, which meant they were unbeatable.

Jared won his singles semi-final on Saturday. The match lasted only seventy-two minutes. An hour later, he and Connor destroyed their opponents in their doubles semi. That meant Jared had to play two finals the next day. I worried that he didn't have enough energy left in the tank to carry him through both matches, but he reassured me over the phone that he felt fit.

That night, I couldn't sleep. My mind chattered at warp speed. I tried to use meditation to calm my thoughts, but I couldn't even slow them down, let alone stop them. I felt that this final might be his only chance to win a professional singles title in the majors. Even though I am a Buddhist and don't believe in a god, I found myself pleading with something out there in the universe to please give Jared that win.

If he could maintain a high level of consistency while playing this all-out-assault style of tennis, the trophy belonged to him. But I knew that Jared had been riding the crest of a momentum wave, and like all waves, sooner or later it would come crashing down. Few players can maintain that kind of peak performance for long. That is why the top players compensate by playing smarter, more consistent, high percentage shots. They rarely go for big bombs.

Final Sunday turned cool and blustery. Carrie arrived only minutes after Shar had finished our therapy session. We crowded into my kitchen. Shar steamed rice while Carrie and I prepared a spicy bean-curd dish, Mo Po Tofu, which my mother had taught me to cook. She always said that hot things restored the spirit, so I loaded it up with peppers in case Jared lost. I loved how the scent of scallions and chili sauce saturated the apartment.

After dinner, we sipped a French Bordeaux while waiting for Jared's final against Nicolas Adelmann. The phone rang. I fished the receiver from its cradle, and Jared barked in my ear like a rabid dog. At first I didn't recognize his voice. It seethed with hostility. He finally calmed enough to explain that Karl Diefenbach had paid him a visit. Diefenbach had pulled Jared's wildcard entry for the Rome, Madrid, and French Open tournaments.

"Nonsense," I snapped before I had time to think, adding, "Diefenbach gave us his word." But I already knew it was true. I took the news like a lightening bolt, jaw rigid, heart pounding, lungs struggling to draw air. Carrie and Shar stared at me, both their faces molded into blank expressions.

Diefenbach allowed Jared to play next week's Munich tournament because the draws were already published, but Jared would have to qualify in Rome, Madrid, and Paris. The qualifying events for these tournaments, however, were already booked solid. For Jared to play, at least one quallie would have to pull out, which was unlikely.

Diefenbach didn't give a reason, of course, but I knew that Jared had played far too well to risk giving him free entry into the more prestigious Masters Series and Grand Slam tournaments. Strings were pulled to keep the fag from winning a major title. The strategy was obvious: brush him into the background and allow him to play only the small, unimportant tournaments while devising a way to drive him out altogether.

Diefenbach had waited to tell Jared the heartbreaking news, waited until minutes before Jared was to play the singles final, knowing it would pitch Jared's concentration out the window and cause him to lose. *Smart*, I thought, *very smart*.

I tried to refocus him on the final, assuring him that if he won this tournament and Munich, his ranking would climb to the point where they had to let him play the other tournaments.

He went silent, grappling with the mathematical possibilities. I crouched in my chair, feeling the lie turning in my stomach like a hot blade. I had already done the math, and I knew he needed a minimum of three championship wins to get his ranking high enough for an automatic entry into the top events.

Ensnared by my chair, thousands of miles away, I felt so pitifully small and useless. While waiting for him to respond, I took a cold, hard stare at myself, seeing me for exactly what I had become: a disabled liar who was incapable of helping.

Outside, the wind picked up, thumping on the windowpanes with its soft, ineffectual fists. I became conscious of Carrie's and Shar's stares. They had obviously figured out from my half of the conversation what had taken place. Carrie turned away, unable to look me in the eye. Shar bit her lower lip and shook her head.

After Jared hung up, I switched on the television. They showed highlights of previous matches. I positioned my chair at my computer and began to type an email to Jared. I wrote that he needed to stay focused, we were not beaten yet.

It was a gigantic lie. I backspaced and changed the subject, saying that I was getting by, listing all the things that I had relearned: dragging myself into and out of the tub, cooking on a stove that is at eye level, using the Internet to order groceries, taking out the garbage without spilling it over myself, sleeping alone.

As I typed, I thought how my former accomplishments were now only painful reminders of what I had lost. All that knowledge locked in my head—how to split-step as the opponent hits the ball, how deep to bend the knees during the serve, how to jump back to smash an overhead—made useless by a bullet.

So be it. My life was now confined within these walls. I had relearned many things, but I hadn't learned how to help my man from half a world away. I grappled with the puzzle but drew a blank. My ineptitude astounded me.

The match started, and Jared began to lose, badly. His timing was off, and he sprayed balls everywhere but in the court. A fresh anger washed through me. My man needed someone to encourage him and fight his off-court battles. That had always been me. But, I reminded myself, that life was over.

If all I could do, however, was stay home with only this one-eyed link to Jared, I would surely implode. I knew how to play pro tennis but lacked legs. People with worse disabilities than mine played tennis. I'd watched them at city-sponsored events for the disabled. I marveled at their courage, but I instinctively knew, having played at the sport's pinnacle, that I would never play wheelchair tennis.

As I watched Jared lose the first set in record time, I wondered if I could coach without being able to play. Could I share my knowledge without being able to demonstrate? I dismissed the thought, but a moment later I reconsidered. Would learning to coach from a chair be more difficult than learning how to cook dinner or sleep alone? I pushed off, gliding past Carrie to the remote control. I switched off the damned television.

The room went silent except for the sound of my chair as the momentum carried me to the bay windows. Behind me, Carrie and Shar gathered their things.

Billowing clouds of low fog drifted over the bay like a fluffy comforter being pulled over a mattress. A sharp, crescent moon edged above the Bay Bridge, and to its right, Mars shone brighter than the cluster of stars surrounding it. It was the kind of night that made me long to run barefoot on wet grass on the Marina Green and lose myself in the fog.

I cranked the handle until the window stood wide open. Cool air reached in and took hold of me, and with it came the scent of mist and saltwater and a hint of spice from the roses in the garden. I leaned over the windowsill and peeked at the patio two floors below.

Thoughts gnawed at my insides like a live rat swallowed whole. Could I help rather than hinder? I struggled with the question long after Shar and Carrie said their goodbyes and the front door closed.

The pressure in my head built until something burst. I whirled my chair away from the window and pushed off, bumping into the back of the television. I snatched the wires from its back-plate and heaved the damn thing onto my lap. Its weight was substantial, but my legs couldn't feel it. I turned and pushed off toward the open window, building up speed. As I struck the windowsill, I heaved the TV with all my strength.

A moment of sweet silence hung in the air, then an ear-splitting crash rose from the garden. I didn't bother to look down. I glided back to my computer and continued my email. *Jared*, I wrote, *I am just beginning to realize what I'm capable of.*

CHAPTER 22

I SPED past a stream of anesthetized-looking travelers that stretched the entire length of the terminal corridor. They all glanced at me, seemingly embarrassed and fearful as they scurried out of my way. Did I scare them in the same way that drunks and beggars do? Did they cringe at the idea that, but for the grace of their god, the same thing could happen to them? I wanted to know what was going through their minds. They all had that same weary and frustrated look of people on the move. Some had come to the end of their journey. For others, this was merely a pit stop before moving on. We swam against the flow, salmon fighting their way up stream. Carrie pushed my chair as fast as people could jump out of our way. Shar lugged a backpack and a carry-on case in our wake.

I read in the newspaper on the plane ride across the Atlantic that Jared had rallied his concentration in the second set and won the Barcelona championship. He surpassed that achievement an hour later by winning the doubles final with Connor. That was a colossal relief. It proved that Jared was mentally steadfast and didn't need my emotional support. Now I could focus on getting him those three wildcard entries that Karl Diefenbach had reneged on. I had no idea how to achieve it, but I had no choice. This journey had an inexplicable importance, and I vowed to risk everything.

Cold fear crept into my gut, like those gigantic swirling butterflies before a championship match. My fear came from the uncertainty of the people around me. Even though I was in a post-9/11 airport, my experience in Miami made me feel as if any one of them could have slipped a gun by security—a man in a tan trench coat, a blonde lady lugging a backpack, three soldiers in their dress uniforms. What if they recognized me? Away from my apartment and adrift in a world of religion-bred hatred, you never knew. My only confidence came from knowing I would not make this journey alone. In this grand game of life, I partnered with Jared, and doubles was the game I played best.

I scanned the terminal, not missing a detail as this new pursuit unfolded. The Munich airport resembled a shopping mall: bright, austere, designed to move foot traffic and lure shoppers into stores. It resembled every airport terminal I had ever seen: sparkling duty free shops, fast food restaurants, bars serving tankards of beer at nine a.m. to men in business suits who sat next to neo-hippy backpackers. We passed luxurious fashion shops—Gucci, Chanel, Hermes, Versace, Giorgio Armani—where narcissistic patrons primped like Hollywood starlets on Oscar night. Only the information signs posted in German gave any indication of which country we were in.

We reached gate twenty-eight as flight 402 rolled up to the ramp. Carrie positioned me across the waiting room, facing the exit ramp. She stood behind my chair with her tense fingers digging into my shoulder blades. Shar hid behind her, ready to jump out and surprise Connor.

I gazed across the terminal, feeling a thumping in my chest. A man wearing a blue security uniform sauntered by, two Muslims under headscarves, five Japanese tourists dressed in loud Hawaiian shirts—in a world of religion-bred hatred, you never knew. A shiver raced across my shoulders as a dozen people sprinted out the exit ramp and cut across the waiting area.

Jared emerged, sporting his habitual lightweight blue suit and soft hair brushed across his tan forehead. He looked weary and thankful to be off the plane. Directly behind him marched Spencer, fresh as spring rain. Jealousy leaped through me as I, once again, wondered if they had behaved themselves. I dismissed the thought. I simply didn't care. I was back with my man, and only that mattered.

They followed the crowd toward the baggage claim area. As Jared shuffled across the carpet, I couldn't peel my eyes from him. I loved his inner strength, his calm dignity. Our eyes met. He stopped dead. A heartbeat later, he dropped his carry-on bag and began to run. The force of his taking me in his arms knocked my chair backwards and it tumbled over. He held me aloft, my feet dragging on the bluish-green carpet. I felt his heart thumping and heard a muffled sigh.

"Bastard," he whispered, burying his face in the curve of my neck. "Why didn't you tell me?"

I felt an extra two or three pounds around his waist since I'd seen him last. He and Spencer had not eaten properly, and they had probably hit a few beer halls. *That stops now*, I thought. I would make him eat right, work him hard during practice, and have him in fighting trim before the Italia tournament. Assuming I could get him into the Italia.

Spencer jogged up and dropped their bags. His broad smile made me laugh at myself for being jealous. He leaned close and gave me a tender, loving kiss. It amazes me how much emotion can be conveyed by simply touching lips.

Someone screamed from across the room, and I froze. It was Connor's voice as he came out the exit ramp and saw Shar. She literally leaped into his arms. Roy, J.D., and Harman gathered around them, visibly dumbfounded.

I nibbled on Jared's ear before whispering, "With you two calling every night, I thought it would be cheaper to fly here and save on the phone bill. Are you surprised?"

"I ought to slap you silly." He gazed at Carrie and smiled. "Thank you. You have no idea what this means."

Carrie shook her head. "Don't thank me. Wild horses couldn't hold him back."

Spencer hauled my chair back upright, and Jared set me in it. He knelt beside me and kissed me again, ruffling my hair with his rough paw.

"Come on," I said. "Let's pick up your luggage and grab a cab. I want a sausage and sauerkraut dinner before we hit the hay."

"Amen," Jared said.

Wheeling along the corridor, I happened to see Karl Diefenbach gliding toward the first-class lounge. He wore an impeccably tailored gray suit with a burgundy handkerchief peeking out of his breast pocket. His neatly groomed head swiveled away from me, studying something down the corridor. I followed his gaze to see the bouncing hips on a trio of young stewardesses.

My euphoria fled. Anger rose from my solar plexus, driving right up through my brain. I grabbed my chair's wheels and lunged forward. I breezed up to the door of the first class lounge just in front of Diefenbach. I spun around to face him. Jared and the others ran to catch up. Diefenbach glanced left and right, as if determining the most convenient escape route.

"You gave us your word." I almost succeeded in keeping the emotion out of my voice, even though my heart pounded.

"I can't tell you how happy I am to see you—" He suddenly blushed. "My apologies," he continued. "I was about to say: on your feet again. But you're obviously not."

That velvet voice could charm the skin off a snake—or anyone who prefers tone to substance—but it didn't charm me. *I don't know how*, I thought, *but from here on, I will change his life as well as my own. Both he and I will think of our lives in terms of before this moment and after it.* I wanted desperately to start by smacking that patronizing smile off his face. "Obviously."

"It's terribly good to see you out and about. We must do lunch." Diefenbach became lavish, his standard response anytime he felt uncomfortable.

"Just because I'm in this chair does not make me less formidable. A wounded animal is the most dangerous." My voice became even and flowing, betraying none of my excitement.

"The ATP and I did everything we could to protect you. You have only yourselves to blame."

"I don't believe that, and neither does my lawyer. The ATP could and should have done much more," I persisted. "Speaking of my lawyer, I'd like to introduce Carrie Bennett."

Carrie hid her surprise like a Broadway actress who had just been thrown an impromptu line. She stepped forward and held out her hand, saying how she had looked forward to meeting him.

I stared into his cold gray eyes and he into mine. I saw them flicker when he realized that I was on a mission to battle him personally. He broke our gaze by glancing at Carrie's outstretched hand. He removed his wallet from his inner coat pocket, extracted a card and, instead of shaking her hand, slipped the card into her fingers.

"That is the law firm you'll want to contact regarding the shooting." He turned back to me. "I told you that it was dangerous to push me. You have no idea what you're up against."

"Whatever it is, I promise to make myself a unique problem for you and the ATP."

"I've just flown in from Japan, where I heard a curious expression the Japanese use for people who don't conform: 'the nail that sticks up needs to be hammered down'."

"You're going to need a bigger fucking hammer."

"Daniel, I don't want a battle. That helps nobody. Let's meet for lunch and talk about the summer hard court schedule."

"The only way to avoid a battle is to give Jared those wildcards."

He scowled as his fists rested on his hips. "I'm afraid that's out of my hands."

"Well I'm certainly relieved to hear that," Carrie said. "My practice really needs a drawn-out, expensive case like this. The publicity alone is priceless. A huge, mega-rich organization like the ATP openly discriminating against gays and the disabled? Wow! And the longer it drags on, the more publicity there is. I figure we're talking a hundred-million-dollar settlement, easy."

A distrustful frown crossed Diefenbach's carved lips, but his eyes made no comment. A pause stretched into an awkward silence before his voice rose a dozen decibels. "If you think you can draw the ATP into some convoluted legal farce, you'd better think again. I've discussed these matters with our legal team, and they assure me we are on firm ground."

"Oh my goodness," Carrie said with a sadistic little laugh. "We're not simply going to sue the ATP for negligence and discrimination. There are the tournament sponsors, the tournament organizers, the security firm hired by the tournament, the gun manufacturer that made the weapon, and that's just for starters. We're even thinking about suing the French for inventing the game of tennis in the first place." Carrie's lips spread into her most confident smile. "Win, lose, or draw, by the time I'm through with you, Mr. Diefenbach, no company on this planet will risk sponsoring one of your tournaments."

CHAPTER 23

JARED lifted me onto the bed and fumbled with the buttons on my shirt. I ran my fingers through his hair, becoming excited. I needed him badly, and he obviously felt the same. I pressed my hands to the sides of his head and kissed him. Pulling away, I said, "Much as I want you, I've been traveling for fifteen hours. Let me unpack a few things and take a quick bath. After that, I'm all yours."

"Don't unpack. You fly home tomorrow," he said, unable to look me in the eye.

"I came to help. I can get you into Rome somehow."

"It's too dangerous, and besides, you should be at home recuperating. It's too soon for you to be active."

"You want to lock me away where it's safe while you flirt with danger?"

"It seems that way."

"Danger's over here, and I'm over there."

"Let's not do this now. We can argue in the morning," Jared suggested, using his most placatory voice. He stroked my cheek with the back of his fingers.

"Can we?"

"Yes."

"And you'll be objective?"

"Of course."

"Okay, but after we've made love and before we drift off to sleep, I want you to think about something."

"Anything."

"Think about the fact that if you send me home, it's the worst thing you could do to me. I'm dead in that apartment, living moment by moment in an existence I hate. My life, the life I was meant to live, the only life that means a damn, has been stolen from me. I'm not willing to settle for crumbs. If it comes down to a choice between sitting in that apartment like a vegetable or being shot down like a dog, I'll stay and take my chances."

Jared turned his head to look out the window.

I took a deep, audible breath, and continued. "Remember how you were before you started to play again, how you died a little each day, how the pain grew unbearable? Well, that's precisely what I'm going through. If you still want to sentence me to that, I'll go."

His eyes gradually closed, and his brow creased with three deep lines. His urge to make love had vanished. I wasn't sure why—whether caused by anger or painful memories or fear—but something inside him simply shut off.

I unpacked everything in my bag before relaxing in a hot bath. By the time Jared hauled me from the tub, Shar was there for our afternoon therapy session, after which room service delivered our dinner. We ate silently, brushed our teeth, and went straight to bed. He held me to his chest as if he were protecting me from something frightening, and, without a word, his breathing deepened. In sleep, he shifted so that his face rested a few inches from mine. Across the short expanse of white linen pillowcases, I felt his breath on my face, imperceptible except for the warmth he gave off.

Morning's pale light was breaking through the curtains when Shar knocked on our door for our A.M. therapy session. Jared stumbled to the bathroom while she administered my comfort shot. As she rubbed me down, I told her I wasn't sure if I would be on the next plane home or what, explaining how I'd left the ball in his court.

"I'll fly back with you, no problem," she said. "But what a shame after all this."

"Connor needs you more," I said. "You stay."

She kissed me, crossed her fingers, and began my stretches.

After she had gone, I bathed and dressed. Jared and I had breakfast with Spencer and Carrie in the hotel dining room. I took charge of ordering a low-fat, high-carb meal for Jared, and he didn't protest. Neither was there any mention of my flying home.

After breakfast, we put Carrie into a taxi for the airport. She flew on to Rome for a two-week vacation on her own while we drove to the tennis facility. Jared submitted his urine samples for drug testing. I verified that the urine bottle went from him directly into the hands of the independent testing agency, just to be sure.

On our way to the practice courts, I scrutinized the crowd—two tennis players carrying bags on their backs, an ATP official wearing pink-shaded sunglasses, three women wearing polo shirts and jeans—in a world of religion-bred hatred, you never knew.

I noticed something else, something about Jared. He had always been quiet, only speaking when he had something useful to say, but he had become quieter. He seemed to absorb sound rather than emit it. I realized that his silence came from an intensely focused stillness at his core, like a tiger poised to strike.

At the practice court, no more than two minutes after we set our bags down, the press arrived en masse, literally running down the concrete walkway between the courts, pressing from all sides, snapping pictures and shouting questions.

In a forceful, no-nonsense voice, Jared told them to leave us the fuck alone. We were here for a workout and only a workout. He said I was not giving interviews, nor would I answer questions. He explained that if they didn't leave, he would have security remove them.

The crowd hushed, then began to disperse. I knew this would be a situation we would face often, perhaps every day, but there was no way around it.

Jared shot me a look that could freeze mercury.

After they left, we began our standard workout, starting with tai chi. I couldn't perform all the intricate leg moves, but as I directed Jared and Spencer through the meditation, I performed the upper body moves, which helped ease the pain in my chest.

I saw Connor and Shar watching from a distance. He wore his light-blue warm-ups and had his tennis bag slung over his shoulder. She wore a yellowish middle-eastern outfit complete with a black shawl wrapped around her head. I didn't pay them much notice, but I did see a pained expression cut across Connor's face.

Next came the physical conditioning exercises. I was determined to work those extra pounds off Jared's waist. But before we began, Connor strolled up to shake my hand, and Shar bent to give me a tender hug.

Her smoky voice became a croon. "Looks like you're back in the saddle."

"Yippee-kai-yay. That's me, bustin' broncs and takin' names."

"Can you wrangle another hot-blooded colt into your stable?"

"What will Roy say?"

"I'm the star," Connor snapped. "What I say goes."

I lifted an eyebrow and gazed at Shar, who suddenly seemed embarrassed. Yes, her cheeks were definitely reddening.

"I don't want to fight Roy."

"Leave him to me," Connor said.

"All right, work out with us today and talk to him tonight."

A smile fluttered on Connor's lips. His shoulders dropped six inches as his face rose. I guessed what was going through his head. He had played in only a half-dozen tournaments, but he had already realized that the pro tour is a lonesome and stressful affair. Most players are on their own: no coach, no family, few friends. It feels like it's you battling the universe. Being part of a team helps to mitigate that pressure.

I had my men drop and do two minutes of fast push-ups while I told Shar what I had in mind. "Clay court tennis is all about long, grueling points, big strokes, endless running and sliding. It's the most physically demanding surface. Hard courts take a toll on the joints, but clay saps the muscles, and because clay makes the ball bounce higher, the chest and shoulders take more impact, so we alter the conditioning. A good clay workout improves strength, flexibility, and anaerobic conditioning in the upper body as well as the trunk and legs."

Push-ups for two minutes alternated by squats for two minutes. Repeat, repeat, repeat. The squats stretch and strengthen the hamstrings, inner thigh, quadriceps, buttock, and calves. Twenty minutes of that had them panting.

We began an easy warm-up. As they grabbed their rackets and took to the court, Connor draped his arm over Spencer's shoulders and squeezed. The intimate look that passed between them told me that the hard feelings that had come between them had evaporated. They shared that intimacy I saw on the beach that first day. This time I felt no envy, only happiness.

While the boys warmed up, I explained to Shar that most clay-courters are retrievers rather than aggressors. They work longer points, keep the ball in play with safe, loopy shots, and have the perseverance to grind out a five-hour match.

My philosophy was different. On a surface where sliding, moving, and changing directions is challenging at best, it's better to be the player dictating the point, and that means aggressive play. Yes, I wanted them to hit the ball higher over the net and with tons of topspin to bring it back into the court, but the gritty surface slows the ball and affords them an added split-second to get to each ball. That means they have more time to set up and hit a commanding shot closer to the lines. Jared had won his previous matches with that same aggressive style. I simply wanted to improve on what he had already done.

I called them over and reminded them that in ninety percent of all hard court rallies, the ball is struck less than five times. In a clay court match, the average is eight to ten balls per rally. Clay court tennis is grueling, and to win on clay, you have to suffer. Your willingness to push yourself beyond your personal pain threshold is the barometer of how far you will go on clay.

I think that's why Jared was unbeatable and Connor struggled. Jared's fury blocked out his pain, and vengeance drove him past his endurance, whereas when Connor began to feel the pain, he gave in to it.

They began slowly, generating safe, loopy, groundstrokes. I had them notch up the aggression, another notch, up and up until they smashed every ball. They both had great wheels and seemed comfortable moving on the gritty surface, but neither slid into their shots like the better clay courters do.

After forty minutes of aggressive drills, I heard Roy Lin's gravelly voice directly behind me.

"What the fuck is going on?"

Connor ran over as I wheeled around to face Roy.

Connor's sweaty face showed a mixture of joy and fear. He said with mock happiness, "Look, Dad, Daniel is coaching me again. We're having an awesome workout."

"Stay away from my boy," Roy barked, pointing a finger in my face. "We don't need your kind of trouble."

Before I could answer, Connor stepped between us. "I want Daniel to coach me. When I worked with him, my game improved, but I've gone downhill ever since the shooting."

"You're in a slump because you're playing on clay. Your game is better suited for hard courts. You'll be fine once we're past the clay court season. Besides, he can't even walk, how the hell can he help you with drills?"

"Dad, seventy percent of this game is up here." Connor's voice grew loud as he rapped his head with his knuckles. "And he has that seventy percent that you and I don't have." Connor stopped abruptly, keeping himself from going too far.

Stinging silence.

"Dad, I love you," he continued. "You're the reason I'm doing this, but I'm not backing down. Daniel is my coach, my only coach, and I'm not going back on court without him in my corner. You don't like that, Uncle Harman can drive you to the airport."

Roy stood speechless while the blood drained from his face. I knew he truly believed his child could never have spoken to him in that manner and tone of voice. Truth be told, I was equally shocked. We all were. That didn't happen in Chinese families. It gave me a pretty good indication of just how scared and lonely Connor had become.

Roy stuttered, "I'll catch a cab to the hotel. We'll talk more tonight." He stalked away. Uncle Harman reached over and patted Connor's shoulder. He also shook my hand and told me he was happy that we were all working together again. He glanced at Spencer and smiled with his eyes.

We finished our workout with thirty minutes of serving practice. I felt that both my boys were working too hard to win points, and it would sure help to get some cheap points now and again. To that end, I wanted to increase the velocity of their serves by having them use a lower toss and abbreviated take-back to get them serving consistently in the upper 120 mile-per-hour range. That would ensure more unreturnables and also make it easier for them to control the rally if the ball did come back.

While Jared and Connor ambled to the locker room to prepare for their afternoon matches, Spencer wheeled me into the stadium to watch Jared's first round against Mariano Delores from Argentina. He was a respected clay court specialist, so I thought this match could easily go the distance. Connor's first round was on an outer court and would go on about the time Jared's match would probably finish.

When I first saw center court from the perspective of my chair, a lump lodged in my throat, making it difficult to breathe. The burnt red dirt is not really clay but made from crushed brick often called terre battue (the battle ground). A black net dissects the court into two equal halves, while snow-white lines define the rectangular boundaries of the playing field. Between the lines and the spectators' seats are the game's peripherals— chair umpire, lines judges, ball kids—taking their positions like chess pieces on the board. I loved the absolute orderliness of it, the precisely defined battlefield, bound within the rules of the game.

We waited only fifteen minutes before the players strutted onto the court. Jared wore all white clothes, a red bandana, and his now trademark red slashes on his cheek—his war paint. He looked ruthlessly intimidating.

Even more menacing was how he carried himself. I had seen this new, brutal persona on television, but now I witnessed his metamorphosis right before my eyes, and it scared me. I could not fathom how the man who had held me so tenderly through the night could be this paint-wearing fiend.

As they began to play, his savagery became even more evident. It allowed him to dominate his opponent. He never doubted that he could win every point. He sometimes turned his fury on himself, but he knew that he couldn't be outgunned. He had supreme confidence that he could squash his opponent like a bug, and with Jared, it was obviously personal. He got cranked up like nobody else in the game. His new tenacity and grit were without equal. Tennis was his Roman Coliseum, and he became its fiercest gladiator.

He crushed Delores 6-2, 6-3, in an hour and twenty minutes. We now had ample time to make it to Connor's match. As Spencer wheeled me down the ramp and out of the stadium, I tingled all over. For the first time, I wholly believed that Jared had what it took to be the best player in the world.

EUROPEAN tennis fans knew nothing of Connor Lin, but they took notice that afternoon. He played the Swedish veteran, Thomas Lundy. Smart money bet heavily that Connor would go down in straight sets. To everyone's surprise, mine included, Connor won the match 6-0, 6-0 in fifty-three minutes. Reporters in the pressroom joked that he played like he was double-parked. I suspected that he was furious with himself for hurting his father, and he poured that fire into his game without losing focus.

In fact, his focus sharpened to a razor's edge. I'd seen him do that before. With heightened intensity, his game radiated flair. He played by deviant rules of physics, pushing the envelope of what is physically possible, rules he made up himself seemingly on the fly. Awed, Jared and I kept turning to stare open-mouthed at each other, but I questioned whether or not Connor could maintain that intensity once his anger subsided.

Watching him lift his game even higher in the second set, I felt a shimmer whiff through my head, becoming white-hot and, like liquefied metal, slowly oozing down the length of my spine. When it hit my testicles, my whole body shook violently. I now coached two of the top players on the planet, perhaps even the top two, and how exciting it would be when, not if, they met in a Grand Slam final.

That night, as we retrieved our key at the hotel's front desk, the clerk slipped Jared a cable that had arrived an hour earlier. Jared opened the envelope and read silently. Somewhat dazed, he passed the note to me. It was from Carrie. She had arrived in Rome and had gone directly to the tournament site, where she demanded to see the tournament director. She had somehow bullied him into reinstating Jared's wildcard entry.

Sitting in that ornate lobby, I almost wept. A concerned bellhop asked in broken English if there was something wrong, something he could help us with. We laughed.

We found out later that my stunt at the airport, pretending that Carrie was my lawyer, had inspired her. She told the Roman tournament director that she represented a law firm engaged by the tournament's main sponsor. She claimed the sponsor was concerned that its gay clientele would be angered by their move and that if we were not given the wildcard, the sponsor would withdraw its support for next year's tournament.

You really have to love any woman with balls that big. I felt so lightheaded I thought I would faint. The next thing I knew, Jared had lifted me out of my chair and given me a loving hug as he carried me to our room.

CHAPTER 24

JARED'S elation soon cooled, and his silence returned. We ate dinner in our hotel room with him as talkative as a gravestone. I tried to coax him into conversation by making plans for Rome, but I might as well have been on another planet. Being ignored was my punishment for not flying back home. I knew his silent treatment could last for days, maybe weeks, but I felt determined to overcome it.

He wheeled the dinner trolley into the hallway and shut the door. He stripped down to his jockey shorts, walked to the bathroom sink, and began brushing his teeth.

"When you're finished, let's talk about tomorrow's game plan," I said, attempting to spark some kind of conversation. I thought keeping it tennis related was a sure ploy.

Through the bathroom door, I heard him spit, rinse his mouth, spit again. When he returned to the bedroom, he didn't reply, wouldn't look at me. He strolled to the bed, pulled the covers back, and crawled in.

"We need to talk," I said. "I mean, if I'm going to be of any help, we need to talk."

He switched off the bedside lamp and turned his back to me.

"Unbelievable!" My voice rose to louder decibels than I had intended.

Silence.

"Ignoring me will not drive me away."

Louder silence.

"If I hadn't come, this would be your last tournament. Carrie and I got you into Rome, and maybe, just maybe, we can help get you into the French too."

Deafening silence.

"What's happened to you?"

It occurred to me that Jared's silence was different from the other times he had ignored me. In the past, I could wait it out or lure him into talking with a good tease. But this immutable silence came from Jared's new battle-hardened persona. The fortitude I had seen in his tennis game now reared its head in our bedroom. This formidable determination came from an absolute resolve to fight with all his inner strength and crush any opposition to his will. He battled me with the same intensity that he fought the rest of the world.

I wheeled into the bathroom, brushed my teeth, undressed, and turned off the light. Slipping between the sheets, I pressed against his stiff back, holding him with one arm around his waist. At least he didn't pull away. I kissed his neck. I felt the strong urge to say that I was sorry, but that seemed patronizing, and that was the last thing he wanted. I considered giving in, telling him I would fly home, but that was the last thing I wanted.

I had to say something, if for nothing more that to hear my own voice. "If we must fight each other, then we'll fight," I whispered. "But I'm not leaving, and you're not pushing me away like some useless bag of garbage."

He finally uttered a prolonged sigh. A moment later, he turned to face me and, without a word, pulled me into that hollow space between his arms. He began kissing my face so softly that I wasn't sure what he was doing. I thought his kisses would escalate into lovemaking, but after a minute, he simply held me until he fell asleep.

I WOKE to the sound of the door closing. Room service had delivered a breakfast tray. I sat up, squinting against the harsh morning light at the clock beside the bed, and realized I had overslept. I turned sideways, and pain raced up my back, grabbing my full attention. Shar had not come for our sunrise therapy session, I thought, until I noticed a syringe and a bottle of morphine lying on the nightstand. She had come, but Jared had sent her away. He sat at the table pouring coffee. We glared eye to eye. Fresh anger inflamed his pupils so intensely that I braced myself for another silent day.

I gave myself an injection, dropped into my chair, and wheeled to the table. Jared poured maple syrup onto a stack of pancakes, quartered the stack, and wedged a whole quarter into his mouth. The tight muscles in his jaw made a clicking sound as he chewed. He had ordered me a basket of blueberry muffins, my favorite. He poured me coffee without being asked. It was strong and bitter and very hot. The muffins were warm and wonderfully fragrant.

"You should have awakened me an hour ago," I said. "We'll have to hurry. The car will be downstairs in thirty minutes."

No response. He didn't lift his eyes from his plate. *How strange*, I thought. *He is so contradictory that he denies me Shar's therapy and his companionship while at the same time ensuring that I have my favorite breakfast.* I began to hate his thoughtfulness as well as his cruelty.

My attempt at small talk failed miserably, so I tried a different, more blunt approach. "Why can't you make love to me?" I asked in a rush. "Am I so repulsive now?"

No response.

"If you don't answer me, I'm going to throw this coffee in your face!"

His head lifted and his eyes bore into mine. "What if there is another gunman out there? I can't protect you from these fanatics. We proved that in Florida. If you die, what the fuck am I supposed to do?"

"If I die today, wouldn't it be better if we had made love last night?"

"Better is putting your skinny butt on a plane and getting you somewhere safe."

"It's okay to hate me a little. Sometimes I hate you too. I hate your good legs, your strength, your ability to ignore me."

His face froze with pensive rejection.

I said, "We need to fight them, not each other."

He winced, and I knew I'd hit a home run. "I fought them just fine before you came."

"That may be, but you're forcing me to be a cripple, and I've had enough of that. Don't you see? I can't fight the demons in my head sitting alone in our apartment. I need to be with you."

"I put you in that chair by not backing down. You died on that operating table, and they brought you back. Do you know what that did to me, the idea of me killing you?"

"That's why you've ignored me?"

"The hospital staff wouldn't let me see you, wouldn't even tell me your status. They said I wasn't family, so I had no legal rights. When your parents came, they told us you had a thirty-percent chance that the brain damage would make you a vegetable. When we got a second chance, I vowed I would never put you in harm's way again."

"I'll take that risk," I said, but the lump in my throat made me wonder if that was true.

"You want everything to be the way it was, and it can't. The world has changed; we've changed. There's real danger lurking out there. These fanatics are not just trying to stop us, they're trying to kill us."

"You're right. I'm not the man I was. I'm not nearly as strong now, and I can't deal with being brushed aside. On top of that, these pain medications fuck with my head. Half the time I'm not sure what's real. I know I'm being overly dramatic, but, tell me, could you live with yourself if I shot up a whole vial of morphine or swallowed a bottle of painkillers? I'm not threatening you. I'm saying that I'm unstable, and there is danger no matter what we do."

He suddenly looked stunned and, for the first time, not sure of himself.

I took a couple of deep breaths. "And let's discuss the flip side. If they kill you, who is left alone? Who has to go through life sitting in this fucking chair, lonesome and unwanted? You think I can deal with that any better than you? You have always been the taker, the selfish one, and that's always been fine with me. But goddamnit, I have needs too."

I sat in the silent aftermath, glaring at his face, which was framed by the tasteful blue wallpaper. He stood, threw his napkin onto his half-finished pancakes, and stalked to the bathroom.

I felt a knife twist in my gut. Until that moment, I would have never believed I could commit suicide. But once I had actually voiced the possibility, and considering my drug-induced mood swings, I realized I was more than capable.

On the other hand, he was right. I was trying to turn back time, an impossible undertaking that could only end in failure. The whole situation somehow felt like an unsolvable puzzle, the sound of one hand clapping.

THE beautiful cloudless day attracted a crowd of gay fans and a few diehard reporters who hadn't gotten the message. They hovered around our practice court snapping pictures and cheering us on.

That normally put me in a fine mood, but I couldn't melt the iceberg that had crystallized inside me. I had come to help not only Jared and Connor, but myself. To do that, I needed Jared's support, which at the moment was nonexistent. He hadn't said another word since breakfast. He did everything I asked on court, letting me direct the practice, but it felt like screaming into a black hole, because nothing came back.

I noticed him scanning the crowd the same way I did, scrutinizing the two in leisure suits carrying briefcases, a man with a cast on his right arm, the elderly man walking with a limp. In a world of religion-bred hatred, you never knew.

I needed to get these guys working up a good sweat, but I was freefalling into depression.

Finally, Connor shuffled up and put a hand on my shoulder. "Hey, which planet are you on?"

I shook my head and looked up, as if seeing him for the first time that day. "Sorry," I said. "Let's move on to cross-court drills. We'll start with backhand to backhand."

"I'm going to pretend you didn't say that," Connor said, rolling his eyes. "Whaddaya think we've been doing?"

"Sorry." I glanced up, feeling a stab of angst.

Connor said, "Let's work on the game plan for my match."

"Right," I mumbled, as I pulled my scouting notebook from my bag. "Who are you playing?"

"Shit." Connor spat the word and turned his back on me.

Laughter erupted behind me. I swiveled my head to see Roy Lin among the spectators flashing a full set of small white teeth. He caught his breath and barked at Connor, "Hey hotshot, how much are you paying your big-time coach? If you double his salary, maybe he'll remember which tournament you're playing."

Connor's eyes narrowed. "Give it a rest, Dad. Everybody has a bad day."

"Not on tour," Roy hissed. His voice sounded deadly. "On tour, you can't afford bad days. You give it a hundred percent, no matter what."

"Dad," Connor said, his voice seething.

"No, Connor," I stopped him. "He's right. I'm doing more harm than good."

Jared ambled over. He still wore that stony, expressionless face, but compassion singed his voice. "Have Harman drive you to the hotel to pack. You fly home tonight."

"Let me watch you play this afternoon. I'll leave first thing tomorrow."

Spencer wheeled me through the fans and into the players' cafeteria. I bought him a coke and myself a tea. We sat there, silent, until Connor's match time.

Connor played on an outer court. We wheeled my chair to the edge of the court, four feet behind the chair umpire. Roy, Harman, and Shar sat in the stands directly behind me. A dozen gay fans recognized me and lined up for autographs, which I scribbled onto programs, hats, arms, even tennis balls. They all wanted to touch me, telling me how sorry they were and that they were so very proud I wasn't letting this stop me. I felt worse with each well-wisher.

Connor followed Argentina's Alberto Silva onto the court, and, after the coin toss, they began their warm-up. Connor wore his trademark Hollywood dragon shirt, and he had a bounce to his step that made me hopeful. Once the battle began, I had no problem zeroing in on Connor's play with a critical mind, even though I felt Roy's laser eyes boring into the back of my skull.

Connor's demeanor on court had changed. Now that he had regained some confidence, the showman in him reemerged. His swaggering, fist-pumping, tenacious theatrics had the fans cheering. He was becoming the Chinese equivalent of Joshua McEwan, the hot-headed macho Aussie, minus McEwan's grating edge. He pumped himself up for every point, and the fans adored him. They encouraged his showmanship, and that energized him. He clearly wanted to impress them. That was not a problem as long as he stayed focused.

The real problem showed up late in the second set. Up a comfortable break and serving at 5-2, he began to cramp. His fragile legs had taken a beating during those drawn-out points. His quads and hamstrings simply broke down. He needed a week's rest and a month of strength training, but that was not an option.

He won the match, but only because he pulled two aces out of his hat to win the last two points. Had Silva returned either ball back into play, he would have easily won the point and eventually the match, because Connor could no longer run.

As we listened to Connor during his post-match interview, Shar told me that every night she massaged his legs for an hour. We discussed his workout schedule, trying to find a way to lessen the load and give his legs a much-needed rest.

Half listening to her and half listening to Connor, I realized that he had become even more adept at handling the media, but his answers were somewhat banal and carried an undertone of boredom. He had learned that the press always asked the same six unimaginative questions after each match: How did you prepare for this match? What was your game plan? What was going through your head when you slumped in the second set? How does it feel to be in the next round? What do you expect in your next match? Do you think you can win this tournament?

The questions seldom varied, and after a few tournaments, most players find it difficult to sound enthusiastic or spontaneous. It was clear that in Connor's eyes, the media's sparkle had begun to tarnish.

We waited for Connor to shower and change before we moseyed over to watch Jared's match against McEwan. As usual, Jared came out wearing all white. His eyes burned with intensity, and his freckles glowed the same color as his bandana and war paint.

The match mutated into a loud, emotional, frustrating dogfight. Right from the first game, McEwan questioned every close line call, arguing with the chair to sway the decision in his favor. That ploy had always gone against Jared, but on clay, the ball leaves a clear mark in the dirt, so every time McEwan questioned a call, the chair umpire inspected the mark before making a valid call. It dawned on me then that part of Jared's confidence on clay came from knowing that the linespeople couldn't cheat him out of points.

Jared won the first set in a tiebreaker, and McEwan smashed his racket in a violent outburst. Jared remained cool, oblivious to McEwan's gamesmanship. While we waited for the second set to begin, Connor leaned into me and asked in a voice low enough that Roy couldn't hear, "What's up with you, and why is Jared flying you home?"

"Look, Connor, I'm not discussing Jared's and my problems with you, okay?"

"I have a right to know. You brought that weak stuff to the court today and made me look like a fool in front of my dad."

He had stood up to his father, and I let him down. Of course he had a right to know. I took a deep breath. At the same time, I stared at Jared, seeing the war paint slashed across his cheeks and that frightening calm deep inside him.

I had held so much inside ever since the shooting, and now I didn't know how to put my exasperation into words that made any sense. I realized that Shar's advice to seek mental therapy had been right on target. It was a mistake to come here in such fragile condition. Connor's eyes were liquid clear, no pity and no judgment, only a desire to understand.

Okay, I thought, *I can do this.*

As Jared began serving the second set, I recounted Jared's rejection, how being with him felt like screaming into a black hole. The silence created feelings of loneliness and uselessness.

Connor listened without interrupting. Talking about it helped, and I surprised myself by saying much more than I probably should have; what started as a trickle began to pour. When I wound down and came to a stop,

I saw the scoreboard: 5-4 with McEwan serving to stay in the match. I had talked for almost an hour.

We watched in silence until the game went to deuce.

Connor said, "My gut says that the reason he's freaked out is that he's embarrassed about being coached by someone in a wheelchair. You know, deep down he believes you're inept."

"Maybe. Who knows?"

"Stop coaching him. Just work with me."

Even though Jared had a match point, I stared at Connor.

"You heard me. Stop kowtowing to him and show him you can do the job by coaching me. When I kick his ass on court, he'll know it was because of you."

I smiled, liking his arrogance. But I shook my head and watched Jared win the point and the match. Cheers erupted from several hundred fans. Jared raised his arms in victory, but he didn't look our way, didn't acknowledge us.

Connor slid his arm across my shoulder and gave me a squeeze. He whispered, "Even if I don't kick his ass, he'll know that you plan to get on with your life, with or without his approval, which is exactly what you need to do."

His words rang true in my heart. I glanced away, knowing what I needed to do but also knowing that I did not have the courage to do it. But I had enough courage to stay there and keep trying to help. I would not fly home a failure with my tail between my useless legs.

We're just starting the third set, I thought. *It's time to dig deep, not give up.*

That's when Shar leaned over, and her voice was all honey and soothing. "I told you that you need psychological counseling to help you through this. Well, guess what? Jared needs it as badly as you. You're both floundering in an emotional storm. You need to take a break, go somewhere away from all this and get help, together. I mean, for Christ's sake, darling, it took Seles years to return. You guys charged back in a matter of months as if nothing had happened. Give yourself a break and get help."

Of course she was right. We were both unstable, and understandably so. But I knew Jared would not walk away from a shot at the French Open, and I needed to stay with him. I gave her a sad smile and patted her hand. "Okay. After the French."

"That's a month away. What makes you think you two can survive that long?"

I wasn't sure at all.

While Roy and Harman went to retrieve the van, Spencer wheeled me to the players' lounge entrance behind Connor and Shar. Our men were not scheduled to play doubles that afternoon, so we talked about where to go for an early dinner.

Although no one actually voiced it, we all felt that if our luck held, Jared and Connor would meet in the final, and the anticipation of that had us as giddy as schoolgirls. When Jared emerged from the players' lounge doorway, we were all in high spirits. Even he wore an angelic smile, as if he were thinking the same thing. But when his eyes fell on me, his smile dissolved.

Something inside my chest plummeted. A heartbeat later, anger rose up in its place. If I'd had legs, I would have bitch-slapped his frown into next week. Against my will, I swallowed, absorbing his silent censure, reminding myself of what Shar had told me about Jared needing counseling too.

Over the next three days, Jared and Connor fought their way into the semi-finals of both singles and doubles. Jared continued his silent campaign, refusing to acknowledge me. I worked around his attitude by focusing on Connor. The others—Spencer, Shar, Harman—wallowed in an embarrassed silence of their own, tiptoeing around us.

Roy, on the other hand, kept to himself. We only saw him at breakfast and dinner. As the situation tensed, I wrestled with depression and doubt, but there was no squelching the thrill of seeing both my athletes working toward the final. They demolished their opponents, playing like they were born on the red dirt. Connor's legs continued to break down during long matches, but he somehow found the heart to play through the pain.

It seemed, however, that our run had come to an end. In the semifinals, Jared would play Christopher Drake, the number one player in the world and arguably the best male player of all time. Drake hadn't lost a match to anyone but Jose Lamas all year on any surface. He had the kind of smooth, effortless, all-court game that the rest of the pack only dreamed of achieving in some future life.

Connor's situation looked equally hopeless. His semifinal opponent was the reigning king of clay, Jose Lamas, who hadn't lost a match on clay in two years. It was difficult to imagine Connor beating the hard-hitting superathlete on any surface, but on clay it was impossible. Smart money bet heavily on a Drake/Lamas final, and that is exactly where I placed my chips too. I hoped that my boys would give them a damn good fight, something that would boost their confidence and help them gear up for the doubles final so they walked away feeling good about their losses.

CONNOR narrowly won the first set against Lamas, 7-6. I was thrilled, but I knew the match was far from over. When Connor cruised into a one-break lead in the second set, I began to believe he would win. My pulse raced, and sweat covered my upper lip. But two games later, he began to cramp. He lost the second set because of his hampered mobility. The trainer came out at each changeover to massage his legs, which kept him going.

Early in the third set, he worked through the pain and began to move again, but he had lost the momentum. Connor finished the match, but he lost 3-6 in the third set. The worst part was that his legs were done in. Sadly, we had to pull out of the doubles rather than risk an injury that could sideline him for months.

We were all crushed. I don't think any of us thought he had a Chinaman's chance before the match, but after winning that set and a break, we became optimistic. After shaking hands, he limped to his chair, sat down, and pulled a towel over his head while Lamas took his bows. I wondered which hurt worse, his legs or his heart, but deep down I knew. At the same time, playing that well against Lamas was huge, and once we conditioned his legs, nobody would touch him on clay.

JARED and Drake squared off like gladiators with neither man breaking serve in the first set. The points developed into long, grueling tussles that had both players scrambling and sliding on every area of the court. The tiebreaker went to an electrifying 12-10, won by Drake. The second set carbon-copied the first, except that Jared won the tiebreaker 16-14. The match had stretched over two hours in the hot sun, but both players looked fresh entering the third set.

Everybody was on his or her feet for most of the last set. Jared and Drake achieved the kind of hard-fought, brilliant shot-making that you normally see once or twice in a match, but they played that way on almost every point. The tension heightened with each game. It was like watching Seabiscuit and War Admiral racing down the homestretch, nose and nose, each one expending every last iota of strength and heart. My body rocked with spasms.

Victory came down to a deciding third set tiebreaker, which was the only fitting end to such a gloriously fought battle. I saw something in that tiebreaker that I didn't believe. Jared had gone toe-to-toe with the best player on the planet for over three hours, elevating his game to impossible levels just to stay even, but in the tiebreaker, he lifted his game, and Drake faltered.

Goosebumps enveloped me. I couldn't utter a sound as I watch Jared win every point in the tiebreaker. For those incredible seven points, Jared lifted his game to a level where it was literally impossible to play better, and for me at least, it exemplified the truest testament to what the human will is capable of.

THE next day, a Sunday, Jared played Lamas in the final. Spencer warmed him up before the match while I supervised. Jared still wouldn't acknowledge my presence. I felt excited and furious. He was about to play the most important match of his life, and he refused to share it with me.

The bookmakers gave three-to-one odds that Lamas would pulverize Jared. As predicted, the match was quickly won, but Jared rose victorious, felling Lamas in straight sets, 6-3, 7-5. The crowd, many of whom were obviously gay, went ballistic as Jared smashed a crosscourt winner on match point.

Lamas seemed shell-shocked that he had lost to a fairy on his best surface. I saw something in his eyes, something broken, and I felt a stab of empathy. I knew that sometimes when you're riding a wave of confidence and your expectations are in the stratosphere, a bad loss can crush your heart, and you are never the same after that. Lamas's eyes held that look.

Jared glowed with a radiance that I'd never seen before. Standing in the center of the court with his arms held high, he basked in the crowd's adoration. He turned in slow circles, making eye contact with seemingly everybody in the stadium, everyone except me. My elation nose-dived into something painful.

During Jared's victory speech, he congratulated Lamas for putting up a great fight. He thanked the tournament organizers, the sponsors, the crowd, even the ball kids. He didn't mention me or any of the others in our camp. We all felt slighted.

By the time Jared had finished his interviews, showered, and changed, the doubles final was deep into the second set. The stadium was packed. Only a few people wandered toward the parking lot. Our little group huddled outside the players' lounge. The others moved from foot to foot, smiling and patting each other on the backs. I stared at the setting sun as it dipped toward the rooftops. The sinking feeling in my gut grew worse.

Jared finally emerged wearing a sports shirt and jeans. He held his trophy in his right arm and his tennis bag slung over his left shoulder. A few reporters had hung around to get an interview, but Jared brushed passed them. They had also wanted to interview me, but I had begged off, saying that Jared was the man of the hour.

He strolled toward us with a proud smile. When our eyes met, as before, the smile melted. He turned and walked back to answer questions from reporters that he had already bypassed, making us wait another ten minutes. My stomach folded in on itself, knotting into a heavy solid mass. I had to do something, anything, to change our situation. If things kept going as they were, the pain would consume me. When Jared finally waved off the reporters and approached our group, I saw with suicidal clarity exactly what I must do. I looked him straight in the eye and said:

"I want to know just what the hell is going to kill that bug you have up your ass. Tell me what will make everything between us all right again."

"I already told you, but apparently you only hear what you want to hear."

Everyone stood around us, steeped in embarrassment.

"I quit," I said, failing to keep my voice matter-of-fact. I sounded reckless, and my hands trembled. Did he notice, I wondered?

He simply stared at me.

"If you're too damned good to be coached by a cripple, then you're too damned good, and that's fine. From now on, I'm coaching Connor, and you can go fuck yourself."

I could see his simmering hostilities were about to boil over, and the prospect of getting it all out both thrilled and terrified me. A stray nerve kept pulsing in my neck, reaching up to spread a tingling sensation over my skull, but he merely clamped his teeth together and walked past me, heading for the parking lot.

I'll give him one week, I thought, *one tournament*. We would go to Rome, and I would work with Connor. I would show him just how capable I was, desperately hoping that he would come back to me and that we would make things right again. At the end of the Rome tournament, I vowed, I would either have a lover, or I wouldn't.

CHAPTER 25

RESPLENDENT Rome—a silky blue dome vaulting over sun-baked piazzas, Bernini fountains, crumbling monuments, stone churches, a labyrinth of shop-lined streets.

I love Rome. Like San Francisco, it spreads over seven hills, but the similarity ends there. The architecture, climate, even the inhabitants' musical chatter whiffing down the narrow streets all have a different texture. Romans are charmingly unhurried; they lounge in piazzas, trundle down sleepy back streets, and take joy in simple things. They love drama and seem to over-emphasize everything just so they can make an eloquent show in the telling. This was Rome, its ancient beauty and expressive people, half enchanted isle and half tourist trap. It infused me with an intoxicating sense of adventure.

Emerging from the train, I saw two hundred fans pacing the platform. Someone shouted Connor's name, and they surged toward us, begging for autographs and throwing kisses. A handful of reporters were intent on rooting out the scoop of how a gay athlete felt playing in the Christian capital. Connor repeatedly exclaimed that he was not gay, but they shook their heads and asked the same question in a different way, as if Connor had not understood. Finally, a squad of police cut a swath through the fans and led us to waiting taxies.

We checked into separate rooms at The Ingleterre, a wonderful hideaway a few blocks from the Spanish Steps. The elevator was ancient and cranky and so small my chair filled it. I ascended alone while the others waited. The whole time I rode in that box, I feared getting stuck between floors and not be able to escape.

Later, I felt strange—lonely—sleeping by myself in an unfamiliar room, but that seemed a better alternative than tolerating Jared's condemnation.

Harman arranged for a van to pick us up. The driver maneuvered the narrow city streets with practiced ease, although he used his horn so often that I became rankled long before we arrived at the tournament site. I was sure my irritation had more to do with coaching Connor without Jared's help.

Connor, I was sure, felt the pressure as well. This would be his first tournament without playing doubles and without Jared's support. I made that decision for two reasons: to reduce his court time in an attempt to keep his legs fresh, and also to limit my involvement with Jared. Connor would have only Shar, Harman, Roy, and me in his corner.

In the players' cafeteria, the four of us ate fresh fruit and crusty bread and drank strong coffee while Harman went to arrange a practice court. Jared and Spencer sat three tables away gobbling down scrambled eggs and bacon with a mountain of fried potatoes and a tower of buttered toast. It was no secret where those extra pounds around Jared's middle had sprung from.

When Harman returned with our court assignment, we all trooped toward the door. As I passed Jared's table, I stopped next to Spencer, who had just stacked eggs and potatoes on a piece of toast and stuffed it into his mouth, giving him a chipmunk's bulging cheeks. I asked him to hit with Connor. He swallowed, a loud gulp, and shook his head. He explained that he had already agreed to hit with Jared, who had a court reservation for the same time slot. I smiled, told him no worries, and wheeled to the door.

All the way to the court, I searched the passers-by for a player or coach who could hit with Connor, but by the time we reached the court and Connor began his stretches, I had not seen a single one. Connor looked sideways at me as he stretched, somewhat nervously, and Roy stood at the courtside railing with a loud smirk cut across his face. While Connor performed his tai chi, I continued to scan the growing number of onlookers for a hitting partner to snare—still no one.

Connor opened his bag and removed a racket. I swallowed hard and asked him to pull one out for me. He shot me a look. A moment later, a grin fluttered across his lips. He handed me his racket and grabbed another, then loaded his pockets with balls. I laid the racket across my lap and wheeled onto the court, positioning myself at the service-line T. A murmur rose from the spectators.

"We'll take it slow and easy. Keep it in my hitting zone."

I wondered if Roy still wore that sneer, but I didn't dare look. Instead, I wiped the sweat off my forehead and swallowed the lump in my throat. Connor pulled a ball from his pocket and looped it over the net. I kept my eyes glued to the ball, trying to shift my clunky chair sideways with one arm while swinging my racket with the other. I completely missed the ball.

I stared at Connor. He nodded. I nodded back. He pulled another ball from his pocket and floated it into my hitting zone. I swung and missed again. I instantly realized how large a part the legs played in racket timing, and without legs, I had no timing. I hung my head, staring at the red dirt. Spectators mumbled. I decided to quit the farce, thinking Connor could work on his serve while I scrounged up someone to hit with him. I turned my head, knowing that I'd see Roy gloating, which I did.

More importantly, I saw Jared and Spencer striding down the sidewalk that led between the courts. They were about to pass. I whirled back to face Connor.

"Once more."

The ball looped over the net, bounced three feet in front of my chair, and soared into my zone. I had my racket back, and I swung up and through the ball, sending it back to Connor's forehand. He eased it back to me, and I hit it again.

"Keep it coming into my forehand so I don't have to move this damned chair."

We kept the rally going for twenty more balls, forehand to forehand, until I clipped the net and the ball dropped on my side.

"Okay," I said. "Backhand."

We had a thirty-ball rally on the backhand side until Connor sprayed the ball too wide. I smiled, thinking I was getting my timing down as long as I didn't have to move the chair.

We both moved behind the baseline and began another rally, hitting the ball deep and with more pace. After a half dozen rallies, I found that I could maneuver the chair a bit to adjust to a wider-hit ball, but it proved especially difficult, because my wheelchair was the run-of-the-mill hospital type and not designed to move over dirt. It was not only tedious, but so awkward that while leaning to hit a ball I tipped the chair over and tumbled out. Connor ran to help me.

I glanced at Roy. His smirk had vanished. Jared stood behind him, a statue. His mouth hung slightly ajar, and his eyes gleamed with mist. I sent Connor back across the net. I would not give up while Jared stood there. I felt him, felt his presence like an oncoming train.

I finally had a weapon to fight against his silence, one that made an impression, and I found that gratifying indeed. I had gone beyond words and shown him that I would not be stopped. With or without him, I would move on with my career.

Seeing me struggling to control that damned chair while hitting balls across the net moved his heart. I saw it in his misty eyes. I couldn't tell if he felt pity or respect or outright anger, and I frankly didn't care which. At that point, I just wanted desperately to make some kind of impression on that iceberg in his chest. I bet everything that I would win him back by pushing myself all the way, even if it meant making myself a target.

It became a good workout for Connor. He was motivated to show the others we were an effective team, so he honed his concentration in order to keep sending the ball directly into my zone, making it an exercise in precision ball control. He performed better than I could have hoped for.

As the morning passed, I began to move better, prepare faster, and feel the ball through the swing. My timing magically emerged, which allowed me to stay in the rallies longer and hit with more pace. As my control improved, I began feeding him combinations—a deep ball to the backhand followed by a short ball to bring him to the net for a put-away volley.

After two hours—a span in which I ate the dirt six more times—I hit the proverbial wall. Exhaustion let my old adversary, intense pain, grab hold and shake me until my bones rattled.

I wheeled to the sidelines and downed a fistful of painkillers. Connor trotted over. He had a healthy sweat glistening on his forehead. I hadn't given him the kind of intense warm-up I would have preferred, but that was a good thing considering his fragile legs. He had worked reasonably hard and seemed ready for his afternoon match.

He won that match convincingly, which demonstrated to me at least that, with practice, I could do the job. So fuck all those courtside spectators—Jared and Roy included—who had stared at me with pity in their eyes.

That night in my hotel room, one floor below Jared and up to my chin in hot water, I still felt a deeply satisfying glow—no doubt helped by Shar's comfort shot. I could lose the man I loved, but I was no longer useless. I could make a difference in someone's life, if only my own.

Later, I lay in bed trying to imagine Jared sprawled on top of me, and that was what I saw as I slipped into sleep.

THE next morning, Connor and I were on court, working on tactics specifically geared to beat Jared. Connor was on the opposite side of the draw from Jared, and assuming that they both continued to win, which I did, they would meet in the final. It's always dangerous to look ahead, but I wanted Connor fully prepared and confident if he faced Jared on championship Sunday. It felt treasonous pulling out all the stops in order to crush the man I loved, but I felt that was the only way to get him back on my terms, to show him I could do the job.

I didn't line up a hitting partner for our first hour on court. I wanted to feed him balls myself while we worked on a different tactic that would give Jared fits—Throw Sand in the Eyes, Sail over the Charging Tiger, Cut off a Wing.

No one knew Jared's tendencies better than me, which meant that no one knew how to exploit his weakness as fully as I did. And I found that with more practice, I was capable of showing Connor these tactics.

I was, admittedly, being selfish—gambling on Connor's chances in the tournament in order to prove I could be an effective practice partner. In my defense, I had arranged a hitting partner for the second hour of practice so that Connor could hone what he and I worked on with someone more capable. The more we worked, the more adept I became at directing the ball and the more my confidence grew. But when forced to lean for a ball, I continued to tip the chair over and tumble out. After the last tumble of the day, I looked over at the courtside spectators and saw Karl Diefenbach glaring at me.

Connor ran to help me back into the chair, and I told him to hit some serves while we waited for the practice partner to arrive. He gathered some balls as I wheeled over to where Diefenbach stood. I was covered in sweat, panting heavily, and dusted with red clay. He, of course, looked flawless. Even in the Roman heat, his navy-blue suit looked pristine, as did the scarlet handkerchief in his breast pocket, giving him a hint of flair.

"You're really quite mad," he said. "You must have some kind of death wish."

"Just trying to do my job, like all the other coaches."

"You've managed to pull one over on me, but I can assure you, it won't happen again. For your own safety, I will prevent Jared from playing another tournament."

"I wish the hell you'd stop looking out for us."

"Somebody has to protect you. It seems you're incapable of doing it yourself."

"If that were really your intention, you'd increase security for all the players. But you're not doing that, are you? You're focusing on us, which smells suspiciously like discrimination."

"I don't want to see anybody hurt, and I certainly don't want our sport damaged either. And off the record, lying your way into this tournament has only made you a very powerful enemy."

"Like I didn't know that already? The question is, what's changed?"

He strolled off with majestic, confident strides. I scanned the spectators for the twentieth time that morning. A Japanese couple in matching straw hats, thirty or forty gay men, a man wearing a polo shirt and chinos who I assumed was reporter because he was constantly writing in a notebook. Everyone looked harmless, but in a society of religion-bred hatred, you never knew.

TWO days later, Connor showed up on court looking like he was expecting to receive a spinal tap. His energy levels were low, and his mood was down the toilet, which was strange, considering he was winning his matches. I tried to pump him up with encouraging remarks, but they had no effect. Ten minutes into the warm-up, and I knew we were wasting our time. Whatever the problem, we needed to get him over it, and quick. I called him to the net.

"Connor, what's wrong?"

"Talk about a non sequitur."

"This is ridiculous. You're going to tell me what's eating you before we hit another ball."

His eyes dropped, and he seemed to study his shoelaces.

"Connor?"

"That bitch is seeing someone else," he hissed.

Yes, I thought, not surprised. I had seen her dwindling interest in Connor, her wandering eyes. She was clearly impressed by European men. But it hadn't really registered until he pointed it out.

"Shar?" I said, rather stupidly. "Are you sure?"

"Sure enough."

"So you haven't actually seen her with anyone?"

"I can smell him on her."

"What will you do?"

"I'm going to drop that fucking slut like third period Spanish. I mean, fuck, she's the one who needs me, not the other way around."

I couldn't help but grin. "Right, and you're this upset because she means nothing to you."

"I'm gonna punch her teeth down her fucking throat."

"Okay, look at it from another angle. On Monday, we leave Rome, and she'll leave whoever it is behind. As long as she comes back to you, is it really that huge an obstacle? And suppose you win this tournament? You know, show her you're still a champion. That would go a long way to make you more attractive than this other schmuck." *Or girl*, I thought but didn't actually say.

He nodded, reached across the net, and laid his hand on my shoulder. "Looks like you and I are in the same boat, only for different reasons."

"Right. And the best outcome for both of us will come when we win this damned championship. That will get them both back on our terms. So let's get to work. Okay?"

"Okay," he said with a slight grin.

AS EXPECTED, both Connor and Jared won their matches right through the semifinals, beating all the big guns along the way: Drake, Lamas, Gardener, Montoya, and McEwan. It was six days of the hardest work I had ever done, and if someone had told me a month had elapsed, I would easily have believed them.

A keen wind blew in on Final Sunday, and I knew it would give both players fits. Connor and I hit the practice court early to review our tactics under the blustery conditions. I didn't arrange a hitting partner that day, because I wanted Connor to have an easy workout, to keep his legs fresh for the final.

We worked for thirty minutes before I noticed Connor checking his watch. Nothing registered until I saw him do it again and again. *He's worried about Shar cheating on him*, I thought. I wheeled to the sidelines and grabbed a bottle of water. When he jogged over, I asked him why his mind wasn't on the warm-up.

Without answering, his head jerked up, and he looked past me. A grin lifted the corner of his lips. I heard a voice behind me, Jared's voice, sharp and cutting like a scalpel.

"So this is it?"

I swiveled around and glared at him. It was the first display of anger I'd seen from him all week, and I was taken aback, not quite knowing how to respond.

"You're not backing down? You're going to train my opponents to beat me, no matter what?"

"It seems so," I managed to respond with an unsteady voice.

His chin trembled. I couldn't tell if he was angry or fighting back tears. My plan had worked, to a degree. All week the pressure had grown until, hours before the final, he erupted. "You really think you can sit in that fucking chair and teach pro-level tennis?"

Something solid and heavy lodged in my chest, and I didn't trust myself to answer, so I simply shrugged my shoulders, trying to seem as nonchalant as possible.

Long, silent seconds ticked by. People around us looked away, as if steeped in sudden embarrassment, yet Connor grinned like a Cheshire cat. I could hear rock music coming from the stadium sound system. It was Tina Turner singing, "What's Love Got To Do With It."

"Because if that's what you think, you damned well better think again. I'm not about to let you train my opponents in that crummy chair."

My eyes watered. I wanted to scream at him, scream anything. I opened my mouth, but no sound came out. Then something peculiar happened: he smiled. It was that same comical smile that I saw as we were falling together at the shooting.

He stepped sideways, and I realized that he had been blocking my view of a wheelchair, a sporty model specifically designed for playing tennis. It had a lightweight titanium frame and thick wheels that were narrow at the hips and flared outwards so they didn't get in the way of swinging arms, and they gave a wide stance so that even I couldn't tip it over. Its front wheels were tiny and built for quick maneuvering. It had a seatbelt to keep me from falling out no matter how far I leaned for a ball. Wrapped around the stubby backrest was a canary yellow ribbon with a huge bow, and a note was pinned to it that read, "We Love You."

"You need a better chair if you intend to keep coaching," Jared said. His voice broke, and I knew he had choked up, probably crying, but I couldn't take my eyes off the chair to see. It was the most amazingly beautiful thing I'd ever seen—excluding Jared, of course. My head went numb. I literally couldn't form a single thought. I could only stare dumbly at that magnificent chair.

Spencer ran over, leaned down, and hugged me. "Ready?"

That heavy thing lodged in my chest suddenly quadrupled in size. I looked up into his beaming face and nodded. He pushed me toward it, and as he did, he told me how Jared had searched everywhere in Rome, but couldn't find one, so he had this one flown in from London. It was top of the line.

As he pushed me next to the chair, Jared leaned down to help. I threw my arms around his neck and hugged as he lifted me. We stood like that, nailed together, squeezing the life out of each other while merging into one being again. The crowd began to clap. Most weren't sure what was going on, but it didn't matter.

"I love you," I croaked.

"I know. Don't ever leave me again."

I nodded my head against his shoulder and turned to dry my eyes with my sleeve. Spencer ripped the ribbon from my new chair, and Jared lowered me onto the seat. It felt like riding on the back of a Tomahawk missile. Spencer handed me my racket and gave me a push. My chair whispered onto the court, gliding like a dream.

Connor hit a ball toward me, and I was on it in a flash. The chair seemed to respond on its own. After five minutes, it had become a part of me, and I couldn't fathom how I'd ever managed to play in my old chair. Jared stepped onto the court and began hitting balls. He hit just out of my reach so that I had to scramble to reach each ball. It was fun, as fun as any other time I had played tennis when I had legs.

Once again, I played the game I loved with the man I loved—the movement, the feel of the ball on my racket, the sound of the ball being struck, the hustle to get into position for the next ball—it was a ballet, albeit a little slower paced than before, but equally as enjoyable.

But I caught myself. Here we were only hours before the big final, and we were goofing off. *Time to get back to work*, I thought, *to ensure they both get a proper warm-up*. I opened up my heart, put this new joy inside a treasure chest, and closed the lid. I became the Parris Island drill sergeant once again.

As I barked out orders, Jared and Connor gave each other sideways glances while trying to suppress their smiles. I sailed off the court and let them warm each other up, as we had always done. They responded enthusiastically, and a surge of excitement ran through all of us, like an electric current flowing through metal rods all linked together. Even Roy, Shar, Harman, and Spencer felt it.

It was more than preparing for the final. It was being a team again, like having all the right numbers pop up together on the winning lottery ticket.

AS MY players showered and changed, the rest of us made our way into the stadium. I was reluctant to leave my shiny new chair, but I wanted a ringside seat, so Harman and Spencer carried me down the steps to the coach's box. We all crammed together and watched the stadium fill to capacity.

The gay men came out in force. One group waved rainbow flags and camped it up for the television cameras. Their pride at having one of their own in a final was contagious.

The players emerged to a thunderous ovation. Jared wore all white except for his red bandana and his war paint. Connor sauntered across the court with the embroidered dragon shimmering down his back. They were both intimidating and ravishing. At the net, waiting for the coin toss, Jared bounced on the balls of his feet like a prizefighter ready to brawl. One look at Connor's face showed that he got the message loud and clear.

I hardly took a breath during the warm-up. By the time the match began, I felt dizzy, on the brink of fainting. I made myself breathe as I watched Connor execute our game plan flawlessly. He broke Jared in the first game and never looked back. Even though Jared played well, controlled the points and fought hard, he didn't win a game in the first set.

In the second set, I watched Jared lose another game, and my heart sank. His wheels were turning, trying to figure a way to turn things around, but I knew he couldn't do it as long as Connor stuck to our game plan. Jared couldn't blast his way through this match. He could only hope that Connor would lose his concentration, which was possible but unlikely. *Not this time*, I thought. I had prepared him too well.

Therein lay the rub, the turning knife in my gut. Jared needed to win this match in order to earn an automatic entry into the French Open, the one thing in the world beyond me that mattered to him, and in my selfish bid to get him back, I had effectively robbed him of the opportunity. And with Diefenbach resolved to derail him, this could very well be his only opportunity ever. My mouth went dry, and I became nauseated, feeling like a traitor as I watched him lose game after game.

Would he blame me? It didn't matter: I blamed myself. My head sank until my chin rested on my chest.

Jared won a game, then another, but Connor held serve to go up 5-2. That's when it happened: a miracle. At least I thought it was a miracle at the time. As Jared served to stay in the match, Connor's right leg cramped up as tight as a steel rod. The combination of all his hard running and the stress of being so close to winning broke down his fragile legs. He limped to the chair and called for a medical time-out. The trainer gave him pills, water, a leg rub. The match continued with Connor still limping. He couldn't really move, at least not like he needed to.

Jared seized control, easily winning the next three games to even the second set at 5-5. Connor's other leg cramped, and it was back to the trainer. During the first cramp, I had wondered if Connor was throwing the match to ensure Jared qualified for the French, but I now saw the agony etched across his face. The cramping was real, and it was costing him the set, but there was a slim chance that he could work through the pain in the third set and still win.

That was when it hit me. This was no accident. Once Jared had figured out that he couldn't overpower Connor, he began to run Connor side to side, front to back, run, slide, run, slide, run, run, run. He had known how to exploit Connor's weakness just as well as Connor knew how to exploit his. As understanding blossomed into admiration, I heard the chair umpire announce that Connor had withdrawn due to severe cramping.

Everyone in our players' box floundered in a jumble of emotions. Jared walked over to shake hands, but instead he bent and they hugged for a long, emotional few moments. The spectators cheered. I told myself to be happy. Both my players would play the French, and both had a legitimate shot at winning.

Jared had ridden a seventeen-match winning streak that earned him two tier-two and one tier-one titles. That pushed him into the upper echelons of the game. He was now seeded sixty-fourth in the world. By ATP rules, they were required to let him play the French. We couldn't play the Madrid Open because the draws were already set, but we would play the French. Jared had beaten the game's top players, and in doing so, had beaten Diefenbach and the other bureaucrats as well.

OUR last day in Rome, a Monday, we wandered down ancient streets, sightseeing. Jared and I were anxious to see Michelangelo's Moses, the

Vatican, the Sistine Chapel, and the handful of Caravaggio paintings that hung in churches sprinkled across the city.

On our way to the Vatican, we sailed across a scorching piazza that boasted a Bernini fountain ringed with outdoor cafés and colorful umbrellas to protect their patrons from Sol's heat. There were only a handful of people in the piazza: a lesbian couple strolling with their arms around each other, two young children pulling at the arms of an old man while begging him to hurry, and a group of Korean tourists snapping pictures in front of the fountain.

Uncle Harman finally pulled his eyes from his Frommer's Guide and pointed to the crumbling baroque church that towered above the other gray stone buildings. "That church has a Caravaggio, the Madonna dei Pellegrini."

"I'm game," I said.

"I'm for getting a gelato while you check out Madonna what's-her-name," Connor said.

The others opted for a café. They trooped to the closest umbrellas and huddled around two shaded tables. Only Jared nodded at the church. He pulled me up the stone steps backwards, and we passed into the sanctuary's cool twilight.

That time of the morning, there were few worshipers in the pews. One gray-haired woman, on her knees and dressed in black. She bowed over a prie-dieu and performed her devotions at the first chapel on the left. Two chapels away stood twelve tourists gazing at the Madonna dei Pellegrini. Four spotlights illuminated the painting, and the tourists reminded me of apostles gathered around a shimmering Jesus ascending to heaven.

Jared wheeled me across the cracked mosaic floor as I absorbed the splendor of the imposing domed ceiling supported by massive columns. At the front altar, an ornately vested priest lit candles, and beside him, a cloud of incense billowed up and dissipated through the cavernous cathedral, giving the air a sweet, sacrificial odor.

The cluster of tourists retreated a few steps so that Jared could wheel me to the front of the chapel for an unobstructed view.

I gazed up at the painting with the same rapture as I'd seen on their faces. The standing Madonna held an overly large child in her arms while two elderly peasants bowed at her feet. The detail was awesome, right down to the dirt on the peasants' toenails. Caravaggio's masterful use of light gave the picture a realism that drew me into the scene, as if I were kneeling beside the peasants. I could almost smell the musty odor of the Madonna's robes.

The spotlights suddenly shut off, and the chapel fell into darkness. The lights were controlled by a meter at the side of the chapel that must be fed coins to keep the lights on. I sat in the dark, waiting to see who would feed the meter. Neither Jared nor I had any coins, so we watched in disappointment as the entire group of tourists marched away, leaving us to the cool dim.

We waited, hoping others would come to feed the meter. Jared knelt beside me and took my hand. Minutes passed. The coolness felt wonderful, and somewhere behind the altar, a boys' choir began a Gregorian chant. Their high-pitched harmony filled the cathedral and fused with the incense-laced air. Over the voices, I heard Jared utter a deep sigh.

"In Florida, I should have backed down," he said, his voice scarcely a whisper. "I put you in that chair."

"Honey, it wasn't your fault."

"I wouldn't blame you if you hated my guts."

"You've got to let go of this guilt."

"That's the reason I tried to send you home. I couldn't stand seeing you in that chair, knowing I put you there. I died every time you looked at me."

His voice broke with emotion. I knew he had to talk, get it out, work past it. The pressure had built to the point where it had to spill over. There in the darkness, I let him tell it all: the pain, the fear, the guilt. It surged out.

"I'm so ashamed. I wanted to lock you away because I couldn't stand seeing you like this. And then when I saw you tumbling over on court, over and over, not giving up, I realized how strong you are, stronger than I'll ever be, and pitying you was a waste of time."

I pulled him closer, pressing my face into the soft curve where his neck merged with his shoulder blade. We held each other in the dim stillness until I heard footsteps approach, the *clunk, clunk* of coins dropping into the meter. The chapel blazed with light again. I glanced at Jared's face. Two wet trails streaked his cheeks. We gazed up at the Madonna holding her baby.

I wanted to tell him it was okay, but I knew that words could not heal his torment. He needed to work it out himself, internally. He would. I was sure of it.

We both would, together.

CHAPTER 26

DIEFENBACH did stop Jared from playing the Madrid Open, which unwittingly turned into a boon. Jared had been peaking nonstop for four weeks and, although he seemed fit, his leaden eyes revealed his exhaustion. The physical demands of daily clay court matches coupled with our off-court emotional battle had taken a toll.

Connor could play, but I decided to pull him out to give his legs a rest. Not playing the Open would give them a two-week breather, ensuring they would be fresh for the French.

I kept wondering how Jared would play at the French Open. He had carried that load of guilt inside of him, and it had created a blinding rage that had spurred him on to become a top player, using his self-hate to crush his opponents. But now that he had talked it out, he seemed to have purged that rage. Could he still play with the same intensity? I was dying to know, but I wouldn't find out until he played again.

We flew to Spain for our respite. During those weeks off, I planned to work my boys only enough to keep them sharp. We would drill at about sixty-five percent of their normal practice and play level, keeping them honed but also allowing them to recuperate with plenty of good food and leisure.

Harman, efficient as always, found a villa for hire seventy-five miles northeast of Barcelona. It dominated a bluff covered with olive trees and overlooked the Mediterranean. The stately blue and white house was built solid to withstand the winter storms that pounded onto shore. It had a lovely red-carpeted staircase floating upward in swan-like curves. There were sixteen high-ceilinged rooms, each with a view of the water. The floors were made of honey-colored oak. Although each room had electricity, they used oil lamps to light the rooms, which gave the place a dreamy glow. And best of all, it had two clay courts just up from a white-sand beach.

To get to the Villa Baraka, we drove through the nearest town, Palamos—a colorful community at the edge of the sea. From a distance, the village roofs resembled a rust-colored cape spread on the shore between olive orchards and silvery-blue grape arbors terracing the hillsides.

We arrived in the early evening, driving a Volkswagen van with tinted windows, and were ushered into the Villa Baraka via the front door, passing through a spacious hall that led to a drawing room. A large oval table dominated the center of the room, and armchairs and sofas upholstered in silk, with that sepia color silk takes on with age, were grouped around the walls. A large and lovely landscape hung over one sofa, its massive gilt frame glowing softly in the low light. The room smelled the way I imagined a Turkish bazaar must smell: incense, dust, burnt charcoal, and wood (cedar? mahogany?) and underlying it all, the sweet scent of cut flowers slowly decomposing.

We were received by a flatteringly courteous Baroness von Friedemann. The Baroness, in her mid-nineties and weighing no more than a handful of feathers, wore British tweeds, a double strand of lustrous pearls, and, over her ashen-silver head, a colorful lilac scarf that seemed as sheer and frail as her body. She spoke with an Austrian accent and was still handsome at her advanced age: high cheekbones, paper-fine translucent skin, and lips that looked like carved ivory. Time had fashioned her face into a benevolent mask, reducing it to an essence, as a grape becomes a raisin. Her pale gray eyes captured my attention, intelligent, proud, and hard as cut diamonds.

"Welcome," she said, "to the Villa Baraka. Did you have a pleasant journey?"

"Pleasant enough," Roy Lin said.

"Did you fly or come by ship?"

"We flew," Roy continued. "A good flight." For Roy, that meant a short flight.

"You must be famished. There is plenty to eat, and you have time to freshen up before dinner."

The estate had no butler but rather a reedy twenty-year-old, obsequiously obliging houseboy named Alma, who had emigrated from Tangiers. His lean face was the color of lightly creamed coffee, and his eyes vaguely recalled the Moorish conquerors. He dressed in Arabian style robes of white linen, with a headcloth held in place by what I later learned was a ring made from camel skin. He wore no shoes, which allowed him to move about the house as silently as a sea breeze.

We had the Villa Baraka and the beach to ourselves, and if we wanted some nightlife, Palamos was a forty-minute stroll down the road.

We arrived well past our normal dinner hour, but the Spanish tend to eat late, so we had time to retire to our rooms before dinner. Each couple had their own bedroom, including Spencer and Harman, who shared the small corner room at the end of the hall. Our room was airy, with a huge four-poster cherry-wood bed, bare oak floors, and two French doors that opened onto a balcony that overlooked the Mediterranean.

Since the guest bedrooms were upstairs, Jared carried me to our room. Alma deposited our bags inside the doorway. He moved to the dresser and lit an oil lamp. Orange-yellow light flickered on the walls. He smiled and bowed as he closed the bedroom door on his way out.

I instantly loved our room's rustic beauty. Jared eased me onto the bed and flung the French doors wide open. The salt-misty breeze flowed in to mingle with the scent of white roses standing in a vase on the chest of drawers.

Jared moved around the room, studying every detail. My eyes followed him, loving his inner calm, his manliness, his strength. He turned to go downstairs and bring up my wheelchair, but I reached out and grabbed his arm, pulling him onto the bed.

"Leave it," I said. "Up here is just you and me. No chair. No reporters. No tennis. No reminders."

He grinned and began to unbutton my shirt. He must have noticed the pain spreading across my face, because he left the bed long enough to pull my morphine kit from my bag and prepare a comfort shot. I reached for the syringe, but he said, "No." He wanted to do it.

We slowly undressed each other as my pain retreated. He pulled the green bedspread back, and we slipped between cool Egyptian cotton sheets. We made love while the sea breeze washed over us.

The dinner bell rang. We ignored it.

Most times, after we had made love, we would lie in each others' arms to enjoy the aftermath, but this time, we had no sooner finished than Jared jumped off the bed and found two cotton robes hanging in the wardrobe. He tossed one to me, donned the other, and, scooping me into his arms, carried me out the door, along the hall, and down the back stairs. I held onto his neck as we crossed the garden and headed for the beach.

The evening sky had turned a pure shade of purple. The stars had not yet appeared, and in the distance, we saw men from the town gathered around their boats to prepare the nets. A few minutes later, they hauled their boats into the surf and glided across the water, leaving a green trail of phosphorescent light. The same light inflamed the surf and made the night seem magical.

We sat at the water's edge. He untied the knots holding our robes, and they fell away. Lifting me in his arms again, we dashed into the boiling surf, diving into an oncoming wave of green light. We swam underwater until we found a warm pocket in the cool water. Breaking the surface, we floated lazily in the shallows.

After months of being trapped in a hospital bed and that chair, a prisoner without legs, I was suddenly and magically set free to frolic. I glided through that liquid environment. My arms were all I needed to swim like a seal pup. Deliciously liberated, I became Baryshnikov performing impromptu leaps, plunges, and pirouettes.

The sea felt like a thousand silky fingers caressing my nakedness. Jared playfully splashed a handful of water in my face. The air shattered with brilliant phosphorescent light. We tumbled about in luminescence, were covered with it, radiated it. Seduced by the splendor of it all—this freedom, a lavender sky, swimming naked with Jared—I began to tremble.

Jared came from behind, pulling me into that hollow space between his arms. The cool surf swirled over my skin and mixed with the heat from his body, igniting an inferno inside me. I spun around, and we kissed. I lost myself in that kiss, became nothing but lips touching lips and the frantic beating of the universe—or was it only my heart?

He carried me to the beach and laid me on the sand, smothering me with more kisses. I merged with the sand under me and his stone hard body over me while luminescent water swirled over us. It all coalesced into a sensation of ferocious love. The weight of the sky, the sea, the universe pressed from all sides, crushing us together with such agonizing ecstasy that nothing but our hunger for each other survived.

Later, as the tide rushed out, we lay with limbs interlocked, listening. The sea's roar held a unique quality. It had a density that squeezed my eardrums, as if I drifted a hundred feet under the surface of the water.

Jared said, "We should live like this all the time."

"You're insane. Life would be too glorious."

"Let's do it. I mean it. After the French we'll move to Spain, somewhere along the coast. We'll get Spanish citizenship and marry."

I nuzzled my face into his shoulder. In a world where most people, gay and straight, were not getting married, but rather becoming partners—as if being a committed couple were a ballroom dance competition or some risky business venture—here was a man who wanted to marry me, who wanted to say, "Until death do us part."

"You really are insane," I whispered.

"Why shouldn't we? It's what I want."

I smiled into his shoulder. *Yes*, I thought, *I want it too.*

Clouds had rolled across the sky, and rain began to fall. Jared scooped me in his arms again and carried me further up the beach. We leaned our heads back and let the rain pelt our faces. We kissed and kissed until I began to shiver. I'd never felt so deliriously happy as being held in his arms with the cool rain falling on us.

"After the French," he whispered in my ear, and I kissed him again. We donned our robes, and he carried me back to the villa, up the stairs, and down the hall to the marble bathroom. He filled the tub and got in with me. We horsed around like boys in the first blush of puppy love.

"God, how I missed you," he said, rinsing the lather from my hair.

AFTER drying me off, we wrapped ourselves in bath towels, and he carried me back to the bed. I lay on my side, propped on one elbow, running my free hand up and down his smooth flank. After a few minutes, I had him flexing and squirming on the cool sheets.

He leaned his head back and laughed. I pressed into his body. We rolled this way and that, tangling in the sheets. He turned serious, and we made love again—fragilely, with obscene tenderness. We prolonged the buildup until it hurt. The whole universe turned frantic. I remember with an appalling clarity the weight of his driving body, his consuming heat, my gasping for breath, and his animal-like grunts echoing in my head as we climaxed together.

Around midnight, a scratch sounded at the door, hardly noticeable. I thought it might be a mouse. The door swung open and there stood Alma, holding a tray crowned with fine-cut crystal glasses filled with mint tea, bowls of bean soup, and a loaf of crusty bread. He carried it to the table on our balcony and told us with an impish smile that he had also delivered dinner to Harman and Spencer, who had also ignored the dinner bell.

We thanked him, and he bowed, turning a shade of scarlet I could see even by the lamplight. He started to say more but stopped. Jared and I smiled at each other in the embarrassed pause that followed, and Alma quickly left, closing the door as silently as he had opened it.

The rainclouds had blown over. Jared carried me to the balcony to enjoy our dinner by the moonlight. He sat me near the railing and caressed the back of my neck with one hand while sipping his drink with the other. The tea was hot and fragrant and opened up my head so that I seemed to breathe easier than ever before.

A light on the ground floor room caught my eye, and I turned my head to see a bare-chested Alma standing beside the Baroness, who sat in a chair by the window. She was dressed in her sleeping gown and looked as if she were already dreaming. I nudged Jared, and we both watched Alma open a small paper container on the table next to her chair. The container had a cut of white powder inside. Beside it he placed a spoon, a lighter, and a hypodermic needle.

We both froze, too surprised for words. The Baroness turned her head, and her eyes fixed on the powder. Alma expertly melted down the solution in the spoon, filled the hypodermic. Gently, he hunted for a usable vein in her arm and gave her the injection.

She laid her head back, eyes closed, her face clouded over with a relaxed and easy pleasure. Alma moved behind the chair, but now he held a brush in his hand. He pulled the pins holding her hair, and the silver mass fell about her shoulders. Ever so gently, he teased out the tangles from her long strands until it spread like a wave of silk across her thin shoulders. As he brushed, his lips moved as if he were absentmindedly counting each stroke to himself.

I felt an immediate bond with this ancient lady. The fact that we both required our comfort shots to face this world of pain made me love her in a sisterly way. I also wondered if her white powder held more comfort than my vial of morphine.

Well after midnight, with dinner a pleasant memory and the breeze becoming chilly, we heard Connor and Shar's voices echoing through the wall, harsh, with abrupt accusations and retaliations.

There was a moment of silence followed by a bang that must have been their heavy wooden door slamming. I snuggled closer to Jared, and he kissed me. I knew we were feeling the same sense of gratitude for having overcome our fight.

I wondered what it was that bound us together, this thing we call love. I had no words for it, no way to define it or even understand it. It was simply some desperate yet fragile force that had grabbed hold of us and would not let go.

I closed my eyes and let sleep take me, still wondering what it could be and whether it would still be there in the morning.

CHAPTER 27

SUNRISE cast orange rays across our bed. I woke to the feel of warmth on my face and Jared stroking my bullet wounds. His touch left a queer sensation on my damaged flesh. I winced when I turned toward him, and he hurried to give me my morning comfort shot. As the pain receded, he nuzzled his face to my wounds, kissing my scars one after the other. Warmth flowed from my center into him like a mountain stream tumbling to the sea.

We made love again.

In the tender aftermath came another scratch on the door. Before we could cover ourselves, Alma flung open the door and breezed into the room carrying a full breakfast tray. He stopped dead in his tracks, eyes growing large and his mouth forming a perfectly round "O." His confusion was evident as he struggled to decide if he should back out or proceed.

"Would you leave that on the terrace, please?" Jared said.

Alma dropped his head, staring wide-eyed at the tray, and shuffled to the table on our balcony. His eyes never left the floor as he scurried back across the bedroom. The door made a whooshing sound as it closed.

We burst with laughter, peals of it. When our mirth ebbed into calm smiles, we donned our robes and Jared carried me onto the terrace. We sat at the table with me on his lap.

"Are you going to spoon feed me too?" I took his ear in my teeth and bit down hard enough to get his full attention.

"If that's what you want. This morning you get the royal treatment, whatever it takes to make you happy."

"I'm already happy."

"Happier."

"Impossible."

"Is that a challenge?"

I rested my chin on his shoulder and glanced across the garden, past the glass conservatory to the long, golden beach and the sea beyond. The water shone a bright blue all the way to the point where it merged with the sky.

On the beach, Shar led Connor and Spencer in their morning workout, running at a brisk pace on wet sand. I knew that Jared should join them, but I was not willing to let go of him, not yet.

On the other side of the garden, opposite the conservatory, a barefoot woman dressed in a patched-together grey dress rocked on the stoop outside the kitchen door. She hummed a perky tune while plucking a fryer; the feathers lazily floated from her hand like smoke on the wind. She looked to be in her early twenties and built like a wrestler. Her face had a dark brow with rosy cheeks and rosier lips, and her raven-black hair cascaded down her back like a waterfall. Later, we learned that she was Sara Domingo Sanchez, our cook.

We feasted on poached eggs on toast, yogurt, and a variety of sweet rolls, washing it all down with rich coffee and fresh-squeezed orange juice. Both the breakfast and the setting were so delicious that neither Jared nor I wanted it to stop, but by nine o'clock, Shar appeared at our door for my therapy session. Jared crawled into tennis clothes and joined Connor and Spencer on the tennis courts while Shar worked on my muscles. An hour later, we joined the boys on the courts.

Connor was quiet and sulking, while Spencer outshone the morning sky. I wasn't sure when he and Harman had become lovers again, but the fact of it made me glow.

My goal for our two-week retreat was to find a way for Connor to win points without his legs taking such a beating. For me, that meant shortening the points by coming to the net and with better footwork. All the great clay courters slide into their shots. That allows them to work less, because they take fewer steps to the ball, and it also allows them to recover with minimal effort.

The other thing clay courters do is stay behind the baseline, because coming to the net on clay is a sure ticket to be passed. That's true if the approach shots and volleys are deep, but if you chip a short-angle or a drop shot, it's a smart play and ends the point quickly. So I planned to focus on sharpening their skills of sliding, drop shots, short-angle chips and volleys.

We worked moderately hard until noon. Connor and Jared were already becoming somewhat comfortable sliding into their shots, so we spent more time perfecting their drop shots. Jared was all business, as usual, but Connor continued his sullen preoccupation. I guessed his moodiness had something to do with the shouts rumbling through the wall the night before. Spencer tried to cheer him up and keep him focused, which didn't help.

From noon until teatime, the hottest time of day, the Villa Baraka experienced what Truman Capote once called "white midnight." Everybody moved inside, the shutters were drawn, and a drowsy sleep stalked us all as we retreated from the sun.

In the hushed mid-day, there was only the pale sunlight peeking through the shutters and the unbroken heat. I laid atop cotton sheets, stroking Jared's sweat-moistened body, the windows open to the sea, watching the waves march toward us, relentless, like ticks of a clock counting down the time until the villa came to life again.

Spencer used the hot siesta hours to work online, bent over Harman's laptop to manage Jared and Connor's websites and respond to fan emails. The hate email had greatly diminished since coming to Europe. The European gay men had become aware of us and were lavish in their support. We received invitations from all over France, Italy, and Germany to stay at gay-owned guesthouses, enjoy free meals at restaurants, even people offering to put us up in their homes. Some admiring fans suggested we get to know them intimately, while a number of long-term couples applauded our monogamy and what we were doing for professional sports in general.

At five p.m. sharp, the Baroness presided over high tea in the conservatory. Her ashen-silver hair was gathered into a tight bun behind her narrow head and was held in place with two chopsticks. That, combined with her Kimono-like, peach-colored dressing gown, gave the impression of an eighteenth century Japanese geisha. Her double strand of pearls, each one as large as a marble, completed the impression. She was never without them, her pearls, and she often absentmindedly twisted the strands around two fingers as she spoke.

The French windows let the afternoon sunlight pour through in amber-gold waves. A huge oak table dominated one end of the room, and at the other stood a polished, ebony grand piano.

Everyone sat side by side on antique sofas and love seats, looking rather awkward, while the Baroness arranged flowers and Alma set an elaborate array of refreshments on the table: silver teapot and strainer, delicate bone china, crystal champagne flutes, tongs for the sugar cubes, embroidered napkins. It was a grand treat for me, and I could tell from the sparkle in her eyes that the Baroness enjoyed it more than any of us.

We began with icy bottles of Bollinger champagne accompanied with cucumber sandwiches, toasted baguette with pâté, oysters, and strawberries from the garden. The Baroness ate nothing.

"I never eat," she told us. "Never."

She sipped from a flute, seeming to exist only on the sea air and champagne as she presided over the conversation as a conductor directs an orchestra.

She clearly enjoyed talking, but never about herself, which shrouded her in ambiguity. She talked about her villa, every aspect of it, as if it were a lover that dominated her thoughts. "The Villa Baraka," she said, "the name comes from Africa, like so many wonderful things in Spain. It means 'house of blessings'." She went on to give us a detailed history of the house and the surrounding area. As she began to tell us about Alma, her voice dropped to a husky soprano, and her lips twisted into a sideways smile.

"Ah, well, Alma, he came from Africa," she said, as if that explained much. "He responded to an advertisement I placed for a cook, but after a single meal, I knew he was an imposter. When confronted, he confessed that he was on the run from his family, who were forcing him into a marriage with someone he detested. He was desperate not to go back home. Well, there I was." She waited for a comment, and when none came, she said, "How could I have turned him out? I made him the housekeeper, and he seems to have a talent for it. He has many talents." Her smile widened, and Jared and I exchanged amused glances.

She turned to me. "You are lucky to live in America. Ah, New York. It is delicious. The parties, the opera, Broadway. It is the center of the world: lunches on Park Avenue, dinner at Radio City, and champagne, champagne. Everyone was so gracious, so kind. The doctors said I could not stand the excitement at my age, but what do those fools know?" She lifted her flute with her brown, bony hand and sipped while the mantel clock chimed.

"Speaking of excitement," she said. "I suppose you will all want to taste the nightlife of our humble town. The nightclubs are not particularly innocent, and I am sure you can find whatever interests you. They go from dark to dawn, which is not surprising, considering that the townspeople nap all afternoon and no one dines before ten. There are a number of excellent eating establishments around the main square, which truly is the heart of the town. Anywhere else, and you eat at your own risk." She thought for a moment before adding, "The marketplace is a wondrous place to browse, but be forewarned, these locals have great pride and are not afraid of strangers. If you question the freshness of the fish, the sweetness of the figs, or the ripeness of the olives, you risk a loud and heated scolding." She smiled and glanced around the room. "These Spaniards intimidate me so."

After tea, Jared played piano, Schubert, at the Baroness's request. He played poorly, with many sour notes, which was not surprising after so long an absence from his own keyboard. As he played, the breeze flowing through the open windows became stronger.

The Baroness turned to me and said, "We call this wind the Levanter. The Moors used it to sail here from the eastern end of the Mediterranean."

As the wind strengthened, the force of it brushed my face. The wind that brought the Moors to these shores also brought the smell of the desert across the water from Africa. I closed my eyes and took a deep breath, envisioning veiled women in the Kasbah with the mountains on the horizon. This wind that once carried men in search of gold and adventure teased me with its promise of freedom.

But it was an empty promise. I remained imprisoned in my chair. I noticed the Baroness scrutinizing me and felt myself blush.

"You are caught up in the world's most hideous lie," she said out of the blue. Her face wore an expression of mockery, and I wondered if she were pulling my leg.

"And what would that be?"

"Simply this: that at a certain point in each person's life, he loses control of what is happening to him, and he becomes controlled by fate. It's so easy to believe. It takes all the responsibility away from us, and we like that. But it is only a lie, a truly insidious lie."

CHAPTER 28

THAT first week, every day carbon-copied the previous one. We spent most of our day in the sea, swimming: in the mornings before and after our tennis practice, when the water was pale as champagne, and again in the afternoons before tea-time, when the water seemed as sluggish as chowder, and at night before a late dinner, when the water was dark and satiny. We swam on sunny days and during showers, high tides and low. Our tawny bodies grew dark while resting on the sugar-fine sand just beyond the water's reach.

My skin, pallid from lack of sun after the shooting, turned a brownish yellow, lion-colored, except for the spider's webs of untannable scars decorating my side and back—the scowling mouths of bullet wounds and thin surgical incisions to repair the nerve damage.

Without the power of my legs, I could not keep up with the others in our many swimming races, but what I lacked in speed and gracefulness, I made up for in stamina. I loved frolicking in that liquid environment, and I always stayed out until Jared finally hauled me to the beach over my protests.

After a long swim, I had nothing left—no energy, no warmth, no joy remained—making me realize that I must take life in small, measured doses, like the pain medications I took six times daily. But the sun, the saltwater, and exercise also had a healing quality, and it seemed that if I could only stay there long enough, I might wean myself away from all those medications. I imagined being drug- and pain-free. How grand life would be. I amazed myself with how my priorities changed from one week to the next.

Roy and J.D. never came to the beach. Both retired to the conservatory after breakfast, where they read the papers, first page to last, meticulously scanning every article. Alma brought two papers from town each morning: the International New York Times and Barcelona's English paper, The Sun. They finished reading sometime before lunch, and during the siesta hours, Roy withdrew to his room until teatime, while J.D. spent his afternoons playing high-stakes gin rummy with the Baroness.

Connor jokingly suggested that Roy spent the afternoons writing his memoirs, how he became the impetus behind creating a tennis star. I reminded Connor that Roy was a driving force behind his success and that Roy did indeed deserve a great deal of credit.

I would sometimes join Roy and J.D. on my way to or from the beach. Whenever Roy and I talked, it was always about neutral subjects: the weather, the food, the Middle East crises, or Washington's latest embarrassment. He refused to discuss my work with Connor or anything having to do with tennis.

After five days, both Roy and J.D. had had enough downtime, and J.D. claimed he couldn't afford to lose anymore at cards. They decided to leave us to our leisure and fly to the Madrid Open in order to hobnob with clothing representatives and sponsors.

The Sunday beginning our second week at the Villa Baraka, we braved the afternoon heat to have a picnic at the beach. If it got too hot, we reasoned, we would simply lie in the cool surf. Jared and I, Harman and Spencer, and Connor and Shar followed Alma two by two out past the tennis courts and onto the sand.

That afternoon, a huge cloud of seabirds gathered in the sky, looking like a malignant tumor festering over the steely-blue sea. They hovered and swooped over the water, making me think that a monstrous school of fish were knifing just below the surface. Those birds, raven black with swan-like necks, fell from the sky, beak first, plunging into the water.

Beyond them, a schooner with blood-red sails smudged the horizon, heading toward the town where fishing boats moored in the shallows, their masts tilted and their sails lashed down.

We had invited the Baroness to join our picnic, but she coughed gently into her handkerchief and informed us that she never went out and repeated, for emphasis, "Never."

The afternoon turned blustery. We took shelter in the recesses between some dunes and brought out an impressive array of accessories: folding chairs, beach towels, a soccer ball, and a picnic hamper the size of a steamer trunk.

Alma had packed and carried the hamper himself, and he struggled with its weight while staggering across the powdery sand. He spread a candy-striped canvas tarpaulin over the sand, opened the hamper, and began to unload its contents: bottles of chilled white wine, containers of egg salad sandwiches, tubes of salami, bowls of olives, and bright yellow pears. He clamped a wine bottle under his arm, inserted the corkscrew, gave a quick, sharp pull, and poured wine into crystal glasses. No plastic at the Villa Baraka.

Jared carried me on his back and sat me on a corner of the tarpaulin. I lay braced on one arm with my legs sprawled awkwardly to one side. The others spread out our bright blue towels, stripped down to Speedos, and applied sunscreen to their reddish-brown skin. By now, we were all used to swimming together in the buff on that deserted beach, and the boys donned Speedos that day solely for Alma's benefit.

Shar didn't wear a swimsuit but rather a sheer, silky wraparound skirt that covered her hips but left her breasts exposed. Her skirt tied low around her waist and billowed open with each gust of breeze, revealing her athletic legs all the way to her crotch. After a week of tanning, her skin glowed as lustrous as sealskin.

Alma ignored her, but that she would expose herself in front of a straight man turned Connor's face beet red.

She set a folding chair close to Alma and began to read a book, but after a moment, she pushed her sunglasses up into her hair and held out her arm, taking a glass of wine from Alma. She tasted it, grimaced, and said something to Alma that I didn't hear, but I saw him shrug and smile, showing a full set of even teeth. Across from Shar, Connor buried his legs in the hot sand. He pounded the mound with his palms, giving it a good spanking.

"It's getting hot," Connor said. "Let's play some ball in the surf."

"You go ahead," Shar said. "I'm going to stay here and enjoy the heat, my book, and the wine." She leaned back in her chair and crossed one leg over the other, dangling her flip-flops in the breeze. Connor slapped the sand again but made no move toward the water.

"The sun's intense," he told her. "You should cover yourself." When she ignored his suggestion, he took a full glass of wine and drank it like water.

The sun grew stronger, and the sand radiated its heat, glimmering like snow and giving off an intense scorched smell. Jared had fallen asleep, and I saw that the ridges and planes of his chest and stomach had turned dangerously red. I grabbed the tube of sunscreen and woke him by applying a generous amount to my hands and smoothing it onto his skin.

A voice called from somewhere down the beach; a dog barked. The wind dropped, and everything became still. The whole universe seemed to tilt sideways. A cooler wind rushed off the water, and the shadows of fast-moving clouds sped over us.

Alma served lunch and opened two more bottles of wine. We tried to get him to drink, but he smiled and shook his head. While we munched on sandwiches and olives, he drew a little square carpet from the hamper and laid it over the sand several feet from the tarp. He faced southeast, folded to his knees on the carpet, and bowed three times while chanting a prayer. We all watched with interest, but Shar seemed utterly fascinated.

Alma finished his prayers, rolled up his carpet, and poured us more wine. Connor sipped at his fourth glass.

Shar leaned closer to Alma and asked, "Tell me about Islam. What are you praying for?"

"Miss, the Prophet gave all people the Koran and gave the faithful five obligations to satisfy during their lives. The most important is to believe only in the one true God. The others are to pray five times each day, fast during Ramadan, be charitable to the poor, and once in a person's lifetime, they must make a pilgrimage to the holy city of Mecca."

"You've been to Mecca?" she asked.

"No, Miss. I am going this year. I have the money saved and am waiting for Ramadan."

Shar's smoky voice dropped lower. "Wouldn't it be exciting to experience Mecca during their holy festival?" she said to the rest of us.

Connor jumped to his feet, spraying sand everywhere. "Damn you. Is it necessary to embarrass me like this?" He slurred his words only slightly.

Alma looked away and began to pack the hamper.

Shar's eyes grew hard, and her voice chilled. "What crawled up your ass?"

"You flashing your tits like some Bangkok bar slut and flirting with the fucking hired help."

"Maybe I like the 'fucking hired help,' as you call him, because he's not as crass as you are."

"If I'm so crass, why are you with me?"

"I'm wondering the same thing myself, darling."

"I'll tell you why. You're using me."

"Using you! You couldn't wait to sniff my panties. You begged for it like a dog."

"Of course I wanted you. I still do, but I don't like sharing. You flirt with every swinging dick that struts by. I know you were seeing someone in Rome. How do you think that makes me feel?"

"I never said this was monogamous. Most men prefer it that way."

"You're using me to make a name for yourself. I'm the star. I'm the one people pay money to see. You're a leech, a bloodsucking leech making a name for yourself on my talent."

"Bloodsucking leech?"

"Would you rather I said dicksucking whore?"

There was a moment of silence as Shar lifted herself out of her chair and cocked her arm. She swung her hand in a quick arc, delivering a no doubt stinging slap to Connor's face.

Connor stood in a silent rage. For an instant, I thought he would smack her back. We sat motionless, averting our eyes. Shar took a step back, studying Connor's reaction, and suddenly laughed, a brutal, humiliating bark of laughter. "You're such a child, darling." She snatched her clothes and her book, holding them tightly in the crook of her arm. She wheeled around and marched back to the villa. Alma trudged behind her, balancing the hamper on his shoulder while struggling through the soft sand.

Connor stalked the other way and plopped down at the water's edge with his back to us, staring out to sea.

We glanced from one to another with that oh-shit-what-to-do-now look on everybody's face.

Spencer stood and rambled after him. He sat beside his friend and drew an arm across Connor's shoulder; their heads came together. Silent and unmoving, they sat locked together with their backs to the world.

Finally, they rose and waded into the breakers. When the water climbed waist-deep, they leaned forward in unison and began to swim out past the boiling surf to the calm swells in the deeper water. Jared, Harman and I watched, casting uncertain glances after them as their bodies cleaved the water like dolphins. They swam further and further out until we couldn't see them. Long minutes stretched into half an hour. I became increasingly nervous.

"I think we should go after them," Harman said, "but I can't swim very far."

Harman and I turned to Jared, who climbed to the top of a dune. Shielding his eyes with his hands, he scanned the sea. I experienced a dozen agonizing seconds until Jared said, "I see them. They're way the hell out there, but they're coming back in."

While we waited, it clouded over and began to drizzle, lightly at first but steadily growing heavier. By the time they reached shore, a steady rain fell. Harman high-stepped through the surf and took Spencer into his arms while Jared plunged into the breakers to pull Connor to the beach.

I threw Jared a towel, and he draped it over Connor's shoulders. Connor's lips were a pale shade of lavender, and his body shook in spasms. Jared wrapped his arms around him, trying to transfer his body heat. Connor pulled away, snarling that he didn't need our help, that he could walk back to the villa on his own, which he did. He stumbled along on shaky legs, but he managed to stagger up the beach, past the tennis courts, and into the villa.

The air remained warm regardless of the rain. Jared sat at my side and held me close. Connor's stunt had affected him deeply; I saw it in his eyes. The thought of death had him thinking about the shooting again. I glanced over at Harman and Spencer. They lay on the sand with their bodies intertwined, kissing. I wanted to do the same with Jared, and I was about to suggest leaving them alone, but Jared had already come to that conclusion. He crawled to his knees and pulled me onto his back.

He carried me piggyback along the shore for a half-mile, our bodies streaming with rain. The storm's intensity grew, and Jared began to stagger like a drunkard. We toppled onto the sand and laughed like lunatics, mostly from relief that the boys had made it back unharmed.

We were halfway to town along a deserted section of beach with nothing but sand, sea, rain, and each other.

Jared leaned into me and pressed his lips to mine, opening my mouth with his tongue. His lips, his whole body, had the clean, pure taste of rain. Even my body smelled rainwater fresh. The odor of painkillers oozing out my pores had washed away. For the first time since the shooting, I was able to totally forget that it had happened—no pain, no drug smell, no need of legs—just me and Jared and the cleansing rain.

He peeled my trunks down over my ankles, and his muscled body covered me like a living quilt. He impaled me. With the rain slashing at Jared's back, he pressed me into the sand. I held him, feeling safer and happier than at any other time in my life. He began to moan, and I bit his shoulder, trying to divert his attention so the moment would last as long as possible; a lifetime would have been too short. The bite only spurred him on, and he bucked with force. His mouth covered mine. I struggled to breathe. He pulled back and began to laugh, a deep and contagious laugh.

Shifting his weight to his knees, he lifted me in his arms and ran for the surf. A moment later, a wave bowled us over, depositing us far up the beach, plastered with sand and seaweed, chilled to the bone, wrestling like schoolboys but still laughing. I pulled myself onto his back. He bent to pick up our wet clothes before carrying me back to the villa.

We indulged in a hot bath, dry clothes, and bean soup with crusty rye bread in the kitchen—graciously served by Sara Domingo Sanchez, because Alma had vanished. It was not long before Harman joined us, letting us know that Alma had driven Shar to a guesthouse on the town's square and that Spencer was upstairs tending to Connor, who had raided the liquor cabinet as soon as he got back to the villa.

"For someone who doesn't drink, he sure put away a lot of expensive brandy," Harman said. "He's dead drunk now."

"Did he say anything?" I asked.

"Most of it incomprehensible, but I caught 'fuck her' several times before he passed out. We carried him upstairs and plopped him into bed."

Later, while Jared and I lay in bed with the French doors open to the storm, I heard Connor on his balcony, bent over the railing, being raucously sick into the garden below while the rain bombarded him from above. I thought of sending Jared to his aid, but I was certain that Spencer was still there, helping as best he could.

CHAPTER 29

THE storm raged through the next two days. Most of that time I sat in our room, staring at the wind-driven sea as brilliant bolts of lightning danced over the darkened water. Living in California, I had never experienced such extraordinary displays of lightning and booming cords of thunder. The villa trembled with each thunderclap. That magnificent violence challenged my senses, and I relished every minute of it.

I felt the rest did both my boys some good, and it granted Connor time to recuperate from an obviously painful hangover.

On that second stormy day, Roy returned without J.D. Lambert. Connor's pitiful condition drove Roy into a frenzy until Harman explained the circumstances, after which he seemed quite relieved, perhaps even grateful. He strolled about whistling a lively tune until he found that there were no papers to read.

Alma, who normally brought the morning papers, had not returned since taking Shar into town. That not only had a humiliating effect on Connor, but the Baroness took to her bed and stayed there, which left all the cooking, cleaning, and serving to Sara Domingo Sanchez.

The storm broke the morning of the third day, and by noon, the sky became a radiant, unbroken blue. We decided to ease Sara's workload by driving into town for dinner. Following our afternoon swim, we piled into the van and drove to Palamos.

Although many of the town's buildings had been built within the last fifty years, the old section surrounding the original plaza had stood unchanged for two centuries. The plaza itself was a beautifully manicured park the size of a city block, and at its center stood an ornate fountain. Tall elms and poplars shaded the square, and in the pockets of sunshine roses grew with voluptuous red blooms. A stone church dominated the north side of the square overlooking the plaza, the town, and the sea beyond.

To the south stood the Hotel Excelsior, two elegant stories with wide, sweeping balconies on both levels. The square's east and west sides were lined with sidewalk cafés where patrons ate under multi-colored umbrellas. There was a barbershop as well, two formal restaurants, five saloons, and several less-prestigious guesthouses.

We arrived during siesta. The shutters were drawn, and a drowsy calm stalked the streets. Dogs slept under the café tables. Pigeons perched in an elm and made soft cooing calls, as if trying to lull us into sleep. We sat on benches under shade trees and waited for the cafés to reopen.

The heat had broken, but sweat still dripped steadily under my cotton shirt.

At five o'clock, the plaza came alive. The doorman at the Hotel Excelsior opened the thick wooden doors and stood under the purple canopy. A dozen couples appeared at the tables, sipping beer and munching tapas. The barbershop opened for business, although there were no customers yet. Dogs sniffed around the cafés, looking for handouts.

We picked the most prosperous-looking cafe and crowded around a cane table, ordering beer, shrimp cocktails, raw octopus, and oysters on the half-shell. As the waiter scurried to the kitchen, we sat back to watch the people.

A number of patrons assembled under the umbrellas, glancing our way while affecting a studied indifference. These well-to-do citizens had long, straight backs that arched upwards, and their skin looked alabaster pale. Many had sandy-blond hair and eyes like a sailor's, with that sparkle that seems to reflect the sea.

A clutch of youths recognized Jared and Connor. They came begging for autographs. I noticed a mask falling over Connor's face as he answered their questions. Yes, it was an exciting match. Yes, he planned to play the French. No, he had never played Ernesto Montoya, but he had played Jose

Lamas. I'd never seen him act so bored with his fans. Or was it something else? His eyes kept roving the square as he talked.

Across the street, three teenagers began strumming guitars while a fourth played a mandolin and sang. His voice soared above the instruments as they played their mercenary songs. The sun sank under the rooftops. It was so picturesque that it might have been a scene from a movie.

Spencer told a joke, trying to tease Connor out of his doldrums. A beer later, Connor relaxed and even flashed a momentary grin. We ordered another round and more tapas. As the waiter set down new glasses and plates, Connor turned to watch a group gather around a table on the other side of the café. I followed his gaze and saw Shar and Alma sitting with three other men. I touched Jared's leg and nodded in Shar's direction. He glanced over and rolled his eyes.

"Shit," Jared said.

Connor's scrutiny grew less than polite. He focused an aggressive gaze on Alma, and it was returned in equal measure not only by Alma but by all the men surrounding Shar. They stared straight at Connor with an unspoken challenge.

I couldn't help thinking how similar Connor and Alma seemed, the proud cock of the head, the sad fear in the eyes that their body language tried to mask, the same feelings of wanting to possess Shar, who could not be possessed. I wondered if Connor could see the resemblance too.

I drained my glass. "I feel like a stroll. Connor, how about wheeling me around the plaza?"

When he didn't respond, Spencer offered to do it. I shook my head and touched Connor's arm. "Connor, walk with me?"

At that moment, Shar touched Alma's chin and pulled his face around to look at her, ending the stare-down. She said something we couldn't hear. A moment later she laughed, a burst of stinging laughter that we heard all too well.

Connor stood up and spun my chair away from the table, wheeling me down the street toward the Hotel Excelsior. We passed the musicians, and as we did, the mandolin player began a solo to his own accompaniment, a love song popular a few years back about a love that never fades. The guitarists joined in, strumming their instruments, and one accompanied the mandolin player's tenor voice with his husky baritone.

Connor pushed my chair faster. As we hurried along, the serenade melted into the hum of other night noises, and Connor slowed our pace again.

Behind the Hotel Excelsior's balustrade, on the ground floor terrace, every table was occupied. Well-dressed patrons sat with a casual air. Their banter drifted up in clouds of gay noise and made me hopeful that tonight would prove to be something special.

In fact, it was already special. The almost-full moon shone down on the plaza and along the streets. The townspeople strolled about, chatting and smoking. Children chased each other around the fountain.

"It's a beautiful night. Wouldn't it be grand to be out on the water, sailing?"

Silence.

"Something tells me you left your thoughts back at the café," I said.

More silence.

Okay, I thought, *try a more direct route.* "Connor, do you want her back?"

"Yes."

"What are you prepared to do?"

"Whatever it takes."

"Do you know what women value most in a man, what everybody secretly values?"

"No, but it sounds like you're about to tell me."

"Dignity."

"Dignity?"

"That means self-control," I said. "Ultimate composure while in torment. Ladies eat that up."

"I want to kick his ass into next year and drag her back home."

"Right. That approach worked so well the first time that now he's with her and you're wheeling me around the square. Connor, you blundered into an emotional outburst that embarrassed her and made you look foolish. Do you really want to repeat that?"

"But how can I get her back? She's over there laughing at me."

"There is nothing you can say to her; words can't fix this. You have to show her that you're more man than she gives you credit for, more man than Alma."

"How?"

"Show her you're hurt, that she punctured your heart, but that you're quietly enduring the pain. If that doesn't get her back, nothing will. And even if it doesn't work, at least you've shown her you can survive her. She'll have more respect for you."

By the time we passed the barbershop, we both had fallen silent. I enjoyed mingling with the locals. Connor didn't say another word until we had completed a full loop. He guided me right back to the table and sat beside me. The waiter had deposited a new round of drinks, and I noticed that Jared had switched to soda water without my badgering him.

The musicians had finished a series of love ballads, and the mandolin player strolled through the café while holding out his straw hat with such a display of humility, bowing with lowered eyes and softly grinning while tiptoeing between the tables, that it was impossible to refuse him. I tossed some bills into his hat and thanked him. His grin spread into an obsequious smile as he put his hat on and rejoined his troupe. They began another round of ballads.

Roy said, "I hear there are Chinese restaurants in Paris. I can't wait to eat good food again." Before he finished speaking, Connor was back on his feet and stalking toward Shar's table.

I am sure he had a simple desire to say something to her, not even knowing what that something might be, but I could tell from the tension overtaking his body that his anger had taken over. Harman and Roy jumped up, but before they could stop him, he began to shout. "You fucking slut. How dare you leave me like that? I need you, goddamnit!"

Alma leaped to his feet, pummeling Connor's mouth with one fist and the left eye with his other. I flinched at the force of the blows and began to pray that there were no broken bones. Connor's head knocked backward. He lost his balance and landed solidly on his butt, dazed.

The men around Shar shared a loud bray of laughter. A half-dozen older men sitting at nearby tables cackled too. Alma loomed over Connor, ready to continue the drubbing, but Roy and Harman converged on Connor. Each took an arm and lifted him to his feet, then guided him back to our table.

Blood ran from his lips.

"So much for dignity," I said.

Connor looked away. He tried to speak, some kind of apology, no doubt, but he could only mumble through his numb lips.

Roy said, "Let's take him to the van. We can eat back at the villa."

"You go ahead," I said. "I'll pay up here and join you."

I called for the check and waved Shar over. She whispered something to Alma. He glared my way as she strolled over.

She sat beside me. "Sorry, darling. I didn't want trouble."

"No need to apologize. Connor's hot-tempered, immature, and in love. I'm sure you remember what that feels like."

"Will he be all right?"

"Let's talk about you."

"Me? I'll be fine. I plan to hang around here another week or so before moving on. Maybe I'll go back to Rome, or Venice. I've always wanted to see Venice before it sinks."

"You plan to take Alma with you?"

"I hadn't thought about it. He's a sweet kid, but probably not. Why?"

"He means nothing to you?"

"Should he?"

"He means a great deal to the Baroness. They had something going until you came along. Now she's got no one."

She looked away. "Shit!"

"Buddhist law," I said. "Every action causes an equal reaction to everything around it. It's a lesson I keep learning over and over, it seems."

"Even if I dump him, there's no guarantee he'll go back to her."

"No, I suppose not."

She took my hand. We both smiled, a sad smile of parting, probably for the last time. She leaned over and hugged me. "Take care of him."

"I do what I can. If you ever need my help, don't hesitate."

All the way back to the villa, we were quiet except for Spencer, who mumbled that we needed to put some raw meat on Connor's eye if he was expecting to see the ball anytime soon.

FRIDAY, our last full day at the Villa Baraka, began quietly enough. At sunrise, Connor tapped on my bedroom door. I had agreed to let him take over my physical therapy sessions since Shar had abandoned us. Connor had watched her perform the procedure and was interested in doing it himself. He still harbored the idea of treating the sick and injured someday. He wanted a taste of that experience, I supposed, to see if it was truly something he enjoyed.

Jared slipped on his running shorts and shoes. He and Spencer dashed off for a run along the beach while Connor administered my comfort shot, which held a little less comfort than I was accustomed to. I laid on my stomach while he worked in a relaxed yet intent fashion. His touch was soothing, his manner caring. He poured liniment onto his palm and gently rubbed it over my ribbons of scar tissue and into my skin. It felt so good, so sexual, that I groaned every time I breathed out, an involuntary sound coming from deep within.

"Is that too much pressure?" he mumbled through a swollen lip.

"It feels better than Shar ever dreamed of."

He worked his thumbs into my shoulder joints and along my sides. The pain inside me retreated, and a soothing warmth spread through the hollow space it left behind. He massaged his way down my left leg and up the right, turned me over, and repeated the procedure on my front side. This time I could see the glow on his face as his hands kneaded my muscles. His eye was dark and swollen, his lip puffed up and plum-colored. But his damaged face radiated a benevolent glow that I'd not seen before, on him or anyone else. It felt like he was making love to me in a non-sexual way.

Sunlight poured through the open windows, and a soft breeze stirred the fragrant air. Shore birds called from far away as my mind drifted within his touch.

As he rotated my leg to stretch the muscles, he mumbled, "I cut down your dose of morphine, and I think you need to cut the number of painkillers you take too. I mean, I'm no doctor, but shouldn't we try to wean you off these medications? Just a little at first and see how you feel?"

His tone was caring. More importantly, he made sense.

I began to think that Connor was born to be a healer. I wanted to tell him so, but I also didn't want to lose him as my client. So I kept silent as he performed my stretches.

Before he left, he took my hand and smiled. "How was that?" he mumbled.

"I think you would make a competent doctor." I couldn't resist being honest.

His smile widened. I wondered if this little spark had reignited his old dream.

Alma had returned sometime in the night, and he delivered breakfast on our balcony as soon as he saw Jared and Spencer run up the steps. Jared and I enjoyed a quiet breakfast while we watched the golden sunlight tumble over the Mediterranean. We spent a vigorous two hours on the court. After, we all hurried to the beach to cool off with a swim before lunch. Even Roy joined the fun.

Roy's pale yellow skin shone bright against the blue, blue water, and it was the first time I ever heard him laugh at nothing, seemingly for the sheer joy of hearing himself. Connor looked more surprised than anyone, but I became suspicious. It was too out of character. Something was up, something only he knew about, and I began to worry.

During high tea, the Baroness showed me her small but impressive collection of crystal figurines: ballerinas, cherubs, dragonflies, hummingbirds. She had twenty in three different curio cabinets around the conservatory. Each cabinet literally burst with prisms of color in the afternoon sun that played through the French windows, the figurines seeming to dance a slow, intricate ballet within a sea of colorful light.

Her favorite, she said, was a smoky green angel, Baccarat, made in 1820, with beautiful translucent wings as sheer as any butterfly's and little spikes sticking out of the body. "This one," she told me as she placed it in my hand, "is called Sebastian."

It glowed like some rare emeralds I had seen. I smiled and agreed that it was the most extraordinary piece in her collection. "It must be wonderful to have a hobby that you love," I said.

"Love, yes. Wonderful, hardly. It is my curse." She drew a long breath before continuing. "There are always so many rare and magnificent pieces that one does not have, and they are all terribly expensive and hard to acquire. It is funny how the mind always migrates to the hundreds of pieces one does not yet own, rather than simply admiring the ones one does have."

Yes, I thought, understanding perfectly.

"Most of the serious collectors' pieces were crafted before 1900," she said. "I started collecting after my husband's passing. Back then, they were out of fashion, and one could find bargains, but no more."

I handed the figurine back to her, and she placed it on the shelf.

I was about to ask how much a piece like Sebastian cost when J.D. Lambert burst into the room, his face white as a sheet. He set his briefcase on an empty loveseat and opened it with a flourish. Extracting two stacks of contracts with little yellow sticky arrows to show where to sign, he handed one stack to Roy.

"They sweetened the deal after you left. Six million with Adidas and another million and change with Canon cameras. Daniel hit the nail on the head, they weren't offering even half that when I talked to them at Indian Wells. He said to wait until after the French, and look what it got us? An extra four million. My God, Daniel, I could kiss you. And that's just for starters. I'm talking to Faberge about a new fragrance, and Rolex left a message on my cell just an hour ago."

"It's not after the French," I said. "That's two weeks away."

Roy had known this was coming, and he had said nothing. I knew that's what had changed him, the cause of his good humor. He had finally gotten exactly what he wanted.

"The best news is," J.D. continued, ignoring my comment and handing me a stack of papers, "Nike offered Jared a ten-million-dollar deal, and HBO wants to buy the rights to your story. They'll publish a biography through Random House and do a movie. It might even turn into a mini-series."

"What story?" Jared asked.

"You know, being the only openly gay man on tour, the shooting, going on to win all these tournaments. They're already working on the manuscript. They want to send the writers over during the French to interview you both. You're solid gold, Jared, twenty-four karat. They've offered two million, but I think they'll go twice that. I'm waiting to hear back from Columbia Pictures and DreamWorks before we sign with HBO."

Jared stared at me, neither smiling nor frowning, his eyes empty and dull. He echoed my thoughts when he said, "How can they write a story that isn't finished yet?"

A disquieting silence fell over us, soft and dense. I felt torn in two. On the one hand, I was thrilled about the Nike deal, and visions of all those medical bills going up in smoke made me giddy, but my other half was angry because HBO and Random House wanted to write a final chapter, bind us in hardcover, and close the book. I felt that we were just getting started, hardly past the second chapter.

"Will Nike come through if we back away from the book and movie?" I asked.

"To be honest," J.D. said, "right now it's kind of a package contract. It was really Nike that got HBO on board. They're looking to get a ton of publicity out of the whole deal."

Roy cleared his throat and asked rather abruptly, "Connor is as good a player as Jared, and he's won a Masters Series. Why are they offering Jared so much more?"

"Marketing is a fickle business, Roy," J.D. explained. "The movie, for one thing. All this has little to do with skill on the court. It's about charisma, good looks, and being a winner. I call it the 'Pizzazz Paradigm,' and that's what translates into fat endorsements. Some players have pizzazz, and some don't. Andre and Pete had pizzazz, but not Chang. Maria's definitely got pizzazz. Lindsay has a fabulous game and has won more prize money than any other woman, but she lacked pizzazz. Connor's good-looking, and his personality on court excites people; they want to be him. He's also Chinese, and China is jumping into this sport with both feet. In a few years, it could be more popular than badminton. That's why they've offered him more than Alec Gardener."

J.D. smiled big, but when Roy continued to frown, he said, "Now, Jared doesn't have pizzazz. He's like Christopher Drake. His personality is reserved, cool, and he lets his stick do the talking. But he has a huge gay following, and gay fans have lots of disposable income, and this war paint thing he does is pure marketing genius. It makes him unique and enhances his warrior image. By the way, I'm checking into whether we can patent his war paint idea before some cosmetic company gets it first. Combine all that with the movie and the book, and we're golden. Better. Pure platinum."

J.D. smiled as wide as Kansas. "Am I good or what?" He looked at me and Jared. His smile faded. "What? Trust me, no one can get you a better deal than this. You're set, we all are."

"J.D.," I said, "this is overwhelming. We appreciate what you've done, but Jared and I need time to think this over."

"What's to think? This is what it's all about, the golden egg, the bottom line, right?"

"J.D.," Jared began. "Daniel is right, this is overwhelming. We owe you so much. You saved our lives, for Christ's sake, so we want to give this deal careful consideration. Daniel and I just need time to talk. I don't want to commit to anything until after the French."

"Sure, Jared. Whatever you say. There's plenty of time. Just tell me one thing. Are you guys talking to other agents behind my back? Be honest with me, I can take it."

I wheeled over and held J.D.'s hand. "Like Jared said, we owe you our lives. You're family. When we sign a deal, it will be with you."

Tears welled up in his eyes, and they sparkled golden in the afternoon light.

The Baroness sent Alma to fetch a bottle of Dom Perignon and a tin of Beluga Caviar.

Roy grasped my hand with his stubby fingers, saying, "I know we've locked horns in the past, and I've not given you the support you needed, but that stops here. This deal would never have happened without you. I don't have what it takes, and you do. I'm so damned grateful, I could kiss you myself. From here on, no matter what, I'm behind you all the way."

For a split second I thought he would kiss me, but he merely shook my hand. *Funny what money does to people*, I thought.

As the champagne poured, we all toasted our good fortune. Jared and I sipped just enough to be polite, then Jared carried me to our room and laid me on the bed. We peeled off our clothes. I had lost count of how many times we had made love in this special place by the sea, but this time we only held each other. I felt his skin against mine, noticed how his breath tingled across my neck, listened to his heartbeat thumping the same cadence as mine.

I knew we were experiencing the same fears: that if we signed the contracts, our lives would change dramatically in ways that we could not foresee.

The main issue was that we would be required to attend all the major tournaments, which would mean globetrotting for ten months out of the year, just when we had started to nurture our little dream of moving to Spain, getting married, and living in a house by the sea. I could feel that dream disintegrating into a fantasy that would remain just that.

We held each other until we heard the dinner bell.

Jared had food brought to our room, and we ate on the balcony by lamplight. The town lights glimmered in the distance like candle flames dancing on the wind. After dinner, Jared sat me on the railing, holding me close to him as we gazed out over the dark sea.

I wanted to tell him that we could have our dream, that we didn't need the money, but I knew it was not about money. In the world of professional tennis, there is much more to proving who is top dog than winning titles. I sat there wondering how to reel him back to our little dream.

And if I succeeded, could he truly be happy with only that?

AFTER my morning therapy session with Connor and before Jared and Spencer returned from their run, I sat on the balcony eating our last breakfast at the villa. Glancing into the garden, I saw Alma sitting on the kitchen stoop smoking his hookah. The sweet tobacco smell drifted on the breeze and into every room of the villa. He smoked with an expressionless face, as if his whole being was intent on listening to the sounds that the wind carried off the Mediterranean.

Forty minutes later, Jared whisked me downstairs, and I sat in my chair while Alma loaded our luggage into the van that would take us to the train station. While I waited to be lifted into my seat, the Baroness glided down the stone steps like an apparition. She knelt before my chair, and I saw that her eyes were red. I wasn't sure if she hadn't slept, or if she had been crying, or if she had just taken her own comfort shot, and I didn't dare ask. I took her frail brown hand in mine, and she pressed a white box into my palm.

"A gift," she said, tilting her head to one side, "to remember us by."

I lifted the cover to find the smoky green figurine that was her favorite: Sebastian.

"I can't accept this. You're being outrageously generous."

She turned on me with an unblemished candor in her gaze. She glanced up at Alma, who stood waiting to help me into the van, before saying, "Nonsense. I know it was you who returned something to me of much greater value."

I continued to protest weakly, "This is your favorite. Please, some other."

"I may be wrong about you. You may be too young to appreciate Sebastian. Most men treasure defiance in the face of adversity. I believe it is only with considerable age that one sees that triumph can only be achieved through virtue: convinced of his righteousness, the youth clenches his jaw against the arrows ripping at his flesh and piercing his heart. Dignity under fire is the only true achievement. That is why I want you to have Sebastian. He reminds me so much of you."

A sparkle of joy tinged her laugh before she said, "Besides, my dear, you will be doing me a great favor. You see, I must limit myself to only twenty pieces. Otherwise I would spend my entire life acquiring more and more of these little gems. It becomes a cruel obsession. But by taking this one, you grant me the enormous joy of finding a replacement. Please, do not rob me of this pleasure. I look forward to it so."

"I don't know how...."

She cut me off. "Thank me only if you have the willpower to cherish this one, the one given, and not crave more. If the bug bites and you become a collector, you should spit in my eye, because I have placed a terrible curse on your head."

CHAPTER 30

THE train swept us from Barcelona to Paris, passing through ancient towns built of stone, olive groves climbing the hills in orderly rows, and vineyards speckled with field hands in straw hats. The French farms and pastures all had that immaculate look that made me think that they just popped into existence the moment I saw them, pristine and perfect Monets, one after another, not a blade of grass out of place. Each time a postcard scene emerged, I wanted to stop time so I could etch each detail of it into my brain, but the train sped on, leaving me with a sense of loss until a new scene emerged.

I was right to come to Europe, if only to once more experience the wonder: how this landscape seamlessly bridged past with modern, blending castles and legends and traditions with bullet trains and businessmen in Italian suits chatting on cell phones about the political situation in the Middle East. Crossing and re-crossing this time bridge brought me a sense of amazement.

As the train drew closer to Paris, I watched the sky, assuming that before we actually reached the city it would cloud over and begin to mist, if not outright rain. It didn't even occur to me that it wouldn't happen, because this city had always greeted me while swathed in a lead-colored shroud. But the sky remained liquid blue, and I finally yielded to the notion of arriving at a city I had never experienced before.

Paris is a myth, a dream one experiences while one is there: the low, beautifully carved buildings, lovers strolling down the Champs Elysees, the sidewalk cafés, street artists, tourist boats lazing down the Seine, and ooh la la, the cabarets. It was like drifting in a balloon high above and removed from reality. They say Paris is the city for lovers, and if that means, as I assume, that it is a beautiful fantasy, then I heartily agree.

For almost a year, in the tones of worshipers before a shrine, we had talked of playing the French Open. At last, we were only hours away from stepping onto the red dirt of Roland Garros.

Several hundred gay men had gathered at the train platform. How they knew we would arrive on that train is anybody's guess. I suspected the Nike representatives were responsible, an attempt to drum up some free publicity before announcing we were signing with them. Whoever tipped them off, we were caught unaware. Several people in the crowd held signs in English that said "We love Jared" and "Go Jared and Connor."

Jared took me in his arms and carried me from the train. A cheer went up, and we were mobbed, literally crushed, by the fans pushing to get an autograph. A dozen police muscled their way through the mass of shrieking fans and escorted us to a line of taxis.

We were whisked across town to a charming family-owned hotel, Le Fleurie, on the left bank, a half-block off Blvd. Saint Germain. I halfway expected a crowd to greet us at the hotel, but when our convoy pulled around the corner, the street stood empty. I glanced at Jared and returned the same relieved grin that he flashed me.

The lobby and dining room were tiny but comfortable. There were several excellent restaurants within a two-block radius, the Latin Quarter was a leisurely ten minutes away, and the Marais was just across the river.

Jared and I checked in, and I wheeled into the only elevator, a tiny coffin-like interior of mirrors that started at about the level of my neck and reached to the ceiling. My chair barely squeezed in, and I had to reach around to push the top button, marked 5. The elevator door sighed and closed, but nothing happened. I sat there staring at my distorted face in the mirror. I hit the button again and again until, after a nervous hesitation, the elevator rattled and began to rise with a rather loud hum. I was instantly afraid that that damned box would get stuck between floors and no one would intervene to help because they didn't understand English, but the box jerked to a halt on my floor, and the door rattled open.

Our room was only slightly larger than the elevator, truly one of the smallest hotel rooms on the planet, even smaller than the rooms in Tokyo. But even though there was no room to maneuver my chair and only one person at a time could squeeze into the bathroom, the room had a certain charm: modern furniture, original oil paintings, and when Jared lifted me in his arms, I could look out the windows and see the tip of the Eiffel tower climbing above the rooftops.

Jared suggested that we demand a larger room, but I said no, it didn't matter. I didn't plan to spend much time in the room, and when we were there, I wanted to wrap Jared around me like a blanket. As far as I was concerned, it was perfect.

Jared changed into tennis gear, and I maneuvered into the elevator again. We met the others in the lobby. We had planned to have lunch at a nearby café before catching the subway to Roland Garros for a few hours of practice, but after being mobbed at the train station, we were all afraid of being recognized on the streets. Roy suggested we hail a couple of cabs and drive directly to the courts. Harman volunteered to stop for sandwiches so we could eat at the courts.

At the tennis complex, we saw a mob of protesters assaulting the front gates. *Oh no*, I thought. *I can't face another scene like the one in Florida.* I glanced into Jared's watery eyes, and he took my hand, pulling me closer.

There must have been two thousand people carrying signs and punching the air with their fists. The signs were all in French, so we had no idea what they said, but the angry shouts clearly broadcast the mob's outrage.

But something didn't quite gel. Sprinkled through the crowd were a sizable number of gay men. In fact, the entire gathering looked like something I would expect to see in the Marais, which didn't make sense. Why would gay men be protesting? *Perhaps it has nothing to do with us*, I thought, somewhat hopefully.

Our taxis whisked around the corner and sped to the players' entrance. At the gate, we flashed our credentials, and the guards waved us through, but two other guards blocked the road just inside the gates. The driver leaped out and retrieved my chair from the trunk. Jared helped me into it while Spencer grabbed the tennis bags.

Karl Diefenbach strolled up. He resembled an undertaker in his signature black Brioni suit, black silk shirt, and black tie. The only color besides his pasty face and hands was a flash of a purple handkerchief in his breast pocket.

"Jared," Diefenbach said. "I'm afraid you won't need your tennis gear. In fact, I'm here to confiscate your ID badge."

Connor, Roy, and J.D. crowded around us.

"We made the cut," I said. "You can't keep us from playing." Although I spat out the statement, my voice went up at the last word, making it a question. I suddenly felt as if the ground shook under me.

Diefenbach smirked once, then again. "I take it you haven't read today's newspapers?"

"We don't read French."

"Well make a fucking effort to keep up with the latest developments."

So, I thought, *Diefenbach is angry. Good, now we're all angry and we're all trying to hide it.*

Diefenbach pulled a piece of paper from his coat pocket and unfolded it. "Jared, have you been taking any medication?"

"None, why?"

"No cold medicine, pain medication, muscle relaxers?"

"Zero to everything, why?"

Diefenbach's eyes narrowed on Jared as he mused aloud, "So your blood's as clean as a whistle? You're sure?" He didn't bother to hide his sarcasm.

"Why don't you cut the crap and tell us why you're here?" I said. My growing concern began feeding my anger.

"I'm afraid it's completely out of my hands. You see, the drug testing at the Rome tournament revealed high levels of testosterone and also traces of a performance-enhancing drug in your blood called"—he pulled his reading glasses from an inner coat pocket, slipped them onto his face, and read something toward the bottom of the page— "androstenedione, which elevates the body's production of testosterone. I'm afraid Jared has been suspended from professional tennis pending a hearing to determine the validity of the testing. I should tell you, if they rule against you, they'll disqualify your win at the Italian Open and slap you with a two-year suspension."

Oh God, I thought. Because of our fight, I hadn't gone with Jared in Rome to ensure that nobody could tamper with his blood and urine samples before he handed them to the independent testing agency. *Fuck! Fuck! Fuck!* Fuck me and my stupid pride. That's why the gay men at the front gate were protesting. They must have already heard the announcement.

"That's bullshit, and you know it," Jared said, his voice seething.

Diefenbach shook his head in amused disbelief. "What I know is irrelevant," he said, and his smirk widened into a smile. "Perhaps you're forgetting something. Perhaps you went to the doctor's for back pain and he prescribed some medications, or you had a cold and you took some over-the-counter supplements to keep your energy level high, not knowing what was in it? I can live with a story like that. The inquiry board might go easy on you."

"I did nothing of the kind, and you know it. You framed me, you bastard."

"So you're sticking to that story? Oh well, I'm afraid I must ask you for your players' badges." Diefenbach held out his hand, but he couldn't resist adding, "I told you not to fuck with me. I would have let you have a small piece of the pie, but you got greedy."

"You can't take our badges," I said. "I'm Connor Lin's coach, and Jared is his hitting partner. I assume Connor's drug test wasn't tampered with as well? That would be too suspicious, now, wouldn't it?"

Diefenbach lowered his hand as his double smirk turned downward. "There comes a time, after all the fucking around and whining, when you're reduced to accepting the inevitable. You were outgunned from the beginning. I'm a jackal. I let the young lions roar and swagger about and take down the buffalo, and while they're still strutting about, I sneak in and steal the prize. You might as well leave now with your dignity intact and save me the effort of pounding the last nail into your coffin."

"The game is not over," I said. "We're just starting the fifth set. Becker said, 'The fifth set is not about tennis, it's about heart'."

"Very well. Enjoy your workout. Connor, I wish you the best of luck in this tournament, and if you still wish to play doubles, I can arrange for a new partner. And by the way, if you'd like a coach that can help your career instead of hinder it, I can arrange that too."

Connor set his lips in a firm line. Roy stepped toward Diefenbach and said in a calm voice, "We'll pass on that offer, Mr. Diefenbach. And I think you're overestimating yourself with that jackal comparison. From my point of view, you look more like a weasel, and I don't think you have a clue what the real prize is. Good day, sir!"

Diefenbach clasped his hands in front of his chest, as if he were granting absolution. He turned and walked back toward the administration building.

"Thanks," I said, turning toward Roy.

A fire blazed in Roy's eyes. He had a kind of quiet rage that made him look dangerous. "I told you we would go to the French as a team, and that's what we are, to the bitter end." He narrowed his angry gaze directly on me and said, "You've been dicking around with that bastard long enough. It's time to squish him like a bug."

"He's the most powerful man in pro tennis," I said, not bothering to hide my anger. "And in case you weren't paying attention, he just squished us."

"There are more powerful men than that two-bit pimp," J.D. Lambert said.

"Who?" I snapped.

"Old business wisdom: you need a dirty job done, go to the money. Roy, didn't you tell me your relatives in China were big wheels at the Nike clothing plant?"

Roy nodded.

"I have an idea," J.D. said. "Let's all meet up in Chinatown at seven for dinner." He grabbed Roy's arm, and they both jumped back into the cab.

There was nothing to do but perform our practice and pray that J.D. could pull a rabbit out of his hat, or in this case, an elephant out of his ass. By the time we were assigned a practice court, Uncle Harman had arrived with chicken sandwiches made with crusty French bread and cartons of potato salad. We all gobbled down the meal before getting down to business.

A gloomy shroud hung about our court, and it was hard to keep the men focused. They kept smashing the beans out of the ball to work through their disappointment. We practiced from two to five, a long and grueling workout.

Several reporters came by, wanting the inside story on the doping charges, and Uncle Harman handled all their questions while I focused on the workout.

When we finally quit, we had barely enough time to scurry back to the hotel and clean up before dashing across the city to meet Roy and J.D. in Chinatown.

Even though Paris has hordes of Chinese restaurants, Chinatown is only a three-block area of Vietnamese restaurants, grocery stores, and shops. It didn't take long to find Roy and J.D. Lambert. They were seated at the window table of the fanciest-looking restaurant in the neighborhood, and at the long table with them sat four other men dressed in fine-cut suits. They were the only Caucasians in the restaurant. As we passed the window, Roy waved us in.

The dining room clamored with the conversations of two hundred diners using twenty different dialects and clattering plates from thirty waiters who all looked fresh off the boat from Ho Chi Minh City.

Spencer wheeled my chair to the head of the table, and J.D. gave me a light one-two punch to the shoulder. He was in one of those happy moods that made me wonder what he knew that I didn't.

Roy had to shout to be heard as he made the introductions. The men in suits turned out to be two representatives from Nike, Bob Guillam and John Hackett, and two reps from Adidas, Phil Peters and Mike de Jong. We all ordered the Pho Special, a noodle soup that is a staple in Vietnamese culture.

The suits all nervously glanced at one another, wondering, no doubt, what the hell they would be eating. I was mildly amused at their obvious display of fussiness over the unfamiliar surroundings, but before I could blink twice, they opened their briefcases and whipped out thick contracts, slapping them on the table.

"Before we sign the contracts, I want two guarantees," Roy said, and he held up two fingers. "First, this drug scandal with Jared disappears and Jared gets reinstated in the tournament with a public apology from the ATP. Second, Diefenbach gets the axe. I want that sleazy son of a bitch fired, tossed out on his ass without a crumb."

The smiles on the suits vanished.

"Roy," Hackett said, "be reasonable. There are some things we have no control over."

"You're the money in this sport, and money controls everything. Those are my terms, and I won't budge."

"I'm confident we can persuade the ATP to drop the drug charges quietly and let Jared play. That's in everybody's best interest," Guillam said. "I'm willing to guarantee that." He smiled and held out the ten-million-dollar contract to Jared.

Before I could shout "yes," Roy shook his head, saying, "Not enough."

Phil Peters spoke up. "Listen, gentlemen, even if we could persuade the powers that be to fire Diefenbach, we wouldn't do it, because that would create a political situation between our companies and the ATP, and we can't afford that." He held up both hands, palms facing upward, and smiled that same kind of thin-lipped smile that Diefenbach used.

Roy's back visibly stiffened, and he shook his head, not budging an inch.

Roy was the one making demands, but I knew J.D. was the one who had orchestrated whatever plan they had up their sleeve.

J.D. Lambert spoke for the first time. "Gentlemen, I'm sure you noticed the thousands of gay protesters out front of the stadium today. What do you think will happen if someone leaks to the press that Nike and Adidas are backing the ATP on these phony charges? I think that could create a gay boycott of your products."

Everybody became still as J.D. continued. "We all know that gays have no influence in the world of sports or politics or manufacturing, but there is one industry that they do control: the fashion industry. Gays are the trendsetters, and what they wear, everybody wears. If we organize a gay boycott against your companies, by this time next month, every gay man and woman on the planet will be showing off their new Reeboks and

Pumas, and a month after that, you won't be able to give your shit away. You can partner with us and everybody wins, or you can lose market-share, which translates into a ten-billion-dollar loss next year."

The hush at the table deepened, made even more conspicuous by the constant blare of the other tables' conversations. The suits glanced from one to the other.

"Did I say each?" J.D. added. "I meant to say, 'lose ten billion dollars each'."

The hush became deafening, but the suits weren't convinced we had the power to create a boycott, and neither was I.

Finally, Hackett said, "I'm sorry, we don't respond favorably to threats. Perhaps this was a mistake." He gathered his contracts and slipped them back into his briefcase. The Adidas executives quickly followed his example.

My heart sank. A note of panic crossed Jared's face.

"Gentlemen," Roy said, his smile suddenly looking sly, "I didn't want to bring out the heavy artillery, but you leave me no choice. No doubt you've heard that two hours ago, a general strike took place in Nike's Beijing clothing plant. What you don't know is that by now, the same has happened in the Adidas plant in Shanghai. In fact, you can expect your entire Chinese operation will be shut down by Monday, which will halt your entire clothing manufacturing. How many millions a day will you lose?"

"What does a plant strike have to do with signing contracts, and how the hell did you know about that? The press hasn't picked up on it yet."

"I can make that problem go away," Roy said, ignoring the question.

"How?" Hackett asked softly, giving Roy his undivided attention.

"Like most Chinese families, I have relatives in high places. You fuck with one Chinaman, you fuck with us all."

Roy began to sweat. Hackett watched him coolly, appraising him like a professional gambler across the table. Even in that noisy restaurant, I thought I could hear the nonverbal exchange passing between the suits— *is Roy for real? Did he really cause the strike? How else could he have known about it so fast? Can he really shut them all down, and if so, how much will that cost? Would the Chinese government really support such tactics? How important is it to them to have Connor in the top ten? If Roy can do this, what other cards does he have up his sleeve? Or is this a huge bluff, and if so, how can we break him without risking a general strike? Most important of all: is a pawn like Diefenbach even worth taking that risk?*

Suddenly Guillam and Hackett seemed to come to a silent agreement. The other two picked up on it and nodded, but nobody spoke a word.

The waiter danced by and deposited four plates, each holding fresh ingredients to add to the soup: bean sprouts, basil, lime wedges, and jalapeno peppers. All the suits stared at the platters, no doubt wondering if they were starter salads. To their relief, another waiter swung by with a tray holding frosted glasses of Singha beer.

Hackett held up his glass to the table and cleared his throat. "The ATP will drop the drug charges and reinstate Jared by tomorrow morning. They'll announce that it was an error with the testing and give Jared the public apology he deserves."

"And Diefenbach?" Roy growled.

"Diefenbach is out. He's a loose cannon that we can no longer afford. We'll see to that detail as soon as the tournament is over, you have my word on that."

"Right after the trophy presentation," Roy said. His voice was forceful but no longer a growl.

Hackett choked on his beer, but he recovered and nodded. "You can take that to the bank."

A wave, no, a sea-swell of relief swept through me. I took Jared's hand and squeezed it as hard as I could, and he leaned over and hugged me.

"Now," Hackett said, his face breaking into a thin smile, "can we sign the contracts before the soup gets here?"

Jared took the contract and opened to the page with the little yellow arrows. He stared at Hackett and asked, "You're sure your company doesn't mind sponsoring a fairy?"

Hackett shook his head. "We had a saying on the farm when I was growing up: 'If it doesn't scare the cows, who the hell cares?'"

A chuckle made its way around the table. Jared bent his head, as if in prayer, and signed the contracts. As he raised his head, a smile creased his face. Connor signed his own set of contracts, and the two players glanced at each other. Jared winked. He handed the company copy of the contract back to Hackett.

Guillam reached over and shook Jared's hand, and mine. "How does it feel to be a multimillionaire?" he asked.

I had never really thought that I would become rich. Tennis was never about the money, but rather, it was about doing something alongside Jared that we both loved. But in the moment that it took Jared to squiggle his signature, my future medical bills vanished, and we would never again be concerned about money. I definitely felt a rush. It wasn't the money so much as it was that we were finally, after all the battles, getting the same perks as the other top players. We had more than arrived, we were established now, and the realization was dazzling, like the Big Bang had gone off in my head and created a new and wondrous universe. I was literally stunned.

Through the numbness, I heard Jared say, "Like the weight of the world has been lifted off my back. Now we can afford to hire bodyguards to keep this one out of harm's way." He looked at me as his hand squeezed the back of my neck.

"You should have read the fine print. That's covered in the contract."

"Fine print? What fine print?" I asked, my euphoria suddenly turning to concern.

"I mean that whenever either of you is at a tournament site, Nike will supply four armed security personnel devoted to your protection. We're investing ten million dollars in you two, and we intend to protect our investment."

"I'll drink to that," I said, reaching for my glass.

Connor held out his set of signed contracts, but before Peters could snatch them from his hand, Uncle Harman reached out and grabbed them.

"Sorry," Harman told Peters, "but I need to review the numbers before we hand these over. I'm sure everything is aboveboard, but it's my job to ensure everything is as we agreed. It will only take me a day or two."

Peters shrugged his shoulders. "Take your time, but keep in mind we want to announce this new partnership before the second week of the tournament."

Two waiters appeared at our table with steaming bowls of soup, and we scrambled to make room for them. I glanced around the long table at our happy band, which had gone through so much together. Everyone had a triumphant smile and felt the joy of the moment except for Connor. After signing the contracts, he had become quiet, and a shadow of disappointment veiled his face.

I was certain that Connor's sudden dark mood stemmed from losing his dream of becoming a doctor, because signing those contracts had flushed those dreams down the toilet, and he was visibly grieving his loss. That was the first time I knew for sure that he really preferred medicine to tennis and that he signed the contracts because he simply couldn't disappoint his father. I felt sorry for him, but now there was no turning back. Grandfather Lin had been right, and deep in the back of my mind, I heard him whisper, "I told you so."

CHAPTER 31

ON THE first morning of play, a Monday, the gay fans began to gather at the gates of Roland Garros in the gray predawn. There wasn't a vacant parking place for a six-kilometer radius. They came from France, England, Italy, Sweden, Germany, and Spain; virtually every European nation had representatives among the gay fans. Even hundreds of gay Americans had made the trip over to the ancient side of the Atlantic. Street hawkers sold tickets at ten times their normal price, and they had no tickets left at ten o'clock when the gates flew open and thousands and thousands of resplendent fans surged into the complex. The media coverage over Jared's drug scandal had been a call to arms. The gays came in record numbers, and they made it clear that they had come to cheer Jared and Connor. The organizers were stunned and overjoyed to cash in on this new gold mine.

We began our morning practice session at eight thirty, so only a few dozen people, mostly other coaches scouting us, were on hand to watch us work out, but when Jared stepped onto Court Suzanne Lenglen for his match, the stadium was filled to capacity. I scanned the crowd, and even though I had two armed security men behind me, following my every move, I was still nervous. In a world of religion-bred hatred, you never knew. It turned out that my bodyguards, Bruno and Gunther, were not only both German, they were also both gay. Nike was taking every precaution to keep their investment safe.

Jared wore white with his signature red-striped war paint on his cheeks, and as soon as he appeared on court, a multitude of frenzied fans, also wearing red-striped war paint, leaped to their feet and cheered, blowing horns and noisemakers. I expected fireworks to burst overhead. It was a gay pride parade, Carnival, and Saturday-night clubbing all rolled into one celebration.

The crowd's roar didn't subside until Jared and his opponent, Carlos Ortega from Argentina, began their five-minute warm-up. I couldn't help getting misty-eyed. Jared had been lifted to hero status within the gay community, and his legions were out in force to support their man. Electric waves of pride surged through me as their cheer rose to a deafening pitch. We had traveled a long, bumpy road to experience this, and the joy of the moment became overwhelming.

Spencer and Harman sat to my left, and they must have felt the same emotions, because Spencer almost crushed the life out of me with a bear hug. Harman grabbed my hand and gave it a meaningful squeeze. Even Connor, who sat to my right with Roy, gave me a hug.

When the match started, the tension in the crowd became unbelievably tight, like the strings of a Stradivarius. The fans hung on every strike of the ball and savagely cheered for every point Jared won. They had come to watch their man battle the straight establishment, and Jared gave them their money's worth with interest. The match turned into a grueling, hard-hitting dogfight. Ortega loved to smack the ball hard, and that fed right into Jared's strengths. Jared countered with a barrage of angles, running Ortega from side to side before smashing a bullet down the line.

All my concerns as to whether Jared still had the intensity to play at the top of his game were laid to rest. He was in peak form, and the gays ate it up like raw meat fed to lions. They went riotous when Jared smashed an ace up the centerline to win the match.

Because Connor and Jared were on opposite sides of the draw, Connor wouldn't play until the next day, making Jared's win our only match that day. Roy and I cruised through the practice courts to scout Connor's first-round opponent while Jared had his post-match interview. Thirty minutes later, we all piled into a van and left for the day. Even though we now had full-time bodyguards, I was still nervous about spending any more time than necessary at the tennis facility.

We arrived early the next day to get our practice session in before the gates opened. We hung around the players' lounge for a few hours, downed a quick lunch in the cafeteria, and prepared Connor for his first match. Jared hit with him for twenty minutes on a practice court to warm his muscles and shrink the butterflies in his belly. While the others wandered out to court six to wait for Connor's match, Spencer and I accompanied Connor back to the locker room, reviewing the game plan one more time. As we arrived at the players' lounge, we both patted Connor on the back and wished him luck.

A look of fear crept onto Connor's face, and I could tell he was feeling sick to his stomach. I remembered that look from the first time he played Jared on the show court of the Windsor Club.

"Connor," I said, "you'll do fine. Just stick to the game plan."

"I feel sick," he said. "I mean really sick, like I might barf on court."

Spencer took Connor in his arms. "Come on, Con. Pretend it's me across the net."

Connor pressed his forehead into Spencer's shoulder and mumbled, "I love you."

"I know."

"I wish I could be the kind of man...."

Before he could finish, Spencer pulled back and lifted his index finger to Connor's lips, shutting him up. "You're exactly the kind of man I want you to be: a champion."

Connor glanced down at his sneakers and shook his head. "I don't care about the others, but I don't want to disappoint you two."

"Connor," I said, taking his hand and squeezing, "did I ever tell you about Mats Wilander?"

He shook his head.

"Mats was a middleweight groundstroker with fierce powers of concentration, just like you, and he accomplished something that even Borg couldn't do. He won this tournament the first time he played it in 1982 as an unseeded seventeen-year-old. He did it by being utterly unflappable. During this tournament, I'm calling you Mats."

Connor smirked with an undercurrent of joy, obviously liking the comparison. "Call me any damned thing you like. You earned the right."

"Ok, Mats, enough of this sentimental hogwash," I said. "We'll see you at the court."

Spencer pushed me through the crowd toward court six, with Bruno ahead and Gunther following. As we came abreast of the line to get into the already-packed bleachers, we jerked to a halt, and I sensed Spencer's whole body stiffening. I turned my head to see him scowl at the line of people waiting to get in. Following his gaze, I saw why. Shar Paulot stood in line with her arm laced around the waist of a young Latin man. Carrie Bennett stood directly in front of them. I wheeled over to Carrie's side.

"Fancy meeting you here."

"Well, hello, stranger. What a wonderful surprise."

"Darling," Shar said, "I'd like you to meet Raoul. He's a painter from Guatemala."

I introduced Spencer, who nodded his head without a word or a change of facial expression.

"I ran into these two in Rome, and we decided it would be a lark to show up and cheer our boys on," Carrie said.

"We were hoping to watch Connor," Shar said, "but it doesn't look like we'll get in."

"We have a couple of empty seats in the players' section," I offered.

"That might upset Connor," Shar said. "I wanted to just blend in with the crowd."

"He'd be happy to see you, I'm sure of it."

She looked at Raoul, and a note of doubt crossed her face.

Raoul said, "You go. I'd rather go to court central and watch Maria. She's such a fox. Meet me at the front gate after the match and we'll go someplace more interesting." He bent and kissed her before strolling off.

"You do like the young ones," I said.

"It's a control thing. I like to have the upper hand. But he chain smokes; kissing him tastes like licking an ashtray. And he always wears that regretful smile, like he'd rather be somewhere else. It's maddening."

Spencer wheeled my chair around and pushed me toward the players' section. Shar and Carrie walked on either side of us. Shar asked, "Did he take it hard?"

"Ya think?" Spencer hissed before I could respond.

"I didn't mean to hurt him. Everything just derailed, and I couldn't stop it."

"No one blames you," I said.

"Humph!" Spencer mumbled.

"How's his game?"

"His legs are rested, but he hasn't played a match since Rome. He could be vulnerable. Let's face it, he played great with you in his corner, and he played like crap without you. He's still so fragile."

Music played over the loudspeakers, Paul Simon's "Learn How to Fall," and I noticed it for the first time.

"Wish I could do something to help," she mumbled.

"Try an apology!" Spencer snapped.

"He'd spit in my face."

"Maybe not," I said. "Love has a way of working through that kind of stuff."

She paused, and I could tell she was surprised by the word "love."

Spencer wheeled me as close to our seats as possible. Bruno lifted me in his arms as if I were a bag of feathers and carried me the rest of the way, sitting me beside Jared. Roy, who sat on the other side of Jared, leaned forward with his eyebrows lifted almost to his hairline, watching Shar slide down the aisle to sit next to me. He nodded at her, keeping his lips pressed together. Jared reached across me and shook her hand, telling her, "What a pleasant surprise." He did the same for Carrie. Bruno and Gunther sat directly behind us.

A cheer followed Connor and Philip Seaborne, a French veteran and a crowd favorite, onto the court. Connor strolled to his chair and dropped his bag. He pulled out a racket and tapped it against his palm to test the tension. When he glanced our way and saw Shar, his expression turned icy. He turned his back on us, and I saw the dragon on his back move in a serpent-like coil. I suddenly regretted inviting her. It became obvious that she would affect his concentration.

As the referee tossed the coin, I glanced around, looking for a hole for me and her to crawl into, and noticed that Uncle Harman was missing.

I nudged Jared's ribs. "Where's Harman?"

"He left town on some personal business. He'll be back in a few days."

"Nobody tells me nothing these days."

"Nobody tells me nothing," Jared mimicked my whine. He smiled.

During the five-minute warm-up, Connor became flustered, and I suspected it was because of Shar. I touched her arm, ready to suggest that she leave, but before I could say anything, she pulled a handkerchief and a tube of lipstick from her purse. She spread out the pristine white cloth and used the lipstick to write on it: "I'm Sorry!" and, underneath that, "I love you!"

I waited, hoping the note would help.

Connor finished his warm-up serves and walked toward his chair. Shar held up her handkerchief as he glanced our way. He came to a full stop, staring at those little red words. His face froze, perfectly still, with that beautiful sheen of sweat reflecting the sun's rays. Finally, the ends of his mouth lifted into a wide smile. He sprinted to his chair with a new energy.

Connor won three sets in eighty-six minutes. It seemed as if he couldn't wait to get off the court. As soon as the players had shaken hands, Connor bounded into the stands to hug Shar.

"You're back?"

"You want me?"

"Baby, I'm miserable without you."

"Tell you what, darling. I need to take care of some personal business and pick up a few things at my hotel. I'll meet you somewhere for a quiet dinner, and we'll talk."

"I have a better idea," Connor said. "You go take care of your personal business, whatever his name is, and then bring your bags to my hotel. We'll have dinner in our room after you unpack. Deal?"

She hesitated, smiled.

They shared a sensual kiss while the fans erupted with ear-shattering cheers. The embroidered dragon on Connor's shirt seemed to undulate in an erotic dance while clinging to his spine. The TV cameras zoomed in for close-ups, and the announcer was broadcasting something over the loudspeaker, but I couldn't hear what. *After this moment*, I thought, *there will never be any doubt in anybody's mind of Connor's sexual preference.*

When Connor finally became aware of the clamor that his kiss was causing, he blushed, not quite so red as an apple.

THAT night, as Jared soaked in a hot bath, Spencer knocked on our door. At first I assumed he was simply lonely because Harman was out of town and Connor was holed up in his room with Shar, but he sat on the couch, opened Harman's laptop computer, and showed me an email that had been sent to Jared. It was the same picture that had been sent before the Sony Ericsson tournament—a drag queen in full makeup with his throat cut from ear to ear—and scrawled across the bottom of the photograph was a message: "We have unfinished business!"

CHAPTER 32

THE first week of the tournament flew by like a whirlwind. Jared won his matches easily, demonstrating that he was a top contender.

At the beginning of the second week, Jared played Jose Lamas, the defending champion. After beating Lamas in Rome, Jared couldn't wait to play him again. It turned out to be a routine win for Jared. Lamas walked on court with fire in his eyes and looking for revenge, but he couldn't get his game going. Every time he would string a few good strokes together, Jared would crush him with a bullet angling out wide, just out of his reach.

Jared made only six unforced errors in the first set, feeding Lamas only scraps, and certainly not enough to make a meal. At the beginning of the second set, Lamas already had that whipped dog look in his eyes, the same look I saw in Rome. By the middle of the third set, Lamas's mind was on the jet home. Jared's easy win over Lamas convinced everyone that Jared had become invincible on the red dirt; the pawn had become the king, at least on clay.

Connor, as usual, struggled with each match. After that first win, he suffered through three five-set matches in a row. In each one, he would outplay his opponents to win the first two sets and then get nervous and lose confidence. He spiraled downwards, losing the next two sets, then lifted his game enough to tough out the fifth. Each match he put in a gutsy fight, proving he had heart, but I began to worry. It is a common saying in tennis that you can't win a Grand Slam tournament in the first week, but you can sure lose it, meaning that you can wear yourself down too early in the tournament and have nothing left in the tank for the homestretch.

In the doubles, my boys pummeled everybody. I knew that if Connor's legs held together, they would at least win the doubles championship. As for the singles, I still wasn't sure; Roland Garros has a history of early round upsets and surprise finalists. Form and ranking don't hold up here like they do at the other Slams. Regardless of my uncertainty, it had proved to be the most exciting week of my life, and every second I was there, at courtside or being wheeled through the crowds, I was frightened to death.

I told Carrie about the "unfinished business" email. She begged me to tell the others, but there was no way to keep Jared and Connor playing at the top of their games if they had to deal with that additional pressure. In fact, armed bodyguards or not, I was sure Jared would send me home if he knew. I did tip off the bodyguards, and to my surprise, they wanted a copy of the email, telling me that they could track the sender down. The only problem was that it would take a week or two, even with help from the authorities.

So I sat in my chair, surrounded by bodyguards, trying to stay focused on the tennis and support my players, but not a minute passed that I didn't scan the crowd—a fat man wearing a shiny silver cross around his neck while standing beside the women's restroom door, a woman in a dark blue business suit with a scowl on her face, a Chinese man wearing a heavy coat on a hot day—in a society of religion-bred hatred, you never knew.

The one thing I did know was that if people out there were trying to hurt us, the deeper into the tournament my boys went, the greater the risk. I was praying my bodyguards would identify these jokers before anything happened.

Another issue added to my chronic anxiety: Joshua McEwan, the hot-headed Aussie, had begun mouthing off during his press conferences about his disdain of playing fairies. He had lost his second-round doubles match to Jared and Connor, and that left him seething. He won his singles matches easily, and he and Jared were on a collision course to meet in the semifinal.

The press speculated that it would be the match of the tournament. They queried McEwan about the outcome, and when he openly showed his contempt for Jared, they egged him on. It was Indian Wells all over again; people took sides, and the press fueled the fires to build up the drama. I was seemingly the only one dreading the semifinal confrontation, but not because I though McEwan would win.

True to form, on the second Wednesday of the tournament, both Jared and McEwan won their quarterfinal matches to set up the longed-for meeting in the first semifinal. Jared was excited about the match-up and mentally prepared himself to play his most aggressive tennis ever. He didn't simply intend to win; he wanted to humiliate the Aussie and to shut his mouth for good.

On the day that Connor played his quarterfinal match against Eduardo Flores from Chile, Uncle Harman surprised us all by returning to Paris. Why he had left town he wouldn't say, but before he arrived at Roland Garros, he swung by the airport and picked up Connor's grandparents. They had flown in on the slim chance that Connor would make it into the final.

Harman and the grandparents arrived just as Connor and Flores marched onto the field of battle. We were sitting in the first row, and when Connor saw them, he rushed over. Reaching up and taking his grandfather's hand, he gave it a gentle squeeze. Joy replaced the sickened look on Connor's face, and I began to hope that it would spur him on to win over a very tough competitor.

Once again, though, Connor won the first two sets with an array of beautiful—and deadly—inside-out forehands, his new signature shot, and dropped the next two sets with the same old story of crumbling nerves and wobbly focus. By that point, I had become confident he would win, but I also knew his legs were taking a beating.

Sure enough, Connor raised his game and cruised to a commanding lead in the fifth by using his quick feet, shot variety, and his own personal flair. Watching his flashy play style, I had to shake my head, remembering those first few months of working with him, when there was nothing flashy about him, when underneath he was somewhat shy, slightly self-conscious, and prone to nibbling on his nails. A year later, his expansive confidence, effortless power, flawless footwork, and deft angles made him one of the sport's most spectacular shot-makers.

He won, as I predicted, but as he jogged to the net to shake hands, I noticed a slight limp. I looked closer. Yes, he was definitely favoring his right leg. It was especially troublesome considering he needed to play his semifinal doubles match with Jared in just over an hour. He also needed to play his singles semifinal match the next day, Friday, without the benefit of the usual day of rest.

The good news was that if he won his singles semifinal match against Christopher Drake on Friday, he would have Saturday to rest before the final on Sunday afternoon.

I turned to Shar. "You see that?"

"I'm on it," she responded, with the same note of concern I had in my voice. "I'll pump him with fluids and keep him on the massage table until it's time for his doubles."

I leaned closer to her. "I'm very happy you're back."

"What about you?" Carrie said. "You should continue your physical therapy conditioning."

Connor had not given me a therapy session since coming to Paris. Remembering those stretches made me realize with a shock that, even though I had slowly reduced my comfort shot to nearly nothing, during the last week, I had hardly felt any pain. Between worrying about the "unfinished business" email and with the rest of my attention riveted on my players' needs, I had not given my body a thought. Even when I was engrossed in a match and forgot to take my medication, I still didn't notice the pain.

Was my body recovering to the point that I could stop swallowing a mountain of pills every day, or had I merely acclimated to the pain like passengers aboard an ocean liner acclimate to the rolling of the ship? Either way, I smiled and shook my head no.

We killed thirty minutes at the players' cafeteria catching up on the news from home that Connor's grandparents could tell. Harman got us a practice court, and I supervised Jared while Spencer warmed him up. Jared needed to carry Connor through the match—to cover most of the court and, more importantly, he had to keep the points short. Ideally, we needed a quick straight-set win so Connor didn't aggravate his injured leg.

We ambled back to the cafeteria to wait for Connor, but when we arrived, he and Shar were already sitting with Roy, J.D., and his grandparents. They all had such glum looks on their faces that I thought Connor must have sustained a serious injury.

I wheeled over to see what had happened only to find that Connor was physically fine. As it turned out, Grandfather Lin had been busy the last few months getting Connor accepted into Stanford University, and he had just handed Connor the acceptance papers and told him he was starting in the fall term.

"But how?" Connor whined.

"I convinced them you would make a fine tennis coach for their team if they enrolled you. If you do well, there will be no problem with being accepted into their medical school."

Connor looked to his father, but Roy stayed surprisingly quiet, turning his head away. Connor turned back to his grandfather and explained that he had no intention of giving up his tennis career yet. Medical school would have to wait five or six years. He was now a star and on the verge of breaking through the top ten. He could become one of the game's all-time greats, like Laver, Borg, and Sampras. He could become a source of pride and inspiration for Chinese people the world over.

The old man shook his head. "How great can you be playing a game? Sacrificing yourself to save people's lives, that is the only great profession. And you, Connor, not even two years ago gave me your word that you would become a doctor if we could find the money for school. This is your dream!" The old man glanced at Roy, back at Connor, shook his head again. "Harman, take your mother and me back to the hotel," he said flatly.

We all sat as still as mannequins while Uncle Harman led his parents out of the cafeteria and they disappeared into the crowd.

Finally, Roy clasped Connor's shoulder. "The old man is out of touch. He doesn't understand how important this is."

"He understands perfectly," Connor responded.

"I hate to break up this family moment," I said, "but we have a doubles match on court one in ten minutes. Let's deal with this later."

Court one is the most intimate show court at Roland Garros. It's called "the Bullring" because of its circular shape. As my two bodyguards carried me down to the players' section and sat me beside Roy, Shar, Carrie, and Spencer, I felt the sinking feeling that Connor's sudden dark mood would lose them the match. Once the opponents identified Connor's weakness, they would drive every ball at him.

Sure enough, Connor came out of the blocks sluggish, and the opponents picked on him. Jared played awesome tennis to stay even, but Connor couldn't lift his game enough to give them the edge they needed. They lost the first set 3-6. I became angry, not with Connor's lack of concentration, but at Grandfather Lin for butting into Connor's business without being asked. With each shot that Connor missed, my anger rose until steam was coming out of my eyeballs.

During the first game of the second set, Jared began to favor his left leg until it became a noticeable limp. He called a medical timeout at the changeover, and the trainer rushed onto the court, taped Jared's ankle, and the match resumed. Jared continued to limp, and now he had a beaten dog expression on his face. I hung my head. *My God*, I thought, *we came so close, and now both my players are damaged goods.*

As the match wore on, however, Jared and Connor began to win game after game, holding serve and breaking their opponents easily. Between points, Jared winced in pain as he limped, but during the points, he scampered like a gazelle.

It finally dawned on me that he was faking the injury to convince his opponents that he was the weaker player so they would direct the balls to him, like the mother bird pretending to have a broken wing to lead the fox away from the baby chicks. Amazingly, it worked. I kept expecting the opponents to wise up, but by the time they did, my boys had a break in the third set, and that momentum helped them close out the match.

That was it. With the help of some brilliant gamesmanship, my boys were in the doubles final. Assuming we could get Connor's head back on straight and keep his legs from cramping, I was once again confident the title was ours.

We spent the rest of the day and evening preparing for the semifinals: downing fluids, long stretching massages, carb-packing meals, and early to bed.

Jared held me pressed to him through the night, not letting an inch come between us. He slept well. I know, because I didn't sleep at a wink, nuzzled to him, listening to his deep, sonorous breathing.

The next morning, the sky threatened showers, but by play time, the clouds had broken, and patches of blue were rapidly growing. There were only two matches on court central that Friday, and each of my boys was in one of them. The crowd seemed the same as at every other match:

screaming in a dozen different languages, some faces contorted with hate while others lionized us. The gay fans all wanted to touch Jared, shrieking teens and hopeful men. Some even asked for my autograph.

There is a sizable Asian population living in Paris as well as an equally large gay population. The Asians—mostly Chinese and Vietnamese—turned out to cheer Connor on just as the gay fans supported Jared.

Jared's match with McEwan was first up, and I watched with interest to see which of his two favorite rackets he would select, Thumper or Bambam. He chose Thumper.

Jared came out of the blocks on fire. He ripped the cover off the ball with every stroke from behind the baseline. He dominated McEwan with monster forehands and teeth-jarring serves.

To McEwan's credit, he played a flawless retrieval game that was every bit as breathtaking as Jared's attacking style. Almost every point turned into a twenty-ball rally. It was grueling for both the players and the fans.

They kept everyone in the stadium biting their nails for five hours. The fans had sore necks from tracking the ball and sore hands from clapping at every point. The tension grew tighter with each game. In long matches, a player's performance goes through peaks and valleys, but not this one. Both players executed flawless tennis, long, pounding rallies, pushing each other to come up with brilliant shot-making, until deep into the fifth set.

Jared managed to break McEwan at five-all to serve for the match. They were both hurting. McEwan's face was twisted into a grimace. Jared's body was relaxed, but the pain made his eyes smolder and his mouth hang open, showing teeth like a parched jackal.

A prickling sensation covered my scalp as the determination from both these gladiators awed me. This was Jared's moment, and I watched him collect himself, push his pain aside, and become an animal running on pure instinct and heart. He won three out of the next four points, which gave him two match points.

Cold chills washed through me as he wrung out every last drop of energy his body still held. He won match point by drawing McEwan into the net with a drop shot followed by a perfectly placed lob on the baseline.

The entire stadium leaped to its feet. My body went limp with sweet relief. I hadn't even realized how tense I had become until that moment of release.

Jared pumped his fist as he jogged to the net and held his arm out to shake hands, but McEwan would not admit defeat. Joshua ran to stand in front of the linesman who called the ball good and began screaming in his face. He dashed over and pointed to a spot just outside the baseline and about a foot to the left of where the ball had landed. McEwan transformed into a wild man, screaming for a full minute with Jared still standing at the net with his arm extended like a kid waiting at the counter for the soda-jerk to hand over his root-beer float.

I didn't know what to think, but I knew that Jared had won, and that was all that mattered. The replay showing on the big screen confirmed the ball was good, but the French don't use technology to overrule line-calls. Instead, the umpire climbed down to check the mark. He trotted to where McEwan still pointed. Meanwhile, the line judge who made the call ran out and pointed to the correct mark on the baseline.

The crowd really heated up, stomping feet and yelling as only the French can.

After checking both marks, the chair umpire pointed to the out mark that McEwan claimed was the mark and lifted one finger in the air, ruling that Jared's winning shot was out. The crowd roared. Jared stood at the net, stunned. His extended arm dropped to his side. As the chair umpire shimmied back into his perch, realization of what happened hit Jared. He let out a scream and called the umpire a homophobic fuck, letting lose with a tirade of curses.

The crowd booed and stomped, but it was not clear if their anger was directed at Jared, McEwan, or the chair.

The umpire turned on his microphone and gave Jared a warning for audible abuse. The stadium went berserk, like a bomb exploding. I have never seen anything like it before or since. It sounded like the ending of the world. The umpire sat there looking down at Jared like nothing was wrong, like Jared was a clumsy ball kid that had just tripped and fallen at his feet.

Jared put both hands on the net, just standing there, smoldering, glaring at McEwan while things quieted down, which took about ten minutes. Jared wasn't moving a muscle, and McEwan had a little smirk on his lips.

I felt angry that Jared had been cheated out of match point, but he still had another match point coming. This was no time for him to lose his cool. He needed to keep it together.

Jared sauntered to the baseline to serve at 40-30 and lost the next point with a double-fault. McEwan's call was still festering under his skin. He lost the next point as well, giving McEwan a break-back point to even the match. McEwan let go with a "COME ON!" He began windmilling his arms to pump up the volume of the frenzied crowd.

Jared had obviously lost his composure, and I was afraid now he would lose the match as well. He gave me a cold stare, reading the thoughts that must have shown clearly on my face and becoming even more livid at my lack of faith. He walked, slowly and deliberately, to his seat, pulling Bambam out of his tennis bag and dropping Thumper on the dirt. He tested Bambam's tension with the palm of his hand and walked back to the baseline to serve, quickly looping a ball deep in the box. When it floated back, he sliced a drop shot into the center of the court and followed it in.

Even with McEwan's tired legs, he managed to get to the ball but was only able to put up a weak lob. Jared backpedaled for the easy overhead. He had the whole court to hit into, and all he had to do was keep it in play. McEwan stood paralyzed at the net, Bambi in the high beams.

I saw it happen in slow motion. Jared cocked his arm, and he swung with all his strength, letting out a chilling yell as he spanked the ball as hard as he could right at McEwan. The ball must have been traveling at over 150 miles per hour when it smashed into McEwan's face, shattering the left side of his jaw. Teeth and blood and bits of flesh flew across the court, spraying a red trail across Jared's white shirt.

McEwan fell, knocked dumb, like a fighter who had taken too many jabs to the head. The fans grew silent. Jared stepped to the net, his eyes riveted on McEwan.

I couldn't help but wonder if he had purposely hit that drop shot to set up the smash, but the truth was, I really didn't want to know. He had won the match rightfully minutes before, and they had robbed him, just as they had done earlier in his career. This time, he might have decided that all bets were off and he would win any way he could, but I hoped not.

Regardless, I'm sure he didn't mean to hurt McEwan as badly as he did, but I also knew that all his pent-up frustration from years of bad line calls went into that overhead swing. I'm surprised the ball didn't rip McEwan's head clean off.

The umpire called for the trainer and leaped out of his chair to help McEwan to the sideline bench, but it was clear that McEwan would not continue the match. The whole side of his face was badly damaged. It took the trainer only seconds to determine that Jared's last strike of the ball was a knockout punch and that McEwan had lost. The umpire made the announcement, and the fans erupted again.

Jared held his arms high in victory, and all around him, pandemonium ensued. Thousands of gay fans vaulted onto the court, lifted Jared onto someone's shoulders, and paraded him around in a victory lap. They surged in behind Jared, as if his wake created an irresistible vacuum that sucked them along.

Security guards swarmed onto the court to break up the riot, but the fans ignored them. All I could hear was the thrum of blood in my ears. Jared shouted at the jubilant crowd, but his words were drowned by the uproar.

I believed that the crowd's euphoria was spurred as much by seeing McEwan lose as by seeing Jared win. McEwan had been virulently anti-gay, but he had been belligerent as well, ill-mannered and foul-mouthed throughout the match. It was true that the weather had been excessively hot, the match grueling, and the stakes high, but Jared had played under the same conditions and managed to keep his dignity until he was cheated out of match point.

The upside was that it would be a long time before McEwan's mouth would be back in championship form.

CONNOR'S semifinal against world number one Christopher Drake proved a different experience altogether. The paucity of long rallies and classic clay court grinding made the match go very fast, even though, like Connor's previous matches, it went the distance.

The raucous afternoon crowd of 32,000 all cheered loudest for Connor, the underdog, even though he was on the receiving end of a righteous ass whipping.

For two sets, Drake played nearly flawless tennis, pounding winners with uncanny precision. Connor repeatedly ran down balls that seemed to have already passed him. Clearly in his zone, Drake played like an impeccable champion, which was why he was number one. Watching his effortless footwork and awesome shot making, I not only assumed he would win, I began to fear for Jared's chances in the final.

But in the third set, almost imperceptibly, things began to swing Connor's way. His groundstrokes began finding the lines, and Drake began to miss just enough to erode his supreme confidence. Connor had figured out exactly what Drake would do with each stroke. His acute sense of anticipation got him to each ball with remarkable efficiency, and by taking the ball early, he afforded Drake very little recovery time between shots.

The crowd roared all through the third and fourth sets as Connor played flat-out, like a demon on fire, making an impressive comeback by winning both sets in tiebreakers. In the fifth set, his growing confidence allowed him to move forward, staying inside the baseline, where he could create sharp, oblique angles. He experienced a mental breakthrough during that comeback: going toe-to-toe in the fifth set with arguably the best player of all time, Connor glimpsed for the first time what he was capable of—and so did I.

Unfortunately for Drake, he saw it too. For the number one player to go down to a rookie in a Grand Slam semifinal would be a devastating blow. I could see that thought worming its way into Drake's head in that fifth set, making him tight and irritable, which made him aim closer to the lines and miss a few easy shots. He kept fighting, but he couldn't derail Connor's momentum.

In the end, Connor beat the world number one by breaking him at love and, on his own serve, reeled off four aces in a row. Connor threw his racket spinning into the air and caught it by the handle with a wicked smile.

The reigning king had fallen, queens and rooks and bishops had all been cast aside. Only my two pawns remained on the board. Game over, I won. It was impossible to describe that feeling: those first few minutes after I knew that both my boys had miraculously accomplished what we set out to do. I couldn't form a single thought. I was reduced to simply feeling the glorious universe around me as it all aligned into one magnificent sea of tingling joy. I became bodiless, a feather of perception floating on the breeze.

If I had thought about it, I would have admitted that getting to that moment was worth all the hardship, the discrimination, the shooting, the rehab, and the brief breakup with Jared. That journey I would make again, just to experience that supreme joy for a few heartbeats.

I looked at the stunned faces around me, Carrie, Shar, Roy, J.D., Spencer, and Harman. A line from Shakespeare's Henry the Fifth floated up into my numb mind: "We few, we happy few, we band of brothers." Yes, Agincourt: we had come to France to take what was rightfully ours, and through guts and guile and skill, we had humbled our contemptuous enemies.

THE doubles final seemed more like an afterthought. After the women's singles final on Saturday, my boys played the men's doubles final. It was an America verses France affair, with Jared and Connor playing the team of Boyette and Seaborne, the number two doubles team in the world.

Jared felt so confident after winning the coin toss that he asked Boyette if he'd rather receive serve or be broken. It turned into a tense match with my boys giving as good as they got. The opponents broke Connor's serve late in the third set.

The French team had already dismissed my boys when they went up 5-4, 40-30 in the third set. Serving at match point, Boyette had a questionable shot called out. The replay confirmed the out ball, but Philip Seaborne reacted badly, throwing a high-decibel tantrum worthy of a four-year-old, which progressed into a mental meltdown.

Given a second life, Jared and Connor didn't hesitate to pick up their game. They blew through the Frenchmen to win the next three points and the next two games to win the doubles championship.

I glanced over at Roy. His eyes were wide and shining as the shock of it moved up from his chest to his head. Tears slid down J.D.'s cheeks. He kept dabbing his eyes with a handkerchief and laughing to himself.

I was in less shock than everyone else. I had predicted my boys would win, even though they gave me a hell of a scare when Boyette served at match point. *This is it,* I thought. *My boys are Grand Slam champions, and no one can ever take that away from them.*

That night, we all wanted to celebrate, but because Jared and Connor had their singles final the next day, we opted for an early dinner in the hotel dining room with a bottle of Dom Perignon and two tins of Beluga Caviar. I limited my boys to only one flute of champagne each.

It was a happy gathering, the kind of joyful party a group of close-knit passengers have on the last night of a dream voyage. Laughter vaulted to the chandeliers and undulated back through the glittering room. I didn't even know what I ate. It didn't matter. We raised our glasses to the future. Today and tomorrow were stair steps to greatness, to legend. Nothing could stop us.

At nine o'clock, we put the party on hold until the bigger celebration tomorrow. People left the table in twos and threes to go back to their rooms until there was only Grandfather Lin, Connor, and myself left sitting at one end of the long table. I poured myself another flute of champagne, and Connor poured his grandfather a cup of green tea.

Grandfather cleared his throat and stared into Connor's eyes. "I am not a greedy man," he said, speaking so softly I had to lean closer to hear. "I desire nothing further in this life for myself. Nor do I have any wish to see you wallow in wealth and fame, but if that is what you desire in your heart, I will raise no objections. From the depths of my being, I believe that medicine is the noblest profession. Had I had an education, I would have studied medical science myself, but I'm an ignorant man, and I was not even gifted enough to ensure that my own children became doctors. If tennis is what brings you joy, however, then you have my blessings. But for many years now I have believed that what is in your heart is a genuine desire to heal people, to comfort the sick. If that is true, it pains me to see you going down this other path."

Grandfather Lin took hold of Connor's hand. "But I have a confession I want to make to you, something that I have told no one ever before, and I ask you to listen carefully to what I am about to tell you." He sat staring into Connor's eyes for a minute, as if trying to gauge exactly how much the boy could handle, before he continued.

The old man told of how he, with his mother and father, had taken refuge in a cave during the Japanese occupation of his country, becoming prisoners in that secret cave for over a year.

"For most of that time, we did nothing but lie on stone beds, cringing in the murky light filtering through the mouth of the cave, breathing an evil stench and letting our minds wander.

"Every night I sneaked out to scour the village for food, but there was none. Anything that was edible had already been eaten by the soldiers. I gathered grass, an occasional rat, insects, even meat from corpses."

It took no time at all for his family's flesh to waste away, leaving them little more than skeletons with eyes protruding from their skulls. He described how, at night, his heartbeat sounded loud in his head, pounding with an offbeat and desperate rhythm.

He began hearing a voice that echoed in the pit of his stomach and reverberated through his entire body. It was almost as if the sound of his own heartbeat began saying words, but it had such an intimate and fatherly tone that he at first assumed that it was his own father talking.

"The funny thing was," Grandfather Lin said, "that the voice was so friendly and my father had always been so stern, so I quickly realized that it couldn't be my father. My father had been a doctor, a professional, and respected in the town, and that made him proud and demanding. For my father to suddenly address me so warmly was too shocking, and I soon realized it was my own heart speaking to me. And what it said was, 'After the war, take your family to America, the Golden Mountain, where they will all have the opportunities to follow their dreams'."

At first, he said, that fatherly voice only spoke when he was feeling delirious, but after a few months, the voice became constant, retelling stories that he had heard growing up, gossip about family members long gone—and always reminding him that he must take his family to America.

The voice spurred on his nightly forays into the town. Soon he began to stay out longer each night, loath to return without something of value that would help achieve his dream after the war. At times he became so depressed that he thought about killing himself, walking out into the river and letting the current take him, but fulfilling this dream kept him from it.

One night during his wanderings, as the eastern sky paled, he climbed down into a ravine to drink from a stream when he noticed movement on the far bank. He stealthily crossed the water and found a girl, dirty and shivering, but still beautiful with the blush of ripeness. Her name was Chew-Gen—Autumn Pearl. He took her to the cave and made her his wife.

Chew-Gen's induction into the family increased his desire to accumulate treasure—porcelain, books, fancy silk clothing, gold fillings from corpses' mouths, swords and rifles and coats from dead soldiers— anything that would help get him to America.

During those times, he found he could be happy, clinging to his new wife during the long, cold days and planning how they would live once they reached the golden shores. The voice became more insistent, issuing short, terse commands, prompting him to go out and find food, to provide for his family, to store up more treasures. It was that driving voice that gave him the courage to sneak up behind a soldier one night and cut his throat in order to steal food.

"I murdered a man," Grandfather Lin said, as simply as he might have said, "It was a cold night."

Still the voice urged him on, ordering him to steal, and the resonant beauty of it was irresistible. Soon the cave began to fill with everything except food.

Connor had heard all this before, and he looked bored at hearing it again, but he was not prepared for what followed, the never-told conclusion of his Grandfather's story.

"When Chew-Gen's morning sickness began, it threw me into a panic. How could she possibly grow a child with her empty stomach? I redoubled my resolve to find food, but the effort brought little results. That's when I realized the sacrifice that must be made for the baby, for my dream for the family. For the baby to live, the grandparents must become the nourishment to grow the baby. With all of us on the verge of death, it was the only way to continue the family, the only way to fulfill the dream. *The old ones were in so much pain*, I thought, *it will be a kindness to end their suffering.*

"I sharpened a bayonet that I had filched from a dead soldier, but in the end I was not capable of enacting such horror on the people who gave me life, who had cared for and nurtured me. I doubled my efforts to find food, but in the end, it was clear there simply was no food.

"My courage had melted away, but my parents also knew that their deaths would ensure the family's survival. They welcomed this sacrifice. One morning, when I again returned without food, my mother raised my bayonet. The blade had the bluish tinge of cold steel. Before I could stop her, she placed the blade to her neck and cut her carotid artery. She didn't scream, there wasn't even much blood, only the hoarse, choking sobs of someone too weak to react.

"My wife and I drank blood, ate flesh, and our bodies grew stronger. My father refused to eat. I buried her bones in the silt beside the river. Later, I experienced the same ordeal with my father.

"After the Japanese were driven from the land and Chew-Gen and I moved back to the town, to my father's house, the voice never left my heart. Even as the emotional horror and physical hunger faded, I could not escape the voice, telling me to move my family to America."

Grandfather Lin paused for a few heartbeats, looking into Connor's eyes as if asking for forgiveness. He told of how it took all their stored up treasures to come to this country, and how he and his wife sacrificed everything, worked two jobs each so that their children could get ahead and enjoy the benefits of all these opportunities.

"But I had my dream in my heart, and I would let nothing, not even the love for my parents, keep me from achieving my dreams. That is what I want for you, to follow your dream. You have always said you wanted to be a doctor, and I have always supported you on that. And why? Not just because doctors follow a different set of ethics that transcend politics, war, and religion and devote themselves to a life of compassion and human decency, but also because that was the dream in your heart. What could be better?"

Connor dropped his head, could no longer look his grandfather in the eye. But I could tell that Connor was still not convinced. He was holding on to his tennis dream.

"Let me ask something," the old man said. "Do you really like this person you've become? This person who wears black sequined shirts and laps up the applause? This person who uses all the people around him in order to be a star? Do you like this person? Are these changes you've gone through worth the money and fame?"

Connor suddenly looked as if he had been hit between the eyes with a sledgehammer.

All Connor's jealous tantrums sprang to my mind, the drunken binge, getting knocked on his ass, the times he had abandoned Spencer, his back-talking to his father. I felt suddenly embarrassed for him, as well as something remotely like pity, because I think he was remembering those incidents too.

"Connor, I did not come here to watch you play tennis. I'm taking your grandmother back to China to live out our last days in the land that gave us birth, the place where the bones of our ancestors rest, and where our bones will rest too. So this is my last chance to bequeath something to you. If tennis is your dream, I'm happy for you.

"But if you're going down this path simply to keep from disappointing your father, I say that you must follow your own heart. He's a man, and he will get over it. I have never regretted what happened in that cave. I have followed my heart all these years, and I can tell you that it's the only thing that brings lasting happiness. You must do the same. If medicine is what's in your heart, money and fame are nothing more than a finger-snap. Look deep into your heart, then decide what your life will be. Will you do this for an old man who is going home to die?"

Connor wiped a tear from his eye. His face grew softer, as if letting go of all its apprehension at once. He took the old man into his arms and gave him a long, loving hug.

I suddenly thought about my own father and how I had harshly judged him over the years, and I wondered how many secrets he had hid from me.

"Grandfather, it is too late. I've already signed the contracts. I'm legally committed to play pro tennis for the next seven years."

"It is never too late to do the right thing," the old man whispered. "While I lived in my cave, I became adept at sneaking out at night to steal other people's treasure." He winked, pulling a set of papers from his inside coat pocket: Connor's Adidas contract. "Harman was planning to give these to your sponsors on Sunday, but he misplaced them." Grandfather Lin's face split in half with a wily smile that showed his pearly dentures.

Connor took the contracts and held them close to his chest as if they were precious to him. "What about Dad? It will break his heart."

"Leave him to me," the old man said with a confident grin.

Connor ripped the contracts in half, and again, and again, until they were shreds. He threw the pieces into the air to let them float to the ground like confetti. He gently took the old man in his arms again as the shreds of contract fell about their heads and shoulders. "Thank you, Grandpa. I'll be a damned fine doctor, I promise."

CHAPTER 33

IT WAS cold that morning. The mist was clammy and pricked my skin. Beneath the press of gray sky, I rolled myself onto court central in the heart of Roland Garros to study the sky while wondering if the rain would hold off long enough for my boys to play their final match.

The stadium stood empty of fans, but the caretakers had been there since before dawn, half hidden in the mist, preparing. I heard an occasional shout and the incongruous clapping of plastic seats being lowered and wiped. The workmen had that air of efficient superiority derived from the common experience of knowing the inner workings of something totally mysterious to ordinary mortals, like stage hands who know precisely which levers to pull to make the magician disappear.

Sharing that empty stadium with them on that particular Sunday morning, I was very tempted to scream, to let go with a triumphant shriek and listen to the echo ricochet off the green plastic seats.

Jared and Connor followed me onto the court to perform their half-hour warm-up before match time. They kept their warm-up jackets and sweatpants on. I was bundled up but still felt the chill. They stood at opposite sides of the net at the service line and warmed up like we had done a hundred times. It was most likely the first time in the history of Grand Slam tennis that two players facing each other in the final actually warmed each other up before the match.

They took their time working their way back to the baseline, as if they didn't want to rush even a second of this experience. Connor had decided to retire after this match. This would be his only appearance in a Grand Slam final, and who knew what fate had in store for Jared? We all savored the moment. Whatever nervous energy they were feeling burned off in the first few strikes of the ball. They both became relaxed, moving well and swinging with broad, clean strokes.

A quiet joy came over me, and, as if somehow linked to the feelings churning in my gut, the heavens opened and sunlight spilled onto the court. Warmth radiated over us, and in minutes, our jackets came off and I knew it was going to be a beautiful day.

I had gone over the different game plans with both my players, and I knew they were each eager to jump out to an early lead and dominate the other. Jared felt his heavy serve and pounding groundstrokes would give him the edge. Connor hoped that his foot speed and ability to keep the ball in play would frustrate Jared and allow him to take charge.

I knew the deciding factor would be each player's resolve. At the business end of the match, one player would crack and the other would hold his nerve, proving who was the undisputed champion of clay court tennis for this moment in time. It would pivot toward the mentally stronger player, whoever had more heart.

At the end of the workout, both my boys had smiles on their sweat-streaked faces. They trotted over to me, and before they put away their gear, Connor said something utterly unexpected. "If it looks like the match is going my way, I'm going to back off and let Jared win."

Silence hung in the air as Jared and I stared at him.

"Even the runner-up prize money will more than pay for medical school," he continued quickly, with a sudden, nervous edge to his voice. "So I don't need to win, but if Jared wins, he's set for life. He'll never be denied entry into any ATP event for as long as he wants to keep playing."

Jared's face turned a scalded red. "Don't you even think about cheating me out this fight, you hear me? If you don't give me your best game, I'm coming across that net and kicking your skinny ass all the way back to San Francisco. You think I've fought this hard to not play a real final? Fuck you! I don't give a fuck what you do with your life tomorrow; today, I want your best game. I demand it. I deserve it, you deserve it, and so do the fans."

Jared did not wait for an answer. He stuffed his racket into his bag, flung the bag over his shoulder, and stomped off toward the player's lounge.

"I'm sorry," I said. "I know you were only trying to help us."

"No, he's right. He understands what it's about, and he's not willing to compromise."

"Meaning?"

"It doesn't matter who wins. What matters is that you find out what you're capable of. You want your opponent to play his absolute best, to put as many obstacles in your way as possible, so that you push yourself beyond what you're capable of, and vise-versa. You push each other into that zone where you're playing out of your head and you see how high you can fly. This"—he waved his arms around the stadium—"is only a stage to add more pressure, and that pushes you to fly even higher."

Yes, I thought. He was right. You push each other toward perfection so that you both break through your known limits. And no matter who wins, you step to the net, shake hands, and congratulate the other on a game well played.

A light illuminated in my head. It's true, competition is a cooperative effort to drive each other beyond boundaries. That, I realized for the first time, is the only meaningful goal. Images began to flash in my mind: Diefenbach with his condescending double smirk, Roy Lin with his gruff frown, Jared's leaving me in San Francisco, McEwan's boastful taunts, Shar's angry leer, and the shooter's cold red eyes. They had all provoked me into new territory.

I suddenly felt something near gratitude.

I WAITED in the players' lounge, just outside the changing rooms.

Connor was the first to emerge, and for the first time since Indian Wells, he wore the shirt his grandmother had made for him, the powder blue with the embroidered dragon on the back. I smiled. "Blue is definitely your color. That black sequin number really wasn't very flattering."

Before Connor walked to the waiting area, he gave me a long hug. As he pulled away, I slipped something from my pocket and held it out to him: the dark green pendant that Grandfather Lin had given me back in San Francisco.

"Your grandfather asked me to give this to you, for luck. It came from China."

He took the pendant and held it close to his face as if it were priceless. "You know I love you."

"Yes," I said. "I know. Now, you've been playing in Jared's shadow for six months, and this may be your only chance to step into the limelight, so go out there and make us proud."

His smile was fragile and boyish. He spun around and walked down the hall to the waiting area. The dragon embroidered on the back of his shirt shifted from side to side, as if it were pacing back and forth.

Jared strolled over, set down his bag, and lifted me out of my chair. He held me suspended in his arms, and that eased my anxiety. I noticed with a shock that his face was clean. For the first time since coming to Europe, he would play without his war paint. I stroked his cheek, knowing he didn't need it anymore but a little sorry to see it go.

"I'm about to go out there and play my heart out for the next four or five hours, all to justify my existence. And you know something funny? All these years of work and hardship, I've been petrified of losing, but at this moment, I think I'm more terrified of winning."

I knew who would win this match, but I didn't need to tell him. I knew because in my mind, I had already witnessed the entire match played out, point by point, until the end, when the winner raised his racket in sweet glory. I was sure Jared had seen it too, experienced it with me as I was seeing it. How else could he be so relaxed? Where did this power come from, to see every point before the first ball is struck and to know that what you're seeing is true, is truth itself?

"Win or lose, doesn't matter," I said. "This match is not about tennis, it's about heart. Now go out there and show me what you've got."

He gave me a sensual kiss, pressed his forehead to mine. I was sure he was going to tell me he loved me, and I didn't want him to. He had already shown me in so many ways, telling me would be anticlimactic.

Instead, he smiled. "That reminds me," he said. He sat me back in my chair and pulled an envelope from his bag. "While we've been in Paris, I had Harman go back to Spain to buy this for you. Once we signed with Nike, I knew we could afford something special, so don't worry about the cost. It's a little something for our future."

He handed me the envelope. "Hope you like it." He pulled his bag over his shoulder and walked down to the staging area to wait for the announcement. I watched him glide away, more proud of him and more in love than at any other moment.

When Jared turned the corner and stepped out of my sight, I opened the envelope and pulled out two cream-colored sheets of paper: the bill of sale and the deed to the Villa Baraka. For just an instant, I thought I could smell the wind coming off the Mediterranean. I remembered the feel of swimming in the cool surf and making love on the beach, and I smiled.

SPENCER pushed my chair as fast as he could up the ramp and out into the stadium. Bruno lifted me from my chair and carried me down the steps to the coach's box. There, on the end, was Roy, and beside him sat Grandfather and Grandmother Lin.

Bruno and I stopped next to Roy, who had his camera held in front of his face and was already snapping pictures like a madman. Pride poured off him like a fine rain. I felt happy for him. He deserved his pride. I shook his hand and told him, "Thank you." He returned a puzzled stare, but I smiled to myself without bothering to explain. Bruno sat me beside Grandfather Lin and moved behind me to shield me from the crowd.

The old man's eyes were wet as he shook my hand. "You know who's going to win this match?" he asked.

I nodded.

"I know too. No matter what happens out there"—he pointed to the red court with its pristine white lines and black net—"you have won, because you care about the things that really matter."

I wanted to thank him for sharing his cave story with me. I confess I didn't know how he could live so peacefully with that monstrous thing weighing on his conscience.

As if he had heard my thoughts, he said, "Everyone weaves a unique tapestry, using threads of happiness and sorrow, honor and shame, to create a multi-colored landscape that is our past. The secret is knowing that the tapestry is a mirage. It doesn't really exist. There is only now and what is to come. It is life's mystery—and its blessing."

I twisted my head around to glance at Karl Diefenbach, who sat slouched in his seat in the row above me and two seats to my left. I felt a slight pang, something akin to pity. We had beaten him in every way possible, in ways he was not yet aware of, and I knew very well what would plague him the most: he was pushing sixty, and over the next thirty years, he would grow into a bitter old age, then lie rotting in a mahogany box. Time would reduce him to calcium dust and a few gold fillings, and he would fade from human memory.

I shared the same fate, of course, but not Jared and Connor. Long after Diefenbach and I were forgotten, Jared and Connor would live on in archives, in books; their recorded images and voices would be stored among the precious and venerated objects of our time and our sport.

Yes, he had played a good game, stretched me to my limits, but today at least, I had won. One of my boys would be crowned champion and be accepted into the game's elite. It was a sweet victory indeed.

I reached over and shook his hand, noticing his long, slender fingers with the polished nails. "Thank you," I said. "You almost had us. Better luck next time."

Puzzlement spread across his features, and he mumbled, "I'll bet you a hundred bucks that I don't see you at Wimbledon." He smirked, showing he had something up his sleeve.

I shook my head. "I'm quite certain that you're right." I stopped myself from saying more, telling myself not to gloat, to stay humble, and I did.

In the next moment, a crackling sound came over the loud speakers and the announcer introduced the players. Out walked Jared, his bag slung over one shoulder, his arm raised and waving to the crowd. Connor sauntered right behind him in the same posture. The cheers were deafening and continued until they had reached their seats and unzipped their bags. As the roar subsided, a dozen gay men near the top of the stadium started to sing in clear, strong voices.

"We are family."

As their voices rose in volume, others around them jumped to their feet and joined in.

"I got all my sisters with me."

Soon, hundreds, then thousands were standing and singing and stomping their feet to the rhythm. The officials simply stared into the stands, waiting patiently for it to end. They had never seen anything like this happen in a tennis stadium, and they stood bewildered. What they didn't know, and what I was sure of, was that it would never end.

On and on the song went, growing louder and stronger, until every gay man had joined in.

I thought, *Let the game begin.*

EPILOGUE

BENEATH a scrim of clouds on a mid-August morning, I wheel myself onto Louis Armstrong Stadium in Flushing Meadows, New York. My tennis bag sits precariously on my lap, and my opponent glides in right behind me. A cheer goes up from the four-dozen fans in the bleachers. The clapping echoes in this nearly empty stadium, and the sounds wash over me. When I see people standing to cheer, a tingling sensation rushes through my head. My eyes burn and my mouth goes dry, but I check myself, drawing my thoughts back to my game plan and the match I'm about to play.

It is the second Sunday of the US Open tennis tournament, and I am about to play my fifth and final round in the US Open's wheelchair division championships. One more match, one more night, and Jared and I will fly back to our villa on the Mediterranean.

Happily, Jared is not here to cheer me on. I say happily because he is across the courtyard at Arthur Ashe Stadium, preparing to play in the Men's singles final against the world number two, Christopher Drake.

I glance up into the stands and see Spencer and Harman sitting side by side next to Carrie. Connor and Shar sit directly above them, and little Lincoln Lin sleeps in Connor's arms. J.D. Lambert sits beside them with his wife and two daughters. I smile to think that he's finally forgiven Connor.

Someone else catches my eye. To my surprise, in the row above J.D. Lambert's family, stand my mother and father. Both are clapping their hands and smiling. This will be the first professional match my parents will see me play. I feel something the size of a fist grow inside my chest. It presses against my heart. All their voices are rising now, blending together in one booming cheer.

For the past year, I have not only coached Jared to two Grand Slam championships, I have also put my body, my pain, my blood and sweat onto the court to compete with other wheelchair athletes. The work has been hard, and the wins have only recently begun to swing my way, but through all my losses, I have regained my pride as an athlete. It was Grandfather Lin's story of letting nothing stop you from your dream that has brought me back to compete.

My specialized chair whispers its way to the left of the umpire's chair. I love the way it glides. It's made of titanium and handles like a Lamborghini. I look over at my opponent, Donald James, who is extremely stocky in the upper body and nearly as old as I am. There are over a hundred of us competing on the wheelchair circuit, and the top thirty-two have come here to compete for the $50,000 prize. My opponent is seeded number three.

In these last minutes before the warm-up, we are both completing our pre-match psych jobs. He looks calm and confident, but I know that is mostly a façade. Underneath he is as sick to his stomach as I am and probably more so. If my butterflies are like winged hippos, his must be dive-bombing elephants. Even men in wheelchairs hate losing to fairies.

I smile, thinking I will move into the top ten after I whip the pants off him, but I check myself, forcing my mind to refocus on the present. I want to enjoy each moment of this experience and not jump ahead.

I review the game plan again. My game is still that of the consummate retriever. I work and hustle and bust my butt to get to every ball and send it back over the net, letting my opponent know that I can do that all damn day and to beat me he's got to out-work, out-hustle, and out-play me on every point for the next three hours. I plan to stretch him to his absolute limits, and I'm hoping he can do the same to me, because how else can we find out what we are capable of?

Through my forced concentration I hear a rising crescendo of voices, both cheers and boos, giving me a little spike of joy. I glance up and see a few spectators waving rainbow flags, and I realize that many of these fans are here to cheer me on. My excitement mushrooms. I know that thousands of gay fans turned out today, but I assumed they would all be watching Jared play his final.

I unzip my bag and pull out my favorite racket. A green rubber band holds a white note to the handle. I peel the note off and recognize Jared's fine script. It says: "Sorry I can't be there to cheer. Keep your eyes on the ball and your wheels turning. No matter what happens, you're my champion. And remember what Arthur Ashe said: 'If it weren't for the wind in my face, I would never have been able to fly'."

As I dip my head, I feel Mike Morrison's hand on my shoulder. "Are you ready?" he asks.

"You bet."

I glide to the net. Mike tosses the coin and points to me. I call tails, and it is. "I'll receive," I tell them. On my way to the baseline, I pat my racket against the palm of my hand to test the string tension. Perfect. Everything is perfect.

My opponent swings his racket, and I hear that familiar pop of the ball as it hurtles toward me. It comes fast, and I hurry to draw my racket back and strike the ball back over the net. I remind myself that Donald likes to hit with pace. *He's a power player, so be ready*. What he doesn't know is that I love pace: I eat it for breakfast.

The murmur from the fans spills onto the court. I hear Connor's voice rise above the noise, and somewhere in the depths of my mind, I send him a silent thank-you. I've learned so much more from him than he's learned from me. I taught him how to compete, but he taught me why we compete. Now I will carry that to my grave. I may never be a champion, but I will always be in the game, and I will know exactly why I'm playing.

We come to the end of the five-minute warm-up, and Mike Morrison calls, "Time."

We take our positions at the baseline. My butterflies have shrunk to a manageable size, but there is a lump in my throat. Donald and I eye each other from across the net.

He throws the ball high into the air and smashes it on the downfall. It flies directly at me like a bullet. My chair turns, as if by magic, and my racket strikes the ball, sending it back across the net with a wicked slice. The ball drops deep in the court with a little side-spin.

The game is on.

ALAN CHIN enjoyed a twenty-year career working his way from computer programmer to Director of Software Engineering, but he lost interest in computer science when he began writing fiction. He walked away from corporate America in 1999 and never looked back. Since then he has traveled to over forty countries, scuba dived the Great Barrier Reef, tracked black rhino in the Serengeti, and dined in most of the capitals of Europe. Oh yes, and he's published three gay-themed novels and two screenplays.

In addition to writing, Alan is making a name for himself as a literary critic for several online publications which include: Examiner.com GLBT Literature column, *Queer Magazine Online*, and the Lambda Literary web site. In 2007, QBliss magazine awarded their Pride in Literature award to Alan for his debut novel.

Alan currently spends half of the year traveling the globe and the other half writing at his home in northern California.

You can visit Alan's web site at http://alanchin.net and his writers blog at http://alanchinwriter.blogspot.com. You can also e-mail Alan at Alanhchin@aol.com.

More Romance from DREAMSPINNER PRESS

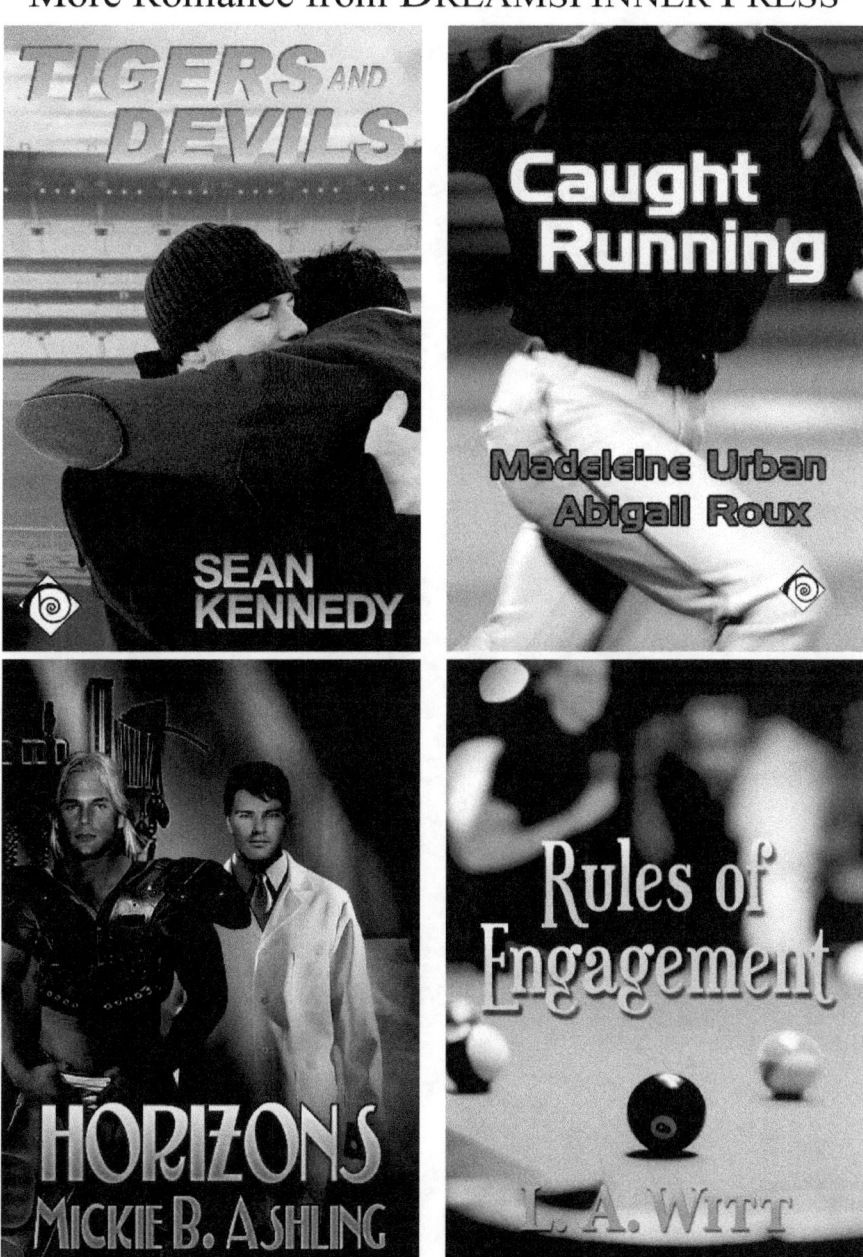

www.ingramcontent.com/pod-product-compliance
Lightning Source LLC
Chambersburg PA
CBHW050035030726
47506CB00001B/289